Praise for [illegible]

'A bright, pacy, readable accour[illegible] extraordinary women . . . Fans o[illegible] this, and it would be surprising [illegible] into a luscious mini-series'

The Sunday Times

'*The Glorious Guinness Girls* has already been compared, and rightly so, to *Downton Abbey*. The two share a delicious comfort-blanket quality, only in the book's case, you do not need to wait until Sunday evenings before availing of its escapist properties.The story combines the intimacy of a family drama, set against the most opulent of backdrops, with sweeping historical themes'

Sunday Independent

'A captivating and page-turning novel about a fascinating family. Fantastic'

Sinéad Moriarty

'Emily Hourican creates a nuanced and complex portrait of not only the Guinness family and their associates, but also of the unstable, ever-changing world they live in. Hourican's meditations on the politics of class and gender really shine'

***Books Ireland* magazine**

'A must for all *Downton Abbey* fans, *The Glorious Guinness Girls* is a gorgeous book, a captivating tale about a young girl caught up in the lifestyle of a family that continues to fascinate – the Guinness Family. A joy to read'

Swirl and Thread

'*Bridgerton* fans will adore *The Glorious Guinness Girls*. Such a charming, moving and gripping read'

Scribbles by Kat

Emily Hourican is a journalist and author. She has written features for the *Sunday Independent* for fifteen years, as well as *Image* magazine, *Condé Nast Traveler* and *Woman & Home*. She was also editor of *The Dubliner* Magazine. Emily's first book, a memoir titled *How To (Really) Be A Mother*, was published in 2013. She is also the author of novels *The Privileged*, *White Villa*, *The Outsider* and *The Blamed*. She lives in Dublin with her family.

Previously by Emily Hourican

The Outsider

The Blamed

White Villa

The Privileged

How To (Really) Be A Mother (non-fiction)

The Glorious Guinness Girls

EMILY HOURICAN

First published in Great Britain in 2020
by Headline Review
An imprint of HEADLINE PUBLISHING GROUP

First published in Great Britain as a paperback in 2021
by Headline Review
An imprint of HEADLINE PUBLISHING GROUP

1

Photographic Sources: Alamy Stock Photo; Getty Images; Mary Evans Picture Library; shutterstock.com.
Line drawing of Glenmaroon by Nick Ellwood

Cataloguing in Publication Data is available from the British Library

ISBN 978 1 4722 7460 1

Typeset in Sabon by redrattledesign.com

Printed and bound in Great Britain by Clays Ltd, Elcograf S.p.A.

Headline's policy is to use papers that are natural, renewable and recyclable products and made from wood grown in well-managed forests and other controlled sources. The logging and manufacturing processes are expected to conform to the environmental regulations of the country of origin.

HEADLINE PUBLISHING GROUP
An Hachette UK Company
Carmelite House
50 Victoria Embankment
London EC4Y 0DZ

www.headline.co.uk
www.hachette.co.uk

For Michael,

who believed in this book as much as I do

Cast of Characters

At Ballytibbert

Felicity Burke, known as 'Fliss'

Hughie Burke, Fliss's brother

Mrs Burke, their mother

Uncle Alex

At Glenmaroon

The Glorious Guinness Girls: Aileen, Maureen & Oonagh

Cloé Guinness, their mother

Arthur Ernest Guinness, known as Ernest, their father

Gertrude Gunn, known as 'Gunnie', Cloé's cousin

Mildred, Ernest's cousin

Kathleen, the housemaid

Thomas, stable hand

Lapham, butler

Robert, footman
Mrs Wood, the cook
Richard, Hughie's friend
Brinsley Sheridan Plunket, known as 'Brinny'

At Burton Hall, Dublin
Henry Guinness, Ernest's cousin
His daughters: Moira, Rachel, Patricia and Heather (known as Judy)

At Number 11 Grosvenor Place, London
Walter Edward Guinness, 1st Baron Moyne, Ernest's brother
Lady Evelyn, his wife, Cousin Bryan, his son

At Number 5 Grosvenor Place, London
Rupert Guinness, 2nd Earl of Iveagh, Ernest's brother
Lady Honour, his daughter
Lady Brigid, his daughter

London Society
Elizabeth Ponsonby, socialite
Teresa Jungman, known as 'Baby'
Zita Jungman, Baby's sister
Brian Howard, poet
Nancy Mitford, the eldest of the Mitford sisters
Diana Mitford, Nancy's sister
Stephen Tennant
Evelyn Waugh

} *Bright Young People*

Violet Valerie French, known as 'Valsie', Oonagh's friend
Essex, Violet's sister
Bert, prizefighter, friend of Baby's
Basil Blackwood, 'Duff', 4th Marquess of Dufferin and Ava

All historical figures are based on fact but as imagined by the author. Apart from the documented historical figures and events, this book, its characters and their actions are the work of the author's imagination. Any resemblance to real persons, living or dead, is purely coincidental.

Prologue

Port of Southampton, 1924

There is a dull thump of flashbulbs exploding, and light bursts behind us, breaking the soft late November afternoon. The newspaper men are here. A thin drizzle, a city drizzle, descends, gathering on the canopy of Gunnie's umbrella and running down the ribs in small rivers. Delicate, less wet than a country rain but dirtier, dragging dust and smoke from the air with it so that my gloves are spotted already. Gunnie's arm is tucked through mine, held tight against the excitement I can feel like a tremor through her.

We have been standing nearly an hour by the chiming of the church spire clock somewhere behind us, staring into the grey sea indistinguishable from the grey sky so that now, when Fantome II appears at last, she is like a ghost ship looming up out of fog, the lanterns at her sides bobbing drunkenly in the wind.

The sails are down, giving her a thin, spidery look; all those extraordinary triangles and rectangles of canvas tucked away. When out and full with wind, they stand in neat formation like pieces of the tangram puzzle Ernest brought back from Flanders. He made me count them once, the sails. I said I saw sixteen, but he said I had missed some and told me then how the moving and arranging of these sails sent the yacht forward and at what speed. He said they were a code that only the wind and sailors understood. It's when he tells me things like this that I remember he is a man with no sons, who must therefore speak to daughters.

The dock is empty but for us and the knot of newspapermen, who have waited even longer than we have. We wait, all of us, for the same reason, although Gunnie and I would never say it. We wait because out there in the gloom, onboard Fantome, is a brightness that lights all our lives.

Forty thousand miles, Gunnie said. Although I can't even imagine what that is. They have seen Panama, the Suez Canal, Fiji, Yokohama harbour. Gunnie showed me on the globe and I looked and nodded but the names meant nothing to me and even when I had all their letters, pitiful few for so many months, still they meant nothing.

Closer to, Fantome looks gay enough, though not as gay as the bright morning they set off, when I waved to them, my handkerchief fluttering long, long after I knew they no longer looked.

'This way, Mr Ernest, sir; over here, sir!' The voice behind me becomes excited as the first figures step down the gangplank. I feel Gunnie twitch, her arm still in mine though I know she will pull away from me at any moment. To be ready for them.

'Over here, please, Mr Ernest!' the newspaperman calls again, followed by another of them, like dogs at a door begging to be let out. Or in. And then, voices mounting in excitement as first Cloé, then her daughters appear, slender wraiths in that treacherous air, 'Look here, Miss Maureen, to me, if you will.' 'This way, Miss Aileen, how was your trip?'

Gunnie lets go my arm and steps forward as the newspapermen move around and ahead of me. I stay where I am and know that the light from their flashing bulbs must obscure me so they cannot yet see me. I watch as Maureen turns one way, then the other, smiling. This is her element, just as surely as the trout at home inhabit the fast-running stream by the back of the stables. Beside her, Aileen is sterner, perhaps cross. She will not do what the newspapermen tell her. Oonagh, they ignore. Just fourteen, hidden by her father, I watch as she peeps out from behind his elbow, and see the laughing look she gives Maureen, turning this way and that for the cameras, and how she is so quick to take it all in. The rain, the grey mist, the empty dock, the flash of camera bulbs.

When they set off, the Daily Express wrote that 'Maureen and her two sisters, Oonagh and Aileen, vivacious young daughters of Ernest Guinness', had left 'Socialist Britain'. Why must they say 'Socialist'? I wondered then. Now, I wonder how different this must all look to eyes that have seen tropical islands and the sun setting over strange lands; surely dawn coming up just as Mr Kipling described it, 'like thunder outer China crost the bay'?

They look so different. Maureen is quite grown up, I see.

Under the cloche hat pulled down at a clever angle, her hair is bobbed and shining, just like Aileen's, and she stands, languid, laughing, completely sure of her new self, just as she was of the old self.

Only Oonagh is the same. That mass of curly hair still, straw boater set back on her head so she can see clearly around her. Those blue eyes that are sometimes silver, sometimes turquoise, too large and bright, until you look into other eyes and find them small and mean. The same eyes on all three girls, the effect so different.

'It's good to be back,' Ernest is telling the newspapermen, who listen with pens poised to write down his words.

'We hear you had many adventures, sir,' one of them says. 'A storm, was it? In Japan?'

'Earthquake,' Ernest replies. 'Destroyed the harbour. Not us, though.' He speaks with satisfaction. I know how he enjoys a test of courage, particularly when combined with skill, but only against machines. He has no time for horses, likes only what can be made to move, tell the time or predict the weather at the touch of a button.

'Glad to be back, Miss Maureen?' one of the men calls out and I think, How quickly they see that she is the one to speak to.

'Jolly glad,' Maureen says, stepping forward a little into the line of flashbulbs. 'You can't imagine how tiring it is, being somewhere different every day.'

There is laughter then and good-natured encouragement to 'tell us more', but Ernest says, 'Better get on. Thank you all for this fine welcome.'

Gunnie has moved forward now and is greeting the family. She's careful not to cry as she embraces Cloé. 'How happy this makes me, cousin,' she says, and Cloé submits to the embrace and says, 'Dear Gunnie' before relinquishing her to the girls, who put their arms around her and begin to tell her of their adventures in a rush. I watch and try again to see how they are different. More – how they are the same. And then, 'Look, it's Fliss!' Oonagh, of course, always the sharpest and quickest. She darts forward, grabs hold of my hand and puts it to her face, then throws her arms tight around me.

~

The motorcars are waiting and we get in, Oonagh, Maureen, Aileen and me in one, Ernest, Cloé and Gunnie in the second and larger. The luggage will follow.

With the doors shut and the rain outside, rugs over our knees and a flask of chocolate, together, across from each other, it is easier. More like teatime at home in Glenmaroon.

'You look so grown up,' I say to Maureen. 'I feel quite shy of you.' I am only a year younger, less than a year, but I do not, now, look it.

'Oh, we had such fun in Paris,' she says. 'Mamma insisted, even though Papa didn't want to stop for so long at all. Monsieur Antoine himself did my hair.' She puts a hand up to those cropped golden curls and pats them. 'Do you think Harrods will be able to keep up?' She folds her gloves in her lap, smoothing the kid over and over with pleased fingers.

'I don't know,' I say. I don't know. My hair is done by

Gunnie, who is clever at brushing and pinning but cannot cut, so I still wear my red-brown curls in the style of Gunnie's youth – Cloé's youth – not this bobbed marvel that is the new fashion.

'But how was it?' I say. 'How was it, really?'

'Fun.' Maureen shrugs. 'You know . . .'

'Filthy food,' Aileen says.

'Too hot.'

'Too cold,' says Oonagh and shudders. 'Remember Spitzberg?'

'Too awful,' Maureen concurs. Then, 'I suppose we'll be in the newspapers tomorrow. Papa will be furious.'

'And you'll find it all very thrilling,' Aileen says. 'Goodness, Maureen, you are vulgar.'

'You like it all just as much as me only you won't say so.'

I look out. The evening is raw and wet, the rain dragged sideways by a rough wind. Behind us, the lights of Southampton dwindle, like a pale hand raised in limp farewell.

'I'll have my coming out next year,' Maureen says after a while. 'Mamma promised.'

'As long as she doesn't have to do anything and Gunnie does it all,' Aileen says. 'And it's my coming out too, don't forget. I've already delayed, because of this trip.'

'Well, it's going to be the biggest party London has ever seen,' says Maureen.

'It's going to be an utter bore – they always are,' Aileen contradicts her. 'All that fuss.'

'Not fuss, fun,' says Maureen with the sullen sound her voice takes on when someone disagrees with her. I can see she is ready

to say more cutting things to Aileen, who will say almost as cutting things back. That dynamic is still there, then – Maureen pretending to be more sophisticated than is even possible, in case anyone suspects her of being young, or inexperienced, perhaps even a little awed; Aileen determined to deny her, because they are sisters and neither can accept that for one to have doesn't mean the other must lose out.

Oonagh must see the row coming too because she leans forward and asks, 'So, Fliss, what have you been doing? Do tell.'

But I can't. What would I tell? That I returned home, and found that it wasn't home anymore? That I counted the days until their letters, then the days until their return so that when Gunnie wrote to Mummie and suggested I join her on the trip to Southampton to meet them, I said, 'Oh, please may I?' too loud and too quick, and saw Mummie's face turn hard and her mouth sharp even as she said, 'Very well.'

'Oh, you know,' I say, 'the usual things. I'm glad you're back.'

'Me too,' says Oonagh, sinking against the upholstery and taking my arm so that the fur of her collar tickles my nose.

Not one of us says Hughie's name, but he is there, beside us, in the car, so close that I think I can smell the Russian cigarettes he smoked and the hair oil from the collar of his jacket, just as it was that last summer at Glenmaroon.

Part One

Chapter One

Glenmaroon, Dublin, 1978

From the first curve of the driveway I see that the house is not loved anymore. It's slack around the edges; tired, I think, of being too much to too many.

A group of women are walking the gravel path that borders the lawn, down towards the river. Bundled into ugly clothes, they have the clumsy shuffle of boundaried living. They stay close together but do not talk much. Behind them, brisk in contrast, are two elderly nuns in unyielding black and white like border collie dogs. This is a care home now, where the Daughters of Charity order the lives of people who are not trusted to order their own.

'Will I come in with you?' he says, stopping the car.

'No. Stay here. I'll come back and get you should I need you.' He takes his hand from the steering wheel and grips my wrist for a moment. The thick blue cords of his veins stand out from the pale skin tinged with grey. Skimmed milk on the turn. The fingers are stiff as they close around my arm, but even so they are more vital than the brittle bones they encircle; the two thin frames of my wrist bones with a hammock of skin dipping between them. How have we got so old?

'Very well,' he says. 'I'll wait.'

The nun who guides me upstairs is younger than the two herding their charges about the lawn, younger than I am, but she's fat and breathes more heavily even than me as we ascend, first the main staircase, then the landing and the back stairs. I've been this way before, the first time I came to this house, sixty years ago. Then, it glowed with the colours of a rich rainbow. The wood of the stairs a deep, pleased gold, scattered with floating patches of pink and yellow light from the stained glass of the large window.

There are so many houses like this now. Big and old and pitiful, like the knuckles on an aged hand, I think.

Up in the attic room, a trunk has been pulled

out into the middle of the floor and the lid prised open. One of the hinges is broken so the lid hangs at an angle.

I know this room. I remember it, from my first night here. It looks even worse than it did. Then, it was bare and grubby with patches of mould. Now, the patches have run together so that the walls are entirely mildewed, and it is crammed full of broken, forgotten things: furniture, china, rotting books, piled up around the edges. Only the bit in the middle is empty; an abandoned battlefield watched over by many ghosts. Beside the trunk, a chair has been left so that I might sit and dip into the contents.

'I'll leave you to it,' the nun says and half pulls the door behind her.

Inside the trunk are yellowing papers, many embossed with the golden harp that tells me they are Ernest's work affairs. The estate agent was right. These are 'Guinness things'. But they don't look of much consequence to me, and I can't understand why first Oonagh, then Maureen were so keen to recover them. Or rather, have me recover them. Even though I know how the newspaper men will turn anything at all about the family into some kind of story.

'Fliss, we must get them back,' Maureen had said, peremptory, on the phone from London. 'You live in Dublin. You won't mind, I'm sure.'

The assumption irritated me – why should I not mind? So much so that even when Oonagh rang, from the South of France, and said, 'Please go, Fliss? I can't bear Papa and Mamma's things to be pawed over by the press', I professed not to understand the urgency.

It was only when cousin Mildred rang, as I knew she would – and almost to the hour, too – that I began to understand how serious they were.

'They don't know what's in the trunk,' Mildred explained, voice cutting crisply across all those transatlantic miles. 'But the nuns say they will give it to a local historical society, and if indeed that happens, reporters will get hold of it, and God knows what will come out.'

'Well, what could come out?' I asked.

'What would I know?' She laughed, and I heard the snap of her cigarette lighter. She breathed in, exhaled. I imagined I could smell the smoke, drifting out through the heavy Bakelite receiver in my hand. 'You're gonna have a much better idea than me.' She sounded so American. I suppose she is American. I mean, she always was, but not as much as now.

'There's nothing to come out,' I said. 'That's just Maureen being dramatic and tiresome and Oonagh being feeble.' But really, what did I know? Perhaps there was something to come out. 'Very well, I'll go,' I said.

'Bring someone with you,' she said. 'In case you have to carry stuff away.' *Stuff*. I imagined Cloé's face, nose wrinkled in distaste, at the word. At the notion that anyone would apply it to items that had belonged to her. I wondered had Mildred chosen it deliberately. A small, late revenge? Although, surely she had had all the revenge she needed long ago? Because Mildred, the poor relation, went off and made a success of her life – first as a nurse in the war, running a field hospital, then as an interior designer, quite a celebrated one, working in London and New York.

'I will,' I said. I already knew whom I would bring. The only person I could bring, because he was the only person who would come.

I bend now and pull the pages about. More golden harps. More dull-looking typed documents. But buried deeper in the tattered nests are pages of handwriting – letters, lists – and scrapbooks, the kind we kept in those days, into which we pasted pictures and sentimental rhymes, postcards, should we ever be sent such things.

I take one out. On the cover are fleshy red flowers, somewhere between poppy and rose, nowhere seen in nature, I am sure. The pages are damp and clotted together, and the clear glue, like varnish, that we used has seeped around and through pictures, covering everything with a cracked yellow sheen. There is a smell of sad old things so I cover my nose and mouth for a moment, but the smell gets in anyway. Breathing it, I can almost see Gunnie's hand, dipping the thick brush into the clear glass pot, spreading the glue busily and pasting pictures.

'Isn't that pretty now,' she might have said, surveying her handiwork with pride. Oonagh, beside her, would barely have looked around. These scrapbooks were yet another of the occupations that Gunnie so carefully cultivated for the girls. 'Maureen's stamp collection', 'Oonagh's embroidery', 'Aileen's crochet'. All, in reality, done by Gunnie or a governess, and displayed as the kind of quiet suitable accomplishment these girls should have; the kind for which they cared not at all.

Some creature, a worm that burrows through old books, has left a series of squiggly holes like trenches dug in the coloured pages.

I turn over the leaves, prising apart those that need it. Sometimes they are clumped together and tear under my thickened fingers. A postcard showing a curly-haired small boy in striped trunks pouring water from a bucket sits beside the programme for a pantomime: '*Tom Thumb* at the Gaiety Theatre'.

There is a photograph of Ernest in his war uniform, another of Cloé in her court dress. Each stares at the camera blankly, and I remember the agony of the wait, the strange suspended length of time for a photograph to be taken then.

The windows of the attic room are loose – the wind shakes them in their rotten frames – and through the gaps I can hear sounds from the gardens below. There is singing, something about Queen of the May. The nuns returning from the river walk with their charges.

I turn more pages. I do not know what I am looking for. All I see are sentimental recollections of childhood, and even at a distance of sixty years, I can catch the smell of that time. Dullness and emptiness, endless waiting, stuck between the schoolroom and the nursery, at ease nowhere. Beating at time with our fists to make it go faster.

Loose among the pages, in some places stuck to them by the leaky glue, are cuttings from newspapers. These must have been added later, I think, because we would not have included them. I pick out one or two. 'Hon. Lois Sturt Fills Role Of Britain's New Queen Of Beauty' trumpets one. I skim the faded type. Somewhere around the fourth paragraph I find Maureen's name, alongside that of Baby and Zita Jungman, and Elizabeth Ponsonby.

The London years of the girls' coming out; the parties and balls, the absurd treasure hunts and scavenger races. '. . . The Bright Young People assembled at 2.30am at some fashionable West End residence . . .' I read, then stop. Enough to live through it once, without reviewing it now from this dank attic.

I turn pages faster, keen now to be gone. There is nothing here, I am sure of it. Nothing that might cause a scandal, but nothing, too, that might not be burned or discarded. Nothing I wish to remember. It's time for me to leave, to go back down the stairs and out the front door, under the crumbling stone portico and allow him to drive me away and know that I will not ever be back.

I close the scrapbook but the activity has been too much for the damp and swollen spine and it pulls apart, pages landing in clumps on my knees and the floor around my feet. I bend with difficulty to gather them, that I might stow it all away and shut the lid of the trunk as best I can, and tell the estate agent to do as he wishes. But in the first bundle of pages I pull up, a news clipping catches at me like a fish-hook. A photo, in the sooty black-and-white of the time. Maureen is in the middle, face turned full towards the camera with that oblique and charming smile. Beside her, Aileen is aloof or looks to be, while Oonagh, still a child, peeks out, grinning, from behind Maureen's elbow. Behind them, I can make out the shape of *Fantome*, the spindly masts stretching up into the dark grey sky, and I know that on either side of the girls stand Ernest and Cloé, although they have been excluded by the photographer. 'Glorious Guinness Girls Return To Britain', I read.

Suddenly, I can sense the choking fog of that day and taste the salt that came in with the sea spray that dashed our faces as we waited.

I remember the joy of their return, the certainty of purpose they brought me. And how long it took me to understand that my life was as real as theirs. By the time I did understand – a very long time after Mummie first tried to tell me on the day I left Ballytibbert – it was nearly too late.

I remember all of it.

Chapter Two

Ballytibbert House, Wexford, 1918

The sound of her skirt was like dry sticks rubbing together. The material was so stiff I thought it might wear holes in itself simply by chaffing as she walked towards me. She was tall, so far above me that I dared not look up and so stared at the ground even though Mummie's voice was in my head – 'Stand up straight and smile' – running down my back, an invisible thread, twitching at my shoulders.

'Wouldn't you like to come and do lessons with my girls?' *My girls*.

Her name was Cloé and everyone spoke it with a special voice, even Mummie, who had no special voices for any but her dogs.

'Wouldn't you like that?' she asked, but it wasn't a question.

I knew her girls. They were three, and they dazzled. Blue eyes and blonde hair. The same but not the same. They had each other's face but with small variations so that looking at all of them together was to see a single treasure hoard split three ways. A store of rubies here, sapphires there, spun gold that together added up to three faces, three stares that were not curious or kindly but almost a dare.

There was Aileen, who was older, almost grown, and Maureen, in the middle, who was my age, or thereabouts – I was then ten, so she was eleven – and Oonagh, the baby at eight.

'Well, that's settled, then,' Cloé said. I hadn't said a thing. She looked at Mummie and Mummie nodded. I didn't know what her nod meant. Was it *yes, that is settled*, or was it the nod she gave to people when she didn't want to answer their questions? The nod she had been giving so often since the news of Papa's death, brought in a stiff envelope so small you would not have thought it could carry so much?

I watched as Mummie handed a plate of scones to Cloé.

'No, thank you.' Cloé waved the plate away. 'But perhaps Felicity would like one?' She smiled.

I knew Mummie wanted me to say *no, thank you* but I didn't.

I took a scone and ate it with jam and thick cream, slowly so that I could tell Hughie later about every mouthful. So intent was I that I didn't listen to what else Cloé and Mummie said, until Cloé stood, the scratching of her dress loud again, and said, 'Gunnie will meet her from the train.'

Who was Gunnie? What train?

I watched from the nursery window as the motorcar moved down the driveway, leaving deep ruts in the gravel that John Hegarty would have to rake over. I wondered if Mummie would come to the nursery, or send Mary to fetch me, and tell me what must happen next, but she didn't.

When Papa died, Mummie said there would need to be changes but she didn't say what, and after a while Hughie went back to school and the changes didn't come, except to Mummie herself, who was sad all the time even when she pretended not to be. The house stopped being careful and quiet and was mostly itself again, and nothing seemed very different except that Papa was gone and the bustle and hurry that always came with him were gone too. Uncle Alex was at the house more, and he and Mummie must have had so much to talk about because they were so often in Papa's study with the door always closed, although I could hear their voices.

'Don't be listening at doors,' Mary said, and I replied that I wasn't. I wouldn't. And indeed, I would not. Except that if I did hear something that told me what would now happen, well, that would not be my fault and at least then I would know.

The afternoon came on to rain, which drummed on the windows and, after a time, began to run down the length of twine Mary had fastened to the wet spots on the ceiling so that drops may twist and chase each other into the chipped white pot below.

I turned the pages of my book and wondered what lessons Cloé's 'girls' did. I could not think.

In the evening I went downstairs to the drawing room and Uncle Alex was there, with Mummie. There was a better fire than in the nursery and I sat on the rug before it with the dogs, who lay stretched out and turned their pink stomachs to the heat.

'How did you like your visitor?' Uncle Alex asked me.

'Well enough,' I said, even though it wasn't what I meant and she wasn't my visitor. 'Why did she say would I like to do lessons with her girls?' I asked after a moment, even though Mummie didn't like me to ask questions, and the drawing room was a place to sit quietly and do a puzzle or read my book while the grown-ups talked.

'Her daughters are close to you in age. She would like them to have a friend. And your mother thinks it is time you had more companionship,' he said.

'I have Hughie.'

'Soon Hughie will go away to school.'

'He is already at school.'

'But soon he will be away for longer periods. Not just for weeks but for many months.'

I didn't know that. I wished it wasn't true. Even with Hughie, four years older, home just for two days of every week, there was so little time to do the things we loved, like putting our ponies, Bramble and Dumpling, over fences and going out with the hunt, even though we were only allowed half days.

I would not go to school, I knew that, because I had asked Hughie.

'Girls don't,' he said. Then, 'Lucky you. I wish I didn't.'

'I have Mary,' I said now.

'Mary is a servant,' Mummie said. 'Not a companion.' In the firelight, her face was tired and her voice full of the effort of speaking.

It was true that there was no one to talk to me much. When Hughie was there, the rules were different. John Hegarty talked to him, about horses and our ponies, and answered Hughie's questions with a laugh. The men on the farm talked to him too, and the fishermen when we stayed with Aunt Agatha by the sea in Waterford. They all knew that Hughie would rather talk to them than anyone else, except for me, and so they talked back, losing the mumbling stiffness that came on them when it was Uncle Alex or Mummie, even Papa, who spoke to them.

'Sometimes it is dull,' I said, carefully, because of never wanting to sound as if I was complaining. But it was the right thing after all because Mummie's face looked less tired and Uncle Alex said, 'Very well, then,' and even I could see the relief.

'Time for you to go upstairs now, Felicity,' Mummie said. I knew Mary would be waiting with my cocoa. She would talk to me. I could tell her stories, and she would say, 'Where do you get your queer ideas, Miss Felicity?' And I wouldn't tell her that I got them from the people around me, from watching them and seeing what they did and wondering, always, why.

Chapter Three

Glenmaroon, Dublin, 1918

The train was noisy and dirty and I didn't like the movement of it, feeling sick and frightened by turns.

I wished Hughie were with me. He would have loved it. All the way to the station in the trap, with John Hegarty driving, I wished for Hughie and his questions. He would have known what to say to John Hegarty, asking how to tie things and catch things, about the war where Papa went and did not come back alive, and the horses that went with him and were still over there, and whether they might one day return.

I thought how stupid it was that Hughie, whose

letters told me he hated school, must go away and learn things he had no interest in, while I, who would have liked to know more about India and Flanders and arithmetic, must not.

The hard, red velvet of the train carriage seats scratched and scraped at the backs of my legs so that they were soon raw and sore. I wanted to sit on my hands, to protect my legs, but I knew Mummie would not like it.

The guard on the train gave me good warning when we came towards Dublin, though he need not have bothered. The change in the air told me, the way it lost its sparkle and was dragged down with the weight of the houses. So many houses, all with their backs to the train as though it had offended them.

I had been to Dublin before, of course. To the pantomime with Hughie and Papa, and once to the Gresham Hotel, where the curtains were as thick as shadows. But never like this, alone. And even though I knew I would be met, by the lady called Gunnie, still I was afraid. How would she find me? How would I find her? What if I could not tell her who I was and she swept out of the station without me, to tell Cloé that I had not come after all? The train was late, I knew because the guard had said it; what if she had left already, tired of waiting for me?

The train stopped, a screech of brakes that said it did not wish to stop. I didn't know where my trunk was. The guard had said he would 'stow' it for me but I didn't know what that meant. The carriage door had closed and the handle was stiff so that I could not now open it. I pulled down the window and put my head out, but my hat had come loose so I had to hold it to my head and could not see properly. I think I might have cried then, even though I was ten and too old for tears. I didn't know where I was and knew only that I disliked this great noisy, dirty place where pigeons flapped ragged wings as they made angry rushes on whatever bit of bread or crumb of cake people had left behind.

Home and Hughie were so far away, even though he promised he would write and visit, and I knew so little about what was to happen to me except that I would stay 'for a time' with Cloé and her girls. What was 'a time'? Even that I did not know.

'You must be Felicity?' She was small and round and whiskery with wet brown eyes like an otter, and she smiled at me in a way that said she was happy to see me. Had been happy to wait for me.

'Are you Gunnie?'

She laughed at that, said, 'I am Cloé's cousin Gertrude, Mrs Gunn. But Gunnie is what the family call me. I think you had better call me that too, don't you?'

'I cannot find my trunk,' I said, and my voice wobbled.

'Why, I have your trunk. See!' And she pointed to a porter waiting halfway down the platform. Sure enough, behind him on a trolley was my trunk that had so little in it other than the silver-backed brushes Mummie gave as a gift when I said goodbye to her the night before.

'I was going to give you these on your birthday, but as you leave tomorrow, I shall give them now and you must remember me when it is your birthday,' she had said.

'Yes, Mummie,' I said. My birthday was not for several months. Was I really to stay so long a time? I thought she would leave then – she doesn't like to come to the nursery – but she didn't. 'I hope you will remember who you are when you are with the Guinness girls.'

'I will,' I said, although I did not know what she meant. She must have seen that I did not understand her, because then she said, 'We can all see what they have. But don't forget what you have.'

'I won't,' I said. And then, in a rush, because I had to know, 'What is it that I have?'

She smiled. 'You'll have to work that out for

yourself, won't you?' I had no idea that it would take me almost a lifetime to do so.

'Come along,' Gunnie said then, and opened the door and helped me as I stepped down onto the station platform.

Outside the station she led the way past a thin horse between the shafts of a tattered hackney cab and stopped before the longest motorcar I had ever seen. It was not the same as the one Cloé came to call in – that was dark green while this was silver – and standing beside it was a man in a grey uniform with brass buttons, who touched his peaked cap when he saw us.

Inside, the seats were of soft leather, heavenly on the backs of my legs after the scratching velvet of the train carriage.

'First, we will make a small detour,' Gunnie said. The car gobbled up streets in smooth lunges, stopping for a moment in front of two tall black gates set between high walls made up of small yellow bricks. On the gates was a golden harp and the word 'Guinness' in fat, proud letters.

'Is this the house?' I asked.

'No.' Gunnie let out a peal of laughter. 'No! This is the factory. This is where "the bread and butter comes from". That's what Ernest says.'

I thought for a long time, then said, 'Is it a bread factory?' in surprise, because I had been told something else. That made her laugh all the more. She patted me on the knee in delight and said, 'Oh, wait till I tell Ernest.'

After that, the drive was long and I felt sick again, but I didn't mind so much. Gunnie talked as we drove, telling me about the house. Or rather, the houses. 'There is a second house,' she said, 'that almost mirrors the first house. The North house and the South house. We live mostly in the North house, which is the newer and the finer of the two. They are connected, you know. By an iron bridge above the ground.' I did not understand at all what she said – why two houses? What bridge? – but I understood the satisfaction in her voice as she said it. It was the same I felt when Hughie did something wonderful on Dumpling or shot a rabbit true and straight; glory that wasn't mine but was the closest I came to having any.

'Glenmaroon is entirely new,' Gunnie continued. 'Ernest likes everything to be modern. There is a swimming pool inside the house, and a cinema. We're nearly there now. We are past the Phoenix Park, which is the largest park in all the world.' Again, there was pride swelling in her voice like a blackbird's song, as though she had made the park her very own self. We were at the edges of the city now so there were fields as well as houses. I felt I could breathe again. We swept through iron gates and past a cottage, up to a large house that was red and black and grey, with pointy roofs like flags flown on a windy day and many chimneys standing straight as rifles on parade reaching into the sky. There was a long lawn and such flowers as I could see were most strictly laid out – none of the abundance of Mummie's blooms and plants here.

'The gardens are in the Italian style,' Gunnie said, leaning close to me so that her words hissed in my ear.

The motorcar crunched to a stop under a stone archway. 'Here we are,' she said in delight. 'And there's Lapham.' A man stood in the doorway. I knew him to be a butler although we didn't have one, but if I hadn't known, I might have thought him part of the house so straight and stiff did he stand.

'We'll go to the small drawing room. The family will be there now,' Gunnie said. She was too eager to get to them to wait for me and I had to trot to keep up with her, along miles of wooden floors so shiny I longed to take off my shoes and slide in my stockings. I wondered if Cloé's girls ever did that. The ceiling above me was a deep red, picked out with swirling white lines. A vast staircase, of the same warm polished wood, led up to a wall of coloured glass prettily etched with flowers and birds. Light poured through it, bouncing off the floor and walls so that it was like being inside Mummie's jewellery box, the one with the inlay mother-of-pearl lid. The smell was the same as the mother-of-pearl box – sun-soaked wood, beeswax, dust, with something precious at the heart.

Gunnie opened a door into a large bright room. Clustered at the far end at a round table set in the embrace of a deep bay window, five faces turned to stare at me: Cloé and her girls, and a tall lady with red hair.

'Here we are, back again,' said Gunnie, hand to my shoulder to gently push me forward. I let her push me although I wanted to resist. The group at the table were so self-contained, so still in the embrace of the window, that I didn't want to intrude on them. I knew my face must be covered in smuts from the train and felt my hair escape my hat in an untidy way. Meanwhile they stared at me. So many pairs of blue eyes, blazing as if the light from the window poured through them too. Cloé's girls dazzled more than I had remembered, now that I saw them in their own house.

'Welcome, Felicity. This is Aileen,' Cloé said. The tallest of the three nodded coolly at me. 'And Maureen'; a flash of laughing blue and heavy golden curls. 'And Oonagh'; the smallest, most solemn-eyed of the three looked at me and I looked back.

'This is Peke,' Oonagh said, holding up a small snub-nosed dog that looked out from behind a thick fringe with popping eyes. I could hear its laboured, effortful breathing loud in the absence of conversation.

'And this is Mildred,' Cloé continued, as if Oonagh hadn't spoken. The lady with the red hair put out a hand. Beside the slender blue and gold of Cloé and her girls, she was large and pale and loose, spilling over her spindly chair towards the floor like syrup escaping from a tin. Her voice when she spoke was deep and with an accent I hadn't heard before.

'How do you do?' she said. 'So you're the famous Felicity.' I did not know what to say. How was I famous? I was not famous, at all, so why would she say that?

'Mildred was born in *America*,' Cloé said, almost wonderingly, as if unsure how such a person had come to be in their midst.

They looked at me, all of them, so I felt I must say something. 'Pleased to meet you,' I said at last. But because I was unsure and unhappy I said it in Mummie's voice – the one that told you she wasn't pleased, wasn't even interested – so that hearing it, they all looked away and I didn't know how to say that was not how I meant it to be.

'We waited tea,' Cloé said after a moment, as

though this were something magnificent. She sat, I saw, so upright in her chair that her back did not touch it at all and even where she did rest, any contact seemed accidental, as though she had allowed herself to perch only lightly, momentarily, while in flight. 'Gunnie, perhaps you would pour?'

There were sandwiches and scones but also tiny iced cakes and a bigger cake and pots of cream and jam and sweet preserves. I watched as the three girls took small pieces of this and that, as if they were not very interested in the delicious things in front of them. As if they saw such things every day. I was hungry but didn't dare do different to them so I took small pieces too although I could have eaten everything on those pretty china plates.

'I'm afraid you will not find our gardens to be as fine as yours,' Cloé said then, to all of us although I knew she must mean me. 'Felicity's mother, Mrs Burke, is a most accomplished gardener. Her father was Admiral Redmond, you know.' Somehow, this was almost always said of Mummie. As if to make up for the fact that she was just Mrs Burke now.

The three girls said very little and I said nothing and after a time Maureen said, 'May I be excused, Mamma?' and Cloé said very well. One by one all three girls slipped away and when they had gone Cloé said, 'Gunnie, would you show Felicity to her room? And then perhaps you would bring me some lavender water? I feel a headache coming on and will lie down before dinner.'

'Of course,' Gunnie said. Beside me, I felt her quiver like a gundog at a shoot, the heady scent of duty in its nostrils.

With Gunnie I walked up the large staircase towards the window of coloured glass so that I felt we would walk into a song or a poem with the glow of it, then around a corner and up another staircase to a wide hallway with many closed doors. A kitchen or scullery maid came towards us from the far end of the hallway, so dirty and bedraggled that I was surprised to see her. At home, Mummie would never have allowed such a creature to be anywhere except the kitchen. I thought she might scamper away at the sight of us, but she came on until she was upon us and said in a voice that was low and thick, 'Shure I can show the young laydy where she'll be sleeping.'

Gunnie stood silent for a moment and then, 'Very well,' she said. 'You may do so.' I was surprised and watched after her as she turned and went back down the stairs we had just ascended.

'This way, Miss,' the creature said. She smiled at me and there were blackened stumps where her teeth should have been, although she cannot have been much more than a child. She led me along the hall, around a corner and to another staircase behind a heavy door that was small and mean and led up and up into the roof of the house. As we walked up, her always ahead, she asked me questions, but her accent was so strange and solid that I could not always understand what she said so had to stay silent more than answer.

We climbed to an attic space that was so narrow we couldn't walk abreast, and dark because there were only a very few small windows set high up in the roof. We walked to the very end where the creature opened a door into a dingy little room with an iron bed and a mattress with bare ticking and a misshaped bolster thrown across it. The walls were discoloured, mottled like flesh on a cold day, and the air was stuffy. The only window was set high up where I could not reach it and, by the cobwebs around it, did not seem to have been opened in the longest while.

'Am I to sleep here, then?' I asked, trying to keep my voice steady.

'That you are,' she said. 'Shure, where else would you be? Is it with the family you thought you'd be sleeping?' And she began to laugh.

I could bear it no more. I knew I had been sent from Ballytibbert because there was no money and no way to educate me – such things happened often to girls – but was I to be some kind of servant? Why had I not been told? What would Hughie say when he found out? At the thought of Hughie, who had always protected me so carefully, I began to cry. All the tears that I had held in on the train and at the station and since leaving home that morning began to fall in thick clumps and sobs escaped me in ragged gasps.

The creature stood and stared at me, no longer cackling but slouched against the doorframe. I wished she would go away and opened my mouth to tell her so when suddenly in the open doorway, like sunlight, Oonagh appeared, breathless from her climb.

'Oh, please don't cry,' she said, face screwed up in sympathy. 'Don't cry, dear.' But I couldn't stop. 'How could you?' she said then, furiously rounding on the creature beside her in the doorway. 'Of all the mean things . . .'

The creature rubbed hard at one of her teeth and said in quite a different voice, 'It was only a joke.'

'Not much of a joke, I think,' Oonagh said, gesturing towards me with a small white hand. 'Honestly, Maureen!'

At that the creature stood up straighter and pulled the dusty cap from her mop of curls. 'Oh, for goodness sake!' she said without a trace of the accent I had found so hard to understand. 'I'm sorry, then. There, will that do?' to Oonagh and she looked at me and grinned a bit. 'But I had you quite fooled, didn't I?'

'You did,' I said, wiping at my face with the back of my hand. Oonagh handed me her handkerchief, a scrap of lace-edged cambric, so that I could dry my tears properly. 'You did.' I began to half-laugh although the tears were there too.

'You mustn't mind Maureen,' Oonagh said. 'She thinks there is nothing so amusing as fooling people with disguises.'

'Well, there isn't,' Maureen said. She rubbed again at her teeth, which I saw were just painted with black, not missing, and grinned again at me. I, my upset almost forgotten now, grinned back.

'Let me show you where your real room is,' Oonagh said, taking my hand.

'I'll come too,' Maureen said. 'No hard feelings, I suppose?'

'None,' I said.

'Isn't Mildred horrid?' Maureen asked as we walked back along the narrow hallway and down the steep stairs. '*The famous Felicity*,' she mimicked.

'Who is she?' I asked.

'A cousin.'

'Another cousin?' I thought of Gunnie, who was '*cousin Gertrude*'.

'We have a great deal too many,' Maureen said. 'So many that it's a curse. The Guinness Curse.'

She laughed. 'Papa has two brothers, Uncle Rupert who is older and Uncle Walter who is younger, and they have children who are our first cousins, and that's only for starters because there are heaps more in different parts of the family.' She said it as though 'the family' were a large wardrobe filled with different drawers and shelves.

'Maureen invented a game in which she scores them all,' Oonagh said. 'And then combines the scores of the whole family to get a total. One year, Uncle Walter's family came out at minus 130 because cousin Bryan did something terrible to my doll, Mary Mercy.' She laughed, but Maureen did not.

'Vile fellow,' she said. Then, 'Mildred is one of our *poor* cousins. From America, whom we must be kind to *because she does not have our advantages*.' She sounded as though she were imitating someone else when she said that, but I didn't know whom.

'Come along,' Oonagh said. 'Your room is beside mine and your trunk is there already. Robert brought it up.' Then, 'May I call you Fliss? Felicity seems so very strict.' She squeezed my hand.

'You may.' I squeezed back. Fliss was what Hughie called me.

Chapter Four

Glenmaroon, Dublin, 1978

'Sister says I'm to ask if you want tea.'

The voice in the doorway startles me and I look up to see a young girl.

'What?'

'Tea,' she mutters. She can't, I suppose, go through the whole sentence again. I think of the neatly crafted formality of the Glenmaroon servants – Lapham, the butler who opened the door to me on my first evening, with his terrifying dignity; Robert, the junior footman, and Kathleen, the housemaid; both kind, but skittish too, keenly aware of the invisible line that fell between us and them, and careful to be always on the right side of it. None so careful as Thomas.

Sometimes we persuaded them to cross over for some game – after all, Kathleen was barely older than Maureen, Robert within a couple of years of Aileen – but they stepped back as soon as they could. That line drawn by privilege must have been drummed into them from childhood. And into Thomas down at the stables, because of his father, more than any of them. He was younger than Aileen but I think now that he saw not a line but a gap, something deep and wide and hungry, and chose never to step across because he understood how much the stepping back and forth, the erasing and redrawing of that gap, blurred the differences and hid them. Hard to see and destroy something if it has been prettily camouflaged.

I suppose it should have been obvious how deeply Thomas resented what was around him. But it wasn't. Not then. Not to me.

Instead, he let Hughie come to him. Drew him in, I don't know how, although I suppose it wasn't hard. Hughie with his natural sense of right, and wrong, his instinctive sympathy, his youth, was ready, and made more so by Papa's death, by the way Mummie drew away from both of us after it, and the way we lived so close to but so separate from the children of the cottages: we could see their misery, but it didn't touch us, even though childhood was often ugly back then.

'No tea, thank you,' I say. But rather than slide back out the door as I expect, the girl comes further into the room, standing with her hands twisted behind her back as though roped together there.

'There's more,' she says, peering into the trunk.

'More what?'

'More of that. In the stables.'

'More papers?'

'Yes. Bags of them.'

'Will you show me?'

She darts a look behind her.

'It's OK,' I say. 'I'm meant to look through them. That's what I'm here for.'

Chapter Five

Glenmaroon, Dublin, 1918

My first morning in that new house – I hardly remembered how I had got to bed the night before, so tired was I – I woke to find a maid laying a fire although it was April. On the small table beside my bed, a cup of cocoa steamed. The bed was high from the ground and I sat up against plump pillows and sipped my cocoa, which was far sweeter than I was used to, afloat on feathers, planning how I might get down without a scramble in front of this neat person in her starched black dress and white pinafore. How I might hide my nightdress, darned so many times, from her swift, humiliating appraisal.

The maid left, after wishing me a 'Good morning, Miss', and I tumbled down from the bed, to walk across a rug that was thick and furry like moss with no worn bits to catch my bare toes. My few dresses had been hung in a heavy wardrobe with great hoops of brass for handles. When I pulled them they resisted my hand, then gave with a sudden capitulation that sent me backwards a few clumsy steps. I dressed in my grey serge from the day before and was wondering what to do and where to go when there was a tap at the door and Oonagh came in.

She was neatly dressed in a pretty blue frock that brought out her eyes, with a white pinafore over it, her hair tied back with a blue ribbon. 'I am to bring you to the day nursery for breakfast,' she said.

Even though we had parted such friends the night before, I think we both felt a little strange again, because she was very formal and I didn't know what to say and she didn't say anything more, just led the way to a bright room where Aileen and Maureen were eating breakfast. Sunlight glinted on the silver knife in Aileen's hand and lit up the orange marmalade on it as though she spread her toast with sticky gold.

After breakfast had finished, as we stood to leave the table, I did what I would have done at home – slipped a slice of bread into my pocket, to have later should I need it. I thought I was quick and discreet, but Oonagh saw me.

'You can ask if you are hungry,' she said. 'You just ring a bell and ask a maid to bring some bread and butter, or even cake.' I felt hot and itchy at being caught doing something that was almost stealing.

The governess arrived, Mrs Spain, and said, 'Let us see what you have learned' to me. 'You are nearly of an age with Miss Maureen so we shall see how you do together.' She spoke fast and arranged her words with precision, snapping them off at the end in case they tried to escape and do something she didn't wish.

I did not expect to do well in the little contest she had in mind, and sure enough, once installed in the schoolroom with its spinning globe and smell of chalk, I found Maureen was far ahead of me in French, arithmetic and English composition, and her handwriting was more elegant. But my knowledge of history – thanks to Hughie – was greater. 'Although it comes perilous near to *politics* at times,' Mrs Spain said, making 'politics' sound like something unpleasant. 'Far too much of Irish battles and rebellions, not nearly enough of our dear kings and queens.'

Maureen, alight with the spirit of competition, was quick with her answers, triumphant in her rightness, reeling off all she knew with an animated smile and a sideways glance at me that said she meant no malice, but was determined to win.

After lessons we had luncheon, then rode out on the ponies. Because I had left Bramble behind, I had a neat grey pony with a white sock called Captain.

I saw at once that, for all they were light in their saddles, the girls did not love riding as I did, and were what my papa would have called 'front door riders', taking delivery of their shining mounts from Sean the groom rather than going to the stables to do their own saddling up. My papa would have dismissed them for this, but I was beginning to understand that for these girls, everything was different. The many rules around what I could do, and say, which I thought were like the strictest laws of nature – that water flows downstream and trees die back in winter – did not exist for them. Even Hughie, whose rules were different to my rules, was bound in ways, but these girls, it seemed, were not.

Later I would come to understand that they had different rules, less visible, just as strict, but in the beginning, all I saw was the immense indulgence they were granted. Their comfort was considered in all things, their wishes consulted. I suppose I took that for freedom at first.

As we rode, I asked them questions, about the

house and how it worked and who everyone was, and tried to understand answers that were too brief – they were both more interested in teasing each other than describing the details of their household. 'Ask Gunnie,' Maureen said at last, clearly bored, so I gave up. But I watched all around me, listened and tried to make sense of what I saw. I felt I must be alert and vigilant in case I be called upon for something I had not anticipated. And I must hide how strange I found this new place; how much I missed the old.

I still did not understand, really, why I was there, and Maureen's prank of the day before had bit deeper than I was able to admit. Was I indeed to be a servant in some way? Or a companion? And if a companion, what, exactly, must a companion do? Was I there to do lessons, as Cloé had said, or to be of help, as Maureen's joke had suggested? And if that, what help could I possibly be?

For each moment of the day the girls had different clothes so that they seemed to be constantly in and out of their bedrooms, changing, repinning hair and positioning hats. I had only my grey dress, and a very old riding habit cut down from one of Mummie's, and when I put the dress back on after our ride and went to the day nursery, Maureen looked me up and down and said, 'Must you always wear that?'

'I don't have many dresses,' I said, and saw her flush red and hot.

'Drat this embroidery,' Oonagh said. 'I cannot make it come right.'

'Why bother?' Maureen said. 'You know Spanish will do it for you, because she wants to show it to Mamma so Mamma sees how well she has been teaching us.' She giggled. 'Spanish' was what she called Mrs Spain.

'How might I post a letter?' I asked. It had been very much on my mind. I wished to write to Hughie and tell him, try to tell him, some of what my new life was like, but I didn't know what to do when the letter was written.

'Just put it on the table in the hall and Lapham will take it,' Oonagh said.

'Who are you writing to?' Maureen asked. The way she said 'you', I saw that she could not believe I had anyone with whom I would correspond.

'Hughie. He is my brother.'

'A brother. Lucky you,' Maureen said. 'I wish I had a brother and not just dull, dull sisters.'

'You almost are a brother,' Aileen said then, looking up from the copy of something called *Vogue* she was reading. At just a month short of fourteen, Aileen seemed very much a young lady, who spoke of going to afternoon dances with other young people, and was excused from lessons with us, although she was still expected to fill scrapbooks and produce watercolours. She had friends, other young ladies, whom she was permitted to visit with Mildred to accompany her, and the makings of a life beyond Glenmaroon, for which she was greatly envied by the younger two. She was bored and distant with us, until she forgot to be grand and aloof, and was nearly as funny and silly as Oonagh. 'You are just as loud and fidgety as a brother. I don't see that we need one.'

'You never see anything that is not right before your face,' Maureen said. 'We need a brother because we are too much the same. What are the differences between us? Three girls? A boy would be something different.'

'I am not the same as you, not by any imagining,' Aileen said with spirit.

'The only ones who see any differences are ourselves,' Maureen insisted. 'To all the rest of the world we are simply The Guinness Girls. You know we are. You've heard them whispering, at dancing classes and tennis parties. As though we are all one and the same. And easily swapped,' she finished gloomily.

'I am nothing the same as you,' Aileen insisted again, glancing quickly at herself in the mirror opposite. It was the kind of glance I would often see her give, in mirrors about the house, but also in windows, even the highly polished silver dish covers at dinner. At first I thought it was vanity that sent her so often towards her own reflection, but then I began to see it was more as though she needed to reassure herself – of who she was, what she looked like. Maureen's vanity was the belligerent strut of a cockerel that knows itself to be the finest in the yard, Aileen's a more hesitant thing altogether.

'Tell more, Fliss? About Hughie,' Maureen demanded then. 'How old is he? Is he clever? Would I like him? Or is he a bore like cousin Bryan?' And even though I was secretly nettled at the way she asked – as if Hughie were hers to discover, a box to ransack – I tried to tell them how brave Hughie was, how much he knew, how well he protected me from the nannies who ruled the nursery when we were younger – who were kind to him and cruel to me so that I understood very early that there was a difference between boys and girls.

'Well, then, I wish dearly that we might have had a brother too,' Oonagh said with feeling. 'Someone to stand up to that awful Nanny Whitaker.'

'Was she the one who made your head bleed with the bristles of the brush?' Maureen asked.

'No, that was Nanny Hawkins, remember?

Nanny Whitaker was the one who said I must eat the porridge made with milk that had gone off, even when I said I should be sick. And then I was sick, and she said I must eat that too,' Oonagh said, hanging her head down so that she was entirely hidden behind the mass of her hair. I heard the disgust in her voice and the shame too.

'Now I remember,' Maureen said, giving Oonagh's arm a squeeze. 'I prayed and prayed that something awful would happen to her. I prayed so hard that I'm certain something awful did, even if she didn't stay long enough for us to see it.'

'But surely Gunnie and your mother would not have allowed that?' I asked, appalled.

'That was before Gunnie came, and when I told Mamma, she said, "Nanny knows best and you must do as she says",' Oonagh said. 'Maureen was the only one who would listen. She tried to take revenge by hiding Nanny's Bible but that just made her more angry.'

'So does Hughie go about on his own?' Maureen wanted to know. 'Anywhere he chooses?'

'Yes, because he is fourteen. And when he is home from school in Newbridge, I go with him.'

These girls, it seemed, were almost never without supervision. If they were not with Mrs Spain, it was Gunnie, or Mildred, or Sean the groom, or Cloé. I thought of the many hours that Hughie and I had, to fill as we wished with only the rule that we must not annoy anyone. We would take our ponies, or walk about the place, and eat the apples that fell from the trees. We would visit the farm workers and the tenants, who might give us tea in rough mugs. We were always hungry, always curious. Hughie talked to everyone we met and told me afterwards what they meant by certain things they said – things called 'grievances' – that he understood and I did not, and that he said were fair even though Uncle Alex did not agree.

The next afternoon, when I went to put on my grey serge after riding, Gunnie came to my room with an armful of dresses. There were navy sailor dresses, pretty percales with white collars, just like Oonagh and Maureen wore, and even a rich red velvet. I had never owned such clothes.

'You can wear this for the drawing room later,' Gunnie said, picking out a soft brown with tones of red and a wide sash. 'It will suit your dark colouring.' At home, no one ever spoke to me about the way I looked, except for Papa, who used to say, 'You are a fetching enough little thing' when he was pleased with me.

'But where are they from?' I asked now about the dresses in Gunnie's arms.

'Maureen,' she said. 'She insisted I bring them to you.'

Chapter Six

The news that the girls' papa was back moved through the house like swallows through a barn; swift and glad, until it seemed it was known in the kitchen and stables as surely as in the drawing room and schoolroom.

Mildred was first with the news. By then, some weeks in, I had realised Mildred was always first with the news if she could be. I saw the sense of importance this gave her. Her large pale face would acquire yet more purpose as she doled out the information, bit by bit, rationed to some system of her own.

'You must be sure to put on good frocks this afternoon, to come down to the drawing room' was what she said, coming to the schoolroom after breakfast one day.

'Why so?' Aileen asked. 'Are there visitors?'

'Of a sort,' Mildred replied.

'Oh, for goodness sakes, Mildred, stop pretending to be the Sphinx,' Maureen snapped. 'Who is it? If it's Great-Aunt Olive, I shan't.' This 'Great-Aunt Olive' was married to a brother of the girls' grandfather, and was 'a great meddler' according to Maureen.

'If you don't, you'll be sorry,' Mildred said, refusing to be robbed of her importance. 'It isn't Lady Ardilaun.'

'Well, then, who?' Maureen demanded.

Mildred paused, faithful to the pace she had decided on. 'It's your papa.'

'Papa is back? Why did no one tell us?' Oonagh demanded.

'Not back yet, but expected any moment, and I am telling you now,' Mildred said, rising to leave, so satisfied that she seemed an even bigger person than when she had arrived.

I had not yet met my host. 'Papa travels a great deal,' the girls had told me. 'He has many things to tend to everywhere.' I was fascinated that they spoke of their father's business with familiarity, even fondness. Mummie, when she told me of it – 'He has a great deal to do with the making of stout' – had said it as though it were something not quite nice.

But Maureen was as happy to boast of that as she was to boast of the quickness of her fingers across the piano keys. 'It is the largest brewery in the world,' she told me. 'The very largest.' And on days when the wind came from the south and there was a thick, sweet smell, like burned treacle, blown from the city out as far as Glenmaroon, she said with pride, 'It is the smell of the factory.' It was she who laughed most when Gunnie told them all what I had said about the bread and butter factory, repeating my words and saying, 'Oh my, that's good!' until Cloé, looking pained, had said, 'That's enough now, Maureen.'

The house knew that Ernest had finally arrived before we did. There were sounds of footsteps on the polished wooden floors, up and down the stairs, doors opening and closing, all with an urgency I had not yet known there. I was nervous and wished that he had stayed away longer so that I might get a little more accustomed to being there. But I dressed in my new clothes and tried to still the pounding of my heart, which threatened to deafen me as we walked down the stairs.

'Papa!' Oonagh was first, running across

the room towards a man who stood by the chimneypiece, one arm draped across it as though it were a favourite hound. I saw a broad face with a small, thick moustache that dragged his nose too close to his upper lip, and clever, curious, light eyes that were the originals of his daughters. The moustache hid his mouth so completely that his teeth, when he smiled, were a surprise flash of white in all that brown. Maureen and Aileen followed more sedately and, in a moment, I understood why when, in response to Oonagh's attempt to throw her arms around him, her father held her off, then took her hand in his and shook it politely. He then shook hands with Aileen and Maureen, and looked on them all with pleasure. He did not see that Oonagh was crestfallen. Or if he did, he said nothing of it.

'My girls,' he said, looking carefully at each in turn the way Mummie did with Hughie and me when we had been sick and might be sick again. Then, 'You are Felicity,' he said, watching me over their heads.

'I am, sir,' I managed.

'You are welcome,' he said. 'Most welcome.' To my surprise he bent to the coal scuttle. I expected he would ring for a servant to stoke up the fire, already blazing well in defiance of the large window open to the evening air behind me. Of a sudden, the room was filled with loud music, a popular tune that I knew, 'Cherry Ripe'. I looked around to see where it came from but could see nothing. Only when I looked back and saw the laughing faces of the three girls did I understand that I was not meant to understand.

'One of my little inventions,' Ernest said, and bent to the coal scuttle again. This time I saw that he pulled a lever. Again the room was filled with the opening bars of 'Cherry Ripe'.

Cherry ripe, cherry ripe,
Ripe I cry,
Full and fair ones
Come and buy.

The music was tinny and not beautiful, perhaps not even completely in tune, but as it filled the room once more, pushing at the walls and ceiling to make space for itself, pushing against the evening air that smelled of night jasmine on one side, and the acrid smoky tickle of lichened wood on the other, I felt it run right through me.

I thought of my papa then, dead in that war where the soldiers sang this song as they unrolled their bedding or cleaned their boots, or so he had told me on one of his leaves home, and I felt hot tears rush to my eyes. I could not raise my hand to my face to dash them, but neither could I let them spill and be seen, and so I had to stop them. At all costs I had to stop them. I looked hard at the carved chimneypiece, following the intricate swirls of the marble as it meandered, concentrating hard on it to divert my thoughts and force the tears back.

Following those curves and swirls, my eyes came to Ernest himself, still staring at his coal scuttle. In his face, as he looked down at it, was all the delight I had seen in Oonagh's earlier when she had flung herself towards him before that arm came out to halt her.

'What have you been doing?' he said, and Aileen and Maureen began to tell him of their lessons and their rides. Cloé, straight-backed on a chair close by, drew Oonagh, whom I saw was still chagrined, to her. 'Give Papa a moment to compose himself,' Cloé said quietly. 'He is only just returned.'

'He is always just returning or leaving,' Oonagh said, hiding her face on her mother's shoulder. But Cloé shook her off.

'Stand straight, child,' she said. 'Do not slouch.'

'How was your trip to London, Papa?' Aileen asked.

'Good, thank you,' he replied.

'And Uncle Rupert?'

'Well. His children send their love.'

'Dear little Honour,' Maureen said with too much emphasis on 'dear'.

'That's dear little *Lady* Honour,' Aileen said with a sideways look at Maureen, who abruptly turned her back on her.

'You have a new cousin now,' Cloé said. 'A baby called Patricia whom they call Patsy.'

'Sounds like a puppy,' Maureen said.

'Maureen Constance!'

'Well, it does,' Maureen insisted, so she was sent back upstairs with Mrs Spain for her rudeness.

'Ernest, may I bring you a toddy?' Mildred asked.

Before he could reply Gunnie said hastily, 'I have asked Cook to prepare a consommé. So sustaining after a journey, I always think.'

'Not at all, a toddy's the thing,' Mildred said with decision.

I saw Cloé look with amusement from one to the other as they waited, near trembling with anticipation. But 'Nothing, thank you,' Ernest said, and I saw them both slump somewhat, before Mildred rallied.

'I have saved you a most interesting article about the price of barley that was in *The Irish Times*,' she said and then, when Ernest said, 'Thank you, I will read that later,' swelled again to her largest size so that Gunnie, beside her, was quite dwarfed.

That evening, Maureen, Oonagh and I sat drinking cocoa before our bedtime. This was my favourite time of the day, I had decided, the half hour before bed when we sat together in the day nursery with no Gunnie or governess, the curtains drawn and the fire lit and lamps glowing on the chimneypiece and surrounding tables.

In that half hour, the chill of the drawing room that was the chill of all the drawing rooms I knew – where our parents ruled and where they asked questions for which there were no answers: 'Are you being good?', or talked about us as though we were not there – was dispelled. Out of their sight, the competition that seized us all in their presence dissipated and we did not need to rush each other, grabbing for the few scraps of their attention, like the dogs at home hoping for a scrap from Mummie's plate.

That night, rain had closed the day down early so that it was quite dark already, and beyond the heavy curtains the windows ran wet. But I didn't mind. At home, I would have thought about the plink of drops into blue-rimmed enamel bowls, the rivers of dirty water running down the hairy length of string in the nursery, the clammy sheets of my bed. Here, the worse the weather outside, the cosier I felt indoors. I took off my shoes and stretched my toes to the warmth of the fire.

'What kind of a cousin is Mildred?' I asked.

'The worst kind,' Maureen said in a flash.

'She came from America some years ago,' said Oonagh, stirring her cocoa thoughtfully. 'Her papa was Great-Uncle Cecil, who was my grandmother Dodo's brother. He had one family and his wife died and then he married Mildred's mother and had another. Mildred's mama came with her, but she is American and worked in a bar' – she was round-eyed at the idea – 'so we do not see her. There is a brother too, but we do not see him either. Mamma said Mildred might live with us. She wanted to change Mildred's name, because she said how dreadfully common it was, but Mildred said she wasn't a dog and refused. At first Mamma was awfully cross about it and said she would send Mildred away, but now she has accepted, and so Mildred is here.'

'And tries a good deal too hard to make herself useful,' Maureen said. 'Always busy about everybody's business.'

'But Mamma says now that she does not know what she would do without her,' Oonagh said.

'That's because Mamma is lazy,' said Maureen with a sharp laugh.

'Mamma is not always well,' Oonagh corrected, but without heat. 'Mildred is the one to organise everything,' she continued. 'Even the packing for

Papa's trips and bathing the dogs. The servants hate her because she is forever questioning them on what they do. Lapham especially.' She began to laugh. 'Mildred cannot understand the importance of his dignity. It is because she is American. Lapham's dignity is like his breathing, there is no place where one starts and the other begins.'

'And where is her mama now?'

'I think she's in service,' said Maureen. 'We don't see her, although Mildred might.' My own coming was so recent, my place in this house so new, that I instantly wondered what Mildred must think of her changed circumstances and those of her mother and brother. Did she mind being separated from them, as much as I minded being away from Hughie? Did she wonder at the difference in reception, and why she had been chosen for this luxury and her mother and brother turned away?

'And Gunnie?' I said then after a pause in which Oonagh hummed snatches of 'Cherry Ripe'. I wished she would stop. My unexpected tears of earlier still worried me. I had to be careful not to let myself be surprised like that again.

'Gunnie is Mamma's cousin. She made a bad match.' Oonagh lowered her voice with the importance of the words. 'He was a scoundrel and he ran away, so Gunnie came to live with us.'

'They must live somewhere, I suppose,' Maureen said, indifferent.

'And the other cousin? Honour?'

'Uncle Rupert's daughter. He is Papa's elder brother.'

'And she is Lady Honour because Uncle Rupert will be Lord Iveagh, and Maureen is terribly cross about it,' Aileen said, coming in upon us. 'And now there's a Lady Patsy as well.' She laughed.

'When I marry, I shall be far better than a Lady,' Maureen said with a flash of irritation.

'When I marry, I shall be free to come and go as I please,' said Aileen. 'And I shall have a jolly lot of fun.'

'When I marry, I shall have heaps of children,' Oonagh said. 'What about you, Fliss?'

'I don't think I shall marry,' I said. The idea had never occurred to me. No one had ever suggested it. It was too new for me to consider it properly. I thought I might ask Hughie what he thought, in one of my letters, then wondered how I could begin to describe all of this – any of it – to him.

Chapter Seven

Glenmaroon, Dublin, 1978

'Come with me,' the girl says. 'I'll show you.'

My knees creak as I stand – this attic is even damper than it looks – and creak again as the girl takes me down the narrow staircase at the very back of the house, the one that goes from attic to kitchen without ever passing through anywhere spacious and formal; a staircase I'm sure Cloé never knew existed.

The kitchen is almost unchanged: the large black range is still there, the deep stone sinks and long wooden table. But a new kitchen has grown up around the old, taking place craftily, like weeds in a neglected flowerbed. Instead of the old worn flagstones, the floor is covered by dirty cream linoleum. There is an electric oven beside the old range, a white kettle plugged in on the countertop and, in the stone sink, a yellow plastic basin. Only the bar of Sunlight soap looks unchanged. There is no more light here than there ever was – a bare electric bulb cannot make up for walls that are too deep, windows that are too close to ground level, and the shadows in the corners are as thick as webs. I expect Cook to step out of them, or Kathleen to emerge with a tray, but there is only a cat.

Two women stand at the long table, peeling potatoes slowly. Their heads are bowed and they stare, both of them, down towards their hands that move mechanically. There is a small pile of peeled potatoes in a chipped enamel basin, and a far larger pile, unpeeled, in a muddy heap beside them.

The women don't look up and we pass through the kitchen and out the door into the yard that was never grand or pretty but is now squalid. Mud is churned thick underfoot and there are old vegetable bits trodden into it. I brace myself for what lies beyond the dirty yard: a tumbled wilderness, I assume. But I'm wrong. The gardens are glorious, smugly abundant, with a hint of lushness that was missing when I lived here and that enhances them. Like the soft collapse that comes with marriage in certain beautiful women.

Not that any of the Guinness girls let themselves collapse like that. All three, certainly in their first marriages, kept themselves smartly vigilant. Perhaps they knew the marriages wouldn't last? That they would need to stay primed and ready, a gun loaded and cocked.

That isn't something I know much about; just one more aspect of their lives that was mysterious to me.

How much we grew apart, I think, as the girl leads me down the gravel path towards the stables. Or were forced apart. By their fortune, and the expectations that came with that, but also by the things that happened to us. By which I mostly mean the thing that happened to us in this house, in that summer that felt like a beginning but turned out to be an end.

It was a thing that happened to all of us but mostly to me. My loss. My guilt. I can hardly blame the girls. Pain and upset were not what they had been made for.

The girl skips ahead, singing a little song to herself. We reach the stables, and here the glory of the gardens ends. The stables are even sadder than the house. Tumbled-down and filthy, a place for scrap iron and bird droppings layered like cement. There is a smell of rotted straw and cat urine.

It's so quiet. It was never quiet. This was a place of constant industry all of its own, a kind of satellite to the larger house. Always the sound of straw being swept, ground raked, hooves clopping, the shiftings and blowings and occasional whinnying of horses, Thomas whistling, the squeaky front wheel of his barrow. Even the birds seem less now than they used to be. Or maybe they are different birds, not the kind that sing but a type that scratch and watch. A couple of bicycles lie against walls and doors. They must belong to the nuns, I suppose. In all that place, they are the only things that look to be still in use.

My shoes are wrong, that's for sure. They aren't the careful high heels of my career years in the publishing house, but they are wrong, nevertheless. Mud like this needs boots. I am ill-prepared. I try walking around the worst of the churn, but the ground is treacherous and what looks solid often is not, drier dirt crumbling into thick spots of muck.

'Up there,' the girl says, gesturing. There is a set of rooms above the tack room, with a narrow outdoor staircase leading to it, just lumps of stone really that jut out from the wall at mostly regular intervals, although an iron rail has been added that acts as banister. Back then, the steps were whitewashed. Now, they are a dull grey. These were Thomas's rooms, I know, although I have never been up to them. We wouldn't have dared climb and knock then, not even Maureen. Instead, in those days, we stood in the yard and called up 'Hulloo, Thomas, are you there . . . ?'

I once saw Hughie come down from there. He must have gone looking for Thomas and I remember thinking how brave he was to go up and knock for him. He stumbled as he came down and I thought he would fall but he didn't.

Now, we climb, the girl and I. She goes first. As I follow, holding hard to the banister, I wonder whatever brought her up here in the first place.

'The Sisters sent me up,' she says, as if she has read my mind. 'They don't go everywhere, but they like to know what's in each room. I look, but I don't always tell them.' She says it with the sudden flash of a grin.

The door has swollen in its frame, is bulging and rotten, and the girl puts her shoulder to it and heaves. The smell that has been walled up in there is so strong that it charges me: horse sweat and leather and the glycerine soap used on saddles and bridles. Resentment, mistrust, the urgency of time passing and the disillusion of too much time passed. This, then, is Thomas's room.

Chapter Eight

Glenmaroon, Dublin, 1920

'Oh Fliss, there is a letter from Hughie on the hall table,' Oonagh said, tapping at my door and putting her head around it. 'I recognise the writing. If you wait, Lapham will bring it to breakfast.' Then, 'I thought not,' she said with a laugh, as I tore off down the hallway in my dressing gown, hoping I would not be seen, unable to wait.

'Fliss has had a letter,' she announced at breakfast.

'From Hughie?' Maureen asked, reaching for a dish of kippers. By now, we breakfasted downstairs with Cloé and Ernest, although he was usually up and gone by the time we came in.

'Yes,' I said. 'He will stay with a friend called Richard Butler, on the other side of the Phoenix Park, for some weeks and he says he will ride over if he may, and see us.'

'Of course he may! Oh Fliss! How wonderful,' Oonagh cried. 'How long since you have seen him?'

'One year and six months,' I said.

'No days?' Maureen asked with a smile. She knew, we all knew, that I could have given days and maybe hours.

'When does he arrive?' Oonagh asked.

'Barely a week,' I said. I couldn't quite believe it: that letters would finally be swapped for the realness of his arrival. That the hand I put out to him so constantly in my mind would clasp a real arm, warm and solid. That we would once more talk together. I would see him, hear him, and Oonagh, Maureen and Aileen would see and hear him too.

And that I could ask him the things that were in my mind. Because Hughie's letters were beginning to change. They spoke of things I didn't understand and that he didn't much explain. He used words like 'retaliation' and 'self-determination' that meant almost nothing to me but that winked and danced on the page like candlelight that flickers in a draught and gives one a headache. He dashed these words off casually as though I should know them, but without detail that would explain them, and so I began to listen for them elsewhere – in the conversations of the grown-ups, in the hints Mildred dropped. Anything that might fill in spaces in a picture I wanted to understand but couldn't see clearly.

And because I listened and paid attention even when I pretended not to, I began to realise that Hughie's words, although not used themselves at Glenmaroon, had indeed echoes, shadowy reflections in the conversations that went on around me, brought in from the world outside Glenmaroon that didn't seem to be as it used to be. They were part of what Ernest referred to with tight-lipped disapproval as 'temporary unrest', and Mildred, with relish, called 'a whole lot of trouble'.

The first year that I lived at Glenmaroon, I had gone home for Christmas – two confusing weeks of trying not to compare Ballytibbert with the house I had become used to; trying not to see the swelling behind the wallpaper in the night nursery; not to notice the smell of dog and earth at the front of the house, boiled cabbage and laundry starch at the back; of trying not to be 'grand' in case Mummie felt the insult. But two weeks, too, of daily talks with Hughie, hunting with him, riding out on days when there was no hunting, sitting in a corner of the dim drawing room in the evenings, watching firelight flicker in his serious brown eyes as he told me that soon he would be old enough to help with the farm, Uncle Alex had said so, and how, when he took it over altogether, when he finished school, he planned to make life better for the workers in the cottages, and most of all for their thin, whey-faced children.

'I'm not the only one who cares about these things, Fliss,' he had said. 'There are others like me. Who see the possibility of a different kind of country, one that is more fair, that can choose to care for all the people who live in it, even those who are poor and hungry.' He was fifteen then, and the warmth in his voice was like firelight, a steady glow, but he was careful to speak quietly so Mummie and Uncle Alex couldn't hear him.

But the next year, although there had been talk that I would go home again for Christmas, Mummie and Cloé between them decided I would not. By then there was trouble in much of the countryside. The fight for independence from the Crown that Hughie had spoken of, which had started in 1916 and been squashed, almost extinguished, had reared up again. There were men who had decided they would sacrifice anything to be free – I knew this from what Hughie said – and that meant shootings and attacks on police barracks, talk of hunger strikes and extra recruits to the constabulary to try to keep order. The countryside, which looked empty, was not. It had men hidden in it, behind hedges and in ditches, men with guns and bitterness. Because of that, I was not allowed to travel alone, and no one wished to travel with me. But I knew that by then I had become useful at Glenmaroon, to Cloé, and that she never could bear to deprive herself of anyone who eased her path.

Half of me had been pleased that I would stay – there would be Christmas parties, entertainments, a cinema show. Maureen and I would wear long dresses and, although we would not yet put our hair up, we would not be children either. But half of me, too, had been sick with longing for home and Hughie still.

His letters told me many things – that Mummie was unwell, although she would not allow it to be talked of; that the great chestnut tree behind the house had been struck in a storm and, in coming down, had quite blocked the way to the farm so that for days they had to climb over the trunk before men came with axes to chop it. That John Hegarty was cross because the horses never did come back from the war, and that he, too, had begun to talk about 'changes', not even stopping when Hughie was in earshot. 'It is everywhere now,' Hughie wrote, 'this talk. Like a thaw or the coming of spring.' He wrote of police barracks destroyed and army convoys attacked as though these were fine adventures, tales of glory to be told out loud around a fire.

There were other stories – a constable beaten in the streets and left there to bleed so that he nearly died while people went about their business – but Hughie didn't tell me those. That news came from listening to the grown-ups around me when I was not meant to be paying attention.

In turn, I wrote to Hughie about the most vivid pieces of my own life: Glenmaroon, the girls, what we did, our lessons, dancing classes, picnics, the visits we paid, the cousins who came to stay. Maureen had been right – they had so many cousins that the house was more often full than not.

There was Bryan, a year younger than Aileen, a gentle fellow with a whimsical sense of humour whose pranks were as frequent as Maureen's, but less cruel, more fantastical. Lady Honour and her sisters, Patsy and now baby Brigid, who came rarely and stayed but little, and who were growing up to be less pretty than the girls of Glenmaroon, much to Maureen's delight. 'They may have the title, but we have the looks,' she told Cloé, and Cloé, instead of reprimanding her as Mummie would have, agreed and said, 'Yes, isn't it marvellous.' The four daughters of Henry Guinness, Moira, Rachel, Patricia and Heather who they called Judy, a girl who behaved like a boy, caring only for fencing and games of running and chasing. These four were almost the same ages as us, and we saw them most often because although they lived on the other side of the city at Burton Hall near Kingstown, they were allowed to take the train to visit, as long as the motorcar was sent to meet them.

But no matter how I tried in my letters, I knew these people were no more real to Hughie than boys at school he sometimes told me about. Only Richard, the friend in whose house he was to stay, felt in any way substantial, and then only because Hughie had described his parents – elderly and timid – who had taken Hughie with them for tea when they came to visit Richard one day. Richard, Hughie had written, had been kind and thoughtful, and thoroughly exasperated by their fearfulness, so that made me laugh and gave me a view of him. Other than that, they were all just shadows on a wall, a collection of their escapades and sallies, with no flesh inside the draping of their outer garments; just, I was sure, as the people of my life were to him. And so I longed for Hughie to meet the family properly, as they really were, so he, too, could know them. And for them to meet him.

'I feel I know him already,' Maureen said, licking jam from a spoon in a way that would have caused Gunnie great pain. 'How many times have you told us the story of the time he rescued the kittens John Hegarty had put in the rain barrel to drown?'

'And how, when John Hegarty found out and tried to take the kittens for a second drowning, Hughie hid them in an empty stable, long enough that John Hegarty said they were too old to drown and must be let live?' Oonagh continued with delight at the fond, familiar tale.

'Tell me again how old he is?' Aileen asked.

'Seventeen on June first,' Maureen said. 'Do you not remember the beautiful sketch Fliss sent him for his birthday?'

'So, nearer in age to me than you, Maureen,' Aileen replied slyly. The rivalry between these two had intensified over the last few months so that anything now could be used in the competition. Aileen was generally far more Cloé's child than either Maureen or Oonagh – looking for Cloé's – even Gunnie's – approval in a way the younger two didn't; conscious always of what was proper, and of her own standing. But Maureen could always provoke her enough to make her forget this, and quarrel as whole-heartedly as if she were back in the schoolroom.

Ernest came in then with Cloé. They were to attend the races that day and I could see that Cloé did not wish to go, for all that she was most elegantly dressed. Her face was pale and the smudges under her eyes said that she had not slept.

'Fliss's brother Hughie is to stay with a friend on the other side of the park. He may ride over and visit, may he not?' Maureen asked immediately.

'He may. But he must be careful,' Ernest said, picking up the paper. 'The unrest is getting worse and many of the roads are not now safe. A house has been burned down in County Limerick, a place called Mountshannon. Burned quite to the ground.'

'Oh, but I know it well,' Cloé cried. 'I used to go to dances there as a girl. It was like going to a ball in a Greek temple.' She paused, lost for a minute in her recollections of girlhood, then, 'Poor Louisa. Lady Louisa FitzGibbon,' she said, turning to us in explanation. Cloé liked the jigsaw of people to be a complete one, with all the pieces fitting neatly together, and for us to understand this jigsaw as intimately as she did. These were the lineages and alliances that she knew by heart like poetry, a flow of marriages between families going back and back into ages too dark for most to follow but lit up for Cloé by these vital threads of connection.

'Well, it is nothing like a Greek temple now,' Ernest said briskly. 'Except perhaps a ruined one. They say the fire could be seen from Limerick City and the place burned for two days straight.'

'I thought it was only barracks that were being burned,' Cloé said.

'It was,' Ernest said.

'Was it tenants that did it?' Cloé looked about her as if even in that sunny morning room such a person might appear. 'How lucky that we have none here.'

'If indeed it was tenants,' said Ernest, 'then it is entirely to be expected. Cannot people understand that land in Ireland will always spell trouble?' He put his newspaper down on the table and settled back onto his heels so that he was taller, arms crossed behind his back, chest pushed forward. It was his teaching-master pose, the one he adopted when he wished to lecture. 'Give the Irish work and pay them, as I do, and all is well. Do not lease them land they see as their own and make them pay you for it.' I wondered what Hughie would think of Ernest's reckoning, because it seemed so different to what he wrote in his letters. Soon, I thought, I would be able to ask him.

'Perhaps it is not safe to go to the races?' Cloé said.

'Nonsense,' Ernest said. 'We will be perfectly all

right. I have no tenants here to hate me; to eye my land and believe it theirs.'

'Very well,' Cloé said, and I saw her draw herself together for the day ahead, where she would dazzle – as I had seen her do so many times – then come home to lie prostrate in a darkened room, or worse, take sick for days.

'Let's go to the stables,' Oonagh said once Ernest and Cloé had left. 'Thomas will be there by now.' It wasn't that we would normally have concerned ourselves with a new servant, but Thomas was a pet project, a plan of ours, like a new puppy or bulbs coming up in the patches of garden we had all been given, and we had noted the day of his arrival carefully.

It had started with Kathleen, the maid in starched white who had brought my cocoa that first morning, who had made me feel so shy, in her neatness, that I had not dared get out of bed because my nightgown was old and worn.

Since then, and as I found my place in the household, I had discovered that for all her neatness and efficiency, she was not much older than me and inclined to be a friend. In fact, I suppose she must have quickly understood that my state was usefully close to hers, because soon she began to seek me out when she was troubled – something broken in her dusting, a bracelet Maureen couldn't find that she was worried would be laid at her door – and I had grown clever at helping without seeming to interfere.

It was to me that she first mentioned her cousin, Thomas. 'His father's dead, his mother isn't well at all,' she said, as we sat in the kitchen one afternoon, Kathleen polishing silver, me waiting for the girls to come home from a visit to which I hadn't been invited. 'Thomas is her eldest, sixteen and well grown and will work hard.' She poured tea into one of the big mugs the servants used, so different from the slender china cups of the drawing room, and she pushed a plate of fruitcake towards me.

I had offered to help with the silver, but she said no, 'it wouldn't be right' with a nervous look at Cook, who was kneading pastry, her sleeves rolled up to show thick red forearms, silent but listening. Cook didn't talk much, there was something wrong with her tongue so that the words came out wet and scrambled, but within her kitchen, the force of her personality and the importance of her job made her as formidable as Ernest in his business room. I was frightened of her, because I couldn't understand what she said, and because she seemed to live there in that dim room that was always hot, the black range glowing like the heart of a fire, day and night. The range burned coal, not wood, so the room smelled of soot under the shifting aromas of every day – bread always in the mornings, sweet baking in the afternoons, meat grilled and roasted in the evenings, vegetables simmering, creamy sauces cut through with brandy. This was where the servants had their tea and took their breaks, but the uneasiness of Cook's presence meant that any confidences were usually exchanged elsewhere: in my room, outside in the kitchen gardens or in hurried whispers on stairs and in hallways.

Because Kathleen wouldn't allow me to help with the silver – although that didn't stop me picking up damp scraps of baking soda and pressing them into the tarnished grooves of patterned handles to help her – I turned my mind to Thomas. 'What happened to his father?' I asked.

'He died four years ago,' Kathleen said and, as I was about to ask 'Yes, but how?', rolled her eyes towards Cook and shook her head just a little so that I didn't. Instead I listened as she spoke about how Thomas was 'good with the horses' and 'did the work of a man'. I knew she told me these things for a reason, and she told them to me with Cook in earshot for the same reason. I was useful in that house beyond fetching and carrying for Cloé or doing lessons with the girls; I was a safe passage for news and requirements, things said and needed, which I could carry with me as I moved about between upstairs and down, delivering the way a bird might, a twig pulled from here and dropped there, a snippet or useful scrap.

Time had settled the question of what I was to be in this household, by making it an idea as elastic as I was prepared to let it. As I listened to Kathleen, I thought how I might try to help. I had a plan. Maureen liked the idea of herself as generous. Indeed, she was generous, until something irritated or distracted her. And she was bored. I knew that if I could appeal to this generosity and provide her with a project – especially one she could undertake more effectively than Aileen – I might succeed.

Sure enough, when I presented Thomas's story to her, Aileen and Oonagh, along with the details of the family's hardship, on one of our walks, finishing with the careful resignation that 'It's such a pity we cannot find him work', Maureen said quickly, exactly as I knew she would, 'Leave it to me. I jolly well can.' And she did. A word to Gunnie, a word from Gunnie to Ernest, because that was how things worked, and now it was Thomas's first day, and Maureen wanted to bask in the happy outcome of her scheming.

By the time we found him, sweeping straw from a horsebox, Kathleen had thanked all of us so often and so profusely that I think Maureen expected Thomas would simply pick up where she had left off – with expressions of his humble gratitude. Instead, all he did was say hello and nod at us and then stand, mute, hands behind his back, waiting.

He was what Mummie calls 'dark Irish', or 'Armada Irish', meaning not just brown hair and eyes, like me and Hughie, but brown skin too, as though covered in walnut stain or as if at the end of a long hot summer by the beach in Wexford. Thin, wiry, with eyes that were steady and alert, he was silent in a way that said he wasn't thinking of things to say, or wondering if we would approve of what he said, but silent because that's what he chose to be.

'How do you like your new post?' Maureen asked at last. I think she hoped still to encourage him to thank her.

'Well enough,' he said and went back to sweeping straw. But not in the way servants usually did – because he was worried we would think him lazy, or because he didn't know what else to say – but almost as if he had dismissed us. And after a few minutes we did indeed leave because what else was there to do? We walked back up to the house without speaking.

'I think it's no wonder he couldn't find work,' Maureen said at last. 'Cross fellow.'

Chapter Nine

The day of Hughie's arrival I woke extra early. I dressed quickly and went out through the sleeping house, passing Kathleen in the hallway and putting a finger to my lips with a smile – 'Shssh.' I hoped to avoid Cloé if I could, at least for an hour or so.

Mildred had decided to study nursing, persisting despite ridicule and opposition – at this stage she was mostly just cleaning hospital wards as far as we could see – in a way that secretly impressed me. Without her, it fell more and more to me to take up some of her duties. Every morning she left in the small red car Ernest had given her, wheels spitting gravel up behind, brakes squealing, and many of my days were now spent in her stead: reading to Cloé, fetching things she might want, writing letters that she dictated. This day, I wanted to escape out into the gardens for a little while before bowing to her needs.

'You know I have come to depend on you a great deal,' Cloé had said just the day before. And even though I did know it – knew that I was quieter, more biddable, than Mildred, and better therefore for her purposes – I felt a warm flush of pride at her words.

'I had hoped you would be a good influence on my girls,' she continued. 'And I see that it is so. Just as you are between them in age, so you are between them in temperament. Oonagh is too shy; Maureen too wild. You are good for both.'

If I was, I couldn't always see it. Not with Maureen anyway. Her insolence had become more pronounced than ever by then, and every fight with Cloé or Gunnie, no matter what it purported to be about – a hat, a dress, a book – was really a push for freedom set against a pull for restraint.

After one of these rows, when she had been more than usually rude and jeering, Maureen slipped her arm through mine as I passed her bedroom. 'I'm sorry I was horrid,' she said. 'I don't mean to be, I really don't. At least not to you.'

'I don't mind,' I said, 'but I think Gunnie might.

Perhaps you could tell her?'

'Oh Gunnie!' She tossed her head. 'She won't remember. She has a head that hasn't a thing in it except what Mamma puts there, and then only for as long as Mamma reminds her. She's like a hen, clucking around a yard for bits of corn scattered by the farmer's wife.' She had laughed, delighted at herself. 'But truly, I don't mean to be so dreadful,' she said. 'Only sometimes I feel I'm drowning in thickest treacle. It makes me cross and hot and mean.' She sounded bewildered at her own inability to escape herself.

'I understand,' I said. I did. There was a curious deadness on all of us at that time, as though we were stuck – between childhood and the world of grown-ups; between what we had been, and what we must learn to be. Only Oonagh was still herself, funny and merry, busy with the dogs, her pony, any local children she could lay her hands on in order to mother and befriend them before abandoning them when they got to be too much work. But even she was subdued by how confined we were.

It was a bad summer, in part because the weather was wet, but in part too because the rumours of trouble were increasing. We were too much indoors, too many games of backgammon and old maid, too much of one another's company without the invigoration of others. Even the Burton Hall cousins, usually so reliable, had said no to a few days' visit, that travelling across the city wasn't safe. And only two days before, a swimming party had been called off.

Ernest no longer spoke so much about the unrest 'blowing over'. If anything, it seemed it was intensifying and there were near-daily reports of ambushes and fires. I had seen Gunnie jump at the sight of a strange man in the grounds, and I had to remind her that it was Thomas from the stables.

I hoped that Hughie's coming would bring us more freedom, more activity and a change of routine. That he might distract Maureen from her determination to find fault and cause rows, and it would blow away the cobwebs that held us all.

Outside, the sun had reached only as far as the bottom corner of the long lawn so the grass was nearly all wet and in morning shadow still. At the end of the garden lay the river hidden behind tall grasses so it was almost entirely out of sight, but even unseen it was a draw, exerting a powerful pull on birds and insects so that there was always a hum and buzz of creatures landing and taking off, swarming and multiplying around and above it. It was the Liffey, the same river that ran, thick and stinking, through Dublin City, sending up foul odours and sucking life from the air with its sullen progress. Here, though, it was swift and clean, smelling of weeds and mud.

I walked about the garden and watched the small patch of sunlight grow and grow, like knitting under the hands of an expert, thinking of Hughie's arrival – he had said he'd be with us after lunch – and the joy it would be to see him again. Soon, Oonagh came down to join me.

'I saw you from the window,' she said, slipping her arm through mine. At ten, she was still tiny, very much a child, but with a growing precociousness that made her seem, at times, quaint.

'How is the alphabet going?' I asked.

She giggled. 'Not well.'

Gunnie, in an attempt to cure Oonagh of her habit of silence – something that was considered a serious worry by Cloé – had tried to teach her a method from her own youth, the Alphabet Game. 'You work your way through the alphabet,' she had said, excited to be offering a solution. 'With each letter providing a topic of conversation, you see? You simply start at "a" and work your way down. By the time you will have to turn to the companion on your other side, you will surely only have reached "o" or "n" and once you turn you can start at "a" again,' she confidently predicted.

'Let's run through now,' I said. '"A" is for?'

'Attics?' Oonagh replied after a moment.

'But what on earth can one say about attics? Or apples? Especially when one isn't to talk about food. Perhaps, I don't know, animals?' she finished wildly. 'How does one even talk to boys who aren't cousins?' She sounded upset.

'It's not so hard,' I said. 'You can practise on Hughie.'

'I tried practising on Thomas yesterday,' she said. She giggled. 'Not much luck.'

It was Maureen who started it – making a game of Thomas's silences, I think because she was secretly annoyed at his lack of gratitude, deference, any of the things she was used to – but Oonagh and Aileen had adopted it enthusiastically. 'I got three words today,' one of them might say. Or 'a whole sentence, imagine!' I didn't join in – I couldn't – but I could understand the appeal, and I confess I followed their progress, to see which of them would triumph. So far, none of them had. Although it seemed to me, watching from a distance as I did, that Thomas was most inclined towards Aileen's polite gravity, dealing better with that than he did with Maureen's excitability or Oonagh's childish charm.

But there was something chilling in the very look that he gave us. Nothing with a name, nothing that allowed a retort, but something all the same, in the air about him and the set of his thin shoulders when we spoke to him. It made Maureen furious, I knew that, although she didn't say it, and because of that she couldn't leave him alone but found any excuse to go to the stables and ask something of him. I wasn't sure which she wanted more – for him to show her the deference she was used to, or to be openly rude so that she could complain of it.

We walked back to the house and I was almost at my bedroom – I planned to change in readiness for Hughie's arrival – when Gunnie called out as I passed the door of the small sitting room, 'Fliss, do come in. I want to show you something.'

This 'something' was the exact brewing of the herbs that Cloé sometimes drank, to ease pain and help her rest. 'Do not pour the water too fast,' Gunnie said, watching me critically as I lifted the silver kettle from the flame. 'And do not leave the herbs to steep too long. You must be sure to pick only the leaves of the thyme, never the stalks because they are thick and bitter. When you ask Cook, tell her no stalks, and only the youngest, most delicate leaves.'

'But you always ask Cook,' I said, setting the kettle down carefully.

'In the future, I mean,' Gunnie said. 'When you are the one to ask.' I opened my mouth to say I wouldn't be, and then shut it again. Because I suddenly understood the look in Gunnie's eyes: the encouragement, and the recognition that lay there. And instead of thrilling to them, I was repelled. *She thinks I'm her*, I realised. *She knows I am.*

Until then, I had thought very little about what might lie ahead for me. I knew I would not come out, like the girls, but that I would be expected to accompany them through their Seasons. And I looked forward to it. We all did. There would be new clothes, parties, excitement, trips to Claridge's and The Ritz. Already we had learned to dance – waltzes and foxtrots, of course, but also, in secret, the new dances that Aileen brought to us with her little wind-up gramophone and a stack of records. Without a dancing master, we relied on her to show us the steps, and practised them with one another while she looked on critically: 'Not like that, Fliss, you look like a dancing bear! Watch Oonagh, she has it; it is the lightest, quickest step imaginable.'

But Gunnie's words suddenly showed me that same future differently – a place without a natural end. Because after all, the point of a Season is an engagement. And then a wedding. For all three of them. And then what, for me, when they were married? Where must I go? With whom? I felt hot at the back of my neck at the ingratitude, but all the same I thought: *I do not wish to be Gunnie* – who, for all that she had been married once was now nothing that Cloé did not allow her to be – followed by what might have been the first fully independent thought of my life: *I will not be her.* I did not have any idea of *how* I would not be her, or indeed what else I might be, but what I knew, I knew very clearly: *I will not be her*.

Chapter Ten

It was well after luncheon by the time Hughie arrived that first day. Aileen was out buying gloves and Maureen, Oonagh and I had been sitting in the window of the schoolroom for almost an hour, because it had the best view of the driveway. We were up on the deep seat with the window thrown wide so that we could hear as well as see. Every few minutes Maureen would climb onto the flat roof of the stone portico over the front door – something she was most strictly forbidden to do – and lean out over the low parapet at the far end of it so as to see further down the driveway.

'Do be careful,' Oonagh called after her. 'If

you fall, Gunnie will be furious with all of us but mostly me and Fliss because you'll be dead.'

'Don't be silly. I'm not going to fall. And anyway, it is low enough that I could almost jump it.'

'Maureen! Do not think of it!' I called after her. In her new mood of recklessness, there was no telling what she might do.

'This must be him,' she cried suddenly. Sure enough, there was a sound of hooves on gravel, and indeed there was Hughie at last, coming around the wild mauve and green of the rhododendrons on a chestnut mount. Beside him, on a big-boned grey, was the friend. Broad-shouldered and tall, he looked, from that distance, older than Hughie, like a guardian or chaperone.

'We'd better run down quick,' Oonagh said, 'or Lapham will entirely freeze them.' She was, I realised, nearly as excited as me.

We ran down those wide stairs, golden and pink in the afternoon sunlight, and made it to the hall in time to see Lapham, at his most dignified, open the double doors wide.

Hughie stepped in, the friend behind him, and looked up. The light from the window of coloured glass fell full on his face so that he was, I thought, someone bathed in gold – like the statue that King Midas so tragically made of his beautiful son, just by touching him. Except that Hughie was alive and vital and freedom itself; an escape from our lonely tower simply by being there.

I threw myself across the final stretch of polished floor and hugged him and knew that the girls and Lapham had turned politely away in order not to see the tears that blurred everything for a minute. Still in the doorway, the friend did the same, turning to stare out into the gardens. The familiar smell and shape of Hughie, even though he was much grown, made that hallway I knew so well seem suddenly strange, and I hugged him again, trying to find, in those moments, some of what I'd lost in the last two years.

'You're taller,' he said, holding me away from him.

'So are you,' I said, dashing at my eyes with the back of one hand while I fumbled for a handkerchief with the other. A small hand pushed something lace-edged into mine. Oonagh's 'kerchief. 'You're quite grown.'

'Not quite,' he said, 'but now that I am not cooped in that school, I soon will be. This is Richard.'

'The friend with whom you are staying,' Maureen said instantly.

'Indeed.' Hughie looked amused and Richard nodded politely at us all.

I said hullo and introduced my friends and felt

shy of everyone as I did so, horribly conscious of Lapham behind me. The man made no noise at all, not even the sound of breath. Then Hughie asked, 'May we see to our horses?' and Maureen said, 'We'll show you the stables,' before Lapham could conjure up Robert to do so.

'Good idea,' I said, 'and then let us show you the gardens.' I couldn't bear to sit in any of the drawing rooms with my brother, throwing words to each other over acres of space, with an audience of Gunnie and Mildred and Cloé, looking back and forth politely at us, as though we played tennis. I knew that would come later but first I hoped to hear something of home from him.

'I'll catch you up,' Maureen said. 'First, I must put on a hat.' She went back up the stairs fast – faster than Gunnie would ever have allowed – so that I was not at all surprised when, not many moments later, a kind of cousin of the slatternly creature that had greeted me on my first day appeared through a side door as we walked to the stables.

'Will ye come this way, surrs,' the slattern asked, holding open the door that was built right into the wall and beckoning Hughie and Richard. Behind her, a smell of laundry starch tried desperately to escape the dark passageway into the summer air.

'What?' Hughie said, startled.

'This way, surr, come this way if ye will. Leave yer horrses with the young ladies and foller me for I have something for ye.'

Richard started forward, moving to hand his horse to me, and Hughie looked bemused for a moment, then began to laugh, head thrown back. The chestnut mare checked suddenly at the sound, eyes rolling, spitting gravel up from cavorting hooves.

'I see scarce a thing that ye might laugh at,' the slattern said with pitiful dignity, so that Hughie laughed all the harder.

'Oh dear, Maureen,' he said. 'You are priceless. You should be on the stage.'

Maureen, who hated her jokes to backfire, said, 'However did you know?' in stiff tones.

'Hard to disguise those blue eyes,' Hughie said, at which she smiled, lighting up instantly.

'Brown are so much easier to render common,' she agreed demurely. Hughie, like me, had dark brown eyes.

Oonagh said, 'Maureen!' shocked, and indeed, Richard looked uneasy, but Hughie just laughed all the harder, and I with him. I was proud that he had seen through her disguise so quickly, instead of being wrong-footed and made miserable as I had been. Proud, too, that he had made her see the joke instead of sulk at being discovered.

'Shall you need to go and change?' I asked Maureen, who was pulling at the drab skirt she had put on.

'Not till we go back to the house,' she said. 'If we do happen to meet Gunnie or Mildred, you must all hide me or I will be sent off immediately.'

We walked on to the stables, slowly, Chestnut, Hughie's horse, blowing gently and butting his back with her head.

'You know you have not yet said a thing,' Maureen said to Richard, who blushed.

'Perhaps because you talk enough for all of us,' Oonagh said quickly, alert to shyness in others.

'Well, someone has to,' Maureen said, then pulled ahead to ask Hughie, 'I had you fooled at first, didn't I? Admit it.'

'For a moment.'

'You are at school with Hughie?' I said to Richard, hoping to give him solid ground from which to proceed; a simple question to answer. I had found this to be a good tactic with Oonagh.

'I have. For several years now,' Richard said. He had a pleasant voice, deep and slow; grey eyes and high colour in his cheeks, as though he had been running hard in a cold wind. 'Hughie was there a term before me and knew his way around. He was decent to me when I arrived as a new boy.' He looked at Hughie and I saw – I, of all people, could not be mistaken – the affection he had for him. 'He spoke so often of you,' Richard said. 'I will not say that I feel I know you, because that wouldn't be quite true, but certainly I'm very happy to meet you.'

'Did he really sometimes speak of me?' I glowed warm inside.

'He did. Often. You are very like each other to look at.' He blushed again, and the colour in his cheeks was like a wine glass, I thought, filled and emptied and filled again.

'Have you any sisters?' I asked.

'No. A brother, many years older, who is in London. My parents are rather older too. It's a quiet house.' He looked at Maureen, ahead of us, who was singing some nonsense song about 'the sky' and 'why'. 'We're happy to have Hughie to stay.'

'I should think you would be,' I said. 'But I hope you will come with him and visit us often.'

Hughie dropped back then. 'Do you still hunt?' he asked me.

'Not so much,' I said. The girls didn't care much for hunting. 'But I ride out most days.'

'We must ride together, so.'

'We all will,' Maureen said. I was surprised. She had shown no interest in her horse recently. She looked alive suddenly, glowing with the excitement of unknown company, a new audience. Under the brim of her hat, her face was lit up, by the unexpected shafts of sunlight, but also an inner fire that had replaced her dull, resentful mood of the last few days.

It was one of those rare summer days, rarer still that wet year, that is almost impossible later to conjure in memory, like trying to hold a stone in a spider's web. That one felt especially blessed – nature smiling on Hughie's coming – and I stretched my arms up high in the air, feeling released from some unseen oppression I had hardly noticed until it lifted. Oonagh saw me and, I think, understood the urge to reach up, reach out, into that air that almost had a touch, like the clearest water, because she gave me a wide grin.

'So how do you spend your time?' Hughie asked.

'The deadliest of ways,' Maureen said. 'We do lessons, and learn watercolour, and I have a stamp collection that Gunnie fills for me. Page by page, stamp by stamp. Soon it'll be the finest collection in the world, and I shall have barely set eyes on it.' There was a teasing petulance to her voice, and sure enough, Hughie and Richard both smiled.

'We have picnics,' I said, to try to mitigate the dullness of her description. 'Parties, visits, tennis, croquet.'

'Deathly,' Maureen insisted.

'We have the dogs to play with,' Oonagh said. 'Our ponies to ride.'

'Friends?' Hughie asked.

'Cousins, sometimes,' Maureen said, almost on a yawn. 'Not at all the same thing. Endless parades of them. Each more curious a creature than the last! A great many Guinnesses marry their cousins. Not I!'

Hughie laughed again and for all that I thrilled to see him, I wondered suddenly would he be bad for Maureen, encouraging her wilfulness and the sharp side of her wit.

A peacock went by then, the quivering rage of its crest softened by the melancholy droop of its tail feathers, and Hughie, looking after it, said softly, only to me, 'I had no idea.'

'Of what?' I asked.

'All this.' He gestured around, at the smooth close-cropped lawns and careful flowerbeds, the high walls, tall trees that spread gentle leaves towards one another in fond greeting, and the house that rose up in the middle of it all, as new and shiny as one of Ernest's clever toys, red brick on grey stone and so many mullioned windows that glittered with the success of the under-servants' efforts. 'How is it, really, to live here?'

'It's very good,' I said. 'They are kind to me, and

very dear.' The others were too far ahead to hear, so I did not blush to say it.

'You do not feel . . . ?' He paused, too delicate of my feelings I suppose to say it: *You do not feel overlooked? Uncounted? An impoverished acquaintance?*

'I do not,' I said firmly.

'I'm glad of it. Because I think it's been good for you,' he said. 'You've filled out, Fliss, and look less as though you had just seen a ghost. It's not just the clothes' – his gaze took in my skirt in soft tweed the colour of heather, identical to the one Maureen wore, because Gunnie now bought all my clothes – 'it's more than that.' He reached out a hand and placed it for a warm moment on my shoulder, then turned and looked back at the house. 'That house . . .' he said. 'I expect a very large and magnificent witch to pop out at any moment.'

I suddenly saw exactly what he meant – something about the pointy black roofs, three in a row, so like witches' hats, although I had never seen it before. I started to laugh. Richard, who had joined us by then, laughed too.

'What is it?' Maureen turned around, instantly wanting to know. I shook my head, but Hughie, less cautious than me, less knowledgeable of her than me, repeated his observation. I waited, barely breathing. Maureen's dignity was considerable, and while she might, occasionally, mock herself, she did not at all care for it when someone else did. And for her, the house she lived in, the horse she rode, the motorcar she went about in – all these things were *her,* just as surely as her arms and legs and golden hair. She narrowed her eyes, looked at Hughie, then at the house.

'I see it,' she said suddenly, 'the roofs?' She pointed, and when Hughie agreed, she said, 'Yes, the roofs,' and began to laugh again. 'Wait until you see inside. The hall is like a cigar box and the swimming pool so like a mermaid's bath that I expect some creature with scales to rise up out of it.'

I saw then that Oonagh was feeling left out and shy – she was twisting the bottom curls of her hair, always a sure sign with her – and was about to say something that might encourage her to join in, when Hughie, who must have seen the exact same thing as me, turned to her and said, 'If there is a witch in this tale, there must also be a sprite, and that is surely you.' And Oonagh looked up at him, eyes shining.

Chapter Eleven

Glenmaroon, Dublin, 1978

It's a mean place, this room that was Thomas's; barely the size of one of the bigger horseboxes, and still has a narrow iron bedframe pushed against the far wall although there is no mattress on it. Two small windows sit on either side of the door, too high to see out of, but at least they provide some light. Not much. The far side, where the bed is, is dark and the wall beside the bed, when I touch it, is so damp that when I rub my fingertips together, they are clammy.

So, this is where Thomas slept. It is worse in every way than I could have imagined. What must Hughie have thought of it, if he went looking for

Thomas and found him there? What could he have thought, going from the deep silks and velvets of the drawing room, to this? I didn't need an answer to that. No wonder everything Thomas told him had heft and value, in a way that nothing said by Ernest – in his shirts and finely woven tweeds, with his cigars and cologne – could have. It wasn't really a choice at all. That's what I understand when I see this cramped, ugly place. The air is wet and stale, but a year of open windows wouldn't make much difference here. Even in the warmest summer it must always have been wet and stale.

I imagine I hear our voices from below – mine, Oonagh's, Maureen's – calling, 'Hullo, Thomas, are you there?' Ready to ask that he saddle a horse, mend a tennis net or mark out lines on the lawn for badminton. Asking always as if our needs were urgent, as if he had no other duties or none that couldn't be postponed, indifferent to how long this made his days or how heavy his workload.

How must he have considered us as he lay on that bed, thinking perhaps of his mother, the TB that wasted her, the little brothers and sister who depended so completely on what he brought home to them?

What did he think of Cloé and her bitter, angular beauty; the untouched trays of boiled chicken and the many days she wouldn't leave her room that below-stairs gossip must have told him of? Even the change Hughie looked for cannot have seemed enough to him.

As I think of the shockingly specific nature of TB, the precise path of its destruction, I remember suddenly how, when Cloé spoke of the discomfort that prostrated her, she always did so vaguely, indirectly, so that I never understood exactly where or even what it was. It had no name, whatever ailed her. Or maybe it was that Cloé had no words to describe those parts of her body that were not hands or feet or face. 'It is here,' she said once, pale hand lightly sketching a portion of her middle, somewhere between chin and hips, but she would neither touch nor name the spot.

'Your stomach?' I had asked, and she winced.

'Please,' she said, 'do not . . .' As though I had said something obscene.

Very early, I began to see that Ernest didn't trust in the truth of her ailments. I recognised it in him, because I found it hard too, to have faith in something I couldn't see and she wouldn't name. No wonder he grew so impatient with her.

'Over there,' the girl says now. She points. At the end of the bed, tucked in underneath it, are two bags, white plastic with 'Quinnsworth' written on them in red. I tug at the top of one and see that whatever is inside has been bundled into another layer, another Quinnsworth bag, turned upside down. Through the plastic I can see more papers. Is it in there? That letter that caused so much trouble; that I caused so much trouble with? It didn't occur to me when I came here that I would find it. I never even thought to look for it. I presumed it long gone. But if so much has survived here in this clammy room, why not it, too?

There isn't anywhere to sit – I cannot sit on that bed, even if it had a mattress, I couldn't; not on Thomas's bed – so I pick up one of the bags. It's heavy, but I can manage.

'What's your name?' I ask the girl.

'Trisha.'

'Trisha, can you carry one? I can take the other. Back up to the attic.'

'I can.'

'Was it you who put them in plastic?'

'No. They were there just like that when I found them. And the Sisters didn't because they never knew they were here.'

'I wonder who it was.'

She says nothing, uninterested, I suppose, in my speculations.

We go around the front this time, and the car is where he parked it. He's still inside, reading the newspaper – *The Irish Times*, spread out so that it obscures the driving wheel – and doesn't notice my arrival. I bend down and knock lightly on the driver's window with my free hand. He rolls the window down and the newspaper crackles as he deftly folds it into a neat oblong. I have always admired his way with a paper. I find they escape me. Once opened to read, I cannot ever fold them again. They crumple and bulge and wrinkle in strange places.

'Do you need me?' he says.

'Not yet,' I say. 'I'm not sure what there is here. If indeed there is anything much.'

'Right. Well, you know where I am.'

'Wouldn't you rather wait inside? I'm sure Trisha would give you tea.'

'No, thank you. I'll wait out here.' Then, 'It's different, isn't it?'

'Very,' I say.

'You know, I can't imagine you, or any of us, here.'

'No, I suppose not.' But I can. That other Glenmaroon is here too, just beyond, shimmering at the corners of my vision so I think that if I turned my head fast enough, strained my ears hard enough, I would catch it, pin it down and hold it fast so that I could look at it and see it clearly.

'What's that?' He points at the plastic bag.

'I'm not sure. Rubbish, probably.'

Chapter Twelve

Glenmaroon, Dublin, 1920

Tea that first afternoon was as bad as I had feared. Aileen, back from town, was full of chatter about who she had seen and what they had said, so that even Hughie seemed unable to think of much to say to her in response. Then a rifle-parade of questions from Cloé and Gunnie and Mildred: Who were Richard's people? What did Hughie intend to do with his time now that school was finished for the summer? How was the weather in Wexford? Were they going to the Horse Show? Richard answered with as few words as he could, so few that I began to admire his talent for silence, but Hughie acquitted himself very well and

I could see the very moment they chose to approve of him – the slight turn of Cloé's head towards Gunnie that was an interrogation: 'Well?'; the faintest nod Gunnie gave that was an answer: 'Yes!'

I wasn't surprised at all when they began to make plans that involved both him and Richard. Planning was what they did, these two. Plans for parties, for entertainments, plans for the girls and their future lives, moving the people around them like chess pieces in a complicated game that, I suspected, only Cloé fully understood although Gunnie did her best to keep up.

I knew how much of their planning was hampered by a lack of young men, and I was proud to have brought them so tangible a gift as my brother and his friend. This lack was not something anyone spoke of, but it was impossible, at gatherings, not to see the absence in the middle, there, in between the boys and the old men, where the young men should have been, would have been, if the war hadn't taken them.

Impossible, too, not to notice other absences – a sleeve pinned across the front of a jacket, a stick to bear the weight that a damaged leg could not, an eye patch so dashing that it was easy to pretend it was simply costume.

Worst of all was the absence in the gaze of some of the remaining men, those who came back from the war and who stood scattered like the standing stones in the fields at home, isolated, slumped, half-grown over by grass and weeds, barely upright in their landscape. Impossible to ignore the way their mothers and sisters sought to distract from the vacancy at the heart of what they protected.

'He is a ruin,' I heard one man say to Cloé of his son, who walked and sat and moved mutely amongst us, flanked by his mother and younger sister; a hollow man, a doll to be taken out and put away at will.

'He is not himself,' Cloé had said firmly, 'but a little more time and he will be well.' She did not approve of speaking aloud of things like that. Things that could not be mended.

And my papa too, among the absent. 'It will be soon over. I'll be home by Christmas,' he had said, kissing me goodbye, and he was, for three magical days, with oranges for Hughie and me in the pockets of his greatcoat and the ringing sound of his steps about the house. But it was not over. And so he went back, and did not come home again.

'Do you play tennis, Hughie?' Cloé asked now.

'I do.'

'When did you learn?' I blurted out. There was no tennis court at home, so we had not played as children. I hated there to be anything about Hughie that I didn't know.

'In school,' he said, pulling a face. 'Games are better than lessons at least.' Cloé nodded in approval. She had a deep dislike of men who were 'bookish'. I had seen her lip curl in scorn at the girls' cousin Bryan, who liked to read fairy stories and novels, and did so openly. 'Richard plays far better than I,' Hughie continued.

'Do you?' Cloé demanded.

The ready colour rose in Richard's cheeks, but he nodded steadily and said, 'I do, yes,' then added, 'but Hughie is the better horseman,' so that I smiled at him. He looked startled, but he smiled back. He had a nice smile, I decided. Slow to start, but slow to fade too.

'Perhaps we will have a tennis party,' Cloé said and already the unspoken calculations were beginning: *how many would come? How many would play? What young men would there be for Aileen?* These were young men for her to practise on. The real young men were in London, where Aileen would have her coming out in a couple of years. We all knew that. But in the meantime, practice was important, so her Season would be a success, and it wasn't easy to find opportunities. That, too, I suspected, was reason enough for Cloé to be glad of Hughie and Richard. They were young, and ineligible, but they were men.

Ernest, when he came in, said that he knew

Richard's father, with a nod of approval, then quizzed Hughie carefully on what he intended to do with the farm, giving advice on the most interesting of the new inventions. Advice that Hughie listened to, asking precise questions about costs and yields so that I saw with pride that Ernest, too, was taken with him.

After that, Hughie rode over most days so that he became an expected part of all we did. After lessons and luncheon were finished, he would appear on Chestnut, often Richard with him, and, if it were fine, we would ride out together, to the Phoenix Park with its wide expanses, empty of all but the deer that scattered at our approach or lurked sullenly among the trees.

Richard, I learned, underneath his high colour and long silences, was perceptive and often funny. But only in the right company. Aileen continued to make him shy – although once she stopped being so very conscious of herself as a young lady, she and Hughie soon fell into an easy friendship, one in which she treated my brother exactly as she treated Cousin Bryan – and Maureen clearly terrified him – 'It is her way of a direct attack,' Richard explained once. 'I never know what she might say, or how quickly she might change the angle of her saying, so that I feel I'm turning and turning about to face her but can never catch up. Hughie is able for it; I am not.'

With Oonagh he was more at ease and with me, once he and I discovered that we could, both of us, talk about Hughie, he was never at a loss. Richard told me things that Hughie never would have – 'At school he was the brightest fellow, able to argue anything with the masters. Asking them questions they could hardly answer, about history and politics and what he called "self-determination of nations".' His admiration was obvious. 'I can tell you, my time at that school would have been very different without Hughie.'

'I'm sure you would have got on fine.'

'I'm sure I should not.'

'His size was against him,' Hughie said cheerfully, when I told him what Richard had said.

'How so?'

'Hard to be so much bigger than the other chaps and be such a good-hearted fellow. Made him a target for some of the less pleasant boys. There was one in particular, a tricky little fellow called Moran, cruel, but small and slight. He would rag Richard endlessly, called him "the Man Mountain" and other, worse names. Richard, twice his size, could not fight him. But neither could he match wits with him, so Moran tormented him, dancing around him like a wasp, stinging again and again, and Richard, like a poor maddened bull, unable to find the source of his pain.' Hughie's voice was light, but I could tell he had been angry at the mocking. 'I had to step in and put an end to that.'

No wonder Richard was devoted to Hughie, I thought. And no wonder he was shy of Maureen. 'So you saved him,' I said.

'Nonsense,' Hughie said.

'You did. I know you did because Richard told me.'

'I'm sure he said nothing of the sort.'

'Not in words, no,' I said, 'but as good as.'

It was a bond between us, Richard and me. I knew his gratitude to Hughie, and I liked him for it. Liked that he recognised it and could express it. But I found we had other things to talk of too. He spoke slowly, indeed I think his mind worked slowly, but his instincts were kind and soon, if we lagged behind the others on our walks, I found myself discussing many parts of my life, the things Gunnie asked of me, the things Cloé didn't ask but expected, the girls and the different ways I worried about them. The only thing I didn't speak much about was myself – what I might do or become – because I had nothing yet to say although I thought about it often. He didn't always answer, but he listened.

Aileen often came with us too, less grand and busy suddenly because there was fun to be had. Instead of begging to be let go into town, or on a visit to Burton Hall, she began to say 'what shall we do today?' and make plans just like the rest of us. Even Mildred sometimes joined us on these rides, managing her heavy grey mare far better than I had expected. She was somehow younger, more pleasant on these afternoons than I was used to, the American in her voice more pronounced, maybe because she tried less hard to sound like Cloé, whose words came out like small, carefully contained explosions, as though she were spitting cherry stones, one by one.

Mildred talked to Hughie much more than she ever talked to any of us – maybe because Hughie asked her those questions that I had never dared.

'Do you remember New York?' he asked one day as we ambled through the Phoenix Park, a straggling group of seven. All around us, the park stretched out, empty except for clusters of trees and flashes of white fencing.

'Yes, I was five when I left. I remember it well.'

'What was it like?'

'A city like a train, always moving, always in a rush,' she said thoughtfully. 'But we were poor there, after my pops died' – beside me, I felt Aileen stiffen at 'pops', the man she knew as Great-Uncle

Cecil, but Mildred, if she noticed, ignored her. 'My mom worked real hard to support us and keep us all there together, but it wasn't possible, and when my brother Cecil got sick, real sick, so they thought he might die, she decided it was time to come over here and see what Pops' family could do for us. She wrote to them and the girls' grandfather said we'd better come quick because he didn't want us turning up later and "claiming kinship when I don't know them".' She put on a stiff, choked kind of a voice.

'And?' Hughie encouraged.

'We did what he said,' Mildred said. 'What else could we do?' She shrugged. 'We came over on the boat and all the way, Mom told us stories of Pops' family and how they had so much money, and I thought she meant like our neighbours in New York, the Russos, who lived in the whole house while our house was divided into five or six apartments and ours was the smallest at the very top.' She started to laugh. 'And then we got to England and we took a train and then a taxi and we arrived at Elveden Hall, where the girls' grandpapa, Lord Iveagh, was.' She stopped and looked at Hughie, full of teasing laughter, but something painful too. 'Have you ever been there?'

'No,' Hughie said. 'Go on.'

'Well, I thought, driving in those gates, that it

was a village, maybe even a town, and that Pops' family lived in some part of it. And then we saw it. And it was like a house cut out of paper that someone had unfolded and unfolded so that it just got bigger and bigger until it was absurd, and I thought there must be nothing behind it, a cardboard front that would fall over if you pushed it. And then Mom said no, it was Grandpa's house. I said, 'All of it?' and when she said yes, well, she says I didn't speak for four full days after that. Not one single word.'

'And did you settle well there?' Hughie asked.

'No,' Mildred said. 'You see, we were there already.'

'What do you mean?' Richard asked, baffled, as indeed I was.

'Well, we were Pops' second family. He married a lady from Australia before he married Mom, and his first wife died, but she left two daughters, and they were already living at Elveden. Mabel and Katy, so pretty and charming and *good*' – she brought the word out viciously – 'so you see, there wasn't any need for us. Or, it felt, any room, in that whole, entire, seventy-bedroom house.'

There was a silence that no one could fill, and then Hughie said, 'What about Cecil?'

'He got better. They said the air was cleaner out of New York and that he would be OK. I didn't think air could make that much difference, but it did.'

'Where is he now?'

'He works in a bleach company.' I didn't know what a bleach company was, but it sounded terrible. 'He was wounded in the war, three times,' she said and I heard how desperately she wanted to paint something better for this brother of hers than the bleach company. How she wanted him to take place in our minds as she saw him, or as she wanted to see him; not, perhaps, as he was. I recognised the urge. I knew it well. It was the urge of sisters everywhere, those of us whose glories must always be reflected, bestowed upon us by our brothers or our fathers. I was happy for that to be so – what glory could be better than Hughie? – but I wondered, for a moment, what it must be like to shine in the light of your own sun, like the Guinness girls, with no brother to always eclipse them.

'And your mother?' Hughie asked. But further Mildred would not go. I saw the sudden glance she gave Maureen and Aileen, and the way she dug her heels into the mare's fat sides. 'Let's canter.'

Much later, when I was getting ready for my bath, Aileen came to my room. After fidgeting for a moment with the water jug and the mirror, swinging it back and forth, she said, 'I didn't know all that about Mildred. Did you?'

'No, I had no idea. Or at least, not much idea.'

'Nor I . . . But what an interesting life she has led.'

'A hard life,' I said cautiously.

'Oh yes, terrible really. But well, you know . . .' She paused, and I expected her to say more, but the dinner gong went then and instead she said, 'Drat, I must dress. I'll be late,' and ran out.

Chapter Thirteen

We had more freedom that summer so that often it was only us, without even Mildred to watch over us. 'It is because Hughie is your brother,' Oonagh said when I remarked on this. 'They trust him.'

'And Richard is so dull, they couldn't not trust him,' Maureen said.

'Unfair,' Oonagh protested, but she giggled and so did I. But then I felt that I needed to stand up for him in some way because he was Hughie's friend, so I said, 'But he is a very decent fellow,' which is how Hughie had described him.

'Just what I said,' Maureen drawled. 'Dull.' Even so, she didn't dislike him, that much I could see.

She laughed at him and teased him, but without any real malice.

Having Hughie and Richard – where we had been a house entirely of girls – was new and exciting. Their coming made us different. We did more. We played croquet, badminton, boules, as well as tennis. We went about more, on our ponies and on foot. And we were noisier. There was more and louder laughter, teasing, jokes – barely a day went by that Maureen did not dream up some new absurdity, everything from a posy of flowers that squirted water to a grotesque fake nose that Hughie smuggled in. She persuaded Robert the footman to wear the nose, to see how long before Cloé noticed. A whole day went by, with Robert's shoulders shaking silently as he delivered trays and took them away again, and then that evening, just as Maureen was about to claim a stunning victory, Cloé, on her way up the stairs said, 'Now, girls, go straight to your rooms. And, Robert, if Maureen should try and persuade you to wear that ridiculous nose again tomorrow, I expect you to refuse. Good night,' so that we knew we were beaten.

On days that we did not ride out, we explored. Until Hughie's coming, I had thought I knew Glenmaroon well, but in fact, what I knew was the new house, the North house. The South house was little used in those days – as an overflow for visitors when there were too many, or when the Walter Guinnesses came from London and Cloé made great show of how they must have their own quarters when we all knew she couldn't stand to be in the same house as Uncle Walter.

'Something to do with someone called Ida,' Aileen had said knowingly to us in the night nursery one evening, although when pressed, she admitted that she didn't know much more than a name. 'I think she's an actress, but what that has to do with Uncle Walter, I really don't know.'

'I thought it was the monkeys,' Oonagh had said. 'Such dear creatures. But so naughty. Especially the gibbon, Miss Gibbs. This Miss Gibbs was a sad, sad creature. Part monkey, part human, or at least believing she was part human, and therefore unhappy – as those who are half of something, not whole, will always be.

But even when the South house had visitors, we never went there – rather, they came to us, and so exploring now with Hughie and Richard, we found rooms that I didn't know, even some the girls didn't know.

'Why would we come here?' Maureen asked, when Hughie teased her about getting lost in her own house.

'Out of curiosity? Because it's here, and so are you?'

'It's all very well for you,' she said. 'You can do as you wish. We have so much to occupy our time.'

'Yes, watercolours and embroidery,' Hughie said. 'That wonderful stamp collection.'

'You may laugh, but you have no idea how tightly they hedge us in with all that,' Maureen said. 'Not an hour of a day but we must be doing something, and all useless. Singing, although I have no voice to speak of and will certainly never sing once I am free to do as I choose. Composition, when mine cause yawns in all who read them.' She laughed. 'I am sure a train timetable would be more entertaining. Oonagh's are even worse – so many stories about dogs! – but Fliss's compositions are very good. She has the knack,' she said, and Hughie smiled at me, but Oonagh, I saw, made a face and I wished Maureen had not chosen to praise me at her expense. I knew she did it because Hughie and Richard were there; that they, men, disrupted the balance of our lives in the same way that Ernest did, bringing, to all of us, that biting need to be first that meant we were not careful with one another.

Or maybe it was Hughie himself and whatever the friendship between him and Maureen was becoming, rather than all men. Because Richard, I soon saw, did not have anything like that effect on Maureen. In fact, he may as well have been a horse or a dog for all the attention she paid him, moving him out of her way as required, giving him things to hold – a shawl, a book – but without really seeing him.

Outside the iron gates of Glenmaroon, the stories of violence grew worse, like rooks that gather at evening, too close and too loud, each new arrival setting the tree branch shaking, and after a while Ernest insisted that Hughie and Richard must be accompanied on their ride back every night, 'because it is not safe'.

At first, Hughie protested robustly, but once he knew it was to be Thomas who rode with them, he was pleased. 'Well, if it's Thomas, that's alright,' he said. 'I don't mind his company at all,' and indeed within a few weeks he was often – too often – to be found down at the stables, talking to Thomas when we wanted him at the house. Thomas, to everyone's surprise, talked back. I could not but wonder what it was they discussed – horses, I imagined, or perhaps farming – but when I asked Hughie, as we strolled back up to the house late one afternoon, he said, 'He is an interesting fellow.'

'How so?' I asked. 'He is Kathleen's cousin and his mother is a widow, that I know.'

'His mother is indeed a widow. His father,

Michael Mahon, was one of the men who was shot after the taking of the General Post Office in the Easter Rising some years ago.'

I squinted against the light, surprised at where our conversation had gone. I had expected a story of how Thomas had proposed some scheme for better farm management, or he had taught himself to read. These were the things that usually interested Hughie.

'His death left them destitute. Thomas is the eldest of four. His mother has TB of the spine and cannot work much although she is a nurse. So Thomas provides for them all, from his job in the stables.'

I shuddered. I remembered Kathleen telling me Thomas's mother was unwell. But I hadn't imagined this. TB was the disease we all dreaded, but I had not yet heard that it could travel from lungs to bones.

'I have heard the families of those men get a pension,' I said. 'Gunnie says it. She is very angry, of course.' I laughed, but Hughie had no time for the patriotic resentments that Gunnie wore like a rosette.

'Well, Thomas's mother is angry too. Her pension is less than the widows of the educated men, although they all died the same way. She gets £1 a week, and she has four children.' He sounded unlike the Hughie I knew, who was moved always to help, yes, but moved by kindness, not anger. This note of bitterness was new.

'But his father was disloyal!' I said.

'To who?'

'To the Crown,' I said, bewildered at having to say something so obvious. 'To us, even. To the war that Papa was fighting in. Dying in.' We so rarely spoke of Papa anymore, Hughie and I, that I worried what he would make of me bringing him up like this. When we talked of him, it was carefully, with neat memories. We did not try to bring him forward into our lives and imagine what he would do or say or think, because it was too hard. The shadows that were our recollections were too faded.

There was no 'real' Papa anymore for me, just a collection of stories that could, really, have been about anybody. The truth was, he was overlaid too many times with images of Ernest by now, things that Ernest had said or done or forbidden, so that I was sometimes frightened to venture a memory, bring forth a recollected tale, in case it was not Papa at all but Ernest whom I had remembered and recast in Papa's role.

I suspected that Hughie had no clear route to him anymore either, so to invoke him in this was new ground. But Hughie didn't respond as I expected.

'That's so,' he agreed, 'but there was no shame, for Michael Mahon, in that. It was not his Crown. He was loyal to the men he fought for independence with, and to the country he believed in. The trouble is, the country he believed in has not been loyal to him. They could help his widow, but they do not, or not enough.'

I didn't understand Hughie. I mean, I understood the words he spoke of course, but not the sentiments that lay behind them. What did loyalty mean when he spoke it without invoking the King or any of the things I knew to be loyal to? And yet, I knew one thing – that Hughie, who had lost a father to war, saw some kind of kinship with Thomas, who had lost too, although in a different kind of war.

'It's hard for him as the eldest,' I said cautiously. I didn't wish Hughie to think I was unsympathetic. And I liked Kathleen well enough to feel kindness towards Thomas, her cousin, even though none of it, I thought, had much to do with me.

'He has one brother, the youngest, determined to become a priest,' said Hughie, 'and two sisters wishing to be nuns. He knows that the duty to provide will remain squarely on his shoulders.' I could hear the admiration in his voice. Hughie, who took his own responsibilities for the farm and Mummie, even me, so seriously.

Gunnie called us then from the house and we

quickened our pace, dropping the conversation and I forgot about it entirely. Until some days later.

'Thomas, I need you,' Maureen called out. We were by the tennis courts after lunch, the three of us girls (Aileen, as usual, had chosen to stay in her room reading rather than spend the day with us), and Thomas had appeared on the gravel path, walking slowly with a wheelbarrow filled with dirty straw. He stopped and laid down the handles of the barrow and waited.

'Can you drive the croquet hoops deeper in?' Maureen continued. 'They are loose and falling down, and Oonagh will use that to cheat if she can.' She gave her most charming smile, the smile that went out from her with the absolute certainty that anyone who saw it would do exactly as she wished.

'When I finish up,' Thomas said shortly.

'But we want to play now.' We didn't – in fact we had not talked about playing croquet at all – and I wondered if Maureen was simply trying to engage Thomas and get words out of him as part of a game. Or more than that; I had seen how it irritated her that he would speak to Hughie and not to any of us.

'I can't now, I'll look at it later,' Thomas said, running his 't's all together the way the servants did so that it came out as '*lookattitt*,' all sibilant, as if he spoke in that hissing language he used to horses.

'Well, I'm afraid we rather need you to "lookattitt" now,' Maureen said. She enunciated carefully until she got to his bit, then slurred the words together in a mocking impersonation of his speech. Thomas remained still and stared, not at her, but at the ground, and I felt mortified.

'I'm busy,' he said.

'You don't look busy,' Maureen replied. 'Or if you are, it's busy doing nothing much.' I think she was inviting him to laugh with her, to acknowledge that he was doing nothing more than pushing a barrow of old straw. But he didn't. Of course he didn't.

I don't know what would have happened then, except that Hughie arrived and must have very quickly understood because he said, 'Thomas, Sean Dolan is looking for you. I have just this minute come from stabling Chestnut.'

As head groom, Sean Dolan's authority trumped even Maureen's and so she said nothing, just tossed her head and turned away while Thomas picked up his barrow and wheeled it by her. That the barrow bumped her ankle as it went by, knocking bone with metal so that she cried out in pain, was surely just an accident.

Chapter Fourteen

Our glorious summer of freedom ended on a day that began like any other. We laid out all our plans like boiled sweets to consider, and we chose the one we liked best: a picnic in South house. 'I don't see why not,' Gunnie said, when Maureen asked if we might take our luncheon there. And so Cook packed a hamper and we carried it with us across the narrow wrought-iron bridge that ran between the houses.

'Come on, Oonagh, I'll walk behind you so you can't possibly fall,' said Hughie, trying to coax her across.

'It's not falling I'm afraid of,' she said.

'What, then?'

'The bridge moves as you walk on it. It is unsteady and makes me feel wobbly, as if I might travel through it into quite another world.' But she let herself be persuaded – proof of how she trusted Hughie – and we went across, one by one. Below us was the road that ran between the houses, along which delivery carts made their journeys, bringing the provisions needed to supply the relentless magnificence of Glenmaroon, and I felt suddenly as if Oonagh was right – that we were moving into quite a different land, a place all our own, like in the book Cloé had given me for Christmas, about a secret garden and the children who played there. Trust Oonagh, I thought, who truly was a sprite, just as Hughie had observed, to see it.

'Look, when it's clear you can see most of the city from here,' Aileen said, stopping halfway and looking down at the swoop of road that led out from under us towards fields and trees and on to rows of grey buildings rising in the distance. Surrounded by an embrace of light and dark green treetops, they looked, I thought, as though some distracted bird had gathered stones instead of eggs to lay in a leafy nest.

'Do come on,' Oonagh pleaded. 'I am certain I can feel the bridge sway under me.'

We went to the Orangery, which had no oranges but large windows that faced the sun and was warm and almost bright, even on that dull day, and spread out our picnic on a plaid rug set over the scuffed and dusty wooden floor. There was a stillness to the South house that I loved. It was the peace of rooms seldom used, without the constant small disruptions of North house, where housemaids and footmen were always coming and going.

Cold meats, preserves, freshly baked bread, cheeses, a raspberry tart and cream. We ate and said how much better the food tasted sitting on the floor, then Hughie lit a cigarette, which he passed to Aileen, and a second for himself. The two leaned back against the battered white wicker chairs we had pushed to the side and breathed out plumes of smoke, baby versions of the damp clouds beyond the window. The afternoon had turned dark, and the rain now threw hard drops in large handfuls at the windows.

'It sounds like someone is shaking the house till its teeth rattle,' Oonagh said with a laugh.

'Sounds like gunfire,' Hughie said, and Richard, beside me, gave him a look.

'Hardly,' he said.

'Why not?' Hughie said. 'There is rioting in the North. Plenty of it.'

'Too much of it,' Richard said firmly, and now it was Hughie who looked at him.

'May I have a cigarette?' Maureen asked, ignoring this exchange.

'She's not allowed,' Aileen said quickly. 'Mamma forbids it until she is sixteen.'

'Well, Mamma isn't here, Miss Tattle-Tale,' Maureen said snappily. Then, 'Very well, Hughie, if you will not give me a cigarette, you must promise to partner me at the tennis party?' And she smiled at him, lashes fluttering delicately over those blue eyes.

'But . . .' Aileen began.

'Not fair . . .' Oonagh said. 'What about us?'

'Let's play a game,' I said quickly, to head off the quarrel so clearly brewing.

'Forfeits!' Oonagh said. It was a game I hated – the volunteering of personal items, a ribbon or hair grip, to be 'auctioned', and then 'bought back' with a poem or song or dance.

I sat and watched them – Richard, so serious in his efforts; Hughie in his auctioneer role making absurd claims for the properties of a bracelet of Maureen's; the funny caper Oonagh put on to buy back her hair grip – and thought how much more like the girls Hughie was than me. For all his seriousness about the farm, and the changes he said were coming to the country, he had the same high spirits and wicked humour as they did, the same teasing sense of the ridiculous, whereas I, it seemed, was serious about everything although I longed not to be.

Outside, the rain had stopped and a small patch of light shone in the east, a bright silver sixpence in the far corner of the sky. I wondered would it reach us, spreading to the size of a florin, then a half-crown, then bigger again, bringing a brief evening benediction of good weather.

'You are very quick to spot trouble.' Hughie stepped out of his auctioneer role for a moment to sit by my side. The others were too deep in the game to notice.

'What?' I said, startled.

'I saw how you distracted those two' – he nodded towards Maureen and Aileen – 'from a row. And I see how careful you are to always manage and soothe all three. And you're clever at it.'

'I suppose I am,' I said. 'I've had time to learn.' I smiled to show I meant no sting in my words. Because it was true, I had learned, by watching carefully, always alert, so that I hardly knew I did it anymore.

'I'm sure you needed to learn,' he said thoughtfully. 'I understand that. But I want you to remember, you do not always need to think about them. Perhaps sometimes you can also think about yourself.' It was so long since anyone had suggested such a thing – indeed, for so long everyone around me had suggested the exact opposite – that I was shocked and could think of nothing to say.

He returned to the game, loudly demanding a better payout than Maureen's poem, and I continued to watch. After a moment, Richard came over. 'Not really my sort of thing,' he said, when I asked him why.

'Not really anyone's sort of thing, I should have thought,' I replied. I said it in the new way I was practising then, drawing out the middle of my words then rushing to close them off at the end, just like Maureen did. I thought I carried it well enough that I could pass it off as my own, but I was mistaken.

'You're not them, you know,' Richard said.

'I don't know what you're talking about.'

'You're not them, Fliss. And you're the better for it.'

I was mortified that he had seen through my effort. 'What do you and Hughie do on the days you don't ride over to us?' I asked, to change the subject. I had meant to ask Hughie, but he was rarely still long enough. And if he was, undoubtedly Maureen was there too to distract him and demand his attention.

'Less than we do here,' he said with one of

his rare flashes of humour. 'Sometimes we go into town.'

'And what is that like?' Apart from Aileen, we almost never went into town, except sometimes to the theatre.

'Dirty, restless. Soldiers everywhere.' He made a face. 'Hughie goes to meetings in damp halls. I execute commissions for my mother and wait for him.'

'Meetings?' I said with a laugh. 'I cannot imagine Hughie going to meetings. Unless they are about farming methods.'

'In a way, perhaps,' Richard said. Then, 'I wouldn't mention them to Ernest.'

'Ernest? Whyever would I?' I asked, astonished. Then, 'And do you not go too?'

'Hughie has stronger views than me,' he said.

'About what?' But he didn't answer me. Not exactly.

'My parents, their friends, they think because their families have been here for generations and they know that the housemaid's father once worked in the stables and took them out on their first pony, that they belong and are loved,' he said. 'But they're wrong. They can't see that the country is ready to shake them off like a dog.'

'But what has that to do with Hughie?'

'I think Hughie is on the side of the dog,' he said.

Before I could ask more, Oonagh called to him: 'Richard! Do come on. It's your go.'

I sat and thought about what he had said, trying to puzzle it out, and because I took no part in the game, I was the first to see Robert push open the door and stand for a moment with a more than usually grave face.

'What is it, Robert?' Aileen asked.

'You're to return to North house,' he said. 'I'm to fetch you back.'

'But why?' Maureen pouted and was ready to refuse. 'We only just got here.'

'Mr Ernest has requested it. He says you're to come at once.'

'But why?' Maureen asked again, exasperated. 'I demand to know.'

'There's been an upset,' Robert said. 'That's all I can tell you. You are to go to the drawing room.'

'Better go,' Hughie said. 'If only for curiosity's sake.'

At the door I looked back at Robert, gathering the dishes together from the floor. Behind him, the sky had darkened again, closing around the silver sixpence like a fist.

All the family were in the drawing room even though it was not yet teatime. Ernest stood before the fireplace, arm thrown across it, an adventurer or seafarer, with Cloé, upright in a high-backed chair beside him, the figurehead of a ship, and Mildred and Gunnie side by side on the slippery blue silk sofa. Between them all was a thick cat's-cradle of alarm, woven in invisible strands by the looks they darted at each other.

Behind Ernest the fire was already lit although it was early, and I watched oily flames gnawing at the pile of heaped logs.

'You may no longer go about without Thomas or Sean,' Cloé said abruptly, and beside me I felt Maureen bristle at the peremptory tone.

'Surely if we are within the walls—' she began, but Ernest interrupted.

'Your mamma is right, and you are to do as she says. All of you. Do you understand?'

'But why?' Aileen asked. The hardship would be mostly hers; of late she had been allowed out in the motorcar with Mildred, to shop and even meet friends for tea at the Shelbourne Hotel.

'Because it is not safe.' There was a silence then, and I think Ernest wrestled with how much more to tell us. 'Burton Hall has been attacked and set alight,' he said at last. 'Mercifully, no one is hurt. The family were locked in the lodge by men with masks over their faces, although Henry is certain he knew many of them. The fire did not properly take, even though those devils packed the house with their ham-fisted, homemade explosives.' I did not know if he was more annoyed at the attempted destruction or the poorly made bombs.

'They call it "Irish cheddar",' Hughie said, stepping forward eagerly. Too eagerly. 'The explosives.'

'Do they indeed?' Ernest gave him a long look, then continued. 'The army arrived in time to put out what flames there were before anything more serious happened.'

'But why would anyone do such a thing?' Aileen asked. 'What harm has Henry ever done? He works in a bank.' She sounded bewildered.

'I am afraid this sort of thing is happening rather more now,' Ernest said.

'Where will they live?' Gunnie, ever practical, asked. I could see her mentally preparing South house for a long visit.

'Henry tells me they will continue to live in Burton Hall,' said Ernest. There was admiration in his voice. 'He says the damage is bearable and they will not be chased out.'

'Goodness,' said Cloé. 'What unnecessary heroics.'

'I do not like the way these troubles are turning,'

Ernest said then. 'There is a fuse now lit in this country that burns altogether too fast. Two nights ago the town of Tuam, in Galway, was burned to the ground. Yesterday there were incidents of retaliatory violence across much of the country, and now the attempt on Burton Hall.'

'But it will blow over?' Maureen asked. 'And meantime, may we still have the tennis party Mamma has planned?'

'There will be no tennis party,' said Ernest. 'And furthermore, in the autumn we will move to Holmbury.'

'Papa, no!' That was Oonagh. 'Please, let us not move.' Holmbury was the house in Surrey. I had never seen it, but all three girls hated it. 'It is the dreariest place on earth,' Oonagh had assured me.

'Please, Papa, not Holmbury,' she said now. 'We'll be terribly good and never stray without Sean or Thomas, and Hughie and Richard will be with us for extra protection.'

'It's decided,' Ernest said.

I looked around. Gunnie was already mentally packing up Glenmaroon, but I saw Mildred look gloomy. I thought I knew why. This would interrupt her nursing studies. And Surrey, anywhere in England, I suspected, was too close to her half-sisters, the elfin and charming Mabel and Katy. They were the poison in her chalice, the bitter tears that mingled with the flow of her life. As I watched, she bit her teeth tightly together and a muscle twitched at the corner of her eye.

'Felicity, I will suggest to your mother that you come with us,' Cloé said, and only then did it occur to me that there had been any chance I might not go.

'Of course Fliss must come,' Oonagh cried. 'We must have some good left to us.'

'Who did the burning, sir?' Hughie asked then. 'Of Tuam?'

'Our forces did,' Ernest said. 'With due provocation.'

'You mean the Black-and-Tan forces?' Hughie asked.

'I mean the Royal Irish Constabulary Special Reserve, as you will properly call them,' Ernest said, voice rising a little like the quick lash of a carriage whip. 'They acted in reprisal for the shooting dead of two constables earlier that same evening.' He stared hard at Hughie, and Hughie dropped his eyes.

'Those poor men,' Gunnie said piously.

'Indeed,' Ernest said. 'The affair turned very ugly and it is not quite certain what may happen next. There is a new Auxiliary Division arriving from England this month, and it is to be hoped they will put down this foolish insurrection so that we may all get on with our business.'

'Where is the new division coming from?' Hughie asked, and I saw him look sideways at Richard, who shook his head, just a fraction so that only someone watching as closely as me could have seen it.

But perhaps Ernest watched closely too. Or maybe the interest in Hughie's voice was too keen and he heard it, because instead of answering the question, he said, 'That's enough of that now. I think it must be time for you two to set off. You have a long ride and you do not wish to be out after dark. I will send Thomas to ride with you.'

Instantly Richard said, 'Of course.' And he put a hand out to Hughie, who stood silent and thoughtful. 'Come along,' he said. 'We must go.'

Later, the girls and I sat together in the half-hour before bedtime, each of us, I suppose, lost in our own thoughts of what a move might mean.

I tried to imagine what England might be like, and I could not. I thought of the extra distance I would be putting between me and Ballytibbert. Me and Mummie. Mostly, me and Hughie. 'When I am older, should you like to live with me?' he had asked me one afternoon as we trailed home on foot, leading our horses after a long ride. The ground was soft and wet, as it was always wet that summer. But the sun had come out for that precious hour the close of day so often brought and poured its store of gold thickly over us and down across the path ahead.

'I should like that above all things,' I had said.

'Damn those Burton Hall cousins!' Maureen said now. 'Always ruining everything.' Although unfair, it was exactly what I had been thinking.

'Hardly their fault,' Aileen protested. 'And I have no doubt Judy would give as good as any rebel if she had half a chance.'

'They needn't have made such a fuss. Running to Papa with their tales of woe,' said Maureen.

'They seem to have made very little fuss, actually,' Oonagh pointed out.

'No, indeed,' Aileen agreed. 'Not even moving out. I wonder why they stay? I wouldn't.'

'Nor I,' Maureen said.

But I thought I understood. These girls had many homes, in two countries. They might prefer one to another – Glenmaroon to Holmbury, or even Grosvenor Place in London – but that choice was theirs to make. 'If that was your only home,' I said, 'I think I see why one might stay.'

I thought about Ballytibbert. Would I stay, if men with rags across their faces and familiar voices came down upon us and insisted we walk out with just the clothes we stood in, then set alight those rooms and halls and stairs; the house where I had been born and where Papa's family had lived, generations of them, before us? Would I? I did not know, could not imagine, but I knew what Mummie would do. Hughie, too.

'Not if it was burned!' Maureen insisted.

'I'd rather stay here, even if it was a bit burned, than go to Holmbury,' Oonagh said. 'We could just close the rooms with the burned bits and live in the rest. Oh, such a shame!'

'Think of the tennis party,' Maureen wailed. 'It was to have been such fun. Mamma promised me a new dress, and there was to have been a machine that made ices.'

'And now we shan't see Hughie anymore,' Oonagh said.

She expressed exactly what I was feeling, but I couldn't allow myself to feel it as she did – so I said the opposite of what I felt. 'We'll be back. Christmas, Easter, summer for the Horse Show. Cloé said so.'

'I know, but it's not the same. Here, we see him every day.'

'But soon he will have to go home, Oonagh,' I said. 'This is not his home. There is school to finish, then Ballytibbert, and Mummie, and the farm. He has plans, you know, modernisations he wishes to make.'

'I know all that,' Maureen interjected impatiently. 'I have already decided that when I am of age, I shall put money into his farm. It will be an investment, like Papa talks about.'

'I'm sure Hughie would never allow that,' I said, surprised.

'We have already discussed it,' she said, 'and he thinks it a very good plan indeed.' When, I wondered. When could they have discussed such a thing? And why had neither of them spoken of it to me? But I couldn't ask – not if they had talked like that and not told me – so I said nothing.

Chapter Fifteen

Glenmaroon, Dublin, 1978

Back in the attic, I tip out the first plastic bag and spread the contents around me. The smell is terrible. Some small rodent must have used these papers as a nest before they were bagged because many are chewed and there are scatterings of tiny black droppings.

'Do you have rubber gloves?' I ask Trisha.

'In the kitchen.'

'Would you fetch a pair?' I cannot bear to touch these papers without them. She nods and goes, and I think that I will give her a coin when I leave. I must ask him how much – it's the kind of thing I never know. Is a pound too showy? It wouldn't do to insult her with too little but too much is foolish. He'll know. He always knows such things. Do all men, I wonder, or is it particular to him?

I try to separate the pages with my foot but they are too nibbled and stuck together so I go to the window again. The front gardens are empty. The nuns and their charges have retired. I think how quiet the house is, just like the stables were, although there must be many more people living in it now than there were back then. Then, it was never quiet, or not as I remember now.

Light is sinking and the tops of the trees have caught at what little there is, dragging shapes through it, casting these as shadows onto the lawns below. The trees are too high. Whoever is tending the gardens so beautifully is not able to manage them. Ernest would never have allowed the overgrowth, I think, and for a moment I am irritated on his behalf.

I'm surprised by how much I still wear the pride of being part of that household, even though the household has long disintegrated, and I was never really part of it.

I thought I was. I think we all thought I was. But by the time I left this house for good, at the end of the last summer, I knew I wasn't. They must have known too, even though we all tried to behave otherwise for a long time after.

How much money must it have taken to keep this place as it used to be? All the immaculate lines and borders, the gleaming windows and paintwork, everything so proudly proclaiming the glory of the Guinness family. The work of many hands every day, scrubbing, sweeping, pruning, polishing; constant vigilance, countless monies.

I confess I was fascinated by their wealth for a time. It's easier to say that now. It was so vast and unwieldy that I thought of it as something almost tangible – an extra person in the house. Or more like an extra creature, some fabled beast – a manticore or chimera – that crouched behind them all, protecting them, framing them. It distracted me and impressed me, for which I was ashamed, but I could not help myself.

Even then, still really a child, I saw what money could do – the ease and luxury of their lives. And I knew what lack of it could do. That was the worry in Mummie's face, the endless conversations with Uncle Alex, and Hughie's anger at the barefoot children we passed on the roads around Ballytibbert. I didn't want wealth, indeed it never occurred to me that I could have it, but I liked to look at the evidence of it and try to understand it.

But I never ever thought about it the way Hughie and Thomas did – a wrong to be righted.

I remember when so many lost money – the

Great Crash, as they called it. It didn't affect the Guinnesses. Except that it affected the way their friends saw them. Even I could tell that. Their wealth, its vastness, had been quaint before the Crash. Afterwards, when so many lost everything, it became an affront.

I don't think the girls ever really understood this.

That was a time of Greats, I think now. There was a Great War, and a Great Crash, and neither was ever supposed to happen again. Well, they did. But maybe nothing is ever quite like the first time?

There is a man far out at the edge of the lawn pushing a wheelbarrow. He is too distant and I can't make him out. I wonder if he is the one responsible for the beauty of the gardens behind the house. And if so, why he doesn't do the same work out front. What I can see from this window is neat enough, but far from the glorious riot at the back.

'Gloves.' Trisha is back with a pair of pink rubber gloves that have seen better days. I dislike putting my hands into them, and sure enough they are wet. I try not to think of what other hands must have worn them. I put them firmly on and begin to pull apart the contents of the bags.

Walking back to the house I had pretended to myself that I would search the bags so as to do the job I had been sent to do – find out if there was anything there that could harm the Guinness girls.

But I don't. I search them for myself, and only to look for one thing.

Chapter Sixteen

Glenmaroon, Dublin, 1922

Holmbury was just as bad as Oonagh made it out to be. Dull, undistinguished, so that nearly two years went by like clouds – vague and formless and drifting. Ernest was mostly in Dublin, Aileen often in London, or on long visits to other young ladies, and Maureen and Oonagh away at school – Mrs Spain hadn't come with us; I watched her pack her bags with sullen fury, a cat put out on a wet day. The periods without them were long and unhappy and lonely and I wondered why Cloé had brought me at all, although she made sure I was busy fetching and carrying for her, reading aloud and listening to her recollections of parties and balls. Even so the days were without interest or shape, so that when word came that we were to leave Surrey and travel back to Glenmaroon for the summer of 1922, where they would meet us, I felt as though I had been pushed into the open again, blinking and weak and grateful, in the glare of a strong light after too long in the cramped dark.

I realised I had forgotten what it meant to be a Guinness in the wider world. Closeted with Cloé in her dim room at Holmbury, brewing potions with Gunnie or listening to Mildred's tales of minor goings-on in the village, I had forgotten what it really was to be part of this family. The journey back to Dublin showed me.

The whispers, the nudges, the excitement carefully suppressed behind deference and an extraordinary *politesse* that gripped everyone from stationmasters to maître d's and even policemen as we moved through them like some royal procession, a train of kings through the desert, these things soon reminded me. We were returned carefully, passed from hand to hand as smoothly as though we had been news, some lip-smacking story, rather than people and dogs and trunks and hatboxes.

I suppose I had forgotten, too, that there was still so much unrest in Ireland. Burnings, beatings, shootings, cruelty, and reprisals that went back and forth, back and forth, like a vicious game of catch, but one where I didn't fully understand the rules. Stories that sounded exciting when described in terms of escapades and derring-do by Hughie, in his infrequent letters, became 'savagery' and 'butchery' if it was Ernest who spoke of them, so that I was confused entirely about who to believe.

The trouble now, Ernest explained to us as we drove across Dublin, through streets flung one upon the other in a gnarled mess, was no longer between the Crown and the men of the country, it was between the men themselves, who could not agree on how to govern. There was, it seems, a treaty that had put an end to the war with the British and granted some kind of independence, but even so it was not acceptable to all and so men now fought about that. 'Trouble is trouble,' Ernest said. 'It matters less who they shoot than that they are still shooting.'

'All that is finished with now, I thought,' Cloé said indifferently.

'So you may think,' Gunnie said. 'But these people can no more govern themselves than a pack of dogs.' The satisfaction in her voice was spread thick like butter. 'The first thing they have done is turn on one another. They are so used to fighting now, they cannot think what else to do.'

As we drove, I saw no roadblocks or Auxiliary troops, no sign of the uniforms of the RIC because the Crown was now gone, but everywhere there were destroyed buildings that lolled like tramps, torn-up cobblestones, and the Custom House, one of the city's few fine buildings, was a dirty, sodden, blackened wreck. Someone had stuck a pole into the rubble from which fluttered the gaily-striped green-and-white-and-orange flag of the new country. Above all that wreckage, it looked like a handkerchief waved in distress.

'It burned for five days, Fliss. And when the great copper dome finally collapsed, I tell you, flames burst out from underneath it and caused it to swell outwards of a sudden, like the sails of a fine ship that have been filled with a billow of air.' That's what Hughie wrote at the time, in a letter that nearly trembled, so clearly could I feel his excitement. *'A tremendous sight – a sign of all that is now finished, and all that will now come,'* he continued. It was a promise made to himself far more than me, I thought.

Ernest, when he spoke of the burning to Cloé and Gunnie, while I listened and pretended not to, had a different view. 'Extraordinary folly,' he said. He was angry but tried not to show it. 'A squanderous show of strength. Five of their own men killed, and centuries of records destroyed, all for a piece of foolish propaganda.' In Ernest's world, waste and recklessness were sins not easily forgiven.

Now, as we drove past the wrecked remains, I saw him turn his head away and look straight ahead as if refusing to acknowledge someone who had insulted him.

Past Marlborough Barracks and there, too, the *tricolore* was flying high. 'It doesn't feel *right* somehow . . .' Gunnie mused as we looked up. But I wasn't sure. I liked the pretty colours, and the sprightly way it threw itself into the wind.

Ernest told us these were now called the McKee Barracks, after 'a great scoundrel', although the building was unchanged, and the warm smell of horse sweat and manure-soaked straw was stronger than ever.

'How strange it is to come back to one's home and find that it is in a new country,' Gunnie said petulantly. 'I do hope it does not hinder you in business, dear Ernest?' She put a little trill on the word 'business', as though it were a curious pet Ernest insisted on owning.

'It does not,' he said shortly. 'I make sure of that.'

'Well, I hope their disloyalty does not extend to you,' she said.

'Wages ensure their loyalty,' he said. 'And we

do not ask too many questions. If they leave for a time, once they return to their jobs, we do not look too hard for reasons.'

'But surely that is dangerous?' Gunnie said, excited at the prospect. 'Why, those men could be murderers.'

'Just as long as they are good workers,' he said.

When we arrived at Glenmaroon, it was evening and the last rays of the setting sun poured through the coloured glass above the staircase. The same smell – beeswax, warm wood – that greeted me on my first evening was there again, cut through with a faint tang of vinegar that told me the windows were washed that morning for our arrival. The same expanse of polished wood, the same low red ceiling with its curlicues of white; 'a cigar box' as Maureen had once described it to Hughie. The girls would be home from school the next day; Hughie would be there soon after. We would be together again.

'I say, look, Fliss has bosoms!' Maureen said by way of greeting the next day, when we were alone finally, without servants bustling with cases and boxes, or Cloé looking critically at each girl in turn. In what used to be the schoolroom and was now our writing room, transformed with new curtains and carpet, and a cunning little bureau that folded into itself, she perched on a small table and laughed at me.

'I'm fourteen, of course I do,' I said. 'And anyway, so do you.' I crossed my arms over my chest. I hated when Maureen, who had no sense of modesty, made jokes like that.

'I do indeed.' She stuck her chest out proudly. 'Aren't they fine? Let's measure.'

'Maureen, no!'

'Oh Teapot, leave her be. Not everyone is as interested in themselves and their charms as you,' said Oonagh. They had new nicknames for each other – Miss Tongs and Miss Teapot. Something to do with the school they had been to and one of the girls there, who was called Violet Valerie French; 'Preposterous name,' Maureen had said, 'but such fun.'

'That's because not everyone has as many charms as me,' Maureen said, tilting her head to see herself in the small mirror opposite. She turned her head this way and that, admiring her profile from different angles. 'Certainly, you don't. Why, in the right clothes you could pass as a boy even now.'

'I don't care,' Oonagh said. 'I don't ever want to be grown up and *womanly*.' She went into peals of laughter. 'How terrible that sounds: round and slow and hardly able to move for all the underclothes. I've seen Gunnie getting dressed – she's like a table laid for a banquet, one starched white layer after another.' She laughed again. 'No wonder she can't keep pace with us. I'm never going to bother with all that.' She stretched her legs out in front of her. 'Oh Fliss, you've no idea how lucky you are not to have been sent to school.'

I didn't tell her I would have been happy to have gone, to have carried on learning beyond what was in the few books they left behind.

'Will Hughie be visiting?' Maureen asked then, eyes demurely on the ground.

'He will. You know he will,' I said. When Hughie wrote to me, now, he often included notes for the girls too; sketches and funny poems for Oonagh, short letters for Maureen, and even though they weren't much good at writing back, I knew they didn't forget what he said. 'He'll be here in a few days.' I didn't try to hide the joy I felt. The years gone by had dragged themselves day by day like a dying creature crawling under a hedge, until we had arrived back here, and then it was as if they had never happened at all; as though I had but closed my eyes for some brief moments and now they were open and all was vivid and in motion again. We had plans, and games, and, soon, Hughie.

'Richard, too,' I continued. 'Hughie is staying

with him again. He is finished with school entirely now and has been studying how to manage the farm. In the autumn he will take over from Uncle Alex.' Along with short letters for Maureen and Oonagh, Hughie also often included something for me from Richard – a few stiff lines hoping I was well that I answered with equal formality.

'Good! Richard can make up the numbers,' Maureen said carelessly. 'And this year, no one shall put off parties. We are promised. Papa has been talking about making a long trip on *Fantome*, but Mamma is not fond of the idea and I jolly well hope she persuades him. I cannot think of anything more dread.'

Fantome was Ernest's new yacht, his latest toy, of which I had written to Mummie, 'She is 139 tons and used to belong to the Duke of Westminster.' Mummie had replied, 'Are there no footsteps so exalted that a Guinness won't seek to step in them?'

'He's been talking about making a long trip for years,' Oonagh said. 'It's no more likely to happen now than Peke learning to foxtrot. Or Gunnie getting married again.' And she went into peals of laughter at the idea, this time with Maureen joining in.

Planning for the party took off in earnest a few days later. 'Perhaps the Burton Hall lot might bring some of their boy cousins? After all, it is the summer and so they will be there.' Maureen, pen in hand, wrote names in two neat columns. 'If so then we will almost have enough, all told, for dancing as well as tennis.'

'Will Cloé allow it?' I asked.

'She has said that we may do the organising. She thinks it will be good for us. She's right. I *feel* it being good for me.' Maureen swung her legs over the windowsill and landed lightly on the flat roof of the portico. Useless to tell her to stop these days. She was alight with the energy of plans to be made, entertainments to be arranged, invitations written and sent, numbers calculated. And because she was a Guinness, and therefore unlike other mortals, she was to be allowed. Lapham had instructions to ask her and Aileen many of the questions that would more usually go to Gunnie and Mildred, and even though Gunnie hovered in the background with offers to help, Maureen's refrain was 'We can do it.'

Aileen, at eighteen, was far less interested, but amused by Maureen's excitement and willing to let her lead. 'It keeps her out of mischief,' she had said to me the evening before, back from a few days' visit to friends in Westmeath. 'Or do I mean, it keeps her from making mischief? You know what Maureen without a plan is like,' but she said it with a smile. Aileen, I had noticed, was being kinder to Maureen that summer.

'It's not seeing her for a while,' she said when I remarked on this. 'All the time she was off at school and I was in London, I missed her. Oonagh, too, of course. So much more than I thought. You know, I have always felt I had to battle Maureen for, oh, everything really.'

'What do you mean?'

'It's that she takes over so much. She can't help it. I am always behind her, hidden by her, even though I'm older. Trying to make people see that I am here too because they all look at her. I have felt so angry with her for that. But once she was gone and I missed her, I began to see that she doesn't so much do it, as it simply happens. And' – with a smile that was a grimace too – 'that I'm never going to win.'

Oonagh solemnly undertook any tasks allotted to her, writing out cards of invitation in her best hand: 'The Misses Ernest Guinness request the pleasure of your company at an afternoon party on June 28th 1922. There will be tennis. And dancing.' Even this, Maureen composed herself, refusing the more formal wording that Gunnie had proposed.

'You make it sound so *casual*,' Gunnie had complained, to which Maureen replied with certainty, 'Not casual. Relaxed. Not stuffy. A party for young people.'

I helped where I could, but even with Mildred finished her studies, it seemed Cloé couldn't 'do without' me, perhaps because I suited her better. My time was torn into smaller shreds like a tissue, none of which seemed to belong to me. Cloé asked for me, commanded me, daily. That I sit with her, read to her, walk about the lawns with her. And I did, although often I near twitched with hidden frustration and impatience, subduing them beneath quiet hands and a calm exterior. Desperate to be with the others, I would chafe at Cloé's restraint. But I did not know what else to do.

'There is so much still to do,' Maureen said now. 'Oonagh, you must decide who will partner with who for doubles. I'm not playing with Brinsley; he's good but is too cutting if one drops a serve. Aileen can have him. I might play with Richard, but I will not dance with him. He is far too clumsy.' She sat at the far end of the roof, on the stone balustrade, legs dangling towards the ground eight feet below. Even then, I said nothing. 'Oh, where is Hughie?' she said. 'He said he would come and practise our foxtrot.'

Watching how eagerly Maureen looked for him,

I thought back to the very first time he rode up that path, still unknown to them and them to him, and how the excitement that had been mine then was all of ours now. Because of that, I felt we, who lived as sisters, were now in fact almost sisters – more than friends, more even than cousins. Hughie was the bond between us, beyond even all the hours spent in one another's company.

'Teapot, you know very well Mamma will never, never allow a foxtrot,' Oonagh said.

'Oh, I know.' Maureen tossed her head and swung her legs faster. 'But that doesn't mean I can't practise, for when she's not around to watch me. After all, she won't always be looking over my shoulder. Or Mildred either.' She grinned, giddy with the spectacle of freedom that approached at a gallop. 'But where is he?' She leaned even further out over the balustrade, so that I swung myself out the window and walked across the portico roof towards her.

'Back,' I said, a hand on her arm. She shook me off but swung her legs around to the safe side and stood up.

'Mamma has a new practice,' she said with a giggle. 'Colonic lavage. Shall I tell you what it is?'

'No,' Oonagh called from the window seat. 'Do not dare to tell us. I shall tell Gunnie if you do.'

'It was Gunnie who told me.'

'Only because you bullied her.'

'Well, you had better do exactly as I say or I *will* tell you, so there!'

'And if you don't do exactly as I tell you, I will ensure it is practised on you!' said Mildred, coming into the room. Mildred had changed since finishing her studies and was lighter, more amusing, somehow younger. I wondered was it because she had a purpose. A place to go, things to do, which were not Guinness things.

'You are to go down. Lady Langtree has called.'

'Very well,' said Maureen. 'Oh, why is Hughie so late?'

Chapter Seventeen

Over the next ten days, I began to see that Hughie was often late, and stayed less than formerly. But he still came daily, Richard mostly with him, the two of them coming up the driveway or through the back gate that led straight from the Phoenix Park, and riding back every evening, often long after dark.

They rode back with Thomas, as they had done that other summer, because, Ernest said, 'Even with General Macready and the garrison still in place, it is not safe.' And Hughie listened to him and did what he suggested, but not for the reasons I thought.

'Thomas knows so much about what goes on,'

he said to me one day. 'He truly knows. Not just what is generally said – gossip passed from place to place or what is written in newspapers – but what is really intended.'

'You mean about the Irish Free State,' I said, parroting the phrase. I knew that was what it was called, even if I didn't know what it was.

'Exactly. The Free State. But it's a state that has been born wrong.' As if it had been a calf or a foal.

'Wrong how?'

'It is incomplete and should never have been accepted. It must be put right.'

'But Ernest says—'

'I don't care what Ernest says. He has no idea what he speaks of. He is a businessman and therefore his judgement is corrupt. It is patriots like Mr de Valera who should be listened to now.'

I would have asked more but Hughie cut me off like someone who has changed his mind about something and began to walk faster. 'Never mind, Fliss, you need not think of those things,' he said. 'In fact, it's better you don't.'

We didn't speak of Thomas again, but it was obvious to me – because I watched, I suppose – that Thomas was just as silent with us girls as before, and the friendship between him and Hughie had lasted. Hughie talked alone with Thomas any chance he could, and Richard noticed, and didn't like it. In fact, I soon saw that Richard tried every way he could to break them up, but always as if by accident or coincidence. I wondered if he was jealous of their friendship. If he was, well, that was something I could understand.

Whatever camaraderie had been between Maureen and Hughie two years before was deeper now and different. He turned to her voice as quickly as to mine. Walked with her when he could, not me. Laughed at her jokes, her many, many jokes, in a way he didn't laugh at mine. In my fairer moments, I accepted that I didn't make many jokes and therefore how could he laugh? But when we were all in conversation together and he looked to her sooner, more often, than he looked to me – well, that I couldn't mistake. Nor could I mistake the way she acted, as though on a stage that had but one person in the audience: Hughie. Everything she did and said and proposed was for him.

If Richard was jealous of Hughie, and it was only a guess that he might be, how much more jealous was I, of them both? Jealous of Maureen's influence on Hughie, and Hughie's on her. So that I felt I didn't know myself anymore.

Maybe we were all different? Richard was less quiet that summer, and he spoke without the hesitancy he had first shown. In fact, he seemed to have settled into himself, comfortably, like a load will settle into a cart once it has travelled far enough. When he spoke to me of Hughie, he did so without his former constraint. He was worried, too. 'He's dazzled,' he told me. 'By the men Thomas knows, by their daring and their talk of the future.'

'It's just talk,' I said quickly, because I didn't like to think of Hughie knowing these men who Thomas knew, perhaps meeting them in the time that we were gone.

And Maureen, too, noticed the time Hughie spent with Thomas, I saw, because once when Ernest said, 'Will you send for Thomas,' as Hughie and Richard were about to take their leave, she muttered, 'They need hardly *send* as Thomas is so much under Hughie's feet,' with a sideways flick of her eyes to me. She blamed him for Hughie being sometimes distracted from her.

Whether she was right or not, I didn't know. Perhaps it was just that we were older, and the country more violent, but somehow politics intruded into that summer, snapping around us like a snare around a rabbit's foot. Soon I came to feel about the word the way Mrs Spain must have felt when she first said it to me over four years before: apprehensive. Unwilling.

I began to realise that all the things I had thought were simply Hughie – his care for his fellow men, his deep dislike of anything he considered unjust, his determination to stand up for those without shoes or enough to eat – were now politics. And that not everyone felt as he did. Soon this kind of politics seemed everywhere, in every conversation, every plan and action so that I was frightened.

When Hughie began to talk openly of a change being needed, of injustice that ran so deep in our society that there was no easy way to root it out – and even though Richard told him, 'Hush' and 'Don't be a fool' – I was more frightened still.

But I didn't know how frightened until something happened that should have been nothing, a little thing, without importance. But wasn't.

Small boys threw stones. It's what they did. Threw them into streams, at trees, at birds, at each other. But they didn't throw them at us. They didn't throw them to hit us. Not ever. That was always how it was, so none of us thought anything when, as we rode into the park one afternoon, Maureen, Oonagh, Richard, Hughie and I, past a knot of dirty city children just inside the gate, slashing at bushes with switches, one of them, maybe ten – although it was always hard to tell with the city children, who didn't grow as we did – in a pair of dreadful ragged trousers, feet blue and bare beneath, and a shirt cut down to fit him, put up his fist. Even when he released the stone and it came hurtling through the air, I presumed he had some other target. Not until Oonagh's horse was hit, so hard that the poor creature reared up in shock – and pain, I'm sure, because later we saw that she was cut, a raw red gash pulsing beneath the sleek brown skin of her neck – and Oonagh, unprepared, fell off immediately.

She cried out as she fell and her horse made to bolt. The other horses were immediately spooked and there were frantic moments of trying to restore calm. Luckily, we were going no faster than a trot, so Hughie was able to grab Oonagh's empty reins and slow her horse while the rest of us tended to our own. Then Richard jumped down to help Oonagh to her feet. Her face was dirty from where she had landed in mud, and I could see her hands were shaking as she tried to brush herself down and put back the hair that had escaped her band, but she said, 'I'm all right, I'm not hurt. I'll get back up in a minute. Just let me catch my breath.'

The thing was, the child still stood there, looking at the mayhem he had caused, and the others stood beside him. None of them ran. Nor did the older ones do anything to chastise the thrower. They all stood and stared and the tallest, a boy, raised his hand and held it in front of him, with his thumb and forefinger aloft at right angles. As we watched, he sighted down the length of his finger and slowly squeezed it in the air, mouthing a word. 'Bang!' Beside him, his companions laughed like hounds seem to laugh when they are chasing a fox, wet tongues lolling out of pink mouths. It was only when Richard started towards them that they scattered, racing off in different directions so that he didn't know which to follow.

'After him,' Maureen shouted. 'The boy with the stone. You'll catch him easily.' And Richard began to run.

'Wait!' Hughie said. 'Wait.' Richard stopped, turned back, then started again, confused. 'Stop,' Hughie called again.

'But why?' Richard said.

'Indeed, why should he stop?' Maureen rounded on Hughie. I was off my horse now too, with Oonagh, who was crying, but more from shock than hurt. I squeezed her hand. The children had all vanished. 'You've let him get away! Well, the minute we get back I will give Papa a description of him. I remember exactly what he looks like, and they will catch him then.'

'If you do, and if that boy is found, there is no telling what they will do to him,' Hughie said.

'He's a vicious monster.'

'He's a child. Not as old as Oonagh, even.'

'But he can't be allowed to get away with this. He must be punished.'

'His punishment will not be light, Maureen. He won't be punished the way you or I would be.'

'You or I wouldn't do such a thing.'

'Maybe not, but nevertheless. Do you want him beaten?'

She didn't answer. I could see she was fighting the urge to snap 'yes' because it wasn't true – she didn't actually want a child to be beaten. We all knew what that was – even Maureen and Oonagh; every one of us was close enough to childhood still to remember the shame that was almost worse than the pain, which lasted even longer than the red marks on the backs of our legs. But neither did she want to back down.

'Don't tell, Teapot,' Oonagh said then, on a hiccupy sob that said she was nearly finished crying. 'They won't let us out alone again if you do.'

'I suppose that's worth considering,' Maureen said grudgingly, glad to have a reason to let the matter drop.

We dusted Oonagh down, wiped her face with a handkerchief, helped her back on her horse and set off again with her in the middle, where she was protected. But the day was spoiled. Something had changed under us, something big, and until now we girls had all been too merry and giddy to notice.

The following day Hughie was late again, so that the morning was spent waiting for him.

'Here he is!' Maureen cried. 'And about time. I will go to him.' She was down the stairs so fast that I was able to watch her through the window fly out the front door and straight to Hughie and Chestnut, as I helped Oonagh gather up her lists. I could hear as she called to him – 'We are having dancing at the party and you have to dance with me because if not I will only have cousins to partner me and, oh, the humiliation!'

He smiled down at her and handed her Chestnut's reins and said, 'Well, of course I will spare you that! And Richard will dance too.'

'He can partner Fliss,' Maureen said slyly, 'because both are tall.' I leaned over the balcony to tell her that being taller than her was no great shakes but Richard looked up as I did so, and our glances met and I saw how much he blushed so I said nothing.

'Shall we go down?' Oonagh asked.

'Yes. And then let's play tennis,' I said. 'We need more practice.' Certainly I did. My playing was very poor. Although I had just about learned the formalities of scoring and changing ends, I had little strength of arm and knew that I was an unpopular partner in doubles.

But as we neared the round of the stairs, Cloé

called out from her little sitting room, 'Felicity, is that you? Will you find *The Tatler* and bring it to me? You might read to me for an hour?'

'Of course,' I said, squashing down a sigh.

As I read, seated in the high-backed chair by the window of Cloé's chamber, half turned so that the afternoon light might fall across the page, I saw them, racquets in hand, cross the lawn below me. Oonagh looked up, saw me, and waved. Hughie looked up too then and grimaced – a face that spoke his frustration, equal to mine, at Cloé's demands. Maureen did not look up. Instead, I watched as she took Hughie's arm and leaned close to him. And I continued to watch as Mildred, coming up behind them, looked from one to the other, then took Maureen's other arm and tugged at it so that she had to let go of Hughie and the link was broken.

'Do pay attention, Felicity,' Cloé said. 'You have already read the phrase.'

That evening, after Hughie and Richard had gone and dinner was over, as we sat in our little writing room and Oonagh made yet another list, murmuring, 'If Bryan and Frederick both play twice with different partners, and if Judy does indeed sit out . . .' Maureen said, 'Does Hughie ever go to London?'

'I don't think so,' I said, too fast. 'He will be busy at Ballytibbert, once the summer ends. With the farm.' Why did I feel such a strong desire to deny her this?

'But perhaps he might come?'

'Perhaps,' I said, 'but I don't know why he would.' She looked hurt. I had known she would. So why would I say it?

'For Aileen's coming out?' Maureen said. 'If Papa asked him? He could stay at Grosvenor Place with us and come to all the dances. Wouldn't you like that, Fliss?'

'I would, of course,' I said. 'But I do not see how it can be done. He will have too much to do. He says himself that it's a Herculean task.'

'We will ask Papa,' she said, jumping up from the window seat as though she would there and then race down the hall to Ernest's study. 'Think what fun!'

'Wait!' I cried. Her request had startled me. I needed time to think. To talk to Hughie. To consider what it meant.

'Yes, Teapot, much better wait til after the party,' Oonagh agreed.

Chapter Eighteen

The next day Hughie did not come at all. Richard arrived mid-morning, alone, and in answer to our questions said, 'He is busy but said he would come later,' and when Maureen demanded, 'Busy with what?' he didn't answer her. In revenge, Maureen snapped, 'Well, you are no good.' And indeed, without Hughie, it was hard to know what to do with Richard. He came awkwardly about with us, and even though I tried to talk to him as I normally would, he had reverted to his most silent self and could hardly get two words out. After a couple of hours, when he said he would go, I felt only relief.

'I'll walk you to the stables,' I said.

'Hughie is gone to another of his meetings,' he blurted out when we were past the house and could not be overheard. 'But I think this time is different.'

'How?'

'He said it was to be the last. That the time for meetings is done with.'

'Well, that's good,' I said. I was still totting up tennis pairs in my head.

'He means the time for action is here.'

'What kind of action?'

'I don't know. But I know something of the man he wishes to take action with. Mr de Valera.'

'But surely all that has nothing to do with Hughie?'

'He believes it does. I fear he will do something rash.'

'Well, we must stop him,' I said.

'We must try,' he agreed.

After he left, I walked slowly back to the house, planning what I would say to Hughie when he called later. How I would warn him to stop whatever it was he was doing, and to stop seeing whoever he was doing it with. But he didn't appear. We waited, pretending not to wait, breaking off all we did to 'check' every once in a while, until finally, 'He is not coming,' Maureen said, face mutinous.

'Something must have delayed him,' I said. 'He

will come tomorrow.' I didn't tell her what Sean Dolan, the groom, had told me: that Thomas was not there either. Had not appeared for work that morning but sent word that his mother was poorly and needed him.

The day after, Hughie and Richard arrived in the late morning. Maureen, going to meet them, said, 'I'm glad that you are prompt today, Hughie. I have a great deal for us to do. The party is tomorrow and I need your opinion on many things.' Steel in her tone told me that she wanted, expected, an explanation. An apology. She did not get one.

'You shall have it, but first I must talk to Thomas,' Hughie said.

'Thomas?' Maureen raised her eyebrows ludicrously high, like Cloé did when she especially wanted you to feel the full absurdity of something you had said.

'Yes. His mother is very unwell. I want to find out how she does.'

Maureen rolled her eyes. Any delay would have made her cross, but that it was Thomas Hughie intended to put before her maddened her entirely. 'Oh sobs,' she said. 'As if every Catholic doesn't have a sad tale to tell. Ask Papa. He will tell you they are the most frightful shirkers but will never say no. Instead there will be an excuse. A sick mother. Or a lame pig.' She laughed, looking at

Hughie, expecting him to laugh with her, as he so often did.

'He is no shirker,' Hughie said. 'Thomas is eighteen, no older than Aileen, and he does the work of a man, with the responsibilities of a man.'

'Hardly,' Maureen said, her voice shooting into the high, cold tone – like the hollow echo of a tall stone tower – that she used when very angry. I watched as, beneath the porcelain surface, her skin grew up a mottled red. 'He seems to spend most of his time talking to you when he should be at work. In fact, I think I shall have him turned off. He is clearly lazy.'

'What a sickening thing to say,' Hughie said.

'He is not *your friend*, may I remind you. He is Papa's servant. And not a very good one, it seems.'

'Maureen, do not!' Oonagh begged, and Richard stepped forward to put a hand on Hughie's arm, but Hughie pushed him away.

'Maureen,' he said, 'there are men who sleep in hedges, or different beds every night; who haven't seen their families in months and they do it because they believe in something. In a great fight that will turn this country into a proud nation rather than a beggarly servant.' I saw him straighten up as he spoke, pushing his shoulders back like Papa used to when he put on his uniform. 'They give their strength and often their freedom, sometimes their lives. Because it is a great cause. Can you not see that?'

'What is that to you?'

'Everything.'

'*Everything?*'

And I knew that he had said exactly the wrong thing. But he looked at her in appeal – to step across the gap she had created and join him where he was, and I held my breath. Because I knew that if she did step across, there would be no coming back. I saw her begin to respond; almost like a sleepwalker, she raised her hand towards his. And then she stopped and sudden fury flooded her face – Maureen's usual fury at anyone who didn't do as she bid.

'No,' she said and dropped her hand. 'No. All I see is a fool who talks bold talk about freedom and great causes, that he has learned from a stable boy.'

'Maureen!' I said, 'You do not mean it.'

But Hughie said, 'Let her speak. Better we hear it.' And so Maureen did – vicious, ugly insults that were harsh and personal and that Hughie made no attempt to stop or contradict, just let them roll out in spiteful waves. Except it wasn't what Maureen meant. I knew that, so did Oonagh. It was what she felt compelled to say, because she was angry and thwarted and couldn't stop herself.

We stood there, Richard on one side with Hughie, Oonagh and I on the other with Maureen, all staring at each other, not one of us able to do a thing to stop them. It was the first row they had ever had. I hadn't thought it possible. In everything, those two had always been in harmony: Hughie amused by Maureen's wit, indulgent of her demands, entertained by her in all her moods, and always capable of turning those moods so that she sparkled where she had sulked. They had been the best of friends for two years now. Hughie, of all of us, had been the one to light her up so that she brimmed with the mischief and excitement that made her irresistible. And now they were quarrelling. Over a stable boy. Or so they pretended.

'I am not even sure of his honesty,' Maureen said at last, and I knew she was in the kind of blind fury that was, for her, a dark tunnel without end point. That she could no more turn back now than I could have walked away, although I longed to leave and could feel Oonagh, beside me, trembling. 'There is corn missing from the stables. I heard Sean Dolan say so. Perhaps we must search Thomas's cottage. Perhaps his mother lies upon it in her sick bed. Or perhaps it is only guns she has for company. In any case, it's time he was sent packing. I will speak to Papa.'

Hughie stared at her and I stared too. Her face was white again, colour drained from it as though the surface of her skin was the muslin Cook used to drain curds from whey. Against the white, the pale blue eyes blazed out like those of a herring gull, cold and hot at once.

'Fliss, I must go,' Hughie said, turning away from us all. And the air behind him was broken into sharp pieces that did not fit together anymore.

We girls avoided each other that afternoon. It was easy to do – our tasks drew us different ways, and we went about them, each with the same relief, I am sure. It was not until the evening that we were together, alone.

'You shouldn't have said it, Teapot, you know you shouldn't,' Oonagh said immediately. 'Not to Hughie.'

'You're right, I suppose,' Maureen said. 'I didn't mean to. Not all of it anyway. I will say I'm sorry' – Maureen never said sorry – 'tomorrow, when he comes for the party. I shall make a handsome apology.' She was, I saw, pleased with herself, with her own willingness to look for peace where usually she would push for war.

So pleased was she that I was not altogether surprised when later, much later, when most of the house was asleep, she tapped at my bedroom door, and thrust a tightly folded letter into my hand. 'For Hughie,' she said. 'You will get it to him, won't you?'

'I will.'

She didn't leave immediately as I expected. Instead, 'It's so easy for you to be good,' she said wistfully. 'And Oonagh. Even Aileen doesn't have much trouble with it. Or at any rate, if she's not good, she is clever at hiding that. But for me – although I want to be, very much sometimes, I find it hard. Everything I wish for seems to put me in the way of being bad. Or what Gunnie and Mamma call bad. My temper, my wretched temper.' It was Maureen's same old refrain.

'It's not that you're bad,' I said.

'Well, if it's not bad, it certainly looks like it,' she said gloomily. 'Take today. I didn't mean to say any of those things. Not one of them. It was as if they had their own life and just poured out of me like that girl in the fairy story where toads fell from her mouth every time she spoke. That's what I felt like. I could almost see them, dropping out, all ugly and warty, and hopping away to some dank spot while you all stared at me in disgust.'

'Not disgust.'

'Yes, disgust. Or something like it anyway. Hughie, too, which was the worst of it. I don't care if Gunnie and Mamma look at me like that. But I don't want him to. But this will put things right.' She began to cheer up. 'And I will be better. I know I can be.'

At the door she paused and turned back. 'Don't let anyone see. And' – suddenly childish – 'don't read it!'

I slept that night with the letter under my pillow. She had glued it down with great blobs of the fishy-smelling glue we used for our scrapbooks. I felt it pulsing through the linen and feathers like something with a heart and guts of its own.

The next morning, Richard appeared even before we had finished breakfast, but Hughie wasn't with him.

'He will be here later,' Maureen said confidently, standing up from the table and giving me a swift look. The letter was in the pocket of my cardigan. I could hear the paper crackling a little as I walked out to meet Richard.

'Well?' I asked him.

He shook his head. 'I don't know. I haven't seen him. He was very angry last night, and this morning he was gone before I got up.'

'But you would know where to find him?'

'I think so.'

I put my hand into my pocket, closed it around the letter, feeling the blobs of glue hard like bone.

And instead of withdrawing it, I left it there. 'I'm going to walk to the stables,' I said. 'Oonagh wants you to help her in the tennis court.'

At the stables, I found Thomas. I didn't know what I would have done if he hadn't been there. Perhaps something quite different. As it was, I gave him the letter.

He took it. As always, he was polite, of course, and willing, but never friendly.

'For Hughie,' I said. 'Please.' He didn't say yes or anything at all. But he took the letter and crumpled it in his fist.

I walked back to the house very slowly, giving myself time to turn around and go back and ask that he return it. More, giving myself time to understand what I had just done. I didn't go back.

Chapter Nineteen

Glenmaroon, Dublin, 1978

There are more newspaper clippings in the bag. Entire pages torn out and folded small, not the neatly snipped articles and photos from the scrapbook. I unfold one, bending back along its spines many times until it is laid out flat. It doesn't tell of parties and treasure hunts. 'Two Brave Men Killed'. I unfold another. 'Problems For The New Government'.

I know this story so well now. We all do. The painful birth of the Irish Republic. The war against the British occupation that was no sooner won, than it wheeled about and became a war of comrade against comrade; men and women who found that, after all, 'freedom' meant different things to each of them. Perhaps all births are painful. I wouldn't know.

It's strange now to think how little heed I paid – until I had to – to what went on outside the walls of Glenmaroon that last summer. I knew there had been fighting, and killings, but these seemed less real than the party we planned. I read the large-print headlines in Ernest's newspaper sometimes, although I often had to guess the endings because the paper was folded on the sideboard and I didn't want to be seen unfolding it to find out how the sentences finished.

I knew there had been soldiers fired on, barracks burned, guns found in all manner of unlikely places – in beds, up chimneys, in rivers (would they not get wet and refuse to work, I wondered) and under haycocks. In the evenings or when we had callers, stories were told of houses that had been burned, not just Mountshannon, where Cloé had danced as a girl, and Burton Hall, but other houses too. But somehow none of it had seemed quite real, to us girls anyway.

Part of this was that the stories were told with levity, as well as shock. I remember one, about a girl called Molly whom Aileen knew from dances, whose house, Ballyrankin, was burned. The story was that her family sat and watched it in their own armchairs, dragged out onto the front lawn, side by side with the men who had set the flames, and then moved into the house next door because, as her father said, 'I would rather be shot in Ireland than exiled to England.'

That one was told again and again, with approval, by the various visitors; it was presented like a calling card or proof of collective faith, although it was always clear to me that neither Ernest nor Cloé agreed with the attitude.

There were other stories, of insurgents dressed as washerwomen and even nuns, lurid with detail that did not seem quite real. No more real than the ghost stories Maureen used to tell by the nursery fire in winter, about thwarted lovers and vengeful hags.

Maybe we were too well protected, too isolated in our splendour behind the high walls of Glenmaroon? I called it 'Glenmarooned' one day to Richard, which made him laugh so that I felt suddenly witty and smart, like Maureen. The house was in view of the city but too far out to be involved with it. And because there was no farm, like at Ballytibbert, and no tenants, those of us who lived there didn't leak into the countryside the way Hughie and I had at home, wandering in and out of cottages and talking with men over gates and low stone walls.

At Glenmaroon we were cut off, a palace in a fairy story surrounded by a forest of thorns. Except the thorns weren't real; they were Cloé and Ernest's indifference, the girls' and my isolated routines.

Only Mildred came and went with any freedom, as I recall. Going shopping, running errands, visiting people in her little red car. Sometimes she would even walk to the small village beyond the walls, whereas Cloé would pass through behind the windows of her motorcar, face veiled or averted lest any try to look at her. Mildred spoke to people who were not 'our' people. She knew the name of the woman in the shop and might even come home with some piece of news she thought would interest us all – some new piece of machinery, the birth of twin donkeys nearby, a sure sign of luck, apparently.

Back then, I thought 'luck' would be luck for all. I was very slow to understand that there was a 'them' and an 'us' – and that any luck they had would surely not be ours.

And even within that 'us', there were sides to take, but I couldn't understand because I didn't have a full picture. There was so much I didn't know. Between ourselves, Aileen, Maureen, Oonagh and I, we never spoke of the trouble. Nothing and no one intruded upon us, so that Hughie was the first breath of outside air that told me all was not well beyond our walls. And Richard the first breath that told me that Hughie's way of thinking was not everyone's way.

Ernest, Richard; Hughie, Thomas. Those were the sides, as I understood them, although of course now I know the matter was more complicated; that even on the side of the Republic that Hughie chose and that Thomas belonged to, not everyone agreed. I picked between them, as best I could, and I picked Ernest – his certainty, his denunciation of all those who fought as 'foolish idealists', regardless of what they fought for – because I had the habit of being told what to do by him. And because in picking him I picked his daughters, and the life we led then, of tennis and tea parties and dances. I picked that because I was too scared not to; scared of what would become of me if I transgressed. For all that Hughie had said that one day I should live with him, I didn't know when that day might be, and I knew I couldn't go home to Ballytibbert and Mummie. I just couldn't.

Chapter Twenty

Glenmaroon, Dublin, 1922

I told no one about the letter, although I felt the knowledge of it burning hot inside me. *Maybe Hughie will come anyway,* I thought, *without the letter. After all, it was a silly quarrel. He must see that now?*

But he didn't come. Not to help with final preparations for the party, not in the afternoon when the guests assembled and we were busy dividing them into pairs and planning who would play first – 'which is well nigh impossible because they will keep wandering off!' Oonagh complained. Nor, worst of all, when the tennis was done, the tea cleared and the dancing had begun.

Maureen didn't ask me what I had done with the letter except to raise an eyebrow at me, to which I nodded. Not a lie.

She danced with Bryan, with Brinsley, even with Richard, who had painstakingly helped all day, even though he knew – how could he not? – what a poor second he was. She was very popular, the gayest person at the party, until she found me alone by the window where I had been watching and asked, 'Is he come?' and when I shook my head, her face flushed red and she set her mouth in a thin line to stop her bottom lip trembling.

She didn't ask for him again.

Richard asked me to dance, and we did, both of us badly. As we shuffled about the floor he said, 'I'm surprised. I thought he would be here,' to which, in spite and in agitation at what I had done, I snapped, 'Must we only ever talk of Hughie?' and saw how I had hurt him.

Earlier than expected, too early, Ernest appeared and said that everyone must leave, at once. 'There has been fighting in the city,' he said quietly to Cloé. I sat beside her then – she had asked me to, so I might fetch anything she needed; we both knew that I would not be asked to dance again – and heard it all. 'The Four Courts has been shelled by Republicans. Buildings have been occupied and repeatedly attacked. Our guests would do well to leave at once before it gets dark, and to avoid the centre of the city.'

Ernest cleared the young men very quickly, politely showing them into Lapham's hands and dispatching servants to ride with them. When Lapham murmured that Thomas had been missing from the stables all afternoon, I saw a flicker of irritation cross Ernest's face.

'If we run to the footbridge, we may see the action in the city,' Aileen said.

'Not that footbridge,' Oonagh said with a shudder. 'Maybe we can see from an attic window?'

'I don't wish to see,' Maureen said, hunching her shoulders up around her ears. 'If the Irish must be stupid enough to always be fighting, one another as well as us, that is their own affair and nothing to me. In fact, I hope that they may blow each other entirely to bits and make an end of it.'

'Oh, come on, it'll be a spectacle,' Aileen said. And so we went to the footbridge – Oonagh would not step on it so we called our accounts across to her – 'There isn't much to look at because it's getting dark, but I can see flashes sometimes and there seems to be a great deal of smoke. And there is rumbling, like thunder, or the hooves of the drayman's horses, if you listen carefully' – until Gunnie chased us away, saying, 'You are to come back home at once!'

So we went to the writing room, too stirred up to go to bed. Aileen was full of excited chatter about the party – who had said what, had we seen how terribly clumsy the Misses Waters were, and that they wore brown woollen stockings and brown boots, but wasn't Brinsley – Brinny – a dear? Maureen said nothing.

'I do wonder what happened to Hughie,' Oonagh said, as we sipped our cocoa. 'No doubt he will come tomorrow and tell us and it will be something strange indeed to have kept him away.' She clung to her cup as though it were comforting, the warm and solid shape of what she had just said.

'He will,' I said. I felt sick. 'Of course he will. There will be a foolish explanation, and we will all laugh.'

Still Maureen said nothing.

Later that night when I had retired and the house was quiet, Mildred came to my room. 'May I come in?' she asked, putting her head around the door.

'Of course.'

She came in, shutting the door quietly behind her. 'I thought you should know . . .' she started.

'Know what?'

'Well, I just thought you should know . . .' Again she broke off.

'What is it, Mildred? Know what?'

'That Ernest has told your brother he can no longer visit here.'

'Ernest? But whyever would he do that? Surely he cannot mind that Hughie quarrels with Maureen?'

'I don't know exactly what happened, but I do know it's not quarrelling, it's politics,' Mildred said. 'Your brother is a firebrand. Always was, but Ernest says he's gone too far now.'

The next morning, after breakfast, Cloé sent for all of us. She sat straight-backed on her chair, as though the spindly stiles were poisoned and would pierce her if she leaned against them. Her face was greasy and chalky and I, now an expert, could tell she had passed a bad night. Gunnie looked nervous, fidgeting with the lace at her wrists.

'Hughie has left word that he will not be back to Glenmaroon,' Cloé said.

'But why not?' Oonagh asked.

'Because your papa has said that he may not.' Cloé believed in truth, no matter how prickly and stark its branches.

'Is that why he didn't come yesterday?' Maureen asked.

'Yes.'

'So it wasn't—' Oonagh began in a rush, but Maureen cut her off.

'Papa cannot do that,' she said. 'He is Felicity's brother. She has a right to see him.'

'Not here,' Cloé said. 'Not at Glenmaroon. And not when she is with you.'

'I'm sure we can arrange—' Gunnie began, looking at me, but Maureen cut her off too.

'Why?' she demanded. 'Why does Papa say such a thing?'

'Hughie holds views that are unfortunate and wrong. You have been together far too much and he is not suitable company for you girls. Indeed, I am surprised at Felicity, allowing all this to go on.'

Useless to tell her that it is because of her demands and insistences, the cold compresses and cups of tisane, that I did not see or understand until two days ago what was in front of me.

'I refuse to be ordered around like this,' Maureen said. 'I shall do exactly as I wish.' She tilted her head back so that she was looking down upon Cloé in her chair and her voice was clipped, insolent, in a way I had heard before. It was the way she spoke to servants who angered her, those she felt were beneath her, even sometimes to Gunnie. It was the way she had spoken to Hughie two days before. But never, yet, to Cloé.

'You will not see him again,' Cloé said, standing swiftly. 'That is all.' Despite the fringed shawl around her, I saw how distended her stomach was beneath the folds of her dress and knew how much pain it cost her to rise up like that in one movement.

'He'll send word,' Maureen said later. 'You'll see. With Richard. Papa didn't say Richard couldn't visit.'

But Richard didn't come anywhere near us, and I watched as Maureen's certainty ebbed away and left her flat and still, a boat from which the tide had entirely retreated. The days after the party were long and slow and vague, as if we didn't know what to do with ourselves and so waited for something to happen that would show us.

'Mr Ernest would like to see you in his business room, Miss Felicity,' Lapham said, nearly a week later. Days in which I had waited, and fretted. I could have written to Hughie, or even Richard – I knew a letter would have been delivered by one of the servants without a question – but I worried that Cloé would see my efforts to communicate as disobedience, and I didn't know what to say. Anyway, that wasn't how we behaved. It was Hughie who called or wrote, I who waited and answered. I wasn't sure how to turn that around. But I had, that morning, made up my mind. If no word came today, I would write to him, and ask Lapham to have someone take it across the park. And now this. A summons.

'Whatever for?' Maureen demanded. 'Fliss, what *have* you done?' Ernest did not much concern himself with our day-to-day existences, certainly not with mine. I did not think I had ever been alone to his study before.

'I'll soon find out,' I said. I tried to sound easy, but inside I was quaking. What *had* I done?

In the business room, it was the fidgeting that I noticed first. Ernest didn't fidget. If he pulled a lever or pushed a button, it was in order to do something. Get something. The purpose was always specific, not aimless. Now, seated behind his desk, he played with a model of a biplane, sending the tiny propeller around and around, first one way then the other, and did not look up at me for some moments.

'There has been an incident,' he said at last. Mentally, I ran through the household for anyone I had not seen that day. There was only one gap. Mildred. Something had happened to her.

'It's Mildred, isn't it?' I said. It had to be Mildred. In that roaring red car.

'It isn't Mildred.'

'Then who?' I leaned forward slightly and gripped the edge of the broad desk. My feet felt a long way from my head, and the space between untethered, too empty, so that I was nauseous.

'There has been a lot of fighting,' he said. 'You know that. Not everyone accepts the new government. Regrettably, your brother has become involved.' I didn't know whether to say I knew or to stay silent. He didn't give me a chance to make a decision. 'All week, there has been violence. In Dublin, particularly. There is talk the army will be called in again . . . And now, Hughie is missing.'

'Missing how?' I asked stupidly.

'He has been gone since the day of the party.' Nearly a week. A week of great violence. 'The Butlers, Richard's people, have been to see me. He hasn't been home. They hoped he was here.'

But you have forbidden him to be here, I thought. I didn't say it. 'Perhaps he is at Ballytibbert?'

'I have enquired. He isn't.' More of the fidgeting, this time with a pen that he wiped the nib of, blew on, then wiped again. 'His horse—'

'Chestnut.'

'—was found wandering and brought home to the Butlers.'

'What does it mean, that he is missing?' I asked at last. I still held the edge of the desk, needing its heft. I pressed it so that it hurt my hand, grateful for the familiarity of pain that came from a hard and physical source.

'I'm not sure yet but I thought you should know. We'll keep looking and making enquiries. When I have news, I will tell you.' He stood up from behind his desk so that I knew I should leave. I had reached the doorway when he spoke again. 'Thomas is missing too.'

By the time I left Ernest's room, the girls had been told. By Gunnie, I supposed. Oonagh put her hand in mine and pressed that tiny handkerchief upon me, then squeezed my hand. Maureen said nothing but the blue of her eyes was clouded grey like a dull day at sea so that I wondered how she could see out of all that fog.

Mummie wrote to me, to tell me not to worry, and then wrote again so soon that I could not but worry. I wrote back, asking should I come but she said no, better stay where I was; there was nothing I could do by coming.

At first, I played out possibilities with the girls – Hughie had been wounded and was being cared for in a cottage; Hughie had been sent on a secret mission, told to lie low so his enemies couldn't find him – but Maureen took no part in these fancies, indeed wouldn't talk about Hughie, and never once asked who I had passed her letter to, so that it felt strange and silly to keep discussing what might have happened.

There was no news, and therefore nothing to say, and so we said nothing.

And what of Richard? He came once. 'I have heard that Thomas got as far as Liverpool. It's possible Hughie went with him,' he said. 'It's also possible that he is still hiding out, sleeping rough somewhere.'

'But why would they run away?'

'There have been many killings, Fliss. Men are dead. More will die.'

'I don't understand.' I said that a lot in those days.

'Hughie chose the losing side and so it isn't safe for him to be where Free State forces can find him.'

'At least he chose a side,' I said, but quietly so that he could pretend he hadn't heard me.

'If he is in Liverpool, he'll be able to come back when all is calm.'

'And in the meantime, he will write,' I said.

But days and weeks and then months passed and Hughie didn't write and we all continued not talking about him. He was gone.

And then Cloé made her announcement.

'You know Papa has been planning a trip around the world, on *Fantome*? He wishes to see Japan. I think we will all go. We will travel to London first, where I have much to do, and after Christmas we will begin the trip.'

I believed that 'all' included me. That I would go with them just as I had done everything with them, these four years. And in the months that followed no one said different so it was only a bare week or so before the date, when I asked Gunnie for a trunk in which to pack my things, that Cloé said, 'I think it better that you stay here, Felicity,' and when Oonagh cried, 'No, she must come with us,' and even Maureen and Aileen said, 'Of course she must come,' Cloé said, 'It wouldn't be fair, you know how Felicity dislikes motion, how sick she feels.'

'I am sure I should get used to it,' I said. My motion sickness was not so bad as all that.

'But what if you did not?' Cloé said. 'No, far better you remain here. And your mother would like to see you, you know,' so that I knew that not only could I not go with them, but that I must go home after all, to Ballytibbert, where I had not been for so long, where my mother didn't want me, and where there was now no Hughie to meet me.

Chapter Twenty-one

Glenmaroon, Dublin, 1978

From that rancid pile of paper I begin to pull out bills for horse feed and farriers' visits, lists of tack and orders for hay. The stained and crumpled accounts of the Glenmaroon stables. If it's anywhere, it will be here.

Everything that happened, those last months, I remember now as like dominoes falling, clicking off each other as they tumbled down. I wonder could I have halted them, if I had been able to see the way they fell? Surely not, but we all like to tell ourselves tales of what could have been.

Why did I not do as I should have with Maureen's letter and hand it straight to Richard? Better still, tell her to deliver it herself? I always was too much in her sway. Look at me now, with this pile of rubbish. Saying no to Maureen was hard, and harder again for me. It went against everything we were to each other, against the pliancy of my nature, and my role in that household.

Some part of my behaviour I understood at the time – even at fourteen, I knew it was one thing for Maureen to break the rules of our society and write a letter, quite another for me to deliver it. The rest, I only made sense of long afterwards.

The truth is, I know now, when I picked Thomas instead of Richard, I did not pick entirely without spite, even though I tried to pretend I did. Instinct – the instinct of a child who has been cast off – told me that a letter like that, written by Maureen, read by Hughie, would become a contract between them. Something that didn't include me.

I had lost enough. I didn't want to lose Hughie too – not to the men he talked about, not to the fighting he said was inevitable, but not to Maureen either, even though I loved her.

Hughie had always been the outward part of me, the part everyone valued because he was a boy and then a man. The part I valued because he was himself. He was like the coat I wore to go out into the world, which protected and warmed me. Without him, I found that I was small and cold; without shape, without weight, without form. I could not stand straight or take an easy step.

He was my first, my greatest, friend. The voice I heard that called me from my cot and urged me onwards in everything: to stand, to speak, to climb the stairs that led to the nursery, tugging at my arm from above when I found the gap too wide to struggle up. On my first pony when I was scared and Papa laughed at me, it was Hughie who said, 'You can do it, Flissy, you can do it.' He was the brave one, the clever one, but also the kind one who told me I was brave and clever too. And because he said it, I listened and because he said it, I believed it. And it was that, more than anything, that gave me force in the world. Without him, I would never have had any at all. Without him at my side, I had to start the next bit by myself, and try to learn who I was when he wasn't with me.

I had tried being like them, the Guinness girls – Richard had noticed; I had been glad he had, because I thought it must mean I was successful – but after Hughie left, I began to see that I had to try harder not to be like them. To understand that I wasn't them, and I shouldn't be them. It wasn't something I understood all at once. In fact, it took me years; all those London years that were the most exotic of my life, where being part of the Guinness whirl was to be at the heart of everything. Years that, when I look for them now, are still so fresh and vivid that I surprise myself when I remember how far they are behind me.

Part Two

Chapter Twenty-two

Grosvenor Place, London, 1924

The Southampton fog that nearly swallowed up *Fantome* trails us to London, picking up smells of industry and coal fires so that by the time we step out of the motor and huddle in under the deep stone portico of 17 Grosvenor Place, it is yellow and oily, the kind of fog that London mixes up so expertly, taking all the ingredients of that great city – the chimneys, smokestacks, buses – and blending them into this thick and choking cloak, flung over houses, cabs, people, so that under it we stumble blind, confused, too close together.

I try to breathe only in small, shallow breaths

because the wet dirt catches in my throat. Oonagh has her nose and mouth tucked deep into her fur collar. 'Pooh,' she says, muffled. 'Like being inside a chimney.' Then, 'I see we're still at odds with the palace.'

It's a joke the family likes to make, because of the way the house sits at a curious angle – the front door set to the side, turned away from the ochre brick walls of Buckingham Palace garden, as if indeed it has hunched a petulant shoulder against that greater glory. And yet, once inside the house, the best rooms all crowd onto the palace side, spacious salons and bedchambers stacked one on top of the other, looking eagerly onto the royal treetops, as if in compensation for the petulance of the door.

Inside the hallway, under the stone staircase that curves up and over our heads, Lapham is before us again. 'I have ordered tea to the first-floor salon,' he says.

'Thank you, Lapham. How good it is to be back,' says Cloé.

Upstairs, firelight glints on the silver tea service, and the curtains are drawn against the damp of the evening. The house, so unyielding when Gunnie and I arrived the day before yesterday, has already begun to relax and spread out in welcome. There is talk of travels, but fleeting, almost as if those long months, the many new places and things, are already fading, losing their reality beside the more solid claims of now.

'I had forgotten the chill of a London autumn,' Cloé says. Hat off, teacup in one hand, she looks pale and holds the curved, bolstered arm of her chair so hard with the other that her knuckles are white. 'And how quickly autumn becomes winter in this city.' She sounds, I think, almost frightened. 'I do not think we will see Ernest for some time. There is so much to tend to now that he is back.' Indeed, Ernest has gone straight to confer with his brother Rupert, some doors down at Number 5; on his way passing Walter, who is at Number 11, so that these Guinnesses might as well own the entire terrace, I think.

'There are problems with the new Irish government,' Cloé continues, 'and something called the gold standard, whatever that might be.'

'Oh, that!' Maureen says impatiently. 'It's perfectly simple. It is a way of fixing money to gold. Papa has explained it all. It is Uncle Walter who has been helping Mr Churchill with it.'

'Well, I hope Walter comes off better from his encounter with Mr Churchill than poor Rupert did,' Cloé says. 'At least he might not bear the scars of it.'

'What scars?' I ask.

'As boys, Uncle Rupert and Mr Churchill shared a governess for some years,' Aileen says. 'And one day they were given a toy harness and coachman's whip to play with. Uncle Rupert didn't want to play, but young Winston insisted, and said he must be the horse. When Uncle Rubert still said no, Winston lashed him across the face with the whip, leaving a scar all along his eyebrow. You must have seen it?'

I have indeed noticed this scar of Rupert's – it creeps up through half his eyebrow like something sliding through undergrowth – but I've never heard this story before and wonder why. Then I see that Cloé is smiling gently at Aileen's telling of the tale, and conclude that Mr Churchill's star must be rising politically, and therefore what sounds to me like a savage defect of personality is being redrawn as boyish high-jinks.

'In any case, Ernest will be mostly in Dublin,' Cloé continues, then looks around as though searching for landmarks that will tell her where she is and what she must do. She lights upon one such with relief. 'Oonagh, do sit up straight.'

'Won't you eat something?' Gunnie asks her. I see that she is desperate to offer something, anything, that might tempt Cloé. I can also see how hopeless the idea is.

'Not a thing, thank you,' Cloé says. 'I couldn't.'

She waves away the plate Gunnie has presented as though to look at it makes her feel sick. 'Pass the sugar.' I watch as she spoons five – I count them – teaspoons into her cup.

The girls wander about the room, picking things up and putting them down, commenting on pictures and photographs, walking themselves through their own childhood from a new vantage point, that of being nearly grown up and long away.

I watch them as they move about, trying to catch up again to where they are, conscious that they have all, even Oonagh, jumped ahead of me. The rhythms of their private language, once as much mine as the lines on my own hands, now sound strange and shrill, an aviary of foreign birds.

'We need to plan my Season,' Maureen says at last, running a hand through her close-cropped hair. Without the mass of locks to balance it, her head is bare and austere, like something stamped on a coin.

'Yes,' Cloé says, voice weary. 'Gunnie will help, won't you, Gunnie dear?'

'Of course I will.' Gunnie glows at the prospect, thriving as Cloé wilts.

'Felicity,' Cloé says, turning to me, 'Richard Butler has asked if he may call. Ernest has given him a job, in the factory office in Dublin, and he will travel to London on occasion.' She looks thoughtfully at me. 'I am in two minds whether to say yes to him or not.'

I don't say anything. I don't know what I think about this. Richard wrote once while I was at Ballytibbert and suggested he would like to write again, but I didn't respond. I didn't know what to say to him, and I couldn't bear that Mummie would see the letters coming in and out of the house. She would never have commented, but she would have noticed. And every time a letter arrived, I knew I would have a moment of hope that it contained news of Hughie. The sickening disappointment if it didn't seemed too much to willingly allow.

Cloé continues to look at, almost through, me. 'Perhaps after all it is better to make a clean break?' she muses. I know she doesn't expect an answer. It isn't really a question. 'But he is an old friend and I suppose to say no would be harsh . . . Very well.' She has made up her mind. 'He may call.' She doesn't ask me, just decides.

Aileen raises an eyebrow and Maureen, who has picked up some bold habits, winks. 'A swain,' she murmurs, which makes me laugh, because this is Richard.

Cloé and Gunnie talk of fashions and escorts, of who is to be invited to the coming out ball and which of Cloé's acquaintances must be told they are in town, and I think how different it is to the conversations during my year and more back in Ballytibbert, where Mummie and Uncle Alex spoke furtively about acts of violence that tore through villages and even families, savage things that happened out of sight and were hardly named, but dominated every conversation all the same.

Everything was hurried and covert. Men with their coat collars turned up, speaking from the sides of their mouths; women who wouldn't look at me, eyes locked to the shawls they clasped around them; children, chanting snatches of jeering songs, who stopped and sniggered when challenged.

Because Hughie wasn't with me, I was a stranger there. Without him, I was no longer part of the life of that place, even though they all knew who I was. Anyone I tried to talk to looked at me in silence and answered in monosyllables. Or maybe it was that Glenmaroon and the Guinnesses had rubbed off on me, like the hairs from a cat.

'Has there been any news?' I asked almost as soon as I arrived at the house from the train on my first evening. Mummie and Uncle Alex were in the drawing room to greet me and autumn was already there with them. The girls had been gone nearly two weeks by then, and I could no longer follow them in my mind.

'Not so close, Felicity,' Mummie said. Instinctively I had moved near to the fire because the room was cold, but I had forgotten her rules – among them that one mustn't ever seek too much for comfort. She herself sat well back, a thin cardigan her only concession to the march of seasons.

'You mean of Hughie?' Uncle Alex said.

'Yes.' Who else?

'Nothing. We are still trying to see what we can discover. But the country is in chaos.'

'Ernest said he has his lawyer making enquiries too,' I said. 'He asked me to tell you that.'

'*Ernest?*' Mummie said. 'Really, Felicity?'

I thought, *How typical that she sends me away, without instructions, leaves me long enough that I have become part of a family that isn't mine – and now sneers because I behave like part of that family*. 'It's what he asked me to call him. A long time ago now.'

'He asked you? And of course you obliged. Well . . .' And she gave a small laugh, like drops of water being shaken briskly from a hand. What was I supposed to have done? I didn't ask. She didn't say.

'What do you intend to do?' she asked me some days later, days in which she let me be, to wander alone and reacquaint myself with all the damp corners of the house. Mary was gone, and not replaced, so even the bits of cleaning she had done were now not done. John Hegarty, who had always been old, was even older, and more surly than before. Only Mummie's garden was in any way beautiful, flowers washed clean by the endless rain, arranged in careful order and delicate profusion. The house itself, I saw, was rotting, from the inside and the outside, so that soon the two rots would meet in the middle and draw it all down into a heap.

Her question took me by surprise. I had thought she would tell me. I was fifteen. What was I supposed to do?

'I don't know,' I said.

'Well, perhaps they will send for you again,' she said, handing me a secateurs to hold. She didn't say their name. 'Or perhaps you will stay here,' she continued, taking the secateurs back. I didn't say anything. There was nothing to say. Just as there was nothing to do. Nothing for me at all, to do or be or become. When the silence had gone on long enough, she said, 'You see. That is why I let you go in the first place.' And I didn't need to ask 'What is?'

'It isn't credible that he will suddenly reappear, you know that?' she said, but gently.

I did know it. With every month that passed, the idea that Hughie would suddenly return to our lives became more unlikely. Once or twice I heard

Uncle Alex talk about 'assuming the worst . . .' as he made plans to continue his care of the farm, and each time I made sure to leave the room. Because as long as I didn't listen to that, and as long as I didn't voice my secret belief – that he would return – I had something to hold close to me. If I spoke it, someone would instantly tell me how it couldn't be, so I kept it quiet. A small kernel of hope that only I held on to. I held it in the same place as I held the fear that I was to blame, so that the one might balance the other.

Back home, where hardship was always close by, I found myself beset with images of him, cold and lonely and frightened, far more than I had been in Glenmaroon, where all was warm and comfortable so that to imagine an alternative was almost impossible. Now, at night, in bed, listening to the mournful wind testing the doors and windows, I thought of Hughie maybe huddled in his coat and hiding out in some abandoned cottage or ditch, and it felt as though he were close by – as if, were I to walk to my window and look out, I would see him in the fields below looking up at me, shivering in the wet night air.

Those days went by in a blur of soft edges, nothing to tell where one ended and another began. Not even the fighting touched us much in Ballytibbert, although news of it was everywhere. The hedges and untilled fields had grown up so high that the house was almost invisible from the road. The number of servants had dwindled to Cook, John Hegarty and a boy who helped him. We didn't go out – there were no parties in those years, or none that we were invited to – and only Uncle Alex came and went from the house. The fighting died down and peace negotiations began in the summer before the girls came home. Mr de Valera's side – Hughie's and Thomas's side – lost, and I wondered what that meant for Hughie coming home. But I didn't ask. Gradually Mummie's fears of being set upon and burned out were calmed. That left my fear – that we wouldn't be. That we would never be noticed again. That the hedges and brambles – those cruel whips of thorn that snaked into and under everything – would finally obscure us entirely.

By the time Cloé's summons – that I return to live with them – came, through Gunnie, I had almost forgotten what it was to have days with purpose and engagements beyond walking the dogs, collecting berries for Cook, and waiting. I was good at waiting, I realised. It was easy, if you expected nothing.

'My Season is going to be dazzling and I am certain to be a great success,' Maureen says now complaisantly, picking up Peke and kissing him full on his wet black nose.

'Of course you are,' Oonagh says, taking Peke from her and curling him up in her own lap, using the dog's paws to swipe the air in front of him like a boxer. 'And Aileen too. Isn't that so, Peke?'

Chapter Twenty-three

Grosvenor Place, London, 1925

Over the next months, as Cloé and Gunnie establish themselves, I feel as if the house in Grosvenor Place is a rock against which all of London wishes to dash itself. There are visits, appointments, lunches, tea, dancing lessons, endless callers surging to the door and sweeping up the stairs in a vast eager tide.

London, I discover, is gay and outrageous and eager to be seen. Lit bright and standing tall, except for those times when fog slouches through the city, muffling and distorting it and pulling it about so that it becomes a place both unfamiliar and shrouded. But even then, the lamps are soon lit and the nodding and smiling and partygoing continues.

The older girls are launched, with all the pomp Maureen demanded. Aileen is spared the usual debs round, because she is older and so, once presented, Cloé gives her freedom that Maureen is denied, to go about with young people her own age, busy with more sophisticated pursuits. Soon she is mocking the childish carry-on of the debutantes, 'as if she's been out for years,' Maureen says, irritated and envious. And indeed, London life suits Aileen; she is like a plant with a stout trellis to grow along. 'It's perfect for me,' she says. 'I know what I'm doing. There are rules, and they are rules I understand; the ones Mamma tries to teach us.' She makes friends easily, and there are young men – no one in particular, but enough, in sufficient attendance, that Cloé has faith that there will be.

I think it is a relief to Aileen not to be compared with Maureen. And to be at a distance once it becomes clear, as it does – to us anyway – that Maureen's Season is a failure. At first only I know it. Gunnie, busy gossiping among the chaperones and boasting of her charges, does not see what I, at Maureen's side, can see. And that is the gulf that exists between her and the other debutantes of the Season.

There are girls' lunches, almost every day, where ten or twelve debutantes sit over grapefruit halves, their mamas having gone out for the afternoon in order to let them play at entertaining. Gunnie has explained these lunches to me – 'They are for the girls to get to know each other before the balls begin, so that they shall have companionship' – but either she has not explained to Maureen, or Maureen has refused to listen, because she is like castor oil in milk. From the first, there is something that marks her as different. It might be the directness of the blue gaze she turns on the world, or a tone in her voice that is too loud, too sure of itself. It might be the vast wealth that shores her up and pushes her on, displaying her as surely as if she were a sparkling ring upon an outstretched hand. Or it might be none of these things. What is obvious is that the other girls cling, like butterflies that are newly hatched will cling to a leaf or twig, to one another. They are afraid to stand out, unable to pull away, their damp wings stuck close. Maureen is unable to blend in.

I am invited with her, or else I am despatched by Cloé, I am never quite sure which. But what is sure, what is immediately clear to all, is that I am not a proper guest. The girl who is hosting will always hasten to explain me to the others present, whispering that I have 'come with Maureen' with a look that means they may all ignore me. Not that I mind. Being ignored is easier.

Unlike Oonagh, Maureen has no need of the Alphabet Game. She always has something to say, something striking and odd and funny. But instead of being charmed by her strange gambits, these girls are alarmed, withdrawing into their little huddles as if she might poke them. Their talk is always dull and careful – the Royal Academy exhibition, what parts of London they are allowed visit safely on their own – until the meal finishes and then, by what seems general agreement, the chairs are pulled a little closer over strawberries and thick cream, and someone, usually the hosting girl, will introduce a more exciting topic, always with a careful play of insouciance. 'Well,' she might say, 'what do you think of Gwyneth, Lord Tredegar's daughter? I hear she has gone missing, dressed only in her pyjamas . . .'

It does not help that those they talk about, with that threadbare effort at familiarity, are too often people Maureen knows or has at least met. And being Maureen, she can't resist pointing that out.

'You see that Lois Sturt has sat for yet another portrait,' a girl called Marjorie says one afternoon at what has been a particularly dull lunch at Cadogan Square. Even the grapefruit half – my third this week – was not entirely fresh. 'I think that is now seven in total.' The envy in her voice wars with pride at being the one to know, to tell. 'And she has bought a racehorse.'

'Dear Lois, she is quite mad,' another says fondly but with a nervous glance around that tells me she hopes no one will challenge this annexed acquaintance.

'Pooh, that is nothing,' Maureen says from the end of the table. 'I bet Lois will not see that horse from one end of the year to the next. Now, my uncle Walter has a house full of monkeys, and a friend, Ida, who keeps a panther in her apartment that will spring if it does not like the cut of a man's coat.' The silence that follows, though short, is of the shocked kind, as if Maureen has cursed or spat.

'Shall we have coffee?' Marjorie says after a moment, rising. Coffee is always taken in a separate room, so that the girls might practise the art of withdrawing. I can see that Marjorie is terribly pleased with her own social *nous*, and that Maureen is annoyed at their failure to answer her. Even disapproval would be better.

'It's true,' I say suddenly, hoping to help her. 'The panther. It's entirely true.' It is the first time I have spoken since we arrived. Some of them are startled, as if I were a painting, or a bird in a cage.

But they do not respond, beyond a few vague murmurs: 'I'm sure . . .' 'How interesting . . .'

Soon, Maureen no longer tries. 'I say, curtseying to a giant cake.' Her voice, calculated to reach up to the panelled ceiling of the ballroom of Grosvenor House, drifts across the neat heads around her. They do not turn. The effort of not turning is in every neck and pair of shoulders. It is the afternoon of the Queen Charlotte's Ball, and we have been here for hours. The girls rehearse descending the staircases in neat pairs, matched as much as possible by weight and height so that their sorting makes me think of Cook, beadily grading currants for a cake. Up and down the stairs they go, then practise their curtseys. They are to sweep down 'rippling like fields of wheat', and curtsey, 'as one; lilies bowed by the wind', as Lady Howard puts it, with a steely glint that tells me it is not at all of lilies that she thinks. I watch from the side of the ballroom, secretly agreeing with Maureen: a giant white cake, topped with 181 candles. It is absurd. I try to catch her eye, but she will not look at me. Maureen likes to be seen in triumph only.

'Graceful, *pliant*,' Lady Howard continues, her voice loud and sharp, blue eyes raking the rows of girls before her and their nannies and chaperones above on the balcony, nodding eager encouragement to their charges and passing peppermints around.

The guards of honour, those girls especially slender and lovely who are to wheel in the giant cake, as though it were a unicorn from legend and they the maidens chosen to beguile it, have been appointed. Maureen is not among them. From where I sit, I can tell that she is furious. And because she is furious, she begins to make mischief. She mocks the cake, the curtseying, the fields of wheat and lilies, anything at all. She looks around to see will any of the other girls join with her, but they do not. They avoid her eyes, concentrating on their curtseys.

'It isn't the cake we are curtseying to,' one of them whispers solemnly. It is Marjorie, the girl from Cadogan Square. 'The cake is symbolic. It's the Duchess of Northumberland, who is to be guest of honour.' She sounds awed.

'And she will be invisible,' Maureen flashes back, not awed at all. 'Swallowed up by white icing. Which we will then swallow up in tiny slices. Why bother?'

'My mama says it is wonderful that the tradition is being revived,' another girl adds piously. 'She remembers her own Queen Charlotte's Ball as a glorious night.'

'How sweet!' Marjorie says and they both step

away from Maureen, as though she might infect them, so there is an empty pocket around her. Until Lady Howard notices and orders it closed: 'Move in, girls, there must be no uneven spacing.'

Later, as the order of dances is gone through, I whisper to Maureen, 'It is such a pity there is to be no Charleston, when you learned it so well with Hughie.' I am desperate to cheer her up, to remind her of a happier time, but I am also desperate to see if she will say his name, allow me to say it to her. He is so little mentioned that I wonder if the girls have been told not to, or if they are trying to spare me upset. Or if they simply never think of him. As for me, the part that waits for word from him, news of him, is intensely alive, no less real than the part that goes about with Maureen to parties and balls and talks fashions with Gunnie. It is just better hidden.

Maureen turns away abruptly. 'Do not let Lady Howard hear you say the word "Charleston",' she says. 'In any case, it used to be called "the Black Bottom".'

'Maureen!' I look around, in case someone has overheard something that would not easily be forgiven.

'Well, it did. I, for one, think it a much better name.'

The more the other debs ignore her, the more

grand and hard and unapproachable Maureen becomes, and only the few, the very few, who know her can see that under her exterior of glittering frost, she is humiliated.

Alone with Oonagh and me, she tells the truth, but only some of it. 'It is not at all as I imagined it,' is as far as she will go, late one evening when we have come home too early to pretend the party has been a success. We sit in Maureen's bedroom with our cocoa. The window is open and from outside comes the teasing smell of a summer night, a painful reminder that we are young and should be out and gay, not sitting inside with mugs of cocoa and tales of a failed party. The birds of Buckingham Palace garden across the way are silent, but only just, and in a few hours they will start up again, singing their hearts out as though they alone must clear the dark and make space for the rising dawn. Sometimes, woken by the sound or still awake because sleep will not come, I wonder that they do not die each morning, hearts burst open by the effort. Meantime, in the silence, it is the wet green smell – trees and grass and deep earth – I notice most.

'How is it not?' Oonagh asks, curled up on Maureen's bed with Peke and a new chow puppy she calls Fidget.

'You know how we talked of it? How we

imagined all the endless fun of parties and lunches and balls and dresses? Well, only the dresses are even a little bit fun. The parties are dreadful. Aileen is so lucky to be spared them, only going if she wants, and then only for as long as she wishes. The girls are frumpy and dumpy and dull – and the men are worse. They have nothing at all to say and do not help one with conversation and when they ask one to dance, it is as if they are doing one the most tremendous favour.'

'Perhaps they are shy,' says Oonagh.

'Not shy,' Maureen insists. 'Simply terrible. You wait, Oonagh, you'll see how bad it is.' She brightens up a bit at that, saying, 'In fact, no doubt for you it will be worse. At least I have enough conversation for two, even if my partner cannot find a thing to say. When it's your turn, you will be swallowed whole by the silence.' She settles back, pleased to have redressed the balance of hurt by pushing some of it onto Oonagh. Maureen unhappy is Maureen mean, always has been.

Oonagh looks alarmed and pulls her shawl closer around her shoulders. 'Fliss will be with me, won't you?'

'Of course I will,' I say, although really, I have no idea if that is true, or indeed what exactly will become of me at all. Already I am drooping under the burden of Maureen's failure – my hiding of it, the responsibility I feel for her, and fear of what Cloé will say, and do, when she finds out, as she must.

Outside, there comes the sound of a deep-voiced motorcar, and we all three go to the window to look out. 'He's home early,' Oonagh says. It is cousin Bryan, down from Oxford. We have been watching his comings and goings – Oonagh with naïve interest, Maureen with envy – from Uncle Walter's house, a few doors down.

Bryan, it is clear, is having a far more gay time than we are. The little silver car chugs around and about Hyde Park Corner and out into Grosvenor Gardens several times a day and through the night, like a fish making its way up and down stream, light gleaming on its sides.

'He's not there to stay,' Maureen says. 'Look. He has company.' There is a girl in the front seat whose short hair is silver in the gaslight. She is holding two glasses and giggling and says, 'Do be careful' – voice echoing easily through the empty air – to a second girl, squashed into the tiny seat behind her, who tries to pour from a cocktail shaker. Bryan runs into the house, then out again with something under his arm that he tosses into the lap of the girl in front, sits back into the driver's seat, and the car roars off again.

'Show-off,' mutters Maureen, as we draw back from the window.

'At least Fliss is having an exciting time,' Oonagh says slyly. 'Tea and walks with Richard!'

'Hardly exciting,' I say. Richard's company isn't exciting, not at all. But it is necessary. Cloé has chosen to treat Richard as a sort of cousin, so I am allowed go out with him, to the park, to tea, in a casual sort of way, as if he is family. And in fact, he is, if not family, certainly familiar. A reminder of who I used to be, who I still am really, buried under all the newness. He is a part of Hughie, just as I am; a part of the life that was Hughie's when last I saw him, and because of that he is necessary to me. Without Richard, it's impossible now for me to remember Glenmaroon, even Ballytibbert, the way they were. There isn't space for the remembering; too crowded out with London things. But when I see him, all that blows away for a bit and I can recall early mornings where the mist drifts up from the ground and the smell of the air when a sharp evening rolls in across the end of a warm day. It wasn't that we talked of Hughie – we didn't, much – but we could have. That's what mattered.

'What's it like, working for Ernest?' I asked the first time he called, when we were left alone by Cloé and Gunnie, who had been polite and thoughtful for nearly half an hour, in ways that made Richard very uncomfortable.

'Not what I expected.'

'How so?'

'Well, I didn't expect to be working in a factory,' he said with one of his rare grins.

'I thought you were in the office?'

'I am indeed, but even that . . . But apparently I am useful.'

'I'm glad,' I said, wondering if Ernest would eventually swallow the whole of my world. I imagined him giving jobs to Uncle Alex, to John Hegarty, to Cook – even Mummie, I thought, with an inward laugh. Would he have given a job to Hughie? And if so, would it have been a job to raise Hughie up to Maureen, or sink him entirely beneath her? But I had no answer for that.

'I like your hair,' Richard said.

'My hair? But it is the same as ever.'

'That's what I like.' I think he was the first person to have really looked at me in a very long time.

We were quiet for a while, Richard turning over sheets of music at the piano while I looked out the window. 'Chestnut is sold,' he said at last. 'I thought you would want to know. My parents held on to her as long as they could, but your mother said to sell . . .' A pause, then, 'Thomas is in Venezuela.'

'Venezuela?' I had only the broadest idea where that was. 'How do you know?'

'Kathleen told me his mother had news of him.'

'Of him or from him?'

'Of him. It's hard to get word back from South America.'

I didn't dare say that Hughie might be there too, or voice any other theories. The hope was too small and precious. I couldn't risk hearing the uncertainty that might be in my own voice. So I said nothing, and Richard seemed to understand because he changed tack. 'How are you settling here?' He moved a little closer towards where I sat, as if my answer might be something better not overheard.

'Very well,' I said. It's what I always said when asked. 'It's easy. There is always so much to do.' But he didn't respond as others had.

'What is it, exactly, that you do?' he asked. He moved his arm so that his hand lay close enough to mine that I could feel the heat of it.

And instead of batting his question off with something vague, I found myself telling him: that I didn't know 'exactly' what it was that I did, or should do. That I worried about Maureen and how she felt, because I knew she would never speak a word of her shame, but I could see it in the droop of her shoulders and the dullness of her eyes. How even more I worried how Cloé would feel when she found out. About Oonagh too, who had little to occupy her and who, I suspected, was unhappy, although I didn't have enough time with her to understand why. That I was relieved to see Aileen at least was content, with a clear space that was all her own where her sisters didn't follow and crowd her. And he listened and nodded and didn't offer solutions but just said, 'You think about them all an awful lot, don't you?'

I didn't answer. I thought of Hughie: *I want you to remember, you do not always need to think about them. Perhaps sometimes you can also think about yourself.* Was everyone going to say that to me? And what, exactly, did they mean?

'May I come back?' Richard asked before taking his leave.

Chapter Twenty-four

As the Season progresses, it's worse. To those who stay at home, there is all the appearance of wild popularity. Invitation cards arrive for Maureen and Aileen together, stiff white rectangles with precise instructions – '. . . company requested . . .', 'at a dinner before . . .' – often two or three for a single evening and as many as ten in a week. They pile up in rows of smooth formality, like a guard of honour saluting the way to some coveted end. They bring the appearance of gay success, but it's an illusion.

We are received in houses that have names that belong to them as surely as the stone and marble of which they are made – Norfolk, Marlborough,

Devonshire. Once inside, saluted and pressed in polite welcome by white-gloved hands, we are left. Gunnie goes to sit with the other chaperones, Aileen disappears quickly with her friends, and Maureen, so buoyant at the leave-taking from Grosvenor Place, sinks.

Up we go, to place our coats, then to the powder room where Maureen, always gorgeously dressed in satin and heavy silks, with white satin gloves to her elbows, fiddles with her hair, her gloves, anything to avoid the shame of an unheralded descent down a staircase, at the bottom of which stand knots of other debutantes and their escorts, voices rising to greet those they are happy to see – 'I say, it's Diana, doesn't she look simply marvellous.' There are no voices to greet Maureen.

Gunnie, swallowed up in a crowd of chaperones who sleep discreetly in their chairs, legs crossed at the ankles, sees none of this. Aileen sees, but only from a distance. She does not approach. Perhaps she's afraid that Maureen's isolation may be catching.

'It's because you didn't do much schooling here,' she says in a consoling whisper one night, as we drive home from yet another dismal affair, Gunnie nodding off in the corner. 'The other girls know each other from childhood, but you do not.'

'Or because you have no brothers.' I falter on

the last word, but only a little. 'I have noticed that the most popular girls are those with brothers, because the brothers have friends whom they already know.' I have seen these girls, envied by all, pretending to be unaware of it, saying carelessly to one another, 'Oh, that's just old Frank. You know what old Frank is like.' Knowing, oh so well, that more than half that tremendous crush of debs turns out night after night in the hope that 'old Frank', or anyone at all, will ask them to dance and save them from the shame of sitting out or hiding in the powder room.

'It's not that,' Maureen says. 'It is that they dislike me.' I say nothing then, but I think she may be right. Maureen is an oddity amongst these demure girls and their taciturn escorts. Even when they wear all white – she included – in that sea of milk she is as noticeable as if she were slashed with scarlet.

For me, the balls are better than the girls' lunches, because I am completely invisible and can move, or sit and watch, as I wish, without the whispered explanations that announce me at the lunches: '. . . lives with the Guinnesses' . . . 'my dear, I don't know . . .'

At times, I talk to other young ladies at the edges of ballrooms or fiddling in the powder room, many of them in agonies far greater than Maureen's.

They are almost as overlooked as I am and wish only for the Season to end so they can go home. I try to tell Maureen about these girls, so that she may know she is not alone, could make friends if she wished, but she won't listen. 'Nobodies,' she says. 'I don't think so.'

Once or twice, I am even asked to dance, by young men whom, I find, are more as Oonagh anticipated them – shy, awkward – than Maureen's description of smug aloofness. But she won't listen to that either.

Even Oonagh would be better at this, I think one evening, watching Maureen approach a group of girls and their young brigade officers at a particularly packed dance in a dusty house in Belgravia. 'I'm Maureen Guinness,' she says loudly, looking around at each of them in challenge. It is exactly like the days when she would say 'Shall we?', looking at Hughie, and put her horse at an impossible fence without waiting for an answer.

Except here, she waits. And at first there is no answer. Finally, 'Not another Guinness,' sighs one tall, dark-haired girl with large shoulders. 'One might as well be at a saloon bar.' And they all move off with that languid indifference that Maureen has none of.

'Why is it that *his* business overrides *her* family?' Maureen demands later of Aileen. 'Mamma is the descendant of a king. A *proper* king. Charles II. Why does that not weigh in the balance more?'

'It makes it worse.'

'How so?'

'If there was money but no family, they might forgive you. Like an American. But both? It's too much.'

'And how do you know, Miss Hoity-Toity?'

'Bryan told me. And he's right.'

'Bryan?'

'Cousin Bryan.'

'You listen to him?' Maureen is scornful. But she's also intrigued.

'He's different now. He knows so many people, and they all think he is tremendous fun. He *is* tremendous fun. He has so many clever ideas of what to do and where to go – not like those ghastly debs dances and dull lunches.'

'They are terrible all right,' Maureen says with feeling. 'And you think Bryan is the answer?' She looks thoughtful.

The next morning, only Cloé and I are present for breakfast. 'How is Maureen getting on?' Cloé asks. She has porridge in front of her and has eaten almost half of it.

'Very well,' I say, head bent over my toast and

marmalade. I've been dreading this conversation. I know Cloé has begun to suspect that all is not well with Maureen's debut, and I worry that she blames me.

'Only one doesn't hear so much of her,' Cloé continues, crumbling a thin piece of toast. It is true. The newspapers, so full of the doings of Diana Cooper and Lady Alexandra Curzon, now say nothing on the subject of Maureen Guinness. 'And one does want her to go about with the right people. To meet the right sort of young man. Perhaps she is too fat?' she says, thoughtful. 'Do you think it might be that? I see that the girls who are admired now are so very slim.' She glances down at herself, a quick glance that takes in the angularity of her arms and chest and lingers on her fingers, thin like the chicken bone that Hansel put through the cage for the witch to feel, and crumbles more bits of toast.

'I don't think she's too fat,' I say.

'We could start her on a course of Savory & Moore's Slimming Treatment,' says Cloé. She sounds excited.

'I don't think she's too fat,' I say again.

'Well, you will keep an eye for me, won't you?' Cloé says.

'Yes,' I say. But she must see something in my face, in my eyes that I don't manage to lower fast enough to my plate, because after a moment in which she takes a tiny mouthful of her porridge, she speaks again.

'I do hope the unpleasantness of the last summer at Glenmaroon is behind all of us?'

'Of course,' I say.

'Good.'

And then Gunnie comes in. 'Fliss, will you go to Mrs Daniels and tell her tea must be early today?' She could ring the bell and have Mrs Daniels, the housekeeper, come to her, but she likes to send me on small errands. I think to show she can.

The kitchens and below stairs at Grosvenor Place aren't like those at Glenmaroon. There, the part of the house Cloé and Ernest never saw was at least as big as the part they did – vast networks of pantries, sculleries, wine cellars, laundry rooms, some unused, some dug right into the earth around the house, out of the way of light, unvisited by any except the servants who worked in them. Here in London, the house is run with tight efficiency from the basement, where there is a kitchen, pantry, larder, the housekeeper's parlour and Lapham's room. And although these rooms are not the airy, pleasant places of above stairs, neither do they look as though they come from a different land entirely, the way of Glenmaroon.

When I venture down, I am greeted politely, but

there is no welcome for me. No mug of tea and plate of fruitcake, no Kathleen to chat with. Here there is Mrs Daniels, a stern woman who could have been conceived as the very opposite to Gunnie: thin, angular, with black brows drawn tight over deep-set eyes. So forbidding is she that I have seen Gunnie run aground in her garrulousness before her, words drying to a trickle after their first gush forth.

No wonder Gunnie asks me to convey her messages. I do better, because I don't expect anything more than 'Yes, miss.' After that, I leave, swinging back through the green baize door that cuts the house in half, into two countries with different customs. At first, I tried to linger below stairs where it is amusing to look up through the iron railings and watch the feet on the street outside: ladies in their heels tipping past, delivery boys with their flat broken soles, the brown Oxfords and patent leather of businessmen. But here the servants won't talk to me and I find their accents hard to understand. Just like the servants at home, they speak two languages – that of upstairs, and their own, only here it's dropped 'aiches and elongated vowels twisted like dough into strange shapes. They can be understood easily if they wish, but with me I suppose they don't wish. Their talk is like a wall put up between us that I cannot see over. They stand up when I come into the plain kitchen with its scrubbed wooden table and cream-painted walls running wet with the steam from the pots and ovens because there is no escape for it – no open window or door to exit through – and stay standing. There is no possibility of becoming friends, and even Robert, who came from Glenmaroon with us, no longer speaks to me much. I suppose his survival in that house means that he dare not. Here, the order is strictly maintained, and within that order, I – for all that I am not a Guinness – am on one side of the green door, and he is now on the other.

That evening, on our way to yet another ball, I say to Maureen, 'Please do try tonight.'

'I do,' she says stiffly. 'I always try.' I know she does. That's what makes it worse. Maureen not trying would be easy – I know that Maureen, from lessons with poor old Spanish, countless exchanges with Gunnie, even her occasional unkindnesses to Oonagh and me. That Maureen I can speak to easily, tease and persuade. But this one – Maureen trying, and failing – is different so that I have no understanding of what to say to her. I am afraid of her failure. And of my own.

Upstairs in the powder room, which is green

and worn like moss that has been too much sat on, I hand her a hair grip and watch as she fiddles with where to place it, delaying, while around us, without us, little groups form, girls darting in and out: 'My dear, I love your dress . . .' They move about us as though we are no more worthy of notice than cows in a field.

Finally, the room empties and we are about to go down. Maureen pulls back her shoulders and tilts her chin upwards. I never admire her more than in these moments.

'Let's go,' she says. Just then, in rushes a girl with white-blonde hair cropped even closer than Maureen's. It's the girl from Bryan's motorcar. Seen properly, she is of an extreme slenderness, with the face of an angel, pale and creamy with a tiny mouth and snubbed nose, and eyes that look violet in the dim green light of the powder room.

'Hullo,' she says, coming to a dramatic stop. 'I didn't know anyone would be in here. I waited till all those Miss Mice went scuttling down. I hid behind some curtains on the landing so they wouldn't see me. Am I all over dust?' She turns her head to try to see behind herself, turning and turning, so that Maureen and I laugh.

'Hold still,' Maureen says. 'We'll do it.' We brush her down gently, patting the silver shimmer of her gown while she wriggles and squirms with impatience. 'There, done,' Maureen says. 'Lucky it was only dust, not cobwebs.' Then, 'What are Miss Mice?'

'You know. Peers' daughters from the country, endless streams of them, like little white mice, their noses powdered and their hair stiff with pins, full of plans to find a good match and make Mama happy. Every Season brings them.' She sounds a hundred years old, although she can't be more than eighteen or nineteen. 'Thankfully, they mostly meet a nice guardsman and go back home to the country, leaving London to the rest of us.' Then, 'I'm Teresa Jungman, by the way. Everyone calls me Baby.'

'I'm Maureen. Everyone calls me Maureen.'

The girl laughs. 'I remember you. From dancing classes. You're one of the Guinness girls, aren't you? I think we're related somewhere.'

Instead of rolling her eyes at 'yet more' family, Maureen nods eagerly. 'That's right. Your mother married cousin Richard. You have a sister.' When it suits her, Maureen can be as greedy as Cloé and Gunnie for the labyrinthine connections of family and marriage.

'I do,' Baby says. 'Zita. She's downstairs. Come and meet her. And then, just as soon as we can escape, let's all go on. I know a much better party than this one.'

Chapter Twenty-five

Later, I find out that Baby always knows a better party. That first night, we spend a few hours mingling dutifully, then give Gunnie the slip and sneak out with Baby and Zita – Aileen with us because it seems she knows these sisters already – to their little white motorcar that has an engine that purrs like a spoiled cat. There is an immediate feeling of the forbidden as we slip out of the big, dusty house and into the quiet streets so that we huddle closer and giggle more. Maureen's eyes are sparkling and she hugs my arm as we squash into the motor. There is not enough room for the five of us so I have to sit on Aileen's knees. She holds me tight and I know she's just as excited as Maureen but will not say it.

At the shabbier end of Eaton Square we go up a cramped and rickety staircase, but once in a dim-lit upstairs flat, it is as if the concentrated essence of all the larger balls is distilled into a couple of tiny rooms. There are girls in slinky dresses made from scarce as much fabric as a nightgown, smoking cigarettes in long holders and shrieking with laughter, while a man Baby says is a poet recites comic verses about people we don't know but have heard of. There's a gramophone and records playing, and glasses are filled, emptied and filled again in dizzying succession with something called Old Fashioneds that to me are very new. The room is small and hot and smoky, and pulses fast with excitement through us, like holding a fallen bird in cupped hands and feeling the disturbing, too-rapid thump of its heart.

Having hurried us up the rickety stairs and shouted, 'Here we are, then,' Baby drags Aileen and Zita off with her.

'It's like we've fallen through the rabbit hole,' Maureen says after a long time in which neither of us says anything at all, just look and look. We stand alone, until a man peels himself away from the Gordian knot of people and walks towards us.

'I say,' he says in a voice that isn't loud enough for the roar of the room so that we have to step closer to him to hear. 'I spy cousins.' It is cousin

Bryan. I look carefully at him, now that he is close, searching for the skittish boy I remember from holidays at Glenmaroon. But he is unrecognisable.

This Bryan, grown-up Bryan, is so beautiful that, like the sun, he is hard to look at. In that crowded room, thick with the smoke of many cigarettes and buoyed up by the voice of a man pouring out song like brandy splashing into a glass '. . . *just like Humpty-Dumpty, I'm going to fall; I'm sitting on top of the world* . . .', this Bryan is a statue from classical times, carved from purest marble, then brought to life using the fresh colours of dawn – pink and gold and palest blue.

But he is also slight, and his head droops a little as though the weight of his own beauty is too much for him. The blue of his eyes is as pale as the palest sea-glass and there is something both abstracted and watchful in there, like a man who peers out from the side of a window, ever ready to dart back because he doesn't wish to be seen.

'Do let me mix you a cocktail,' he says. 'None of that foul champagne Lady Marmoset serves.'

'You mean Lady Meredith, don't you?' Maureen says after a minute; she means the hostess at the dusty moss-green house we have just left whom I remember as being as fuzzy and faded as the mossy furnishings around her.

'Well done.' He smiles at her. 'Indeed, I do.'

'I say, that is good,' Maureen says. She is out to charm. 'Those big disappointed eyes.'

'And the jerky little way she bobs and twitches when she's upset,' Bryan says.

'Or excited,' says Maureen with a giggle. 'You should have seen her when the Duchess of Rutland arrived.'

It is a party no more like the debs balls and girls' lunches than china is like glass. Everything pretty, gentle and sweet has been exchanged for what is bright, hard and glittering. After a while of watching, we feel daring enough to step properly into the room, into the place where the smoke swirls thickest and the music from the gramophone is loudest. Maureen dances and I watch. Bryan comes back and hands us both cocktails, telling us to 'help ourselves from now on', before drifting away. I take a sip. Whatever he has concocted tastes awful to me, but Maureen drinks hers, then takes my glass and drinks that too.

Rather than empty as the night wears on, the room fills further and it is only when I look at a dusty clock standing in a corner that I realise we must leave, must at all costs be back before Gunnie sees that we are gone.

'We need to go,' I say, leaning close to Maureen's ear.

She is beside the poet, who has a mournful face

and droll eyes and says loudly to those around him, 'Anybody over the age of thirty seen in a bus has been a failure in life,' at which they all laugh. A girl older than us, thin and straight as a boy with heavy-lidded eyes and large square teeth, says, 'Thirty! Just imagine!' as if that alone were enough to mark one a failure in life. Her name is Elizabeth Ponsonby, I know, because I have seen her many times in the newspapers, dressed as a sailor, a baby, a circus artiste, always with a cigarette in hand, and those big, square teeth displayed in a smile both hopeful and disdainful.

'Not yet,' Maureen says.

'We must,' I say, tugging at her arm. 'Gunnie!' If we are not back, if Gunnie raises half of London in her alarm at our disappearance, there will be a terrible row, and I will get the worst of it. We find Aileen in an alcove with Baby and Zita, and tell her we must go, and quick. 'Very well,' Aileen says. 'I'm sure Bryan will drive us back.'

'I'll ring you up in the morning,' Baby says lazily, and Maureen instantly says, 'Do!'

We squeeze into Bryan's car and drive through streets that are empty, past houses where bleak squares of light are beginning to appear in attic and basement windows as those who set fires and lay breakfasts wake for the day. Around the edges of the buildings, a grey light pushes at the dark, but it's too early and the dark pushes back.

At Lady Meredith's, Bryan watches us get out of the car, then says, 'Be careful, little cousins,' in his low voice, raises a hand in farewell and drives away.

'The cheek of him,' Maureen says. 'You're a year older than he is, Aileen.' But she says it without edge.

Inside, Gunnie says sleepily, 'There you all are!' The ballroom is almost empty, the band is gone, and those chaperones that remain are gathering shawls and shoes. The girl called Marjorie is exclaiming over a long tear to a tulle flounce, holding up the dress so that the knot of girls around her can sympathise. Maureen gives them a pitying look as we go past, footsteps ringing on the empty wooden floor.

'Did you enjoy that?' Gunnie asks as we walk out into a dawn that is already giving up and retreating behind a drizzle of rain.

'Oh yes,' Maureen says. Gunnie gives her a surprised look.

The next morning Maureen is up early and at breakfast. By the time I get down, she is telling stories of the night before to Cloé and Mildred.

Mildred is rarely to be found at Grosvenor Place these days. She has finished her nursing studies and now has a flat of her own, and a job, working with Lady Colefax, who has, as Cloé says with a sneering laugh, 'greeted straightened circumstances by selling furniture to her friends'. Without, it seems, a backward glance, Mildred has quit the battleground of Ernest and Cloé's attention, leaving Gunnie unchallenged for their approval. Gunnie was first pleased and then baffled; left in possession of a prize that has suddenly fallen in value. Cloé, deprived of one of her comforts, was furious and there were many weeks when Mildred was not to be seen at Grosvenor Place, but good relations are back on, and this morning, she looks, I think, wonderful, in a navy suit with a neat jacket belted tight at the waist, her hair cut into a square bob that isn't Grecian like Maureen's or boyish like Baby's, but rather sleek and purposeful.

'Don't interrupt, Fliss,' Maureen says, waving a teaspoon at me. 'I'm getting to the good bit. The poet is called Brian Howard and he has eyes that droop madly at the corner like a basset hound . . .' She proceeds to describe him with a wit that is just a shade off malicious, and I see that she has carefully muddled the two parties, the ball and Eaton Square, leaving out all mention of the drive there and back, so that it seems as if Lady Meredith's has also been the setting for the poet.

Cloé is obviously pleased by talk of Baby and Zita Jungman – 'Ah yes, "Gloomy" Beatrice's daughters,' she says with a laugh.

'Why Gloomy?' I ask. 'Is it because the girls' father died?'

'Goodness no, child. Best thing that could have happened, because then she got to marry cousin Richard and you know, she was really quite poor before that. In any case, they were divorced long before he died. No, Gloomy is for that deep, slow voice of hers. But the girls were always delightful when little. Now, tell me about Bryan. People do change. Perhaps he has?'

'Oh, he has,' Maureen says. 'Such a sickly, annoying boy. So much better now.' It is as much as I have seen mother and daughter in charity for a very long time.

When they leave, I help myself to kippers. 'Hungry?' Mildred asks.

'Starving,' I say. 'We missed supper last night.' I still don't know which Mildred is – one of us, or one of them, meaning Cloé and Gunnie – so I am careful not to give details.

'You seem pleased with yourself.'

'I am,' I say, 'it's the first morning Maureen hasn't stayed in bed. And last night was the first night I think she had any fun since her own coming out ball.'

'Well, but what does that matter to you?'

'Of course it matters,' I say. Just then Cloé puts her head back around the door.

'Fliss, when you are done, I need you to write some letters for me.'

'Very well,' I say.

'Is that really your plan?' Mildred asks when she's gone.

'What?'

'That. Writing Cloé's letters. Fetching shawls. Carrying messages to Mrs Daniels. Holding shoes at dances and falling asleep in the chaperone's corner. Caring too much whether those girls are happy or not?'

'No,' I say, 'it is just . . .'

'Just what? Until you get married?'

'No, not that,' I say with decision. I have thought – what girl my age has not? – about marriage, but I understand too well that this is unlikely to come about; what kind of match might a girl in my position expect to make? And, too, I dimly perceive that it would be simply the swapping of one drudgery for another. Something in the way Ernest insists and Cloé resists but always capitulates has shown me that.

'Richard from Dublin . . . ?' she asks, head

on one side. It is what the family have taken to calling him, to differentiate from Cousin Richard I suppose.

'I don't know what you mean,' I say. It is true – I don't. Richard's friendship has become important to me; he is what I have still of Hughie. But why must Mildred make that something it is not?

'Well, then? What? Carry on as you are until the girls get married, and you are sent with them like a hot water bottle, posted here and there whenever there is a crisis; a baby, a sickness, a death?'

'I would always be happy to help,' I say stiffly.

'You would, I know you would.' She softens, but only the smallest bit. 'That's what I'm afraid of. You're too happy to help. Do you really want to be Gunnie?'

'No,' I say with feeling, 'I do not.'

'I thought not. How old are you now?'

'Just eighteen.'

'The world is changing, Fliss. No one in this house can see it. Nor can any of those bird-brained friends of Aileen's, but it is. Even the rich aren't so very rich anymore. Taxes are eating into their income, bit by bit.' I have no idea, none at all, what she is talking about, but suddenly, I want to. I want to understand, to be able to answer her and converse with her and know what it all means and why taxes are important. 'The world is going to be different,' she continues. 'You don't need to stay here. This is not what your brother would have wanted you to do.'

Her unexpected mention of Hughie shocks me so that I do not know what to say. But she is right. I know it. I have not forgotten his conversations with me. His quiet distress at the shape my life had taken, and the way it was more absence than shape really, just the bits between other people's lives that they did not terribly want. Like Maureen's hand-me-down dresses and the chores Gunnie didn't care for.

'But where should I go?' I ask. I have thought about this. In fact, it suddenly seems to me that I have been thinking of it since Hughie left. But I have no answers.

'There is something called a Pitman secretarial course that girls are doing now,' Mildred says. 'It is typing and dictation and a thing called shorthand that is symbols to mean words and phrases. I think it might suit you. You're quick to learn and clever with people.'

'I am?'

'Of course you are!' She laughs. 'Who else could put up with Cloé's vapours, Aileen's airs, Maureen's showing-off and Oonagh's brooding?'

'I don't know what you mean,' I say, offended

for all of them. For myself too, because I sound such a very poor creature.

'Yes, you do. But don't be cross. I mean it as a compliment. I'm not good with people.' I begin, politely, to disagree, but she waves at me to be quiet. 'Don't. I know it. I set everyone's backs up. In this house at least. But it doesn't matter for what I want to do. You are, and you are good at managing. I saw how quickly you learned the ropes at Glenmaroon, and how quickly all the household trusted you. There are jobs and positions now for young women. If you do one of those courses, you will be educated and can work and then you don't need to be dependent on this family.'

'Could I really?' I say. The idea is dazzling – I see myself, in a chic suit just like Mildred's, walking quickly along with a sheaf of papers under my arm, busy and needed, but for important things – business things, whatever those might be – not trays and tea and reading aloud.

'You really could. But you must start soon, before you become like Aileen and lose the ability to concentrate entirely.'

'Can you help me to find out?'

'I can. I'll even buy you a new hat.'

Chapter Twenty-six

After my conversation with Mildred, and even though it must be a secret between us for the moment, I am excited by the future she sketched. I think over what she has said – 'the world is changing' – again and again, hugging the words to myself.

She is right. As soon as she has said it, I begin to see that she is right, and wonder how I could possibly not have noticed. It is well into July, the Season half over, and yet London is throbbing with excitement, picking up speed instead of slowing down. It is like a heart that beats more madly, aggressively loud and gay, even as it should be coming gradually to rest.

But Mildred is wrong to say that no one in the house has noticed. Maureen, with those sharp eyes, has. What she sees isn't the same change that Mildred spoke of, but it is enough for her.

In no time Maureen understands that there is no longer any need for Gunnie – 'trotting after me like an old sheepdog' – and indeed that having her will be a hindrance in the world of Baby and Bryan, one glimpse of which has intoxicated her. Just a day or so later, she pulls me aside after breakfast and demands, 'How may I convince Mamma to let me go about with just Aileen and you? We cannot be chaperoned by Gunnie. We will be absurd, when Baby and Zita go where they please, with whomever they please.' She is talking fast, almost breathless with urgency.

'I don't know,' I say.

'But you do see what I mean, don't you?'

'I suppose do.' I did. The people of the Eaton Square party did not go about with chaperones, that was certain. I see again the mocking face of Elizabeth Ponsonby and imagine the scorn in those heavy-lidded eyes. 'Perhaps Baby will know,' I say.

'Perhaps,' Maureen says. 'She is coming to call later. We can ask her.'

But asking Baby anything is impossible. She comes for tea, running, shrieking with laughter, to the door in the dreary London rain and leaving her motor in the street so that Lapham must go out himself and move it.

Shown to the first-floor drawing room, Baby shakes her tight curls, paces about, making little rushes to the window every few minutes 'to see what might be happening' on the street below. She smells delicious. Clouds of Toujours Moi. And refuses to sit down. 'I couldn't,' she says positively, as if Cloé has asked her to fly. With an inward laugh, I can see she will be no help to Maureen in her bid for independence.

Tea arrives and she throws herself forward in an attitude of rapture, saying, 'Such darling sugar cubes, where *do* you get them?', then ignores Gunnie's eager response – 'I think they must come from Fortnum's' – turning instead to Maureen and demanding, 'Don't you just adore things in cubes? So neat, so *practical*,' so that Gunnie becomes confused, thinking that Baby wants to know more about the sugar, which is really perfectly ordinary, and offers to ask Mrs Daniels, until Baby gives Maureen a wide look from those slanted violet eyes, their sly expressiveness so at odds with the inanity of her conversation, which sends Maureen into fits of laughter. Gunnie falls silent then, knowing she is somehow the butt of a joke but unable to work out why or what.

'Is your mother still in Surrey?' Cloé asks

politely, to cover Gunnie's hurt silence. But Baby ignores the question.

'I must fly,' she says abruptly. 'I have a bus to catch. Maureen, do come with me.'

'A "bus"? But where are you going?' Cloé asks in surprise.

'Nowhere,' Baby replies. 'It's a tremendously fun game. Some of us go about on buses, and even the Underground' – she gives a delighted little laugh – 'and we leave clues for the others to find. Today it's my turn to be the hare. Maureen, you can help me. A really good clue is something that is obviously me, you know, but not so obvious that it will be spotted too quickly . . .'

'I know exactly what you mean,' Maureen says, standing up.

'It's a new way,' I try to explain to Cloé, when they have left. 'Lots of people talk like that now . . .' But she stays quiet and I can see that the intense and deliberate exaggeration of Baby's feelings – a kind of game she plays whereby the more trivial the object, the more emphatic the response – is very hard for Cloé, who has a strong suspicion of anything more pronounced than 'charming' or 'rather awful'; phrases that must cover everything, including intense triumph and even tragedy.

'She must be quite the silliest person I know,' Cloé says then. 'She talks nothing but nonsense.'

And yet perhaps Cloé has also caught the music of change too. Maybe she, too, can see that a new way is rising up out of the old constraints, and that Baby is of it, because she does not forbid the friendship. And neither does she entirely resist when Maureen and Aileen begin to slide out of the constant watching and accompanying they have been brought up with. First, it is walks together in the park alone, then trips to Fortnum & Mason or shopping in Knightsbridge, even luncheon at The Ritz.

Or perhaps they are simply fortunate in their timing. Because Cloé now enters one of her 'bad phases' and needs so often to lie prostrate with curtains drawn, painfully preoccupied with how she feels and what she may and may not eat, so that as long as Maureen and Aileen are discreet, as long as they make great play of 'cousin Bryan' and 'Baby and Zita, as good as cousins', even 'dear Fliss, so sensible', nudging me secretly as they say it, they are unchallenged.

Soon it is accepted that we may be unaccompanied, afternoons out need not be accounted for. And then evenings are free too, but here only by a duplicity that sees the girls accept formal invitations, to balls and parties at houses Cloé knows, then slip out after an hour or so and go on – to the Café de Paris, the Ritz bar, a better party or even a nightclub. The following day, just as she did that first morning, Maureen will tell stories of the night, but ones that are artfully jumbled and blended.

'I can't carry on with this,' I say after a few such. It's true. The feeling of doing wrong is clutching at me and every day I wake and expect that Cloé has discovered the deception from her couch. I imagine her saying, 'I am surprised at Felicity, allowing all this to go on,' just as she did once before.

'Oh, don't fuss,' Maureen says. 'No one will find out.' We are walking in Hyde Park and around us the chestnut trees are already turning crisp and orange at the edges. There is the tang of rotting hay in the air that says autumn will come early. Maureen is wearing a new coat with a thick trim of black fox at the neck. It swings loose around her, ending just below the knee, and she skips every step or two with sheer joy.

'They will, Maureen, you know they will. Already I can see that Gunnie knows there is something going on. She gave us a very strange look this morning. But anyway, it isn't so much that.'

'What, then?'

'I am to take a course,' I say at last. I had not planned on telling her. Not yet, although I have talked about it with Mildred, and with Richard, on one of his visits. He greeted the idea with so much enthusiasm that I was taken aback.

'It's the very thing,' he said, when I described the strange squiggles that are shorthand, and what learning them would mean for me. I wondered had he misunderstood me.

'It is a great deal of learning,' I explained. 'There are lessons, and work to do at home. Mildred says it will be hard, not at all fun.'

'The very thing,' he repeated.

'A course of what?' Maureen says now. 'Those powders Mamma takes? They don't seem to do her much good.'

'No,' I say. 'Not that,' even though I know well that she knows it is not that. 'A Pitman secretarial course. You know, like they advertise in the newspapers.'

'Oh yes.' She giggles. '"The System That Stands The Strain". I remember. But whatever for?'

'So I can get a job.'

'A job!' She begins to laugh. 'Like those funny girls Baby and I see on the Underground when we lay our chases? With their satchels and sad, sensible shoes.'

'Maybe without the sad shoes,' I say.

'Oh, but you are serious! It's too bad, Fliss. Why must you do something so frightful?'

'It doesn't sound frightful to me,' I say. 'It really

doesn't. It sounds interesting, even exciting. And you know, I can't stay here for ever.' It's a question more than a statement, something I need to know her response to.

'But you can,' she says. 'Better still, come with me when I get married.'

'Are you planning on getting married?' I tease.

'Not unless whomever I marry can promise me more fun than I'm having now,' she says with a shake of her head. 'But I suppose, one day.'

'I must do this,' I say, serious. 'Please understand, Maureen. I want to.' Her response was everything I hoped and needed, but even though I am grateful for it, I cannot see the future she has in mind except as Mildred dismissed it: *posted here and there whenever there is a crisis; a baby, a sickness, a death.*

'But how will you pay for it?' she asks, ever shrewd.

'I don't know,' I confess. 'Mildred has been looking into it. I think she can help me a little. But I don't know.'

'I'll help you,' she says decisively. 'But only if you help me.'

'How?'

'I will tell Papa that he must pay for you to take this course, and that he must give you an allowance too. And I am sure he will. But in return, you must continue to come with me and Aileen when we are out. This new way is very delicate, you know. We must not upset it. Mamma trusts you. Goodness knows why' – she swats my arm with her gloves – 'but she does. And if you cry off now and go all career girl, then she will look again at where Aileen and I go and what we do, and I don't want that. She might send Gunnie with us! So, a bargain?' She puts out a hand for me to shake, and I do.

'A bargain.' I have no idea how I can keep it – how can I possibly learn all the new things Mildred talked about and still spend nights out at parties? But I shake Maureen's hand anyway, and hope that somehow, these things will fit together.

Chapter Twenty-seven

London now, with Baby, without Gunnie, is a different place. All that great grey solid façade of monumental buildings, with its invariable ballrooms and oppressive staircases, dissolves like sherbet and in their place is a different city. A city of cunning houses and flats and mews, of tiny two-seater motorcars quite unlike the lengthy purring beasts that Cloé and Ernest favour. Of hilarity like the lash of a whip. Invitations sent on a whim and parties got up out of nothing more than eagerness. Of cocktails at 4pm instead of tea, White Russians and Gin-and-Its, of Sidecars and French 75s, cocktails again at 7pm while dressing, at 8pm, and all through the evenings that end at dawn with the promise of 'again!' already rising in the morning air.

This is the London Maureen had been waiting for, had given up hope of; where Baby, Zita and their friends chatter and exclaim like so many small birds, hopping from conversation to conversation, pecking once or twice – 'Too funny!' 'How perfectly sweet!' – then moving on. Here, Maureen's odd, confrontational humour is appreciated. She is an instant success. The new London has new manners, new ways of walking, talking, standing, drinking that are immediately hers. Aileen's too, but she doesn't launch herself quite like Maureen does – perhaps, I think, it is because Aileen did not know months of misery and rejection the way Maureen did. Instead, Aileen continues as she was – in pleasant harmony with Gunnie and Cloé, moving from one thing to the next in a way that leaves everything half-done; 'I'll finish that later,' she says, whether it be a letter she's writing, a magazine she's reading, flowers to be arranged. Rarely does she come back to finish any of them. Oonagh, meanwhile, has grown quieter, but I almost don't notice because there is so much clamour made by Maureen.

I watch her set forth to conquer, and she makes me think of one of Ernest's pleasure crafts, a determined, sturdy yacht, gay with lights and bright with flags, putting out to sea under nothing but the power of the wind swelling its sails, nose turned towards the new land. Sometimes she ducks from sight, dwarfed by some massive swell of water, so that it seems she might capsize, but always she emerges again, righted by her own determination, plunging up and forward with a laugh.

To me, this new London is as strange as the paintings of Mr Picasso – that is to say, incomprehensible – and I wish I had someone to talk them over with, someone like Richard, but he is in Dublin at the brewery far more than he is here, or Mildred, but she is too busy.

Like Mr Picasso's paintings, all the usual bits of society that I understand have here been cut up and rearranged. Here, the girls are angular and sometimes harsh, and the young men are soft and yielding like Bryan, or wild and troubling like the poet Brian Howard. Some are downright frightening. There is a prizefighter, a great friend of Baby's, called Bert, a massive bulk of a man with tiny feet whom she moves around as though she were a wasp with a draught horse, a tiny sting here and there to make him rumble forth in the direction she requires. Girls wear trousers and even shorts, with cropped hair and black-painted eyes, while men wear velvet and sometimes feathers, and everyone dresses as someone else at the smallest opportunity.

There are actors who come and go. Also artists and people known as Bohemians, and even a pretty shop girl or two. There are enough of these that Maureen is able to say to me, 'You see, it doesn't matter about people's fathers here,' in a way that is meant to encourage me to be more bold, but I can't because I can see that even though she is right, she is wrong too. Maybe fathers' titles don't matter as much, or mothers being presented at Court, but other things do, and I am no better at them.

Now, it's things like clever conversation that moves faster than the wheels of a train and with a rhythm that is just as loud and distinctive, a fast clackety-clack of chat that rolls forward, over everything in its path, which Maureen is wonderful at and I am not. There are jokes that are caught up and thrown around, lasting entire nights, getting longer and fatter and more absurd so that they are like an endless game of Chinese whispers that finally no one understands – except one girl, Nancy Mitford, who has bright, droll eyes and a way of talking that is even quicker than Maureen's, who always seems able to remember where the joke began and the point of it – but anyway it doesn't matter because really the joke is just a painted Guy Fawkes trundled about in a cart to draw the gaze, and the real brilliance is in they who pull the cart.

There is a way of being rude that pretends to be funny, and of being funny that is rude, so that often I can't understand which is which. Often, too, I am not even sure that those who speak do. Or that it matters to them. 'See how she looks down her nose,' Maureen says in a loud whisper to Baby when we are introduced to a girl called Brenda Dean Paul – I have noticed that this girl's name is always given in full, as if it were a skipping-song or rhyme. 'Is it because it is so very large that she dare not lift it up for all to see the full size?' I am shocked, but Baby sniggers and says, 'You know, I believe it is.'

The girl, Brenda, has shining dark hair but is so thin and pale that I wonder has she been ill. She doesn't hear Maureen, because she hasn't bothered to wait for the introduction, giving a cool stare and saying, 'Charmed' in a bored voice, then turning towards a young man in a wine-coloured velvet jacket with a bottle of something clear.

'There you are, Evelyn,' she says, holding out her glass. 'No half-measures, darling. Now tell me, are you writing something frightful about us all? Elizabeth tells me that you are . . .'

Even if fathers don't matter in this world,

money certainly does, although Maureen pretends it doesn't. It's a pretence that's easy for her because there is so much of it behind and around her, and the same, I think, for Baby and Zita and Bryan. But there are others for whom that isn't so. I have seen the flicker in their faces at the pattering of notes rained out every night on taxis, cocktails, late-night visits to Claridge's and the Forty-Three at Gerrard Street, owned by a terrifying woman called Ma Meyrick who is apparently 'half-criminal half-countess'. The instant of panic in Bert's eyes when Baby gets up casually from a table littered with empty glasses and drifts away when the bill arrives, calling out, 'Bert, be a dear . . .' as she goes.

But Maureen sees only the things that delight her. And there are plenty of those. 'It's as if we're in a fairy story,' she says, taking my arm as we come home one purple dawn in a taxi, 'and all those dreadful debs parties were a test, and we passed it, and now we've thrown off the enchantment and we're free.' Her vision is the exact opposite of mine – to me, it seems that it is now that we are in an enchantment; a fantastical place of constant gaiety that cannot possibly be real, and cannot be halted, like Mr Andersen's story of the Red Shoes and the girl who danced until she dropped.

The city empties as the Season comes to an end and the debs and their mothers leave for their homes in the country. We who stay are rewarded. It has been another cold, damp summer – 'One may as well be in Ireland' has been Gunnie's refrain – but September brings a spell of warm days when the city is lit with a soft honey glow that seems a gentle apology for the failure of what has gone before. The great houses are closed and swathed in Holland covers and the parks are empty of nursemaids and their charges. The late-gold light slants across the smooth mahogany of conkers and catches in the rough prickles of their shells, and there is a thickening in the air that makes me think of hunting, the sideways step of a horse that itches with impatience to be gone; the smell of sweat and leather and wet leaves crushed under restless hooves. I long, suddenly, to be in Ireland, back at Glenmaroon, even Ballytibbert, where I might ride out and forget every single thing except the sound of the hounds and the cunning of the fox.

'Such a relief,' Maureen says as we walk the near-empty streets of Belgravia. 'Not to be surrounded by dreary people. And such a relief that Mamma is refusing to go to Holmbury. She says she cannot be so far from Dr Gordon. And Papa has agreed because it is easier for him to join us in London when he is not in Dublin. He suggested we go to

Glenmaroon, but Mamma said absolutely not.'

'Hard for Oonagh,' I say. 'She has so little to do here, and I think has been looking forward to getting away.'

'I'm sorry for Oonagh,' she says, 'but I never want to go to Glenmaroon again. I hate that country, and the people in it.' The vehemence is very unlike Maureen. Especially the Maureen of late, who shows no care for anything that isn't a party or a dress or something Baby said, and dismisses anything she doesn't like as 'simply too tedious'. I look at her but she keeps her head down and I can't make myself ask her the obvious question – why?

We still don't talk about Hughie and now I know that we won't. There isn't anywhere to begin. Would we start at the beginning, when he arrived, or at the end, when he left? Would we start with Maureen's loss, or with mine? Because it isn't the same loss, even though it's the same person. And because she won't show me what she feels, I can't show her. It doesn't stop me, of course. Every party I go to with her, every young man who talks to her, laughs with her, dances with her, is Hughie to me for a minute. But only a minute. Each time, I remind myself, fast, of all the ways these men aren't him, and of how well he will compare with them when he comes back.

'You know,' I say instead, 'I feel that Oonagh is not herself.' I've thought this for some time, but only now can I find a time to talk to Maureen, a time when she is neither preoccupied with her failure, nor giddy with her success.

'She does seem more mopey than usual.'

'I think she's too much with Gunnie and Cloé. Too little with you and me and Aileen. Maybe we could think of an entertainment for her? The theatre or roller skating.'

'She'd love that. Poor Oonagh, not so much fun to be her.'

'Why do you say that?'

'Well, you know. The youngest – always left behind. And it was always like that. The mean nannies were always meanest to her. Mamma, who picks at all of us, picks most at her. It used to make me so angry that I would try to fight for her. But that only made everything worse. Instead of protecting her, me trying like that just drew more attention, so I made myself stop.' She shakes her head a little, as if to clear something from it. A bad memory, a clinging bit of cobweb.

'A day out, then, to cheer her up?'

'It's a jolly idea, and I'll try, but I have so little time . . .' And like that, her attention is straightaway gone again, back to Baby and Zita and parties. So typical of Maureen, whose kindness is true and swift but changeable as sunlight.

Later, I search through the house for Oonagh. She has taken to hiding on window seats, tucking up her feet and drawing the curtains across so she can't be seen. Several times, she has startled me in a room where I thought I was alone, only for her to slide out from behind the curtain and make for the door. Sometimes she has Peke or Fidget with her, but often she is alone.

'What are you doing?' I say now, pulling back the heavy velvet curtains of the music room. It is the darkest of the rooms in that house, facing onto the yellow walls of the palace gardens so that it seems to take on their tobacco-ish tinge. Oonagh is sitting with feet under her, turned sideways towards the window, forehead leaning against the glass.

'Reading. Drawing.' There is no book, no sketchpad, beside her.

'Would you like to go for a walk?'

'No, thank you. I have already been around Green Park with Gunnie.'

'You look like you're hiding,' I say.

'Maybe, a little.'

'From what?'

She doesn't answer, not immediately. 'You know, I think I will ask Mamma to send me back to that school, where Maureen and I were.'

'Why? I thought you hated school.'

'I do. But I can't stay here.'

'Why not?'

'I just can't.'

'I know it's dull,' I say. 'I remember Maureen at fifteen, how cross she was. How much she hated having to still do childish things when she felt herself so grown up.'

'Yes, but she was at Glenmaroon, and then she had Hughie.' Oonagh is the only one in the household to willingly say his name.

'We all did,' I say quickly.

'Maybe.' She doesn't sound convinced. 'In any case, it's different now, for me.'

'How?'

'With Mamma.'

'What is it like?'

'Terrible. It's as if I am a piece of embroidery to be unpicked, or a watercolour that has gone wrong, that she can't stop painting over and over, correcting bits, adding bits, washing out bits. She thinks that me not talking is because I'm impolite or sulking, but it's not. At dinner, a few nights ago, I was seated beside a dreadful man who spoke only of engines, and as I sat there, Lapham came to me with a note. It was from her, and it had just one word, in that spidery scrawl of hers: "Talk!"'

'Where was she?'

'At the other end of the table! I looked up and there she was, staring down at me.' She makes her eyebrows high and surprised then, like Cloé's, which makes me laugh. Oonagh, when she wants to be, is a good mimic. She laughs too, but I can see that she scarcely found it funny. And indeed, I can see that it wasn't.

'Did you keep the note?' I say.

'No, I burned it in the dining room fire straight after dinner.'

'She just wants the best for you,' I say, but I cannot muster the conviction I should have that those words are true. I know that the first duty for all us girls, but for these girls especially, is to be beautiful, and the second, no less vital, is to be amusing. But recently I have noticed that Cloé complains about Oonagh more than before. I wonder is it because she has less of a hold on Aileen and Maureen? I don't know, but there is a thin whine in her voice now as though it comes through teeth that are clenched. It is the sound the east wind made, jeering through the window cracks in Ballytibbert. At first, I expected Gunnie to step in, to divert Cloé or stand between her and Oonagh, her pet. But she does not.

'She wants the best,' I say again. Because it should be so.

'I was so looking forward to going home,'

Oonagh says. 'I miss the smell of an Irish evening and the fires of wood and turf, not always this foul black coal that London burns that catches in my throat.'

'So do I,' I say, squashing in beside her and putting my arms around her. And I do. For all that I am busy, and thinking of all the new things I will soon learn, there is so much I miss. 'Perhaps soon we will be able to go back for a visit.'

'Perhaps.'

I don't know when Oonagh asks to go away, or how she phrases it, but I know the answer. It is no.

'You have learned as much at school as will be useful,' Cloé says when Oonagh makes her request some days later. 'Far better you stay here and watch Maureen so that when your time comes you will be ready.'

'I am ready,' Oonagh says. 'As ready as I wish to be. I shall ask Papa. I shall write to him.' Ernest is still away more than he is at home, in Dublin at the brewery, and I feel that in his absence the house is growing wrong, like a tree that branches out in untamed ways. We are, all of us, leaning at strange angles to each other. Gunnie is upset that she may no longer chaperone Maureen and sulks with all of us but most of all with me. Without Maureen to take about, London does not suit her. I had thought a broader, deeper pool would give her energy and purpose – the way a large party of house guests used to at Glenmaroon or Holmbury; that she would expand with the greater breadth around her, but instead, it is the opposite and she seems to shrink.

Ernest says no too, and Oonagh slides further back into the empty corners of the house. She, too, takes advantage of the new freedoms, but uses them to be alone rather than in company. She goes to Hyde Park and even Green Park without Gunnie, stays up late alone in her bedroom – I know, because sometimes when I come in, I hear the sound of the gramophone from her room. I tap on the door, but she pretends not to hear, and I dare not walk in as I would have when we were younger.

Chapter Twenty-eight

Dublin, Glenmaroon, 1978

'I could bring the tea up to you?' It's Trisha again, back.

'That would be wonderful.' I am tired and cold, I realise. My fingers ache as if they have absorbed damp and mildew, even through the pink rubber gloves, from the papers I turn over, looking and looking for what I am now certain must be here.

'I'll bring you a tray,' she says, and I bless her silently, listening to the thump of her feet on the bare boards of the corridor.

I make a start on the second bag, wondering if I should just bundle it all up and take it away with me. I could call to him and he would come and help me. We could put the entire trunk into the back of the car, and I could do this at home where it is warm and there is better light. It's getting darker outside, and the bare bulb that swings overhead at the end of a white cord is cheap and of low wattage. But I don't want all this in my little house, the cosy place that he and I have made together, near the canal one way and St Stephen's Green the other. There is a pear tree he has trained to grow against the back wall where the sun hits, its branches spread out flat against the brick in surrender to the warmth, which produces a glut of fruit every year as if from an orchard. It's the only house that has ever been mine, and I don't want the smell of these plastic bags and rotten paper. I know this kind of ancient damp – it drifts into everything. But also, I realise, I don't want so many reminders. So many jostling, jolting pieces of my past and theirs. Better they stay here. Better the nuns burn it all or give it to the local historical society. Let them sift through and make up a tale for themselves. I know my own tale well enough.

London was different for me when I found purpose. That Pitman secretarial course was hard work, but Richard was right. It was just the thing.

The mornings were early and the journey across London long – first the Underground, then two buses – but once I got there each day, as soon as I was inside that busy room, surrounded by the disciplined clack of typewriter keys and crisp rustle of paper, I was alert and eager.

Immediately I was swept into the bustle of the college, where girls like me, all sorts of girls, learned to type letters that were fast and efficient and neat, to master the strange symbols and system of shorthand that was an entirely new language. I think we felt part of a society of the future, one with an alphabet and customs of its own.

It was only on those bus journeys, rattling through row after row of small houses made of red or yellow bricks, that I began to get a full sense of the size of London. Until then, I had lived in just a few miles of the heart of the city, where houses were large and green parklands plentiful.

As I travelled outwards from that precious centre, everything became smaller and meaner – narrow streets, squat houses, tight pieces of green lawn like linen folded expertly and repeatedly so that sometimes I would think of all those rows of houses pressing ever inwards, ready to topple and crush the delicate soap bubble of privilege at their heart.

It seems ridiculous now, but I knew nothing, nothing at all, of London except what the girls had shown me, so that I was actually surprised to find that there was an entire world that had nothing to do with debs balls and girls' lunches, or even Ernest and his brewery. People who lived lives outside the scope of what Aileen, Maureen and Oonagh knew and whose lives were nonetheless full and rich. To them, anyway. There were men, women and children who were happy, and sad, and desperate, and joyful, who had plans and schemes and hopes, all of which meant as much to them as Aileen's impatience, Maureen's triumphs and humiliations, and Oonagh's *ennui* did in Grosvenor Place.

I shouldn't have been astonished at their existence – I, of all people, who didn't come from the world I inhabited – but I was, at first. And then, after a while, I was pleased.

I hadn't known London was so big, big enough for all of us. Them at the glittering heart, me perhaps somewhere else, more on the outskirts, but able to come and go too. I began to see all the ways in which the bits of London where they would never set foot could be places that I would begin to know. Where Hughie could join me if he came back; places that I could make ready for him with my training and the new skills I was learning.

Chapter Twenty-nine

Grosvenor Place, London, 1926

'Are you awake?' Maureen's words are slow through the early-morning air that is dark turning to patchy light like a badly knitted stocking. These morning visits have become so frequent – she, tapping on my door in the grey hour before early summer dawn has broken – then climbing in beside me, giddy, giggly, to tell me about her night, even as I am thinking about my day. Bit by bit, as her sense of freedom increased, I stopped going to parties with her, so that now I rarely do.

'I am,' I whisper. 'Get in.' I twitch back the heavy satin counterpane and she slides in beside me, dropping a puddle of silver sequins on the floor beside the bed as she steps out of her dress. She is cold like marble and smells of cigarettes mixed with perfume, both beaten back by the warm musty odour of her body and the sickly-sweet patina of alcohol on her breath.

'Such a fun night,' she says, putting her arms behind her head and settling back. It is how she always begins. Everything, now, is such a fun night for Maureen. 'I am perfectly certain we shall be in the *Express* tomorrow because Driberg was there, sniffing about as usual. Stephen wore a marvellous leather jacket with a fur trim, and pearl-drop earrings. You should have seen the eyes popping out of heads in the Cavendish bar. One Old Boy actually came over and said, "You are a disgrace to this country and to those who died in Flanders," in such a loud voice, and do you know what Stephen said?' She gives a happy laugh.

'What?'

'He said, "You mean like my brother Bim? This jacket is his, you know, only I added a little Chinchilla fur. For the glamour." And it's true, he was wearing Edward's old army jacket, and stroking the fur as if it were a dear little pet. The Old Boy went brick red in the face and I swear I thought he might explode. Too funny.'

'But, Maureen, perhaps he had a son who died in the war,' I say, shocked. 'Poor man.'

'What nonsense,' Maureen says. 'That damn war is all any of the old men think or talk about.' Has she forgotten that my father, too, died in 'that damn war'? 'And anyway,' she continues vaguely, 'Stephen's brother did die, you know, at the Somme, so surely that gives him leave?' Leave for what, I wonder. To mock the deaths of others? To swagger through their silent grief as if he is immune? 'Anyway,' she goes on, wriggling closer and putting her cold feet against my legs, 'what's the point when it's finished and done with? You know what Stephen calls it?'

'What?' I say. In this mood, there is no point resisting.

'"The Great Persecution".' She giggles. 'Because he says he is persecuted by streams of retired majors saying what a pity it is he didn't die in it.'

'I don't think that's what they mean . . .' I begin, but Maureen isn't listening anymore.

I get up and dress quietly, by what light there is from outside because I do not want to wake her. Even though I doubt I could if I tried. It is still early but I must cross London in time to be at my training college in Croydon – a place I had never heard of before, of which Cloé said, 'But are you sure it is *safe*?' – for 9am.

Maureen was true to her word. As soon as it became clear that Cloé would not change her mind and rein the girls in tighter, or saddle them with Gunnie to chaperone, she spoke to Ernest. I don't know what she said – I didn't even know she had spoken to him – so that I was taken by surprise when she put her head around the door of the small library upstairs where Oonagh and I were making potpourri from dried rose petals, and said, 'Papa arrived from Dublin last night and wants to see you. He is in his business room.'

'Whatever for?' I asked, against the sudden thump of my heart, remembering the last time I had been called to Ernest's business room.

'Don't worry,' she said, so that I knew she saw apprehension in my face. 'Something nice, I promise.'

Sure enough: 'Please, sit,' he said, gesturing me to a high-backed armchair beside the fire, identical to the one in which he sat, opposite me, so that we faced each other. I looked at the fire in order not to look directly at him. It was a bad fire and I was surprised at the servants, at him. It was a wet evening, one of many that year. 'So you wish to learn typing and dictation?' he asked.

'I do.' There was a pause.

'I think it a good idea,' he said at last.

'You do?' I was startled.

'Yes. Both are useful accomplishments, more so

than watercolour and piano, eh?' He smiled then, and, after a moment, I smiled back.

'I think so.'

'At a time like this it is as well to be prepared.'

'You mean the railway workers' strike?' I said. I had seen the newspapers, and although I did not fully understand what it meant to be 'on strike', I was thrilled to know even as much as I did, thrilled too when he agreed with me.

'Do you know what you will do when you have mastered these new arts?' Ernest continued.

'I don't, but I thought perhaps I might get a job. There are secretaries now, and typists.'

'There certainly are. And very useful they make themselves too. But tell me, Felicity, would you like a Season?'

'What?' I was too astonished at the turn the conversation had taken to be other than abrupt.

'A Season. You could come out next year with Oonagh. I know you are older, but I don't think that will matter.'

'Is it because Oonagh is unhappy? You think it will help to cheer her?' Oonagh had always been his favourite. It made sense that he would deny her – going away to school – only to later propose something else.

'It's nothing to do with Oonagh.'

'I don't understand.'

'It's perfectly simple.' He looked irritated. 'I am offering to bring you out, with my daughter, if that's what you wish.'

Was it what I wished? It could be. I could say yes and allow myself to be dressed and coiffed and presented at Court with Oonagh – thanks to my mother having been Admiral Redmond's daughter before she was Mrs Burke, I knew that was a possibility. I could go to parties, not as a kind of chaperone but as a guest. What might that be like?

I thought of the girls' lunches and the powder rooms of the balls I had been to; the stares and whispers that followed me. Would they become more, or less, if I was to be launched into society with a Guinness? When I lay in bed at night, wondering what all the different bits of me – Ballytibbert, Hughie, Glenmaroon, Cloé's girls – made when added up together, would Ernest's offer change the answer?

The appeal was great. How could it not be? It was like opening a book with a dull cover, thinking one was going to read about tillage or some such, only to find the most magical fairytale inside. But I couldn't say yes. To do so would take me too far from where I was, and where I had been. When Hughie returned, I needed to be somewhere close to where he had left me, the person he remembered, not to have disappeared completely into the dazzling world that Maureen and Aileen inhabited. I could visit, with them, but I couldn't take a step so definitive as the one Ernest suggested.

And there was another reason. If the fault was mine for not getting Maureen's letter to Hughie, then it was Ernest's too, for forbidding him the house and the company of his daughters.

Maureen's letter might have brought Hughie back, or quelled the anger that had sent him out that day. But Ernest's intervention must have added coal to the fire that burned in him. I blamed myself so much that I could only blame Ernest a little, but still, I blamed him. And that little, while it didn't stop me living under his roof, stopped me from saying yes to more.

'Thank you,' I said. 'But no. I'm happy to learn typing and be useful.'

'Very well. I approve the plan. I shall write to your mother and inform her, and reassure her that you will continue to live here with us. If you would like that?'

'Thank you, Ernest,' I said. 'I should like that very much.' I did not blame him so much that I could think about leaving. Certainly not for now.

Because Ernest had said yes and given the plan his blessing before Cloé heard anything of it, there was little she could say or do. I saw that she had lost, again – lost a battle, lost someone of use to her – and because of that, I was sorry. But I forced myself to stay quiet even when she said, 'So you wish to abandon us?' She was thinner than ever, her face curdled yellow like a lemon posset.

'It is not that,' I said gently. 'I am happy to be here. Only that I wish to learn new things.'

'Typing?' She gave a chilly little laugh but said no more. I hated watching her struggle against that sour-tasting knowledge – the impotence of her disagreement; Ernest's lack of regard for her wishes – but I wished too that she would not play out her loss on Oonagh.

I try to explain some of the new excitement I feel to Oonagh, the new way of seeing that comes with my daily departures from and return to Grosvenor Place. The *perspective*, a word that Spanish had explained to us, that comes with going and coming back.

'It's the joy of becoming someone else,' I say. 'Someone who is better than the person you are.'

'I should like that,' she says. Home, for Oonagh, now sixteen, is still a place where she hides behind curtains and in her bedroom, playing endless records and smoking in secret.

'I can teach you,' I say suddenly. 'I can come

home and every day, I can teach you exactly what we have learned, and so it will be as if you are doing the course with me. Everything I know, you will know too!'

'But what will I do with it when I do know it?'

'It doesn't matter,' I say, excited. 'Just knowing will be better than not knowing. You have to do something, Oonagh, you know you do. You won't come out for a year, and meantime, you need a better way to spend your time than walks with Gunnie and Fidget. You can practise while I am away all day, and then we can compare ourselves in the evenings.'

'Very well,' she says. 'Teach me. But let's not tell Mamma.'

And I do, for a while anyway. I bring home what I have learned, and at first she is eager and receptive, her quick mind grasping the basics. 'I shall ask Papa to buy me a typewriter, that I may practise everything,' she says. 'I can pretend it is for writing details of our *Fantome* voyage.'

But one day, when I ask how she is getting on, she says, 'It isn't the same.' She is wrapped in an old fur travelling cloak of Cloé's and wreathed in cigarette smoke, sprawled in the armchair in her bedroom – 'the only place Gunnie and Mamma let me alone' – and when I ask how long she had been there responds, 'I don't know, hours?'

'What isn't the same?' I ask.

'It isn't the same for me as it is for you. You go about, among new people, to new places. You have the excitement of all that. No wonder you learn so fast. I am stuck here, waiting for you. I cannot keep up because I do not have the same excitement.'

'But you could,' I say, desperate to persuade her. There is no colour in her face at all now except those blue eyes, but they are paler too, the fragile blue of starlings' eggs, without the sparkle that used to light them. Her hair is dusty and unbecoming, almost unkempt, and I can see, a little, why Cloé nags at her. Once the prettiest of her daughters, Oonagh is now almost plain. The skin around her nails is ragged where she has been picking and worrying at it so that she has taken to hiding her hands when not smoking, sitting on them so that her shoulders hunch in and up, making her seem thinner, sharper, more awkward. 'You have to do something,' I say to her, just as I have said before, but with greater urgency.

'Well, I can't do that,' she says.

'You can if you try,' I insist.

But she can't. She stops practising, her interest dwindles, and I see books I have lent her unopened in a pile in her room.

Now that Aileen and Maureen are so very much out in the world, tea at Grosvenor Place has become a place where the unexpected and entertaining often occur, and despite the long journey across London from Croydon, I am usually home in time for it.

Lapham will open the door to me and say, 'They are in the drawing room, Miss, but tea is not yet served,' so that I know I can run to my room and change out of the plain, dull dress I have worn for college into something prettier, brush my hair, and make it downstairs in time.

There, I might find just Gunnie and Cloé, gathered close about the tea things, while Oonagh sulks beside the window, like a bumblebee or a butterfly, blundering against the glass, desperate for the invisible barrier to dissolve and set her free into the air, but more often, I find Maureen and Aileen, and their friends. Baby and Zita are regular guests, cousin Bryan too. Stephen Tennant is a great favourite of Cloé's, because she came out with his mother Pamela and because he caresses her with compliments, and so she overlooks his Vaselined eyelids and peacock-blue scarves. Elizabeth Ponsonby, she tolerates, because, she says, of her mother Dolly – 'a bluestocking, yes, but a dear' – but secretly I think it is more that Elizabeth, an odd, angular girl with impulsive humours and excess of energy, is a darling of the newspapers, and a reliable foil for Maureen.

This day, Bryan and Stephen are seated together on the chaise longue with Cloé in a chair beside them while Maureen moves restlessly about the room, leaning over the backs of chairs and peering out the windows. Oonagh is on the floor beside the fire with the dogs. She is, I think, too big now, too old, for the dress she wears and looks awkward, ungainly, unhappy.

'Did you hear,' Stephen says in a confiding voice like honey poured smoothly over the back of a teaspoon, 'Lois has been arrested?' His hair is arranged in shining waves not unlike Maureen's and he wears a pinstriped suit with a gold lamé scarf coaxed into the form of a tie. His hands, sketching vague, fretful shapes in the air, are thin and white.

'Good heavens, whatever for?' Cloé asks. By her voice, she does not know whether to be appalled or indulgent.

'Speeding,' says Bryan, taking up the story. 'She was driving through Regent's Park at fifty-one miles an hour.'

'She was on a treasure hunt,' Maureen says. 'Time was of the essence!'

'And of course, poor Lois, if she stays still in one place for too long, someone will try to *paint* her

. . .' Bryan continues, in such a way that Maureen and Stephen laugh, flashing each other little darting looks. Then, 'Of course the Prince of Wales was on the very same treasure hunt so I don't imagine much will come of her arrest.'

Cloé decides that, after all, she will be indulgent. 'Such antics,' she says.

'Oonagh, if you don't stop brushing that poor Peke, all his hair will fall out and he will look like poor Cecil Beaton, who combs further over each time I see him,' says Bryan. I can see that, like me, he has noticed how quiet Oonagh is, how low her head is bent, and is trying to cheer her a little, but Oonagh is too shy and won't look at him, even though she stops brushing and hides her hands by putting them under her knees. I move to sit beside her.

'That odious man,' Maureen says. 'Always insinuating.'

'Oh, Cecil's not the worst,' Stephen says. 'If anything, he may be jolly useful. *Vogue* have given him a contract, you know, and he talks of doing something called *The Book of Beauty*.'

'How nauseating,' Maureen says.

'Oonagh, look what I have for you,' Bryan says then, putting a hand into his pocket, and holding it out, closed. 'But you must guess what it is.'

'I don't know,' says Oonagh.

'Of course you don't know,' says Bryan with a sigh. 'That's the point. Now, take a guess.'

'I cannot,' says Oonagh.

'Oh, go on, for goodness sakes, guess,' says Maureen impatiently. 'I think it's a box of candied peel.'

'No,' says Bryan. 'Oonagh, your turn.'

'A locket,' she ventures after a long pause.

'No. Last guess. Fliss?'

He smiles at me and I say, 'A book,' even though it cannot be because his fist is closed tight over it.

'All wrong!' He opens his hand and shows Oonagh what he has brought her – a supple brown leather dog collar, studded with brass, and with a clever locking mechanism.

'Oh, the darling collar!' Oonagh exclaims. 'For Fidget! Won't he be the smartest dog? Give it to me now that I may put it on him!'

'Only if you admit that I am a very decent sort of cousin to have,' says Bryan.

'You are better, a little, than you used to be,' she says, strapping the collar around Fidget's fat neck. 'I have not fully forgiven you for my poor doll Mary Mercy, but I am willing to consider it.'

'Your consideration is all I ask,' Bryan says with a bow so that Oonagh, suspecting mockery, turns red and looks down at the dogs again.

'Will you have more tea, Stephen?' Cloé asks.

'Thank you, no,' Stephen says. 'But perhaps I can tempt you to a cocktail, dear Cloé?'

'Let's all have cocktails,' Maureen says, springing to her feet from the low footstool she has been sitting on, face cupped in her hands, staring at the fire. 'Oh, do say yes, Mamma. Stephen makes the most divine Gin-and-Its.'

'Really, Cloé, you are far too dashing to be sitting here with tea,' Stephen says. 'Do let me make one of my little concoctions. So reviving.' He looks, I think, badly in need of being revived. He is draped across the divan, his long form bent into a supple undulating 's', head back, eyes nearly closed. A cigarette hangs between his fingers, so languidly that it looks as though it may fall at any moment, and I can see Gunnie twitching, unsure whether to move an ashtray closer. I smile reassuringly at her. I have seen Stephen and his drooping cigarettes before; somehow, they never actually fall. Those fingers must have more grip than he lets on.

'Very well,' Cloé says with a laugh. 'Why not? Maureen, ring for Lapham and tell him what you need.'

Lapham brings a tray with decanters and siphons, and some slick red, candied cherries that look like small painted mouths, and Stephen flicks the end of his cigarette into the fire, to Gunnie's visible relief, then sets about measuring and mixing with precise and careful movements. Satisfied, he distributes glasses, placing each one delicately into outstretched hands, as though giving us a jewel.

Maureen raises hers up high, looks through it towards the light. 'Divine,' she says. 'One for Oonagh?'

'Certainly, if I may?' Stephen says, looking at Cloé.

'She is too young,' Cloé says, 'but very well. Perhaps one may liven her up a little. Goodness knows, she needs it.' She gives Oonagh a nasty look, which Oonagh ignores. But she accepts the glass Stephen holds out to her, takes a quick sip, makes a face, and takes a bigger sip.

Maureen was right – his cocktails are indeed divine so that by the time we must go and change for dinner we have all had a second, and even Oonagh is laughing and looking around at all of us, her face brighter than I have seen in a long time. She is merry over dinner and only retires to her room when Aileen and Maureen go out.

Chapter Thirty

'Fliss, you must absolutely come to this party with us.' Maureen bursts into the small library where I have taken to practising my typing, because Cloé says the noise of the keys brings on a headache if I practise in my bedchamber, which is above hers.

'Cannot,' I say. 'Too much to do.'

'Nonsense. You are becoming reclusive and I'm fed up with it. You tiptoe up and down the stairs with your books under your arm and miss out on all the fun.'

'Well, you're having enough fun for both of us.'

'I am indeed.' She grins. 'But this time you have to come.'

'Why is it so important?'

'It's a costume party, where we all dress as Once We Were, and I have decided that Oonagh will come with us, and together with Aileen we will go as the Three Ages. Oonagh shall be the child, I will be the schoolgirl and Aileen will be the adult. We will wear the same clothes only with variations, and style ourselves the same. Isn't it a clever idea?'

'It is,' I say. 'Very clever.'

'So you will come? I can lend you a dress. You can even be one of the Ages, with us, if you like. The Four Ages?'

'I didn't say that.' I laugh. 'Really, I can't.'

'But you must. Mamma will never let Oonagh go if you don't come with us. So you see, you must come.'

'Are you even sure Oonagh wants to go?' I ask, hoping that might be my way out.

'She is longing for it. So little for her to do. You said yourself that she was mopey. Well, not anymore.'

It is true that Oonagh seems happier and gayer. Now, when I come home, she is always in the drawing room, and seems at ease with Maureen and Aileen's friends. She does not chatter incessantly as they do, but she listens, and laughs, and answers when they speak to her. Which is often. Baby and Elizabeth in particular have made a pet of her, laughing at her jokes, encouraging her, plying her with cocktails despite her age, even picking up her old nickname of 'Teapot' for Maureen and using it liberally. I can see that, for Elizabeth anyway, Oonagh, sweet and pliant still at sixteen, is far preferable to Maureen's more strident appeal. They do her hair and advise on clothes and shoes with so much excitable charm that Oonagh begins to pay attention to her appearance again. She gets her hair cut and wears it swept back from her forehead in a way that enhances the extraordinary blue of her eyes, and begins to dress in the grown-up clothes that Maureen and Aileen wear – silk blouses and pleated skirts, shift dresses with elegant, dropped waists, gorgeous coats that swing behind her as she walks. She looks, I think, much better than when she was crammed into girlish pinafores; she is finally starting to fulfil the early promise of beauty she showed as a child.

In the evenings now, if the older girls are not out, they gather, all three of them, in a small sitting room beyond the ballroom where Cloé never goes. I pass it on the way to my little library, and there is ever the noise of laughter, records playing, the clink of cocktails being swirled, a host of happy sounds that entwine with the thick plumes of cigarette smoke that drift from the door.

'It's like an emergency that no one has noticed,'

I say one evening, putting my head in. 'As though someone has forgotten to shout "Fire!"'

'Won't you join us?' they call out. 'We are having gin fizzes and Duke Ellington.'

'I can't,' I say. 'I have practice,' and do my best to ignore the cries of 'Fliss, too boring!' that follow me, mingling with the strains of Ellington's ragtime piano, as I go to my books and typewriter, leaving them to chatter and drink and practise dance steps until late into the night.

If Richard is in London, I choose to meet him out of the house, although Cloé tells me he is always welcome. I am too fond of him to enjoy seeing him in company with Baby, Zita, Elizabeth and particularly Stephen. He doesn't shine. Indeed, he sits so quietly that after their first meeting Stephen nicknamed him 'Silenzio'. When forced to talk, to answer a direct question, he blushes and is monosyllabic so that I can't bear the contrast with the light confetti of conversation thrown into the air by the others. It's not just for him that I cannot bear it – indeed, he seems frankly indifferent – it's for myself too. Because for all that Ernest praises him and says he is a 'capable young man who will go far', in his honest awkwardness Richard is too much like me. When we are all together in that drawing room, I feel more than at any other time how out of place I am everywhere. And it is impossible to be there, with Richard, both of us hesitant and rather serious, and not think how Hughie would fit with ease. How perfectly his rapid wit and love of the absurd would blend. And how smoothly he would cover both Richard and I in the fine-mesh camouflage of his charm.

'Now, say you will,' Maureen continues, that note of menace there, the hint of bared white teeth that accompanies a response of no when there is something she wants. 'In any case,' she says, 'you cannot go to that college because of the General Strike, so there!' She is triumphant, believing she has delivered the killer blow.

'Well, perhaps that is another reason not to go to the party,' I say.

'Whyever not?' Her brows draw together in confusion, two thin black lines over the blue eyes.

'Do you not remember your papa saying this was a delicate time for the country and we must all be careful in what we do and how we conduct ourselves?' Ernest gave us all a serious lecture, just days before, in the music room. A long lecture, or certainly for him, a man who prefers instruction to debate, who keeps his conversations to an efficient minimum. He talked about the trade unions and how they wanted to 'bring the country to a standstill', saying they were 'resisting progress and mustn't be allowed'. He said the government had a solid plan to resist them, and that we must all be ready to play our parts and be conscious of the times we were in. Mildred had been there too, nodding along to what he said, shooting looks at me that meant, 'You see, the world is changing, just as I said . . .' Surely Maureen cannot have forgotten?

'But what has that to do with this?' Maureen asks. 'He meant going out to those dear faithful lorry drivers parked all along Marble Arch and Hyde Park Corner, who are keeping the country running, and offering them cups of hot sweet tea and sandwiches. That's all. No one bothers about the strike.'

'Except all those who have come out to march,' I say with a smile. 'Mr Baldwin says it is over a million people.'

'Papa only pays attention because he's bored and needs a new toy. He's become awfully glum,' says Maureen. It is true that Ernest is preoccupied, and I detect again the dread hand of politics in all our lives, but Maureen, of course, does not. 'The gyroscope has been a sad disappointment,' she continues. 'Perhaps he will learn to fly a plane. Now, you must have a costume. The party is in two days, but I can help you.'

I give in. What else can I do? There is no way to resist the ferocity of what Maureen badly wants. No way to turn her from her purpose, or duck so that she leaves me out of it.

Later that evening I see Oonagh and ask her, 'Do you really want to go?'

She says, 'Oh yes! It is part of my new plan.'

'What plan?' I ask.

'I'm going to bring myself out. Quietly and not officially, of course. But I'm not going to wait for next year, for Mamma and Gunnie to do it. There isn't any point when I'm dying of boredom now.'

Chapter Thirty-one

The party is in a house on Regent's Park Road, one of the narrow ones, and seems to be all staircase and heavy wood panelling. It is dark and solid and old, and the contrast with the party guests makes me laugh, because they are light and gay and young. Watching them, I think of rice thrown at a wedding – flung upwards in brittle, polished, delicate handfuls, drifting down to land in shiny, scattered drifts.

They move endlessly. Some are dancing, alone and in pairs, others are simply flinging themselves restlessly at one group and then another, taking snatches of gossip and jokes, like bees take pollen, distributing it throughout the party so that soon everyone is covered in it, breathing it in and out. It is the girls who move most, I see, and particularly the girls like Elizabeth, Baby, Zita, Maureen, whom everyone has a welcome for.

They move so constantly that I find that if I stay in one spot, close to a table that is covered with many different bottles – every guest has brought something; 'it's the new way,' Maureen declared – it is easy to follow them as they loop around and around the room, keeping all the wheels of gaiety in motion.

'What filthy stuff,' says Bryan, beside me, tilting one of the many bottles and squinting. 'I'm surprised at David.' David must be the host, I think. Not that anyone seems to own this party more than anyone else – everyone here seems both equally proprietorial and equally indifferent. 'Let me get you a proper drink,' he says, disappearing.

To my left Ray Starita and his band play 'Brown Sugar'. They might as well have tied lengths of string to the hands, knees and elbows of the entire party, I think, because every note is a twitch that sets the room in motion. I watch one girl with more tassels than dress flapping her arms vigorously, twisting her knees in and out. The music is exuberant, invigorating, discordant, and they love it. It speaks to them about them, telling them that they are young and daring and new and nothing like them has been seen before. It does not speak to them of mud and death and failure, of rising prices and discontent, or of duty and responsibility.

Those who don't dance, talk, and what they talk of is the General Strike, exactly as if it is the most terrific entertainment, put on for their benefit. Some of the young men have joined the London police force as special constables and are keen to present themselves in heroic lights. 'Really, it was nothing,' one of them keeps saying. He has a long nose and is entirely without chin, face dwindling into his lanky frame without interruption. 'Anyone would do the same,' he persists. 'You would, wouldn't you?' to anyone who will listen.

'Isn't it cosy?' says Maureen. 'I do like the feeling that we are in here and anything at all might happen on the streets. Why, there might be a riot if those trade unionists get through,' she says, face glowing.

'Oh, but they won't,' says the chinless young man. 'The police are awfully on top of things, and you know, we are here to protect you if there is any need.'

'Well, I call that very reassuring,' says Elizabeth Ponsonby, who is dressed in a frilled romper suit so short that it shows nearly all of her legs. 'Don't you call that reassuring, Maureen?'

'I do not,' Maureen says. 'I can't imagine how badly off I'd need to be to rely on you, Eddie,' and the young man goes off looking mortified while Maureen laughs.

'Too cruel,' Elizabeth says in delight. 'He's the son of the Earl of Cranbrook, you know.'

It is, I think, indeed too cruel. But there is no point saying that to Maureen, who has grown to love the sharp intake of breath, the pin-drop silence, that follows her more outrageous put-downs, so that she now looks for exactly that, saying things that are deliberately styled in order to shock. That they also wound doesn't seem to concern her. In fact, she seems not to notice that the hurt in the eyes of some of her victims is real, and not pantomime. She is rapidly forgetting that she was ever left on the outside, and how much that pained her.

I go and look for Oonagh, worried that she may be overwhelmed by a party that is noisier, more crowded, than any I have yet been to. If Maureen was quick to discover the secret life of London that was emerging among the select group of Baby and Bryan's friends, gathering speed in the Cavendish Hotel and Café de Paris, then she was not the last. It seems that half of society has woken up to the same lure and followed her here. I see girls I recognise from last year's frumpy debutante parties, Baby's 'Miss Mice', now tricked out in shorts and sailor suits, their eyes blackened and cheeks rouged high up so that they look like sly, startled dolls. I wonder what their mamas must say. Even Marjorie of the Cadogan Square girls' lunch is here, wearing a bonnet and waving a silver rattle madly in time to the music. I think how pleased she must be to be at least in the same room as 'dear Lois', who is dazzling in a Chinese silk kimono and bare feet, her hair held back with a silk headband the exact yellow of a blackbird's beak.

Everywhere I look there are cocktails being shaken and poured, drinks slopping from glasses onto the floor that is by now sticky and filthy, large black-and-white tiles disappearing under a film of grey. People are shrieking, gaily, I suppose, although it is not always easy to tell, and some of the costumes are so daring that I cannot understand how they fit with the theme at all. I spot Brenda Dean Paul – I recognise her at once because of her almost shocking slenderness and that mass of dark hair, in tight shining waves – wearing a very short black dress covered in sequins. It cannot, I think, be anything like what she once wore.

Stephen, himself angelic in a white lace gown and silver paint on his eyelids, must agree, because he says loudly, 'So what is it exactly that you've come as, Brenda, do tell? The Ghost of Virtue Long Past?' I am shocked that he would be so rude, but Brenda just smiles vaguely and carries on dancing.

'That girl has been altogether too long in Berlin,' Stephen says. 'It's starting to show.'

'Whatever do you mean?' I ask.

'Well, you know *Berlin*,' he says confidingly. '*Miles* ahead of us in simply everything.' But I do not know Berlin. I look again at Brenda. She is the one of Maureen's new friends – although perhaps 'friend' is not exactly the word for those two – that Cloé has taken against. 'Something unpleasant about that girl,' she said after the first time Brenda called. 'Don't bring her again.'

Brenda doesn't look unpleasant to me. She looks uncertain. I recognise it, because it's how I feel. For all the sophistication of her dress, her face is still that of a child. Her mouth is painted fire-engine red and set in a careful pout, but that does not disguise the bewildered look in her eyes, as though a camera flashbulb has just exploded in her face and she is momentarily disoriented.

I find Oonagh dancing with a boy in a velvet jacket. 'Are you having fun?' I yell over the sound of Ray Starita's saxophone.

'Oh yes!' She takes a swig of the bottle she is holding. 'And so should you be. Now go on and stop fussing.'

I walk back through the party towards the open front door because the balcony is so crowded that I cannot get air.

Aileen is sitting at the top of the stairs, a jacket thrown over her shoulders, smoking. 'Sit,' she says, holding a hand out to me. I sit beside her, although the stone step is cold and my dress is thin. 'Here.' She must notice, because she takes the jacket from her shoulders. 'We can both sit on this. It belongs to Bryan, but he won't mind.' Bryan, I think, almost certainly will mind.

Below us, a group of revellers are dancing in the hall, shimmying up and down, bumping against each other with shrieks of laughter. The front door is open and I wonder what they must look like to passers-by. Except that it is too late for passers-by.

'What are you thinking, Fliss?' Aileen asks, leaning against me.

'Oh, you know, various things,' I say.

'Tell me some of them.'

'Well, I'm thinking that I've never seen a party anything like this before. And that I am not properly dressed for it.' It is true – I am wearing a plain black linen pinafore dress, almost a gymslip, and I know that in comparison with every other person I am ridiculously, laughably, dowdy – indeed, Maureen told me I would be, when I said no to borrowing any of her clothes.

'It doesn't matter what you wear, you know,' Aileen says. 'You always look the same.' And then, hastily, 'Which is a jolly nice thing. Anyway, go on.'

'I'm thinking that I've never seen people drink so much, including Oonagh, who is drinking from the neck of a bottle like a pirate.'

'Oh, never mind Oonagh. What else?'

'That this is a very jolly party, but I can't imagine how much I would like it if I had been to a party like this last night and had another one to go to tomorrow.'

'Which is precisely what I'm thinking,' Aileen says.

'Really?'

'Goodness, yes. I'm thinking that if I close my eyes, this could be any party, in any house, that I have been to in the last year. That there isn't a single thing Elizabeth has said to me this evening that I haven't heard her say a thousand times before. That Stephen, whom I thought the most exotic, surprising creature alive when first I met him, now I find to be surprising always in the same way. I'm thinking that that whole eager crowd could be transported to the other side of the world and they wouldn't even notice, would just carry on drinking and telling each other the latest scandal.'

'So why come?'

'Maureen persuades me. She likes us being together. She says she cannot be "The Glorious Guinness Girls" alone, can she? But now that she has Oonagh, perhaps she won't go on so if I decide to stay at home more.'

'But Oonagh is too young. Cloé will never let her keep coming out like this.'

'Oh, won't she? Mamma's grip is not as strong as it was. Haven't you noticed? Anyway, she is just like Maureen – she sees the virtue in us being the Guinness girls. And Oonagh is far better suited to all this than me.' There is a pause while she smokes, hunched forward over her knees. Then, 'Perhaps I should have a job. Like you mean to?'

'Why do you say that?'

'I've noticed you have a sense of purpose now, since you have begun to learn your dictation and shorthand. Mildred does too. Always somewhere to go, people who need her. Sometimes I think it must be nice.'

'But you have people who need you too.'

'Not really. Do you honestly think this lot would notice if I didn't appear? Except Maureen, and then only because she wants me for something.'

'Well,' I say, cautiously because I know Cloé would not approve, 'you could have a job, I'm sure.'

'No, it's too late. I am thoroughly spoiled, I'm

afraid.' She leans further forward over her knees, resting her cheek on one and looking up at me. It is, I think, a sad phrase, but she has made it almost jaunty, as if 'thoroughly spoiled' were, after all, a fine thing.

'It is different for me,' I say. 'I must have a job, because I will not be married.'

'Don't be hasty,' she says, looking sideways at me. Then, 'You know Bryan is in love?'

'With who?' My heart, to my shame, beats a little faster.

'She's called Diana Mitford. A sister of Nancy.' Nancy, I remember, is the one with the droll-looking eyes, who says things that are nearly as cutting as Maureen, but somehow wittier; less cruel.

'I didn't know she had a sister.'

'She has heaps. All the same ages as us. Diana is Oonagh's age.'

'Goodness, so she's . . .'

'Barely sixteen. Yes. Bryan met her at a fancy-dress party at their house, Batsford Park, some weeks ago, and can talk of nothing and no one else. I think it's why he's being so kind to Oonagh. She reminds him, a little, of Diana. He says he has found the purpose of his life and swears that the moment she turns eighteen, he'll ask for her hand. You'd think he would be a bore about it, but somehow, he's not. It's rather sweet, I think.' She sounds wistful and stays quiet for a moment. 'Am I awful?' she asks then.

'Why awful?'

'To be so ungrateful?'

'Are you ungrateful?' It occurs to me that this is the most I have ever spoken to Aileen on such a serious note. Always the most aloof of the three, certainly with me, she doesn't easily let on to the kinds of urgent emotions – of excitement or despair – that Maureen and Oonagh trade in.

'I feel that I am. So lucky – everyone tells me, so it must be true – and so bored. Not bored – that's not the right word, that's what Elizabeth or Stephen would say. I mean, I don't know what I'm doing and when I imagine my life, going on and on like this, well, I can hardly bear it.'

'But it won't,' I say. 'I mean, it can't.'

'No, you're right. But all the same, sometimes it feels like I've lived a thousand years already.' She uncurls herself from the knot she has been in and stands up. 'I'm going home now. Do you want to come?'

'I'd better stay with Oonagh,' I say.

'Yes, probably you better had,' she agrees. 'Maureen can't be trusted to watch her.'

Perhaps I am not so good at watching either, because I get distracted – Elizabeth wants to talk to me about something, urgently, but then cannot remember what it is she wanted to say so insists we go upstairs 'to explore'. We walk up flights of narrow stairs, along half-lit corridors, and Elizabeth throws open doors. I expect these rooms to be empty, but they are not, not always. There are sometimes small groups of people, who look up, startled, at our appearance. They sit close together on beds or even on the floor. Sometimes, there are fewer people in the room, just two or three, always very close together, but Elizabeth closes the doors so fast that I see very little.

'It wouldn't do to intrude,' she says with a laugh.

Downstairs, I find Brenda being sick behind a plant.

'Are you all right?' I ask.

'Please don't tell anyone,' she says. Her eyes are bloodshot.

'Of course I won't.'

I offer her my handkerchief.

She takes it, then stares at me for a moment with it held to her lips. Mouth covered like that, her eyes are enormous and so black you could drown in them. 'Can I help you find your coat?' I say.

'Oh, I'm not leaving. Not yet. I'm going to dance some more, and then have another drink.

And then, we'll see.' She looks evasive suddenly. Or maybe I am just tired of never quite knowing what anyone means here. She hands me back my handkerchief, which smells of vomit.

By the time I return to the ballroom, the party is hotter, noisier and stickier than ever. Oonagh is dancing together with Maureen, both of them doing the Charleston with grace and ease. Only I know how long they have practised. There are whoops of encouragement from all around and Ray Starita is waving his baton, conducting the girls. *Perhaps Aileen is right*, I think, *and Oonagh is better suited.*

'Will you dance?' Stephen asks, putting out a hand towards me. The silver paint from his eyelids has travelled down his face, catching along the cheekbones.

'No, thanks,' I say. 'I'm really not very good. I prefer to watch others who are better.'

'A lifelong member of the audience,' he says wryly.

'True, but I don't mind that.'

'Nothing to mind,' he agrees. 'Being always onstage is really rather tiring. Especially when the audience will keep goading one on. Of course, the trick is to ignore them. But not everyone can. Look at Elizabeth, always dancing to every tuppenny tune. She will soon exhaust herself.'

'I worry that Maureen will too,' I say.

'Maureen?' he says, eyebrows shooting high. 'Surely not. She has never danced to another's tune in her life. Or, come to think of it, done a single thing for anyone else. Unless one counts her practical jokes. Which I do not.' I think about trying to tell him that isn't exactly true. Of trying to explain about the dresses when I was a child, and the plans for Hughie's farming, and getting Thomas the job, but it feels too difficult to get him to understand.

At last the band pack up and leave and the house shakes itself free of people, like a dog shaking off water drops. I find Maureen, perched on the edge of a marble table, telling a story about something Gunnie has said to an enthralled group. It isn't a very nice story – in it, Gunnie has mistaken Duke Ellington for an actual duke and is quizzing Maureen about who his people are, '"because I never heard of the Ellingtons, which is most odd"—'

'Where is Oonagh?' I interrupt to ask.

'I haven't the faintest,' she says. 'Asleep on some coats?' And carries on '. . . my dears, her face when she found out that Duke is his name!' The group around her dissolve into loud cries of 'Too funny!'

Oonagh isn't asleep on coats, but she is huddled in an armchair, face chalky with exhaustion, and gives a giant yawn and says, 'Yes, please,' when I say, 'Shall we go?' and holds up a hand for me to drag her to her feet.

We leave all together. Outside, the sun is trying to rise up over the curve of Regent's Park but the angle is awkward, and it struggles.

'Let's go on,' Maureen says to the group that is still thick around her.

'I say, let's go and take a shift at the Hyde Park canteen set up for the strike,' says Elizabeth. 'It's the most tremendous fun. Mostly lorry drivers, but the occasional special constable. We serve them tea from great big urns and hand round plates of sandwiches and sometimes the men get together to sing ballads and it's ever so jolly.'

'I didn't mean that kind of going on,' says Maureen. 'Sounds exactly like work to me. Like having a *job*.' She gives me a look.

But everyone else seems to think Elizabeth's idea is 'splendid', and so they set off, picking their way across the street, clinging urgently to one another, stumbling and hesitating as though it were a fast-rushing river with only stepping stones to guide them. The sun is properly up now, triumphant at having scaled the houses, and follows them, spotlighting their clumsy moments – an ankle turned in impossible heels, a sudden lurch or dip.

'Such a fun party,' says Oonagh, watching them

depart with another giant yawn. 'But I think I'd like to go to bed now.'

'Well, there's no point going on anywhere with you two anyway,' Maureen says, giving my arm an affectionate squeeze. 'So we might as well.' Then, 'I say, isn't Elizabeth *absurd*, with her lorry drivers. So *déclassé*.' It is new with her – this sprinkling of French through her speech – and I think, with an inward laugh, of what Spanish would say, she who tried so hard, so unsuccessfully, to persuade Maureen to speak the language.

'If I didn't know better,' Oonagh says slyly, 'I'd say you're drunk, Maureen.' And, for all that her golden beauty is remarkably intact after such a long night, she is squinting in the hard morning light, and I realise that Oonagh is right. Maureen is drunk. Drunk on her own beauty, her success, the sureness of her wit. But drunk, too, on champagne and gin and whatever was in all those bottles.

Chapter Thirty-two

The strike is over just days later – 'Another brilliant failure,' says Ernest over breakfast. I am up and dressed for college, eager to be gone, back to my typewriter and back to my routine. It is early, and dark even though it is May, because the rain has come in – three days of it now, shrouding the trees and houses in a latticed veil of drops as though a cloak has been thrown over them. He speaks cheerfully, certain that the strike outcome is a good thing – after nine days, the strikers have given up without getting what they hoped for; the promise of no reduction in their wages – but, he adds, 'We are not out of the woods yet. Unemployment is still rising.'

He is more in London these days – there is even talk of moving the brewery from Dublin, although I cannot imagine how such a move could be made – and so often now, it is he and I at breakfast together. Sometimes, Richard travels with him – I begin to see how valuable Ernest finds him, how much responsibility he has – and on those days he arrives very early from the small hotel where he stays, and joins us.

Those mornings, Ernest quizzes me on what I have learned and what more I will learn, and he and Richard both listen closely. Ernest seems satisfied, nodding seriously at what I tell them. At first, in these exchanges, I feel as shy as I ever did of him, uncertain as to what is going on behind that moustache that lifts and twitches so vigorously, uncertain, too, as to what I am to him. Not a daughter, not a niece or cousin, but not a stranger either. Because he asks nothing of me – unlike Cloé or Gunnie – and because I am alternately visible and invisible to him, always unsure which it will be, like a light that flicks on and off above my head at the will of another, I have not learned how to be with him. But bit by bit, I grow accustomed, so that soon I find myself able to have a conversation.

When Richard asks about the other girls on the course and I begin to describe them – their quickness and determination, the schools they have been to, where they live and what their fathers do, their plans for the future – I can see that both he and Ernest are genuinely interested, and that gives me faith in myself.

Sometimes, Ernest will give me a lift for part of my journey in his motorcar. We talk mostly of what is in the news, the rising number of unemployed people and what Ernest calls 'a mood of discontent' in the country. But sometimes it is something in Driberg's page in the *Express* – often Maureen's name, or the name of one of her friends – that will catch his eye, and then he will ask me searching questions about the girls and what they do.

When this happens, I revert, suddenly, vertiginously, to the awkward girl I was. Under scrutiny, I don't know whether to claim that I know everything, or nothing.

Since starting my studies, I go about less with the girls, so I do not see what they do. But Maureen still climbs into bed with me many mornings, Oonagh now too – Aileen comes home earlier than them and goes to her own bed; sometimes so early that I am still awake so she puts her head around the door to say goodnight. It seems as if she would like to come in and talk, because of the way she lingers a little, fidgeting with the door handle, but she doesn't. Maureen and Oonagh, though, chatter through the parties and entertainments, one either side of me, interrupting and contradicting one another, until they fall asleep. And so I do know – some of it, anyway – but I also understand that I know only what they tell me, and that this does not always chime with the little I have seen. My recollections of the Regent's Park Road party are vivid, so that I cannot but paint in details that they leave out in their descriptions of other nights – the number of bottles, the stickiness of the floor, the smaller huddled groups in far-off rooms. I am afraid that if Ernest understands how much my studies have interfered with my shadowing of his girls, he will forbid them. And so I dither, telling a little, not much, evading and obscuring.

'I met Arthur Ponsonby at the club last night,' he says this morning, as we drive out through quiet Ebury Street. 'He is deeply concerned about Elizabeth and says he believes she is made for better things than these extravagant pranks they play. What do you think?'

It is exactly the kind of question I hate. Too direct, with too much hanging on it. I say what I think will reassure him, but I am not surprised when the matter comes back barely a couple of weeks later.

'No, Oonagh, that is not a good card to lead with . . .' It is Saturday and we are playing bridge in the small sitting room off the ballroom. Maureen, in between doing her nails and flicking through *The Sketch*, is watching every card like a hawk, pouncing on any bad bit of play or slip in concentration.

'Do stop snapping. It makes you so tiring to play with,' Aileen complains. 'Haven't you got something better to do? Run around with Baby and Elizabeth laying a wild goose chase?'

'Yes, so that you can enjoy all the fun of it without doing any of the work,' Maureen says. 'Don't think I haven't noticed. You are like a lily of the field.'

'It's hardly *work*,' says Aileen. 'You make it sound like you are miners, when all you do is invent silly clues that send your even sillier friends running from Cleopatra's Needle to Piccadilly Circus.'

'No one asks you to come,' says Maureen haughtily. 'In fact, we should be jolly pleased if you didn't.' The girls say such things to each other at times, as a tease. But this is different. Maureen's tone is icy and Aileen's face is flushed. They stare hard at one another and neither drops their gaze.

'Please don't quarrel,' says Oonagh. 'I can't bear it. And Mamma or Gunnie will hear and then there will be all sorts of trouble. And you know how I hate trouble and shouting, so please.' They are so used to indulging Oonagh that there is silence for a time, with just the whisper of cards landing and being picked up.

But Aileen is thoroughly nettled and cannot seem to remain quiet. 'Wait till Mamma hears about Baby and Zita's latest escapade,' she says after a while. 'I doubt she will be at all amused. And if she tells Papa, well, I wouldn't give tuppence for your chances of more freedom. You'll be back behind Gunnie's skirts in no time.' The pleasure she takes in saying this is obvious, and I wonder when the antagonism between these two got to be so very pronounced.

'What is their latest escapade?' Oonagh asks. 'Has Baby been dressing up as a reporter again? Or as "Madame Vorolsky" with her jewels for sale and sad stories?'

'*I must educate my leetle boy*,' Maureen says, '*Ve haf ezzerysing taken from us by zose cruel Communistes . . .*'

The two of them go off into peals of laughter, but Aileen says crossly, 'It isn't, it's much worse. Wait till Mamma hears. And she will, you know. If she hasn't already. Gloomy Beatrice rang her up first thing this morning.'

Sure enough, it isn't long before Cloé arrives,

sweeping in with a rustle of her skirts, Gunnie in tow, and says, 'Put down the cards, girls, I need to have a little talk with you.' Maureen rolls her eyes, but carefully, behind Cloé so that she can't be seen. Gunnie sees, I know, because she looks away quickly and very firmly. 'I have heard a most distressing tale, from Beatrice.'

'Gloomy Beatrice?' Maureen says.

'Don't call her that.'

'But you do.'

'That is different. It's disrespectful when you do it. But that is not what I came to say to you. It seems . . .' she pauses, whether for weight or courage I cannot tell, '. . . it seems that there has been an unpleasant incident at Beatrice's Surrey house.' Another pause. 'There was a break-in while the family were at dinner. Beatrice's pearls were taken. And Mrs Asquith, a guest that night, had her nightdress burned. In her bedroom.' A snort of laughter from Maureen that she tries to cover with a cough. I do the same, I cannot help it, but fake mine as a sneeze. Looking up, I see that Maureen's eyes are entirely wet with mirth and I cannot imagine how she will hold it in.

'It isn't funny,' Cloé continues. 'The police were called. That's when it emerged that the break-in was by *friends* of Baby and Zita. The girls themselves may even have been involved.'

'Almost certainly,' Oonagh says solemnly. She, too, is flushed with the effort of not laughing.

'Well, I hope you see the gravity of the incident,' Cloé says. 'It was very nearly a scandal. Only a great deal of apologising by all concerned has averted that.'

'Well, that's all right, then,' says Maureen.

'It is not,' says Cloé. 'Do you not see, this whole business has got entirely out of hand? If those are *pranks*, then those girls have a very distorted sense of what is fitting. And if they do – well, I worry that you do also.'

'But what on earth has it got to do with us?' Maureen demands.

'I do not like the way you are running around at all hours of the night, with goodness knows who.'

'But you do know, Mamma, you've met them. Baby, Zita, Bryan, Stephen.'

'Them! Oh, I know very well that you are careful that I meet some of your friends. But do not tell me that is all, because we both know very well that it is not. I only have to read the newspapers to see that you are in company with actors and musicians and all manner of Bohemians. I do not know what you do and I do not know where you go, or with whom. Until now I have trusted you, and indeed the antics of your friends seemed like a lot of high jinks, nothing more. But I am starting to wonder.'

It is, for Cloé, a long speech. She, like Ernest, prefers to deal in short sentences and specific questions or instructions. I see that she is at war with herself – the desire to forbid Maureen, in fact, all three of them, outright, from society that she has begun to find alarming, against the fear that Maureen will defy her openly.

Maureen says nothing, so after a moment, Cloé continues. 'You know I can stop your allowance,' she says.

'Of course. Always money with you,' says Maureen, which is unfair to Cloé. 'Anyway, Elizabeth and Brenda never have any money at all and they seem to live perfectly well. It can't be that hard.'

'They live off you,' Aileen says drily. It is true that Maureen's generous allowance is made to stretch far indeed, making me think at times of a large silk umbrella, with many bodies crammed in underneath.

'It is not come to that yet,' Cloé backtracks hastily. As she has become sicker, Cloé has begun to rely more on Maureen filling the house with amusing people and bringing her news. Gunnie is no good for that, and Aileen is either unwilling or less able, and so it is Maureen she looks to, for entertainment and a hold on the world, even an indirect one, so that now she is torn. 'I would just like you to be more careful who you go about with. Fliss, what do you think of this set?'

All three of the girls look at me, those three sets of blue eyes expectant. Again, I say what I think will smooth things over. 'I think,' I begin cautiously, 'that they are sometimes thoughtless, and certainly giddy, but there is no real harm in any of them.' But as I speak, I wonder if it is true. Of Bryan, certainly, and even Elizabeth, with her insatiable, absurd appetite for fun. Baby and Zita, too, are foolish, and often go too far, but are not malicious. Even Bert, Baby's prizefighter, for all his solid heft, is a good-hearted fellow. But there are others of whom I am less certain. Brenda troubles me. Those stick-thin arms and that vacant gaze; the habits of Berlin that Stephen hinted at, which may have travelled home with her. Even Stephen, who is perhaps not himself bad, but who is a kind of spur to the badness of others. There is always some kind of drama swirling around Stephen, and even though he stays aloof, clear, just about – the hems of his trousers skimming the mud – he is, all the same, the pulse behind it.

'They play at destruction' is how Richard puts it when I describe the scene to him. 'They make a great show of pulling all down around them. But they have nothing to put in place of what they tear apart, and they haven't realised that yet.'

He makes me feel that my vigilance is wise, rather than the foolish caution that Maureen dismisses.

Of course, soon after I understood that Cloé asked, and I answered, the wrong question. It is not whether those frivolous young people are bad; it is whether they are bad for the girls. Bad for Aileen, Maureen and Oonagh. That is what we should have asked.

Chapter Thirty-three

I understand that by quizzing her girls, Cloé, in her stilted way, was trying to articulate a concern that is growing. Certainly among the parents of this set of Maureen's. She may have phrased it badly – too stuck on the shame of the potential scandal to properly spell out that the joke bordered on cruel. The taking of the necklace – of course it wasn't actual theft, just japes – was bad, but the burning of a nightgown – something so intimate, in the very bedroom of Mrs Asquith – well, that had a nasty hint to it. And soon, it seems to me, from my place of watching, that there is a split in the group of merrymakers. There are those like Bryan, who tire of the antics – by now, he can talk of nothing but Diana Mitford, and spends as much time as he can at Batsford because she is not often allowed up to London – and those like Elizabeth and Brenda, who grow ever wilder.

Even in the family, the split is obvious. Aileen, like Bryan, is weary of the endless costume parties and treasure hunts. 'I don't know what comes next,' she says to me one afternoon when it is just she and I for tea. 'I try to imagine, but I can't see it. Nothing is as I expected. I am twenty-two. I can't keep on like this, an unmarried daughter at home, with Maureen and now Oonagh pushing up behind me. I should be married, with a house of my own.'

'Is there no one . . . ?' I ask.

'No. No one. Oh yes, there are plenty of chaps who would, I'm sure, if I encouraged them, but no one who, you know . . .'
I knew. No one who made her heart beat faster, the turn of whose head something she recognised and looked for. No one whose voice always reached her ears even when other voices were so loud and so many that it seemed as though nothing could get through.

'There will be,' I say. 'I am sure of it.'

'I hope you're right.' Then, 'You know Papa thinks very highly of Richard? I think he must be right. We spoke for almost half an hour the other day, waiting for you to come in, and I swear, it was the first sensible conversation I've had in an age. He is a good fellow.' She looks so intently at me that I begin to blush, even though I can't think what I am blushing for and want to tell her so.

Maureen, of course, shows no signs of boredom. If anything, she is more devoted than ever to pursuing this endless ragtag party, a kind of sea serpent with many coils, that pops up now in Belgravia, now in Chelsea, now at the weekend homes of various friends, but is always somehow the same party. The same people, the same excitement, the same antics.

Too often still, I go with her. There are long drives to country houses, made longer by the many stops. 'One teensy-weensy drink?' someone will say, to be answered with 'Oh, I think so.' And then we will find some quiet pub and pile into it, taking up space in front of the fire, loudly exclaiming and laughing, calling for drinks that no one outside the tiny patch of London that is their stomping ground has heard of, followed by much cheery making-do – 'I think cider is just as nice as champagne, don't you?' – some self-consciously gay chatter, and then, 'We'd best be off.' And we are gone, knowing, or not knowing, that behind us are ordinary people, outraged, infuriated, who will talk of our visit for weeks: 'She was wearing *trousers*. Hussy'; 'It wasn't her I minded, did you see *him* . . . ?'

I, unable to be careless as they are, am mortified. More so later on when we arrive at, say, Stephen's home, Wilsford Manor, or Shulbrede, where Elizabeth's parents live, to find their honest efforts to entertain us all are mocked and rebuked as insufficient. Watching the delicately restrained disgust with which Elizabeth's father opens yet another bottle of brandy, before dinner is even served, I wonder how they can. How she can. But they do and she does, and if they notice at all, it is only as a blow in the battle of Them and Us that they are determined to wage and win. I am not Them, or Us, and maybe that's why I see it.

'They seem nice,' I say to Maureen about Elizabeth's parents, Arthur and Dorothea.

'What?' She is confused.

'They seem nice?'

'Do they? I mean, yes, I'm sure they do. Isn't she funny, though, with her creaking knees?'

Elizabeth is blind, or worse, to the insults heaped so casually on her parents. Like Maureen, she cannot let go of the serpent's tail. She is, I think, like one of Ernest's machines that has been over-wound. Unlike most of that set, Elizabeth works, as a fashion model but she is forever changing boutiques. When she tells stories at parties – with much wild exaggeration, to even more admiring laughter – of being three hours late, or falling asleep in the middle of the day, it is not hard to see why this might be.

In between these jobs, she has taken to inviting me to tea, or for a stroll. At first, I worry that she will ask me to help her in her more frantic capers and plan how I might say no, but she never does. Instead, I see her differently at these times, more serious, with something wistful behind the smile that lifts only her top lip, showing teeth so large I wonder how they can fit comfortably in her mouth.

'I like you, Fliss,' she says in her abrupt way, blowing smoke into my face as we sit across from one another at Lyons Corner House on Oxford Street. Elizabeth has ordered walnut cake with her tea that I know she won't eat. 'I may call you Fliss, mayn't I?' I say nothing and she continues, 'I feel that you and I are alike in some ways.' I cannot think of a single one, but again I say nothing, letting her speak. 'We must both make our way in the world,' she says then, so that I understand she is talking about money. Sure enough, 'It is different for Maureen or Aileen or Oonagh, different for a Guinness.' There is a tinny sound of bitterness there. 'Different, too, for Baby and Zita. They have claims on Guinness money. No such comfort for us, eh?'

'Certainly *I* must,' I say. I don't spell out all the ways in which it is ridiculous that she, daughter of an under-secretary of state, says we are the same. 'I plan to get a job,' I say. 'When I have my certificates.'

'So I hear. One of those modern girls? Sharing a flat in Chelsea with other modern girls, all drying stockings over the bath and heading off to work every morning?'

'I hope there will be more to it than that,' I say with a laugh. She blows more smoke at me, mouth pursed like a disappointed baby. 'Gasper?' she asks, pushing a gold cigarette case across the table towards me.

'No, thanks.'

'I forgot. You don't, do you? Why not?'

'I never liked the taste,' I say. 'So will you continue to be a fashion model?'

'Heavens, no. That is just a way to fill time and persuade my mamma, who worries about such things, that I am doing something. It is most killingly boring, you know. No, I shan't keep this up.'

'Well, then, you will get married,' I say.

'Do you know how old I am?'

'No.'

'I'm twenty-six. You see.' I did see. I hadn't known she was that age. 'In any case, I rather think the men I like are not quite the marrying kind,' she continues thoughtfully. 'Baby's prize-fighter . . . now there's a man.' She gives me a look from under those heavy lids and laughs. 'You have no idea what I mean, do you?' I confess that I do not, and she continues, 'It is rather sickening, though, isn't it?'

'What is?'

She doesn't answer. Blows more smoke, crumbles a piece of walnut cake that has arrived on a white china plate and arranges the crumbs into a neat pattern – she has pretty, delicate hands – then says slyly, 'There is a rather delicious irony that the source of their wealth is also the cause of their trouble.'

'What do you mean?'

'Exactly what I say.' She gives another twitch of the top lip, a flash of square white teeth. 'Maureen especially. But Oonagh now too. Although perhaps it's the cause of all our troubles.' I am still baffled, and she sees it. 'If you don't know – you'll have to work it out.'

I think of Mummie, all those years ago: *You'll have to work that out for yourself, won't you?* I hadn't understood her. Did I understand now? Perhaps, a little.

Did I understand Elizabeth? Not at all. Not then.

'I don't see that you have troubles,' I say. 'You are all so very gay.'

'Gay? I suppose we are.' She makes a strange, painful shape with her mouth, lifting it at the corners as though smiling, but without moving the rest of her face so that it is almost a grimace. 'I'm sure we seem to be. I'm surprised you, of all people, don't know the difference. Poor Fliss – so good at watching, so bad at seeing.' She pats my hand with hers, mocking me with the pretence at sympathy. 'Now, shall we abandon this' – she waves a hand in disgust at the cluster of crumbs and half-filled teacups – 'and go and have a drink next door?'

Chapter Thirty-four

'Hot news,' says Oonagh, opening the door of my little library where I am tap-tap-tapping at typewriter keys.

'What?'

'Bryan has a visitor and they are both come to see us. It is Brinny.'

'Who?'

'Brinny. Brinsley Sheridan Plunket, you goose. You remember, from the tennis and dancing party, all those years ago? So you'd better hurry down. And change. If Mamma sees you in that . . . well, *quelle horreur*.' She, too, like Maureen, has taken to sprinkling phrases of French through her conversation, which has the effect of making everything she says more distant and unreal. She is wearing a gorgeous green-and-white-striped dress with narrow pleats and triangular pockets, and looks older, now, than her years; sophisticated and yet gamine, somewhere between bewitching child and elegant young lady.

Stephen has come too, and beside him and Bryan, both so languid and worldly, Brinny is like a door blown open onto a hillside, letting in rough, bracing air and views of wide, heather-sprung spaces. He stands in front of the fireplace, and he has about him a smell that makes me catch my breath – leather, horses, Russian cigarettes. It is the smell of my childhood, of hunting and Hughie; of Richard before he began to work in the office; of men who do not dance all night but fall asleep after dinner, worn out by physical exertion. I had no idea how much I'd missed it until I found it there unexpectedly; fighting – defeating – Maureen's Parisian scent, Gunnie's talc, the bowls of rose petal potpourri Oonagh and I have set out.

Gunnie, more at home in conversation than she ever is with Bryan or Stephen, is enthusiastically asking after what seems like every member of Brinny's family, of whom there is a vast number – 'How is dear Helen? And Moira? And Joyce?' – which he answers with a good-natured 'jolly well'. It is only when she falls silent, having run out of extended Plunkets to enquire about, that Brinny has a chance to hear what Maureen and Bryan are discussing. And of course, it is Driberg's column and the latest antics of their friends. I watch him as he listens – they throw names and tales back and forth like two people batting a brightly coloured ball – and can see the honest puzzlement growing in his eyes. Eventually, they, too, run out of gossip.

'We remember you, you know,' Maureen says suddenly to Brinny.

'I remember you too,' Brinny says, but I think he is being polite.

'You came and played tennis,' Oonagh says. 'And then you danced with Aileen at the party we gave, and she was jolly pleased.'

'Oonagh!' Aileen, I see to my surprise, is blushing.

'Well, he did, and you were.' Oonagh looks around, appealing to Gunnie and Cloé, but neither says anything and Gunnie changes the subject: 'Where do you hunt?' she asks, and again I hear how she rejoices in the solid ground under her, anticipating a response that will make sense. She and Brinny have a reassuring conversation about hunting, and then golf, in which he is apparently much interested, and I can see Gunnie is ready to move on to fishing, or perhaps shooting, when Brinny turns to Aileen.

'Do you race?' he asks.

'Horses?'

'Motorcars,' he says. 'Though horses too.'

'I don't know,' she says. 'Perhaps I do?' And she smiles radiantly up at him so that he is quiet for a moment.

Then, 'Perhaps I may take you all racing, to Brooklands?' He appeals to Cloé, and I can see that she is touched by his assumption that her permission is required. It is a long time now since anyone has asked for her approval.

'I think it a splendid idea,' she says.

'It's thirty miles,' he says, 'but I have a new car, a Delage, that will do that in no time at all. Soon there will be the first-ever British Grand Prix . . .' He carries on, talking racing and motors until Maureen interrupts him abruptly.

'That's enough of that. Now, what shall we do this evening?' and begins to plot with Bryan and Stephen, who has so far said nothing except to murmur, 'How exhausting you make everything sound,' when Brinny recounts how many miles to the hour his Delage will do.

But Gunnie is not the only one to find Brinny's conversation reassuring. 'Such a relief to have someone who talks about normal things,' Aileen says later, as we dress for dinner. She is more than usually careful with her toilette, I notice, asking her maid to zip her into a sleek dress of midnight-blue satin and fixing long diamond drop earrings.

After dinner, Bryan and Brinny collect us and we go to the bar at the Cavendish Hotel, which by now has become a kind of den for Maureen and her set. The poor old majors, who once sat on the fringes spluttering into their brandy-and-ginger-ales as young men in sequins wandered by, are gone, or carefully hidden by Rosa Lewis, the hotel's flamboyant proprietor. Maureen dislikes her intensely but Bryan, amused, insists, 'She's something of a genius, such a divine blend of benign democrat and savage autocrat.' By which he means that Rosa refuses entry at will, encourages her favourites in all manner of excesses, and casually bills whoever happens to be the richest man present – for everything. I am far from a favourite – she is more fond of Elizabeth, and devoted to Oonagh, whom she calls 'sweet child' with true affection – but she tolerates me and will often find me a quiet corner to sit in, for which I am grateful, saying, 'There now, that ought to do you,' absently as she moves off.

The bar is dingy and smells of boiled mutton. I can never understand why these gorgeous creatures choose somewhere so scruffy, unless it is the charm of contrast. And indeed the scuffed wooden panelling and low, smoke-yellowed ceiling offer no competition to the gaudy crowd and their hangers-on who throng here – excitable debs come to sightsee, a smattering of older men whose presence I never fully understand (they watch but do not join in) and the musicians, tumblers and pretty Bohemians who all make their living from the fevered churn at the centre of this group.

Brinny scorns the quiet corner I suggest. Clearly uncomfortable in this company, he is nevertheless not the sort for quiet corners. At the bar he orders a brandy and soda, then looks carefully around, taking his time to consider what he sees. 'It is a Bacchanalia,' he says at last in disgust. Then, 'Is that a girl or a chap?' as a friend of Stephen's with blue-black hair walks by, dressed in a kind of Pierrot suit of trousers and tunic, hair falling onto his forehead and curling down over the ruff.

'A chap,' I say.

'And that?' He points to a girl I have not seen before, whose dark blonde hair is cut savagely short, wearing trousers and a man's dinner jacket with sequins on the lapels, who drifts by with a glass held up in front of her like a sacred light she must follow.

'A girl.'

'Why is it so difficult to tell?' He sounds peevish and I am glad when Aileen comes to join us.

'Come and meet some people,' she says to him.

'Righto.' He looks wary but follows her. I watch as they approach different groups, and I keep watching as they are quickly spat out by one and then another. It cannot be Aileen, I know, so it must be Brinny's hearty sporting talk. That doesn't surprise me. What does, a little, is that each time a group breaks up and reforms with Brinny on the outside, Aileen goes with him. Soon they give up and are back with me at my vantage point at the end of the bar when Oonagh skips over, pulling a girl no older than her by the hand, a neat blonde like a picture on a chocolate box, with golden-brown eyes and a gaze of such exaggerated candour that I find I cannot but wonder what she hides.

'See who I have found?' Oonagh says in delight. 'It's Violet, from school. Violet Valerie French.' Dimly I remember Maureen saying 'preposterous name, but such fun'. Her name, I decide, suits her, the childish-sounding nature of it: 'Violet-Valerie-French'.

'She is not yet out either,' Oonagh is saying, 'but she's like me. She's not waiting. Violet has a sister, Essex – can you imagine? – who is older and brings her about, just as Maureen does with me.'

Violet smiles at each of us, turning obediently to one after another: 'How do you do?'

'Fliss, only guess what?' Oonagh says.

'What?'

'Violet is engaged. Already. To an American.'

'Goodness,' I say. 'Are you indeed?' I don't know what else to say.

'He is called Henry,' Violet says. 'Henry Bradley Martin. I suppose you've heard of the Bradley-Martin Ball, in New York?' She looks around, eager to be modest, and I expect her to be deflated when Aileen says 'no' without interest, but her face gives nothing away.

'Here's Essex now,' says Oonagh. Essex is brunette to Violet's blonde, dark to her light.

'More sisters?' Maureen remarks, as she joins us. Then, 'I say, Aileen, sitting out?' with a malicious look.

'Hardly,' Aileen says coolly. 'Sitting down, for a moment, not out. I would have thought *you* would know the difference.' This, so pointed a reference to Maureen's unpopular days, stings – I can see it does, although Maureen instantly covers it with a toss of the head – but much more unfortunately, Brinny laughs. He cannot know what Aileen means, because surely she wouldn't tell him that. He is laughing to be polite, or because he doesn't know what to say, or simply because he wishes to please Aileen, but it's a mistake. There is a flicker in Maureen's eyes that says she will not forgive, and even though she leaves then, I am not at all surprised when she makes a point of coming back a short time later and saying loudly, 'Look, isn't Elizabeth *drunk*,' in tones of marvel as Elizabeth stumbles past, pursued by two young men in matching chiffon scarves. She is making sure Brinny sees what Aileen would much rather he didn't, certainly not at this stage of their friendship, and that is the loucheness, the accepted visible debauchery of this set.

'Surely not?' Brinny is revolted. 'And if she was, no one would mention it.'

'No, no, just tired . . .' Aileen gives Maureen a quelling look, but it's too late.

'Oh, drunk as a lord,' Maureen says, 'very decidedly. Always is, you know. Unless of course it's uppies. It could be.'

'Maureen!' Aileen now is herself shocked, truly shocked, not pretending to be for Brinny's sake – he is simply confused, as I am, as to what 'uppies' are – and for a minute it looks as if Maureen knows she has gone too far, but even as she teeters on the edge of a conciliation, I see her plunge right over with another indifferent toss of her head.

'Well, it jolly well could. It's quite the thing now,' she says and disappears into the throng.

For all Maureen's mischief-making, it's obvious that Brinny is very taken with Aileen, whom he looks at with a kind of shyness that, I think, surprises him very much.

'You don't think Aileen really cares for all this sort of thing, do you?' he asks me anxiously at one point, when the noise of the room is such that it is like a howling dog straining at its leash.

'I'm fairly sure she does not,' I say, recalling her conversation on the stairs at Regent's Park Road, and watch him somewhat reassured.

We go on then, to a party on Arlington Street that is quickly deemed 'too bogus for words' and then the Gargoyle Club, where we stand outside waiting to be let in while Maureen and Stephen poke fun at a nearby window plastered with bills recommending something called The Funfair Casino.

'The Unfair Casino,' Stephen says.

'I say, that's good,' says Maureen, dissolving into giggles and repeating, 'Unfair Casino, Do-You-Dare Casino' and variations, until Brinny begins giving her suspicious looks.

'I think I'd like to go home now,' Aileen says, looking from one to the other.

'I'll take you,' Brinny says immediately and they leave. I long to go with them but Oonagh says, 'Oh just a little longer, Fliss, please, may I?'

when I suggest it. Violet and Essex are with us too. Oonagh has her arm tucked through Violet's and calls her 'Valsie', and it is clear that they have decided to adopt one another.

The next morning Aileen is full of 'Brinny says . . .' and when Maureen announces, 'I am going down to Wilsford Manor with Elizabeth for Friday-to-Monday,' and Aileen says, colouring pink, 'I might cry off. Brinny has offered to take me to visit his sister Joyce, who is in London,' it is obvious what is afoot and does not even require Maureen to say, 'I see,' in significant tones, or Gunnie to look a question at Cloé that is answered with a smile.

Chapter Thirty-five

Many weeks go by and after all nothing is said. There are trips and jaunts, to flower shows, motor displays, even talk of the Newhaven regatta, and Brinny is to be found almost every afternoon at Grosvenor Place, taking tea and conversing pleasantly with Gunnie and Cloé. But the words are not spoken and so nothing changes. He is still, on the surface, a visitor to all the family – as much a friend to Ernest, say, with whom he talks about the government in Ireland and their unfortunate trade practices, as he is to Aileen. The trouble for him is that, so constant a visitor, but without the protection of being anyone special, he is soon a target for Maureen's wit.

'I know who it is you remind me of,' she says to him one day with a long, considering look.

'And who is that?' His tone, I long to tell him, is all wrong. He answers Maureen as if she were a bothersome child. It infuriates her.

'The Great Oojah,' she says triumphantly, narrowing her eyes and smirking at him, daring him to take offence. As so often with Maureen, the wickedness of her wit is matched only by the brilliance, and I have to bite my lip to stop from laughing out loud.

'From the comic strip,' Oonagh supplies. Evidently, they have discussed it. The Great Oojah is an elephant, from a strip we used to read in Gunnie's *Daily Sketch*. His friends are a sleek black cat, Snooker, and a tiny little blond boy, Don, so that Oojah is forever lumbering in comparison, a genial but clumsy and absurd presence on the page. And even though Brinny looks nothing, nothing at all, like an elephant, there is something in the large chin, more again in the protective way he stands over Aileen, who is small and golden like Don, that means I can see where Maureen's malicious inspiration lies.

'I don't know what you mean,' Brinny says, looking at each of us in turn for enlightenment, reassurance. Oonagh, seated on a footstool, is doubled over with laughter.

'Maureen, how dare you—' Aileen begins, but Cloé breaks in immediately.

'You are being very silly,' she says, and her warning look is for Aileen, not Maureen. It is a look that says, *Make this nothing before it becomes something,* and so Aileen falls silent. 'I think you'd better go and call Gunnie, Maureen,' Cloé says.

'Can't Lapham?' Maureen says idly, but she rises and leaves the room anyway and we hear her footsteps, loud on the apricot-coloured marble of the stairs as she skips down.

Probably, she has forgotten the incident within an hour. But Aileen has not. 'I will throttle her,' she says to me later. 'If she spoils this for me, I will kill her.' There is nothing at all in Aileen's slender frame to suggest menace, but there is so much anger squashed into those words, her face is so horribly white as she says them, that she is almost frightening.

Such is the animosity between the two now, that as Aileen falters in the absence of any certainty from Brinny, Maureen, in response, seems to grow stronger. She expands, is indomitable, splendid, certain, and has entirely brought Oonagh over to her side, mostly by ensuring that she – and now Violet too – is included in all the fun of which Maureen is caretaker and gatekeeper.

'Do you not feel for her?' I ask on one of our walks.

'Aileen? No. Why should I? Because the Great Oojah hasn't done the decent yet?'

'Be serious.'

'I am,' she protests. 'No. If she cannot bring him to ask, well, that's her lookout. Now, what shall I wear to this party? The theme is to be Circuses. I thought perhaps an acrobat . . . unless one were to go as a lion tamer?'

In the end, though, it is Maureen, indirectly and unwittingly, who breaks whatever is holding Brinny back. It is September, and after the disappointments of a chilly summer it is, again, beautiful. A late heatwave holds the city tight, and Cloé, who does not care for the heat, is more than usually miserable.

I have examinations to prepare for, and so I stay firm in the face of Maureen and Oonagh's pleadings of 'Please come, Fliss, do!'

'I can't! I won't!' I say, and no matter how much they make me laugh, Oonagh pulling faces and Maureen leaving little folded notes on my bed in her spidery scrawl with indifferent spelling, I hold firm. Violet, who seems now to haunt the house and is a great favourite with Gunnie, who admires her chocolate box beauty no end and is susceptible to the girl's insinuating ways, adds her voice, saying, 'Oh yes, do!', but without any spark to suggest she means it.

Aileen does not want to go either, but they work on her until she sullenly agrees. 'I wish you were coming,' she says with a sigh, as we assemble in the drawing room for a cocktail before they go out. She is twisting a thick diamond bracelet on her wrist and looks tired, certainly beside Maureen, shimmering in pearl-grey cut tight across the hips flaring to a zig-zag hem trimmed in jet beads that swish and click as she moves. Oonagh and Violet, fizzing with excitement, are dressed almost identically in gold and black, like two lively little bumblebees.

Bryan and Brinny call for them and they leave, spilling noisily down the steps and into an evening that is already deepening, although the heat lingers. Over the butterscotch-dipped trees of Buckingham Palace garden, a flock of starlings are whirling and whirling, picking up speed and mass as they circle. I wave them off and it isn't until after I am home from Croydon the next day that I learn what has happened.

Lapham lets me in and, even though it is far too late for tea, he says, 'They are all in the drawing room, Miss Felicity,' from which phrase, and by the smallest twitch of an eyebrow, I know something has happened.

'Only guess,' Maureen calls to me as I enter, still in my neat navy suit, even though I know Cloé doesn't like to see me dressed like that. 'The Great Oojah has come up to scratch at last.'

No one even bothers to say 'Maureen!' They are all too busy smiling, and Aileen waves me over to sit beside her.

'It's true,' she says, 'he asked me!'

'And?' I say, even though there is no doubt.

'She said yes almost before he'd asked the question,' says Maureen.

'How would you know, you weren't there,' Aileen shoots back.

Maureen ignores her. 'Imagine if he'd only intended to ask "Will you . . . show me the way to Piccadilly?" and Aileen said yes before he got to the end of the sentence. Wouldn't he be sick now? He'd have to run away to sea, or pretend to die in a motor accident, to escape.' She can hardly get her words out for laughing, but no one, not even Oonagh, laughs with her. 'Oh, very well, tell it your way,' she sighs.

'It was the party,' Aileen begins. 'Such a terrible party.'

'Such fun,' Maureen interjects belligerently.

'Terrible,' Aileen insists. 'You know the kind of thing. Utterly sick-making. Girls in silk pyjamas, everybody shrieking. Bottles everywhere, stories that no one ever finishes and every single one of them looking desperately around for somewhere new and funnier to go, some new and sillier joke to play. Brinny hated it, even more than he usually hates such things. But he didn't say anything, you see. He never did because he thought I enjoyed it all. I know this now.' She holds up an instructing finger. 'I had no idea last night, although I suspected, but because he never said anything . . . Well, anyway, Sir Francis Laking was there, a face full of make-up and dressed in a lady's ballgown—'

'He did look divine . . .' Maureen murmurs.

'—such a ridiculous young man.'

'Tallulah Bankhead's *secretary*,' Maureen says. If there is any one person Maureen, not given to admiration, can be said to admire, it is this Tallulah, an actress and an American, I understand, but more than that, the darling of London society, or the bit of it that Maureen cares for anyway.

'Ridiculous!' Aileen insists, and carries on, a story that is interrupted often by Oonagh, clarifying, and Maureen, contradicting, but seems to be that this Sir Francis, late in the evening after too many cocktails, removed the ballgown, and all his other clothes, and began to Charleston entirely naked. At this point in the story, Maureen is screaming so hard with laughter that I can barely hear, but Gunnie, Cloé, even Oonagh, though she tries to hide it, are very shocked. 'You should have seen his—' Maureen begins, and only an immediate 'Enough!', loud, firm, from Cloé prevents her.

It seems that Brinny watched for a while as a group of young men tried to wrap Sir Francis discreetly in a dressing gown belonging to the host, but he would keep escaping and none of the young men were steady enough, or indeed concerned enough, to make any progress until Brinny took matters into his own hands. He joined in, bundled Sir Francis into the dressing gown, tied it tight with the cord and prevailed upon him to sit down in an armchair, then put a rug over him and told him firmly it was time for sleep, at which Sir Francis is supposed to have opened one suddenly docile eye and said, 'Very well, for you, then, but only because you are *entirely* divine,' and nodded off like a child.

Brinny, perhaps fired up with the success of his intervention, certainly egged on by Bryan, tired of all the to-ing and fro-ing, and in love with love, accosted Aileen and demanded bluntly, 'Here, how can you possibly put up with this rot?' to which she said, 'But I can't bear it and simply long for something to take me away from it entirely.'

'And that was that,' Aileen concludes happily. 'At very last we understood one another.'

Maureen rolls her eyes. 'All thanks to Sir

Francis Laking. Perhaps he should be best man at the wedding?'

'Ah yes, the wedding,' says Gunnie in great excitement. 'St Margaret's, of course?'

'Of course,' Aileen says. 'When? Mamma?'

'Next year,' says Cloé. 'That will give us time.' Already she looks drained at the prospect.

Later, before dinner, I seek out Gunnie in her room. She is embroidering, head bent low over her silks in a pool of yellow light from the lamp on her bureau. 'May I come in?'

'Please.'

'Is it a good match?' I ask, leaning against the brass bedpost glowing hot and golden in the light. I am trying to understand how all the 'Improvement Conversations', which I had taken to mean that only the grandest of titles would be acceptable, are now come to this joy at a mere 'Honourable'.

'It will do,' says Gunnie comfortably.

'But she is a Guinness . . .'

'That is true.'

'And so, how will it do?'

'Well, let's see,' she says, settling back, fingers busy, mind busy too as she delicately parses the question of Aileen's marriage. 'The Plunkets are a good family . . .'

'But he is a younger son?'

'He is, and that is a pity. But with what she has

. . . well, that won't matter to them. They are fond of one another.' Gunnie would never speak of love. She would find a word like that melodramatic, almost violent. 'Fond', with a dash of special emphasis, is as far as she will go.

'So it would seem,' I agree with a smile.

'And there is her age . . .'

'Twenty-two.'

'Yes, twenty-two. Twenty-three by the middle of next Season. With Maureen behind her, Oonagh now too. No. It won't do. She needs her own establishment.' Which of course is exactly what Aileen herself said. How do they know these things? Do they feel them, the way the starlings from the previous night's circling know that winter is on the way and it is time to be gone, even though the days have been warm and more like to summer than summer was? 'It's time,' Gunnie says with certainty, and breaks off a peacock-blue thread with a neat snip of her front teeth.

'Where will they live?'

'I don't know. That will be for them to decide. And Ernest, who must buy them a house.'

Maureen, waiting in my room for me, lying face down on my bed kicking her legs up behind her and flicking through one of my shorthand books, is far less cosy about it all. 'Not much of a match, is it?' she says gleefully. 'Only an Honourable. She'll be

"Mrs Brinsley Plunket". Who I imagine as a stout person in heavy purple with giant ostrich feathers quivering in her hair.'

'Which doesn't sound one bit like Aileen. Anyway, she wants to be Mrs Brinsley Plunket.'

'More fool her,' Maureen mutters, and I understand suddenly – it's not the match, or not really. It's the marriage, the wedding, the attention on Aileen and the fact that she has something Maureen doesn't. I want to laugh but I don't. She'd hate it. 'And he's a cousin too,' Maureen says, cheering up a bit. 'How shame-making!'

'You said yourself that almost everyone is a cousin. Anyway, a cousin how?'

'His grandmother was a sister of Grandpapa's. Or something . . .' She waves a hand airily, then rolls over onto her back holding my book above her head and flicks a couple of pages. 'What is all this squiggly nonsense anyway?'

Chapter Thirty-six

Grosvenor Place, London, 1927

Once my examinations are finished, I find a job, in a small publishing company in Islington where I am a 'Girl Friday' to the managing director. A job, I soon find, is not at all like studying. The Pitman Training Centre was a place I went to and left, surrounded by people who could have been made of cardboard so little did they impact me, while my proper life was still at Grosvenor Place. It wasn't real the way that the house and the people in it were real. This job, though, is. It is like a new home and a new family.

There is Mr Pearson, the managing director, whose life I must smooth and simplify. My duties are typing, taking dictation, posting letters, attending meetings and taking notes, keeping his office neat, keeping track of the pieces of paper on which he scribbles ideas and the rise and fall of his temper depending on the time of day and week and publishing schedule.

There is Jennifer, a year older, who has been here a year longer. She is me to Mr White, the editor, and she is able to show me where typewriter ribbons are kept, the nearest post office and how Mr Pearson takes his tea. She is cheerful and pleasant, and delighted to see me. 'One is enough,' she says, rolling her eyes at the closed doors behind which Mr Pearson and Mr White sit at their desks. 'Thank goodness they've brought you in,' and then, putting out a hand to shake, 'Call me Jen.'

Jen knows about the morning tea break and our lunch hour, and the best places to go, whether a teashop or café, and clever ways to make our pennies stretch. She talks so much about our pay and 'making it go further' that I feel guilt because mine does not have to, not like hers. I do not have my board to pay for, as she does. Jen lives at home but gives 'something' to her mother – and even though – or perhaps because – she is my first female friend who isn't a Guinness, or introduced to me by a Guinness, I feel I can't tell her the truth of my situation, and so I am vague about where I live:

'with family friends, near Green Park'. Green Park has its seedier side too, so I am not automatically suspected of luxury.

She likes to tell me when there is a sale on fabric in Liberty, or the best place to buy stockings, and does this in a spirit of survival and sharing so that I am sorry not to be able to reciprocate. But I know of nothing to tell her – that Oonagh buys gloves, in silk and kid, five and six pairs at a time, then leaves them in motorcars all over town? That Maureen scorns to wear the same dress more than half a dozen times and says herself that she 'cannot sometimes get out of bed without knowing I have something new and pretty to put on'?

Already Jen has noticed my clothes, even though these are the most discreet, the oldest, of what I have, but I have told her I am lucky enough to have a generous relative, at which she laughs heartily and says, 'I had one too, an older cousin, but then I grew bigger than her and now her generosity is all for my younger sister,' so that I know it is OK and there is no need to say more. Sometimes she will tease me when we are at lunch and say, 'No second helpings if you hope to keep up that wardrobe.'

I feel ungenerous and sly in my silences, especially because Jen herself is so artlessly forthcoming. Within just a few weeks, I know that there is a father dead in the war, and a brother,

Peter, at home who cannot get a job, one of the millions of men who cannot. I know that 'he is about the house too much and on Mother's nerves frightfully'. I know about the younger sister, Susan, 'the pretty one', Jen says, who is pretty herself with a round face and dark springy curls. But I cannot tell her anything much about myself that occurred beyond the age of eleven. I can tell her about my own father, dead in the same war so there is another bond between us, but I cannot tell her about Hughie, about going to live with Cloé's 'girls', or any of it. I wouldn't know how.

Instead, I introduce her to Richard over tea in the small hotel where he stays, on one of his visits, and he is so exactly the kind of young man that Jen would expect – conscientious, quiet, serious – that he acts as a sort of guarantee; as Richard is, so she presumes the family I live with must be. And even though he has said, 'I can't lie, Fliss,' when I explain to him that Jen knows nothing of the Guinnesses, he is decent about keeping my secret and says nothing more than she asks him, even though I know he doesn't approve of the duplicity.

'Far better to tell,' he says.

'Easy for you to say,' I respond. 'You work for Ernest. That's perfectly simple and straightforward. I don't even know what I would say. How I would describe what I am in that house.' I had never told

Richard that Ernest had offered me a Season, not Maureen or Oonagh either. Mildred was the only one I ever told. 'Interesting,' was all she said. 'He never offered me that.'

Jen is a great reader of 'The Columns', as she calls them – meaning, mostly, the doings of that group of Maureen's friends the papers now call Bright Young People, triumphant to have a name at last, that are recorded almost daily in microscopic fascination and fawning detail. How strange it is to read of Stephen that 'his appearance alone is enough to make you catch your breath'. Or that there have been 'festivities at Longleat to celebrate the coming-of-age of Lord Bath's son and heir, the raffish-looking Viscount Weymouth' and that 'among the thirty people staying at the house was young Maureen Guinness, whose current nickname is "Teapot"', when I have watched her pack and listened to the garbled tale of some joke planned, and to know, too, that already the nickname the *Express* so chummily reveals is out of date, that she is now far more often 'Maggie', which Cloé hates, than Teapot.

Jen is unashamedly fascinated by what she reads, and wide-eyed in her admiration for those she reads about, particularly Elizabeth, about whom she seems to feel almost motherly, taking a great interest in her doings and wondering if any of those mentioned with her might be her 'young man'. 'She looks unhappy. What she needs is to find a decent, steady fellow.' I wonder if a 'decent, steady fellow' would be able to cope with Elizabeth, but of course I say nothing. The more I grow friendly with Jen, the less I feel able to tell her about my tentative place in the world that so entrances her.

For their part, Oonagh and Maureen are intrigued by Jen and my tales of her. 'Why can't we meet her?' Oonagh demands. 'Bring her for tea.' And when I refuse, saying, 'No, really, it is not a good idea,' she persists, asking, 'But why not?' And when Richard lets fall that he has met Jen, she is truly indignant. 'Why Richard and not me?' she asks, until Maureen says, 'Fliss is ashamed of us,' but with a smile that makes me think she understands my predicament.

The trouble, my trouble anyway, comes when Elizabeth, who is modelling and selling dresses in yet another dress shop, this one not far from the office where I work, becomes insistent that we meet for lunch, as we are 'both working girls'. She has a car, which she drives badly, as though it might run away with her, and therefore doesn't take the hint when I say how little time I have and I will never be able to go to her.

'So I will come to you,' she says. 'Couldn't be

simpler.' Except that I must, at all costs, keep these parts of my life separate, and so I put her off with promises of 'later'. I assume she will very quickly be indifferent to my 'later', but she isn't and continues to press. It is summer now and many of her friends are away, so she is conspicuously at a loose end. And believes that I am too, because she knows that the girls, Cloé and Gunnie are on the Riviera.

'Can't you just say you will be away for some weeks?' Maureen demanded when I said I couldn't join them.

'Surely they do not expect you to work through the summer?' Cloé said, as though I were being deliberately difficult. I had the hardest time persuading them that really, I couldn't go, and even when they were leaving, Oonagh said anxiously at the last moment, 'If you change your mind, you will come, won't you?'

'It isn't my mind,' I said, yet again, 'it is Mr Pearson's mind.'

'Well, I think he's the dreariest person alive,' Maureen said. 'You will miss all the fun.'

Violet went with them, and there are many delightful encounters planned, although Cloé is mostly going for a rest, in the hope the sea air will cure what afflicts her.

In their absence, I have Grosvenor Place almost

to myself. Lapham is with the family, and Cook with her sister at Margate so that a skeleton staff of housemaids are all that are to be found.

Chapter Thirty-seven

It's strange to me, how much I like being by myself, and the holiday atmosphere of much of the house being shut up. Ernest, if he isn't on *Fantome*, stays at his club, and very quickly, the remaining servants and I establish that we will, none of us, bother one another. Once I say I'm happy with a cold supper, to be left in the dining room and eaten when I am hungry, and I need no more than the door opened when I return from work and a cup of tea sent to my small library, we all get along beautifully. The house, uninhabited – or lightly inhabited – is a different place. It withdraws and settles down to sleep, falling comfortably into itself as if it, like the servants, trusts that I will not tell tales to Cloé. The sounds it makes, the creakings and shiftings, are muffled and slow, the pattern of dust particles in sunlight dreamy driftings rather than agitated dancings. It is a house in an enchanted sleep.

Richard is in Dublin because Ernest is not. Now, when Ernest's away, he likes Richard to be there in his stead. I know it's flattering for Richard, but I miss his company, his quiet good sense and gentle, clever humour.

Bryan calls sometimes when he is at home, persuading me to come for a drive 'or you will get mopey'. We motor around the park, hood up because it is so often raining, a summer rain that leaves mist behind it so that the days are many shades of grey. He asks questions about Mr Pearson and Jen, whom he seems to find amusing, and about what I do with my time. 'You must be bored' is his constant refrain. 'But I'm not,' I protest. 'Not at all. When I am not at work, I am tired from work, and happy therefore to sit quietly and read, or walk about.'

'You make it sound . . . almost pleasant.'

'It is. You should try it,' I say, teasing.

'Work? Perhaps. I'm not averse. So hard to know what to do, though. What, really, is there for a fellow like me? I do not see my way clear at all. My father wants me to go into politics, but I never could. I would like to write, but he won't stand for it.' Arm out the window, he drums his fingers on the side of the motor with a rat-a-tat sound, peering ahead as though the way he sought might be there ahead of him, shrouded in mist. 'It's a queer world the old men have left us,' he says, rather forlorn.

Once or twice, he brings Diana, now understood to be his fiancée although no announcement has been made, always in company with a sister. Usually Nancy, whom I am shy of but sometimes Pamela, kind and calm, a reassuring reminder that the family – despite Diana's beauty and Nancy's quick wit and sharp tongue – are, after all, human. Not that Nancy is harsh with me – the opposite – she is funny and takes pains to be pleasant, but for all that, it isn't possible not to feel plodding and dull beside her quicksilver mind.

Diana is even more lovely than Bryan said, and mostly silent. I cannot tell if she is young and overawed, or self-important and indifferent.

Elizabeth calls too, more often than Bryan, for longer, and for different reasons. He rarely comes in, instead persuading me out. She walks straight in, heels clacking on the marble, already talking. Puts her hat down on one surface, gloves on another, handbag, often, on a third, lights a 'gasper', demands tea or a drink and continues to talk.

'Such a funny little woman came into the shop today. Quite impossibly dowdy, looking for something she called an "at home" gown. Well, I said, that all depends on where "home" is, Mayfair or Chelsea . . . and she said "Hampstead", so I said, "In that case there isn't a thing here, not a thing, that will do . . ." Hampstead. Can you imagine?' and she lights another cigarette, pushing the case towards me. 'Smoke?'

'I don't.'

'Of course. I forget. What news of Maureen? When are they back?'

'Another nine days.' I have told her this I do not know how many times. I know I will tell her again.

'Come out tonight.'

'No.'

'Whyever not? There is to be a party, Carlyle Square. We are to dress as tramps. I have a darling little 'kerchief bundle on a stick. *Please*, do not say it is because of that job.'

'Well, but it is because of that job.'

'I don't see why you bother. No one else does.'

'No one you know, perhaps,' I say, but mildly. I do not mind Elizabeth's abrupt ways.

'That little Violet Valerie, or Valerie Violet, whichever it is – "Valsie" as Oonagh calls her – went with them, didn't she? Looking as like to Oonagh as like can be, I suppose?'

'What do you mean?'

'Oh, come on, don't say you haven't noticed.' I have. Of course, I have. But I would never say it. 'She sticks like glue and slips around like a little faithful shadow, all the while simply soaking Oonagh up. She makes up to Gunnie and Cloé. Maureen too, although she is wasting her time there. What *is* the plan, I wonder?' She looks at me as though I might know something I am not saying and she can hypnotise it out of me.

'Will you stay to dinner?' I say, to change the subject, and she says yes, and doesn't seem to notice that there is only food for one laid out in the dining room. She loads her plate with cold tongue, pickles, potato salad and hard-boiled eggs, picking through what's there, eating a few distracted forkfuls, then finally squashing a cigarette out on the plate and sitting back as she pushes it away to one side.

'I suppose I may as well tell you as you will hear sooner or later anyway,' she says in a rush, with a strange kind of stiff pride. 'There is to be a frightful scandal.'

'Really,' I say. 'I hear very little. I'm sure you needn't tell me.' The thing is, I'm not sure I want to hear. For all her weary sophistication, Elizabeth looks tense, her thin shoulders are set high and rigid, with her neck hunched forward between them like a wary bird.

'Well, whatever you hear, you must know I couldn't care less,' she says defiantly. 'I may well be on a road that leads nowhere, but perhaps that is better than scratching about in a desert.' I have no idea what she means until many days later when Mildred says bluntly, 'Elizabeth Ponsonby has been carrying on with a married man.'

'You do all right here, don't you?' Elizabeth says now, lighting up yet another cigarette and staring about her. 'Do you miss them?'

'Of course I do.'

'Bet you don't.' She gives me a look from under those heavy lids.

She's wrong. I do miss them. But all the same there is joy in coming back to that half-asleep house after busy days in Islington. To come in without running the gauntlet of Lapham, to walk through the empty rooms and corridors without sniffing the air to try to discover what way the many moods beneath its roof blow. Most of all, to sit alone by tall windows open wide to the evening sun and simply stay there as long as the final gleams last. These wet, dull days so often end in a brief golden glow as though, surrendered and unlooked for, the sun finally decides to remind us that it is here, always here, whether we see it or not.

To sit and breathe in the complicated mix of smoke and earth, wet grass, dusty leaves, flowers that pour out their scent desperately lest chance be gone, and petrol fumes that linger longer on the heavy darkening air – it is a strange kind of bliss. Sometimes I meet Jen and we wander together through town, discharging small commissions for her mother, then take tea in a café or corner house. We talk about the office, the mysterious moods of Mr Pearson and Mr White, our own small triumphs – an important letter found when despair had set in – and disasters – a bus delayed that meant late arrival at the office. I enjoy these conversations. They have such solid ground beneath them. In them, I see a future, one I can touch. There has been talk that I may be allowed to read manuscripts and provide a 'reader's report', and Jen is full of the possibilities this may bring. These possibilities, as she sees them, are pleasingly practical: a rise in my pay, future promotions and what these might mean. Jen is a most reassuring person because she sees life as a series of small steps that are laid out with logic, first one, then the next; unlike the girls of Grosvenor Place, for whom there are leaps and plunges, long periods of nothing followed by a sudden upwards lurch that can leave us all nauseous.

Richard, when I tell him about the reader's reports, is just as enthusiastic. 'I'm not surprised,' he says. He is in London at last and we are walking through Hampstead Heath, nearly deserted now that summer is at its height. He finds London too large and dirty, so likes to go where there is water. 'You have a clear mind, and a clear way of speaking and writing,' he says.

'I do?'

'Yes. Hughie used to show me your letters, the ones you wrote to him when we were at school. Your way of describing the people around you, the place you lived, the things you did – they were so clever and conveyed your life so well, even when you were very young. Hughie would give them to me to read, knowing I would be amused at how you conjured situations and people.'

'I didn't know he showed you my letters. You never said so.'

'I thought you mightn't like to think something written just for Hughie had been read by someone else. But he did, sometimes, and they made me want to meet the person who had written them very much.'

To meet me more than the people I described? Surely not, I think, but I don't say it. I know what he would say in return. What I don't know is whether I would believe him.

Talking to Richard, I find I can see myself more definitely: as a person, with a plan and a future, rather than the vague outline I feel myself to be when I am close to the Guinness girls. I even see possibilities for myself. Maybe it's because he is the only person for whom I am not less than they are. With Hughie it was the same – I was as much as them, more even than them. Until Maureen became more than me.

Maybe it's because I have been talking about Hughie, thinking about him more even than usual, but the very next day, I am out walking when ahead of me, a young man with a quick step and a jaunty lift to his head turns a corner ahead of me, and something in his turn, the energetic swing of his form, catches at me and I stop, dead, but only for a second. Then I speed up till I am almost running after him, even though that was not the direction I planned to go.

I move so fast that by the time I round the corner he is only a little ahead of me and by keeping up my pace soon I am just behind him. It isn't him, I know it isn't, but I can't stop myself from overtaking him. I need to look at him.

I turn my head as I pass, to see his face properly. He isn't very like Hughie – wrong hair, wrong height – so I know that it wasn't even really a likeness that caught me but a longing; a need for someone, sometime, to be him.

It's not the first time. I have seen Hughie before,

several times, on the streets and squares of London. Each time I have thought, *Why not? As well here as anywhere*. Until I see that it isn't him, and then I think, *Of course*.

I never say any of that to Maureen or Oonagh, not even Richard. I barely say it to myself.

'We could get a flat together,' Jen says one day, as we drink tea on our morning break. 'Not now. Maybe not for quite some time, depending on how much we can save. But eventually. I've seen places in Earl's Court advertised and we could afford one if it's small and we're careful. What do you think? I don't see that I can continue at home forever. Susan is to be married, and she and George will both live with Mother. Peter is still unemployed and more miserable than ever. But perhaps you are happy where you are?'

'I am. But, oh, Jen, I think it's a wonderful idea.'

'It wouldn't be anything fancy, mind,' Jen says. 'I've seen those flats and they are really quite shocking, some of them. But we could afford better than the worst of them,' she says, comfortably, 'and it would be ours.'

'I would like that very much,' I say. 'But it will not happen immediately. They will not see it as we do, the friends I live with, and I would not wish to offend.'

And then it is August and the family are back, in a tumble of trunks and tales, of who they met, the parties they went to, the impossibility of bathing when the Riviera was so crowded. Most of all they talk about a queer foreign Countess and her son – 'Italian, so they said; too bogus for words' – who were staying in the same hotel, and how she 'near quivered with excitement' when it seemed as though the son might be getting somewhere with Violet, only to discover that she was not a daughter but a friend.

Maureen dwells with great enjoyment on the moment of unmasking: 'over bridge, and the Countess said in that ridiculous accent, like something from a play – "*They are so seemilarrr, your youngest daughters, Madame.*" And then Mamma said, "What on earth do you mean?" And then it all came out, the Countess thinking Violet was one of us, and the *look* on the trout's face when she saw how much her precious son had wasted his time . . .' She goes into peals of laughter, but I see Violet, always so composed, flinch at the words 'wasted his time'. Maureen, who must have seen too, shows no mercy: 'All those games of tennis, and moving chairs around in and out of shade and fetching drinks,' she continues, 'for nothing!'

'Even afterwards, she would keep saying how like the girls Violet is, as though I might be deliberately deceiving her,' Cloé says on a sigh. 'She said they were the mirror images. I cannot think what she meant.' And they all turn and look at Violet for a second, who says bravely, 'I cannot think either. In any case, I have a fiancé. It was always going to be hopeless.'

She doesn't respond when Maureen says cattily, 'Perhaps it's just as well, then, he never got so far as to ask you. For surely you would have broken his heart with *that* news.'

'What have you been doing, Fliss?' Oonagh asks quickly, to change the subject.

'Very little,' I say. 'Going to work, coming back, rattling around the house, taking walks in the park. It has been very wet.'

'How dull it sounds. But it's all right,' she says, squeezing my arm, 'we are home now.' That's when I realise that although I am happy to see them, it isn't like the last time, the time they went away on *Fantome*. This time my life continued even in their absence.

Chapter Thirty-eight

It's soon apparent that the weeks away have not achieved everything that was hoped. Cloé is still in pain, still secretive and mysterious about this pain. The girls look fresh and bright-eyed, but Aileen and Maureen are no more in charity than they were. In fact, now that Aileen is so very taken up with ordering her trousseau and attending fittings, talking plans with Gunnie and receiving wedding presents, Maureen is more outrageous than ever.

This mostly takes the form of spite: slyly needling at Aileen for making what she sneers at as 'not even a *bad* match – that at least might be exciting – just a dull one . . .' and teasing 'The Great Oojah' so relentlessly that Aileen quietly asks him to stay away from the house. The two of them drop out of Maureen's set entirely, finding new friends among Brinny's sisters and their husbands and cousins – nicknamed 'Oojah's troupe' by Maureen – and we begin to see Aileen very little.

Maureen and Oonagh spend their time now with Violet and sometimes her sister Essex, whom I grow to quite dislike. Inside a graceful form she has a clumsy mind, where snobbishness and silliness vie with each other; now one, now the other on top, and in neither guise do I enjoy her company.

But Oonagh, of course, ever loyal, will hear no harm of either. And neither will she listen when I say, 'Do you not think that Violet has begun to style her hair very like yours?'

'It's the fashion,' Oonagh responds. 'Everyone styles their hair like this.'

'True,' I say, 'but not everyone is so often with you as Violet is. Do you not long sometimes to be without her?'

'Not if it means being alone with Mamma,' Oonagh says. 'Valsie is my screen. While she is there, Mamma can't look and pick and scratch at me as she does when I am alone. Of course,' she adds with a sideways look, 'I would much rather it was you who was always with me . . .'

'I can't, Oonagh. You know that.'

'I know. But it doesn't stop me hoping.' And because of that, I don't say what I have been trying to find a way to say for weeks: *What would you think if I was to take a flat with Jen?* I'll come back to it, I think.

Soon nothing is talked about in Grosvenor Place except the wedding in November and what happens after. Ernest has bought them a house in Ireland, a castle, actually, in Luttrellstown – 'with its very own phantom,' Aileen says, 'and a handsome one at that!' – where they will live. Aileen has declined a London house. 'I cannot tell you how sick I am of this city,' she says when Oonagh asks why. 'It is like getting on a train and finding that one is expected to pedal it oneself. I long to be done with it, as does Brinny.'

But as the wedding approaches, she who has for many weeks now been caught up in the whirl of preparation, too busy to talk to us, begins to linger where we are, finding excuses to be close by. Two nights before the wedding, she drifts into the small sitting room where we sit. For once the French sisters are not with us but with their mother. Oonagh is trying to make Fidget wear a hat, one of Ernest's, while she sketches him.

Maureen is flicking through the Army & Navy catalogue, while I am reading a long article in *The Times* about India's fight for self-governance and trying hard to understand what I read. I know that if I ask Maureen, she will explain it in an instant, but I do not entirely trust the speed of her mind, because I know it picks out only those points that interest her. When she talks about Ireland and the Free State – 'men more at home scrubbing horses or digging ditches, pretending they can run a country' – it is so at odds with the accounts Richard gives of conscientious effort and a painful kind of idealism that I am entirely confused.

Aileen comes in to ask after a magazine she was reading and when told that we haven't seen it, instead of departing, wanders about the room, pulling out books and opening them, then closing them and putting them back.

'What is it?' Maureen asks at last. 'You're like a dog that has lost something, prowling around and sniffing in corners.'

But instead of rising and snapping something back, Aileen says, 'Shall we play bridge?'

'Surely you have better things to do? A trousseau to pack? Wedding presents to gloat over?'

'Burton has done it all' – Burton was the girls' alarmingly efficient lady's maid – 'and I cannot stand Gunnie fussing at me any longer: "Do you think you have enough chemises?" As if I were starting out on a long and terrible journey to a place where no dress shop has ever been seen, instead of moving to live less than an hour from a city that is full of them. All day she has been picking at monograms on linen and lace on hems suspiciously, as if the seamstress might have cheated her. Ugh! I cannot wait for this all to be over.' Her mind, I think suddenly, is very full of endings rather than beginnings.

'And then what?' Maureen asks. 'A lifetime of wedded bliss?' Her tone is mocking, but she makes space for Aileen to sit beside her and begins deftly shuffling cards.

'I suppose so.'

'Suppose? That doesn't sound so very fond. Hardly straining at the bit, are you?'

'Well, it will be strange,' Aileen says. 'I mean . . .'

'Cold feet?' Maureen asks.

'No.'

'So, what is it, Aileen?' Oonagh asks.

'It's the wedding night,' Maureen says with a snigger. 'Her wifely duties. The knock on the door when she's in bed in her nightgown . . .'

'Don't be absurd, Maureen. It's not that.'

'Well, what, then?'

'Just that I've never lived with anyone except

you,' Aileen says in a burst. 'Us. This household, I mean. You know. It's always been us, together. And now it will be me alone.'

'With Brinny,' Oonagh says comfortingly.

'Of course. But all the same. So far away.'

'Lucky you,' Oonagh mutters so that only I hear her.

Gunnie has said Luttrellstown is 'very close' to Glenmaroon, but what good that is to Aileen when we none of us go there anymore, I do not know. Oonagh must read my mind then because she says, 'Perhaps we will come to you. Or close to you in any case. And you can visit here.'

'How strange it will be, to visit where I have lived,' Aileen says.

'It's your home,' Maureen says suddenly. 'Wherever we are is always your home too.' And the two of them exchange a look that is half a smile, half a grimace that carries in it all the months of rowing and snapping at each other, but also all the years of being together in everything. And then the look is gone.

Aileen stands up and brushes down her dress. 'In any case, what I really came to say is, Maureen, please do not be outrageous at the reception. Brinny's sisters are not like you, you know.'

'Meaning . . . ?'

'Only that you will shock them.'

'Oh goodie,' says Maureen, lighting a cigarette with a snap of her gold lighter.

The wedding, at St Margaret's Westminster, is cheerful and well-attended, 'and terribly dowdy, don't you think?' Maureen whispers to me as we walk in behind Aileen. I tell her she is being unfair – which she is. Granted, these are not the extravagantly plumed friends of her set. There is no Stephen Tennant with half-inch eyelashes and gold dust sprinkled in his hair, or Brenda, wriggling out of a floor-length fur to reveal a dress so skimpy it seems hardly to hold together at all; no gaudy shop girls with bold eyes and childish, grasping hands, but they are a solid, pleasant lot, who seem ready to embrace Aileen and clearly adore Brinny.

Mildred is there, large and smart in charcoal grey, and with her Lady Colefax, smaller, more vivacious, looking around in a lively, approving way, 'for new clients' Cloé would undoubtedly say.

Aileen glides down the aisle of St Margaret's on Ernest's arm, almost lost amongst her bouquet of lilies and heavy veil of Brussels lace, and back up again on Brinny's, veil thrown back to show her face, eyes shining, nodding here and there to particular friends among the crowd. As she passes where I stand with Oonagh and Maureen, she puts out a hand in a white lace glove and catches mine, giving it a quick squeeze. I put out my other hand to squeeze back, but she is gone.

Afterwards, there is a reception at Grosvenor Place, a crush of smiling faces all nodding approval of the couple and saying 'you'll be next' to Maureen. 'They say it to make sure it is so,' says Oonagh wisely. Then the couple depart and we who are left behind feel very flat.

'It is always so after a wedding,' Gunnie says reassuringly. 'It will soon pass.' But it doesn't. Cloé is withdrawn, exhausted by the efforts demanded of her, but more than that too. She seems in a state of nerves. I catch her staring out the windows, particularly after night has fallen, holding the curtain aside and peering into the flat inky blackness with a strained look, as though trying to see something she knows is out there. She broods on the changes she sees – a section of Buckingham Palace garden wall that must be repaired, a part of Hyde Park dug up because of bindweed – and those she reads about.

'I see Grosvenor House is to be replaced with a block of flats,' she says one morning over breakfast, the *Daily Express* in front of her. 'I cannot believe it. So many dances I went to there . . .'

'Very smart flats, Mamma,' Maureen says, pouring coffee from a silver pot. 'Much better than that dreary old hen house.' She has not forgiven the scene of her humiliation at the Queen Charlotte's Ball; of course she hasn't.

'They say Dorchester House will go too,' Cloé continues. 'So much change. I feel that if I don't watch out, the very chair I am seated on will be taken by you young people and turned into something else.' She gives Maureen an accusing look, as if she might be personally responsible. 'Or burned, or destroyed simply because you don't like it and are strong enough to break it.'

And Maureen, who should soothe and reassure her, smiles wickedly and says, 'Only if we think it is worth our while. We won't waste our energies on any old path of destruction.'

But Cloé doesn't laugh. To her, it isn't funny but alarming. She is utterly distant from us by now, like a light that flickers on a distant landing, because her sickness and ill humours hold her back.

Oonagh entirely avoids Cloé, who continues to pick at her and criticise, even though Oonagh has made of her shyness something that is endearing and entirely her own. She has turned her silence into a kind of trick that is beguiling rather than awkward, and she is altogether charming. But Cloé will not see it.

'Staring and staring, with those great eyes of hers,' she mutters one day when Oonagh has left the drawing room. 'As if she would like to see right through one.'

And then it is Christmas, and I am still wondering how to broach the fact that I plan to move into a flat, with Jen, when Richard asks me to marry him.

'It seems the brewery will indeed move to London, and I with it,' he says one Saturday morning as we walk briskly by the Thames. I haven't seen him in some time – he didn't come to the wedding, although Aileen invited him. 'I have been wanting to ask you something, but I didn't, because I felt I couldn't ask you to move back to Dublin. But, now that I am to live here, Fliss, will you marry me?' He stops and looks at me, or tries to. I keep walking, so he has to move too, to keep up. I don't want to look at him, not properly.

The truth is, I'm not exactly surprised. I've long known that the people around me – Gunnie, the girls, even Ernest – have expected this. And so I have expected it too. The trouble is, I've never known my answer. Not really. Sometimes the assumption that I will say yes has been as steady and obvious as the belief that he will ask. But other times, I feel only the impossibility of anything other than no.

And now that it comes to it, all I can find to say is, 'That's very kind of you. But you don't have to, you know. I will be able to support myself quite well.'

'I'm not being kind, Fliss. Is that really what you think?'

'Yes. I presumed . . . that, like Ernest, you feel responsible for me, because of Hughie.'

'I love you, Fliss. Maybe that was because of Hughie, at first – but now, for a long time, it is for you yourself.'

'Oh.'

'I'm not asking to marry you because I'm kind' – his rare grin – 'but because I want to be married to you. I can't think of anything nicer.'

And instead of making an answer easier, him saying this makes it harder. It makes my answer more important.

What would Gunnie say, if I were to ask – as I did about Aileen and Brinny – what she thinks of the match? '*Well* . . .' I can imagine her, sitting straighter and pulling all her threads together '. . . *it isn't much of an alliance, and there isn't any money, of course, but he is a good and sensible young man and really, you can't expect more . . .*'

Perhaps I'm being cruel. Or giving cruel words in my imagination to Gunnie, who deserves better.

But if she doesn't say it, the world will – whatever bit of it cares what people like Richard and I do.

Part of me feels that it's too neat – two Guinness dependents tied up together and disposed of – part of me imagines Oonagh's efforts to be pleased for me and Maureen's determination not to be. Another part knows that the time I spend with Richard is time in which I am, invariably, happy, and that I miss him when he is in Dublin and out of reach. One very, very small part thinks for a moment about Bryan before I snap it shut, but most of me wonders what Hughie would think. And I don't know.

I have kept such pace with him in my mind that usually, when I look, I can find an instant, up-to-date reckoning. I know, to the day, how old he is, even though I can't add the years to his face, which remains as I last saw it. I have a whole life constructed for him that runs alongside my own. In this life, he is sometimes back in Ballytibbert, making changes to the farm that are profound and sensible, sometimes in Venezuela with Thomas, a country so exotic that all the details are fantasy. But he is always where I can find him, and I always know what he thinks of what I do. He is content that I continue to live under Ernest's roof. He approved of my Pitman course and is pleased by my job with Mr Pearson. He likes Jen and thinks our living together will be a good plan. I know all of this. But I can't see what he thinks of me marrying Richard. Would it count towards '*you do not always need to think about them. Perhaps sometimes you can also think about yourself*'?

I try saying some of this to Richard, but it comes out wrong. Mostly because the feeling of *my fault* is one I choke on.

'I didn't realise how unsettled you still are,' he says, when I have tried to explain what I mean. 'Because we don't talk about Hughie as much as we did, I made the mistake of thinking you thought and wondered less about him. I'm sorry, Fliss. I will try again to find out what happened and where he might be. Perhaps it'll be easier now that more time has passed. Someone must know something.'

I can't tell him this isn't exactly what I was trying to say, so instead I say, 'Yes, please,' and then, 'May I think about what you've asked?'

'Of course.'

And I do. Although I can see he doesn't believe me when I tell him that I have. Because the answer is no, and I can see he doesn't expect that. It's no because it can't be yes. And if I am sorry for that – and I am – how much more sorry must he be? But I know it cannot be yes. Richard is who I should have given Maureen's letter to, and instead I gave it to Thomas. He doesn't know that, and I can't tell him. But I can't marry him either.

But when I see the sudden misery in his eyes, I have to stop myself from reaching out a hand and saying, 'Wait, give me time . . . maybe . . .' because that would be unfair.

Chapter Thirty-nine

St George's Swimming Baths, London, 1928

'Pooh, what a terrible smell,' Violet says, wrinkling her nose delicately and drawing back from the steps up which we have started.

'Smells like the pool at Glenmaroon,' Oonagh says.

'Chlorine,' I say. 'Horrid. I suppose Elizabeth really does mean to give a party in a swimming baths.' Even as I speak, I wonder why must I always take my tone from her or Maureen. Pretending I am gay and careless when I am neither of those things, not ever, and particularly not since my conversation with Richard, and the very few times I have spoken to him since; short, unhappy conversations that were missing all of our previous ease together. I learned so early on to be as they were, without knowing I was learning it, and now I find it hard to stop myself.

'Of course she does,' says Oonagh. 'When did you ever know Elizabeth to shirk her duties as a hostess?'

'Well, she might have cleaned the place first,' Violet says.

'When did you ever know Elizabeth to properly perform her duties as hostess?' I say, which makes Oonagh yelp with laughter.

'It's so hot, I should think the whole of London will be here, splashing about and trying to keep cool, like birds in a fountain.' She fans herself exaggeratedly with a corner of the thick white bath towel she has brought, as instructed by Elizabeth's invitation, demanding the pleasure of our company '*at St George's Swimming Baths, Buckingham Palace Road, at 11 o'clock, p.m. on Friday, 13th July, 1928. Please wear a Bathing Suit and bring a Bath towel and a Bottle. Each guest is required to show his invitation on arrival.*'

'A bath towel and a bottle? No RSVP?' Gunnie had asked in alarm.

'Much easier to just tell everyone to show up,' Maureen had replied. 'They all will anyway.' Gunnie had looked appalled but said nothing. No one says anything anymore, except the newspapers, who still pretend to be shocked at the various antics, even though they have by now been shocked again and again and again, by the same things.

'I don't see any of that lot showing their invitations,' Oonagh says now, pointing at a group of debs ahead of us, jostling each other good-naturedly on the stairs and giggling loudly at the audacity of being here. These parties of Elizabeth's have transformed in the last year, going from the prickly edges of society, to being almost smothered in the centre. The very matrons who raised chilly eyebrows have become enthusiastic patrons, claiming to find 'dear Elizabeth' 'so original'. And their daughters turn up in such droves that Maureen has begun to grumble and say that all is spoiled, 'only that they do at least bring decent bottles. None of that rot-gut that Elizabeth's strange artist friends palm off on us.' Her gripe isn't enough to make her stay away, but she has begun to be ever more outrageous in order to preserve a distinction between herself and the Miss Mice who are, she says, now 'not nearly mousey enough. Positively bouncing and almost hound-like, some of them.'

These same daughters are piling in, wearing robes over their bathing dress, bouncing merrily along the narrow entrance corridor and shoving each other excitedly. 'I say, there's Brenda,' one of them mutters, and I see, on the other side of the pool, Brenda in a tiny black-and-white spotted bathing dress. She is so slender that her arms and legs seem elongated, like the wrought-iron railings behind her.

'I though the pool would be dry,' Oonagh says, looking at the large oblong in front of us, in which rubber rings shaped like horses are floating, with large, flat flowers, pink and white, some kind of chrysanthemum, bobbing about amongst them. 'No wonder it smells so bad.' Spotlights of red and green and blue dance on the water so that the bobbing horses seem to lurch, strange and savage: Poseidon's creatures.

'Lucky the roof is open,' I say. High above, beyond the sturdy criss-cross iron beams, the glass roof has been pulled apart so that a rectangle of sky, still with enough light to make it a feathery grey rather than black, looks down on us. Above the sharp sting of chlorine drifts the smell of an English summer night.

'But there is no space,' Oonagh says. She is right. The tiled strip around the pool is narrow, and wet. Above us the balconies are already crowded with party guests while at the far end, the viewing gallery is taken up with a band who play 'I Can't Give You Anything But Love'. Close to them, so close that I fear they might all fall into a tangle and over the balcony entirely, are people dancing.

'There you are,' Elizabeth says, pushing past a group of young men threatening to throw each other into the pool. 'Come and have a Bathwater Cocktail. There's a bar upstairs. Although the waiters don't look as if they are taking their duties terribly seriously. I can't imagine they'll last very long. Already I can see them casting off their uniforms and diving down into the guests.' She laughs.

'What's in the cocktail?' I ask.

'Haven't a clue. Stephen invented it. Gin, I think. Lemon. Something in a green bottle that smells bitter.' She takes a swig from the glass she's carrying and says, 'Not up to much really, but such an amusing idea. Drinking each other's bathwater.' She giggles and Oonagh makes a face. 'Now, what do you think? Do tell!' Elizabeth continues, looking grandly around. She is wearing a silk bathing costume, red at the bottom, with a striped red-and-blue bodice, like a very jolly sailor.

'Different,' I say.

'Our best yet, I think,' she says, considering. 'That trick with the invitation was clever, wasn't it?'

'What trick?' Oonagh asks.

'"Each guest is required to show his invitation on arrival",' Elizabeth recites.

'Well, no one asked for ours,' Violet says. She has taken off her robe to show a very tight purple-and-white-striped bathing dress, belted neatly at the waist, and gazes around with an eager look.

'Of course they didn't,' says Elizabeth, top lip raised in glee over those ferocious teeth. 'That's the point! I couldn't care less who gatecrashes – all the more fun! – but they are going to need the nerve to do so, don't you see? That way we weed out the hopeless and amateur.' She is so pleased with herself that we all smile and agree that it is indeed very clever, and only after she's gone does Oonagh start to giggle and say, 'Who on earth does she think actually cares?'

'Where's Maureen?' Violet asks.

'Over there, with Stephen,' Oonagh says. 'Doesn't he look elegant?'

Stephen is wearing a pink vest and blue trousers. Beside him, Maureen, splendid in bright red, waves over enthusiastically. Someone shouts, 'I say, watch this!' and leaps into the pool, followed almost instantly by more, jumping in from every side so that soon the pool is boiling and heaving as they splash and laugh and dunk each other, exclaiming loudly and firing rubber horses around. People have drifted into cubicles as there is nowhere else to sit and small gay groups are forming, dripping girls sitting on narrow benches, young men with towels around their shoulders passing drinks from hand to hand in a kind of human chain: 'Pass this along, would you? Thanks frightfully.'

Despite the open roof, there isn't a breath of air. The noise – music, chatter, the particular type of shrieking gaiety that these bright young people bring – seems to build and build as though trapped and unable to find its way out, like a bird flown into a room, blundering and beating again and again against glass in a hot frenzy, unaware that above it an open window offers cool air and escape.

I climb to the first floor and lean out over the wrought-iron railings, face turned up to try to catch the scant fresh air that blows above me. Below, around the edges of the pool, groups sit with their legs in the water, swinging them gently back and forth in the red and blue and green spotlights, kicking rubber horses and calling out to the rowdy gang in the middle. I spot Marjorie in a tight cap, splashing wildly, and several others from that girls' lunch that feels a lifetime ago.

'Here, drink this.' Maureen leans on the rail beside me and hands me a silver flask.

'Bathwater cocktail?'

She makes a face. 'Certainly not. Wouldn't

touch it. That was one of Stephen's ideas. Strictly for the plebs.'

I take a sip, and splutter. 'Goodness, what is it?'

'Gin-and-It.'

'What's the "It" this time?' I ask. 'More gin?'

She laughs. 'Something like that.'

'Did you bring that with you?'

'I did. You don't expect me to jostle with all those other frights, do you?' She takes a long swig. 'Come and dance?'

'No, thank you. I think I'll stay here and watch.' How much Jen would enjoy it all, I think. Her enjoyment, I suspect, would be far greater than those who are actually here.

Elizabeth is in a cubicle opposite me, into which the largest, gayest group is packed. Drinks and cigarettes are ferried across the tiled floor, sometimes across the pool itself, to keep them supplied, eager hands held out for glasses that are then drained almost in a single gulp. Elizabeth must be telling one of her absurd stories, I think, because their faces are turned towards her, expectant, and she is opening her round eyes wider and wider until I fear they might explode. She looks up then and catches my eye and raises her glass to me. I wave back.

Further along the balcony, Brenda is leaning over the railing too, resting her face on her crossed arms, and I presume that she, like me, is watching the games below but when I walk over to her, I see that her head is turned to the side and angled towards the open roof.

'Having fun?' I ask.

'Hmm?' She stares at me, confused, so that I think she hasn't heard.

'Having fun?' I ask again, louder, but still she stares at me and says nothing. Stares through me, really, as if beyond me and far out the other side is something she needs to keep an eye on.

Below, Baby and Zita wear matching costumes, Zita's black trimmed with white, Baby's white trimmed with black, both very fetching. Baby's prizefighter, Bert, close by them, is almost indecent in his navy trunks. Zita, I know, is soon to be married, and I wonder suddenly what will happen to poor Bert when Baby does likewise, as surely she must. Will she bring him with her, like an old coat for which she has affection, into the newly charmed circle of her married state? Or leave him behind to wait and regret?

Elizabeth's trick with the invitation seems to have worked, I think, inasmuch as the gatecrashers, of whom there are many, are a more peculiar lot than usual. Instead of the polite, almost apologetic young men and girls, these are a coarser gang, louder and more rowdy. They throw girls into the pool with a good deal of energy, and at one point get up a game of water polo in which girls sit astride their shoulders and pelt each other with flowers and rubber horses. Soon the efficient chain of glasses being passed up and down to the balcony is disrupted, and the sound of breaking glass rings out like an alarm.

Chapter Forty

I go in search of Oonagh, and it is only then that I realise there is a good deal of this party happening away from the pool itself. In fact, the pool, and the cubicles around it, are like a stage, and backstage there are many more rooms than I had imagined. Some are tiny, damp places that smell of mould, and others are larger, communal changing rooms that echo with a forlorn booming. In one, Brenda is lying asleep on a bench with her head back against a mildew-stained wall. Beside her a blue paper packet is empty and already curling with damp. I shake her but she is sleeping soundly and doesn't stir. Her bathing costume is wet, and she will certainly catch a cold so I go in search of someone who can help me wake her. I find Stephen, leaning elegantly against a wall, eyeing the rowdy young men in the pool.

'Who are those chaps?' I say.

'I think they work in a factory,' he says, fascinated. 'Marjorie and her chums seem to approve,' and he gives me a naughty look.

'I need you to help,' I say. 'It's Brenda.'

'Oh Brenda,' he says with a faint shrug. 'What now?'

'She's fast asleep, but her costume is still wet and she's going to catch a most terrible cold. But I can't wake her.'

He laughs. 'Oh Fliss, truly?'

'Truly what?'

'You really, truly are adorable.'

'But why?' I say. 'Come and see if you can wake her, or at least find a dry towel and put it over her?'

'Very well, I'll put a towel over her. I doubt we'll be able to wake her.'

'Why not?'

'A little thing Brenda calls Dreamer, of which even you might have heard.' I have, but only very vaguely, certainly not enough to know what it is.

'The blue packet?'

'Indeed. Probably brought from Ma Meyrick's Chinese chap.'

'Is it uppies?' I ask, remembering the funny word Maureen once used.

'Opium.'

'And it makes her sleep so heavily? But why on earth take it at a party?' I was honestly confused, but also frightened. There had been something shockingly defenceless in Brenda's profound slumber.

'Why indeed? Except that Brenda takes it everywhere, her very own most faithful companion. Come along, we go in search of dry towels.'

Some of the musicians have downed instruments now and are dancing with guests so that it is harder than ever to make progress without falling into the pool. Maureen has changed into a gorgeous rust-coloured tunic, and she is dancing energetically with two young men dressed in white with sailor caps. They are doing a routine they must have learned from a review, all in formation together. It's fast and complicated and I'm impressed at Maureen's speed and agility. She winks at me as I go by and calls, 'Mind you don't lead Stephen astray.'

We find a cubicle that has obviously been home to some of the dowagers because it is orderly and dry, and towels are folded in neat stacks, and I realise suddenly that the older generation seems to have gone. We take a couple of towels and put one over Brenda and another rolled under her head. She looks more like a child than ever, wrapped up like that, frail and limp beneath the fluffy white. Her head lolls at a painful angle and there is black make-up smudged under her eyes.

'Should I stay with her?' I ask.

'Certainly not. That's going too far. Go and enjoy yourself. I shall resume watching those frightful factory boys holding each other's heads under water. Any minute now one of them's going to *drown* another,' he says in delight.

I go back to looking for Oonagh, wondering how it is this party is fuller than ever, even though many of the people I know are gone. The glass roof has been closed so that the heat and steam make me think of the reptile cage at the zoo, and the noise is more intense, no longer looking for an escape, but simply building and building like a closed fist. The chlorine smell is mixed now with perfume and warm bodies and something sweet that might be alcohol. The waiters have begun making bright green cocktails that are sickly with a taste of exotic fruit, and the factory boys that Stephen is so intrigued by are pouring them into the pool.

'See if we can't turn the water green, chaps,' shouts one, who is thickset and muscled with arms that hang heavy by his sides, as though the effort of lifting them is too much.

So far, they have only succeeded in making the water grey. Though that may also be the number of bodies churning in it. Marjorie is still there, splashing and leaping. Her hat has come off and her hair is hanging in loose wet curls around her face, but her good humour is undiminished. 'Get him!' she roars at her companions as one of the young men Maureen was dancing with dares to sit on the edge too close to them. Although he is still wearing his white jacket, they drag him into the water and dunk him thoroughly.

I go down into the underground rooms where it is stifling, with bodies sliding past me in the dim light, damp and furtive, the glowing tip of occasional cigarettes like eyes lighting up the wet gloom, burning fiercely then fading.

I find Oonagh at last, and Violet, seated on towels in a changing cubicle, a smaller version of the one where Brenda sleeps. There are slatted wooden benches and a floor of small white porcelain tiles. Something is hissing at the back, some steam valve, I guess, and it makes me think more than ever of reptiles.

'Why here?' I ask. 'I've been looking everywhere.'

'Just for a rest,' Oonagh says vaguely. 'We've been dancing. Those musicians sure know how to throw a girl around.' She puts on an American accent, I suppose in imitation of the musician she has been dancing with, but her voice is curiously flat and the words run into each other like a tired horse that will not pick up its hooves.

'Would you like to go home?'

'Oh, not yet, Fliss! The party isn't over, and I'm eighteen now. I'm going to stay till the very end.' She puts her feet up on the bench and drapes her arms over her knees. Beside her, Violet does the same so that they are two guardian statues, facing one another. I sit between them and Violet lights a cigarette, exhaling long and wearily, and begins to talk about another party, another set of people, from the week before. Oonagh listens and interjects remarks and makes shadow-puppet figures with her hands in the light that comes in through the open door.

'It's so dreary here,' I say after a while. 'Shall we go back up?' The room is starting to depress me, as though the damp were seeping into me from those thick walls, white plaster stained with dark splatters.

'Very well,' Oonagh says. 'We can watch the sun come up through the roof. I want to see how wrinkled Marjorie is.' She giggles and looks at me from under her lashes. Her eyes are huge in the gloom, her pupils black and swollen like raisins soaked in brandy.

She looks unlike herself and I ask, 'Oonagh, what

have you been doing?' before I even understand what I am saying.

'Nothing,' Oonagh mutters, but does not meet my gaze. 'Just something Brenda gave me.'

'Brenda? What kind of something? Some of her powder?'

'She said it would make the evening more amusing,' Violet adds, with a show of weary sophistication.

'But why does the evening need to be more amusing?' I ask, looking from one to the other. 'Surely it is amusing enough? Or not amusing enough, in which case it's time to go home.' When did I begin to sound like Gunnie? I wonder. Neither will meet my eye. Instead they look at one another, quick, covert glances, back and forth, careful not to include me.

'Let's go up,' Oonagh says, starting to uncoil herself slowly from the bench. Her movements are lazy and she is only half standing when a group of rowdy young men are in the doorway. Seeing us, they come in, a crowd, blocking our exit and squashing us into the far end.

'Don't leave now,' one of them says. 'We've only just got here.'

'We must be going,' I say, but they laugh at me and insist, 'You must be staying,' in a high, squeaking parody of my voice.

They are wet and drunk and sniggering. But they are also too many and too large. The light from the doorway is blocked almost completely so the room is darker and there is no space. Oonagh, Violet and I are pushed right up against the bench now.

'Let us past,' Oonagh says, words still slurring together, but the men only jostle closer.

'Sit down and have a drink,' the fellow with the heavy arms says. 'Doug's got some capital stuff, don't you Doug?'

'I do,' says the one called Doug. 'Have a swig of that. Fire-water.' He holds out a bottle half full of a white liquid.

'No, thank you,' Oonagh says, and now they begin to mock her voice, saying, 'No, thank you,' to each other in falsetto tones. The one called Doug tries to put his arm around Oonagh then, saying, 'Well, if you won't have a drink, perhaps you'll have a dance instead.' Oonagh says nothing but she stumbles slightly against him, and I quickly move sideways to put myself between her and him, but he moves and the others give him way, so that he is in front of her.

'Don't be so unfriendly,' the one with the thick arms says. 'We're only trying to be matey, aren't we?' and they chorus, 'Yes, only trying to be matey, no need to get so stiff.' Suddenly conscious of wet, naked arms and legs everywhere, I catch up a towel from the bench, hand it to Oonagh and say, 'Put that around you,' which she does although her movements are slow and clumsy, to a series of loud boos from the young men, who tell her, 'Don't be a spoilsport. Just when we was all gettin' friendly.'

Oonagh is staring at the ground, refusing to look up despite Doug's efforts to lift her chin with his hand. She is as limp as the soggy towel around her shoulders and I think she will fall backwards if Doug keeps edging closer to her like that. Whatever is in Brenda's powder has sapped her resistance because she cannot seem to react properly.

'Will you let us pass,' I say, as distinctly as I can with all the authority I can muster, but they only laugh at me, passing the bottle around between them and taking long swigs.

'I say we carry them out and throw them in the pool,' says the one with the heavy arms, and Oonagh shakes her head mutely and steps closer to me.

'Do not dare think of it,' I say, and they laugh again.

'Whyever not?' one asks. 'Whyever shouldn't we?' He looks around, as if daring anyone to challenge his right to catch up the three of us and roughly bundle us anywhere he wants us to go.

No one does. Instead they nod and repeat what he has said: 'Whyever not, eh?' until I am thoroughly frightened at what they might do next.

'But maybe you're right,' Doug says, when the chorus has died down. 'Maybe we'll stay here and be friendly instead.' He moves in to put his arm around Oonagh again, and again she shakes him off. I catch hold of her hand, planning on simply rushing through the crowd, but the idea of pushing past those bare wet bodies, towing a clumsy Oonagh, appals me and I hesitate. On the other side of Oonagh, Violet, who has more space beside her than we do, suddenly turns sharply and wriggles out under the arm of the man nearest her and darts to the door and away. She has one of the towels with her and I think, *She might at least have left us that.*

'What, going so soon?' they call after her, but make no move to follow. Instead, 'About that dance,' Doug says to Oonagh and now he has hold of her hand, the one that isn't clutching mine. Behind him, one of the men starts humming 'I Can't Give You Anything But Love' and the others join in. Doug pulls Oonagh towards him, then harder when she resists, and I see that I will have to conquer my fear of all that wet flesh and be ready to push and shove because clearly it will come to that, when behind the knot of men a loud voice demands, ‘I say, what is all this?’

The question carries over the coarse jokes, the humming, the hiss of escaping steam and the distant throb of the band. The men turn to see who has spoken, parting enough so that I can also see. In the doorway is a man fully dressed in evening clothes so he appears almost of another species to those dripping in their sodden bathing costumes. Beside him, looking triumphant, is Violet. He is compact and slim but stands entirely at ease, then moves forward with all the sureness of an adult at a child’s party that has got out of hand. ‘Out of my way,’ he says to Doug, who is the only one to try to block his path, and then only for a moment.

‘Just some fun,’ Doug says sullenly. ‘Right, boys?’

‘Well, have your fun elsewhere, why don’t you,’ the man says. ‘Now clear off.’ And to my astonishment, they do, shuffling out, grinning back at us and saying, ‘No harm meant, just fun.’ The man puts out a hand to Oonagh, who is shivering beside me, whether from cold or fear I cannot tell, and to my surprise, Oonagh, who does not much like physical contact, wearing gloves to dance still although no one does anymore, lets go of my hand and takes his.

‘You’re cold,’ he says, and she nods. He takes

off his jacket then and drapes it around her bare shoulders and she looks up at him and smiles, pupils still black and round as swollen raisins.

'Oonagh, this is Philip Kindersley,' Violet says.

'Where were you earlier?' Oonagh asks.

'I'm sorry,' he says. 'I came as soon as Violet told me.'

'Not that,' Oonagh says. 'I mean' – she gestures vaguely at his evening clothes – 'where were you before this?'

'Ah. Lady Howard's.'

'Well, I'm jolly glad you came when you did,' she says and she draws his jacket tight around her.

'So am I,' he says, smiling down at her.

Upstairs, the pool is empty of people and the spotlights turned off or broken. Early morning sunlight pours through the glass roof in an accusing stream onto water that is a dirty grey. Hundreds of champagne corks bob about among abandoned bathing caps and cigarette ends. The flowers have been shredded and pink and white petals are everywhere, discarded in wet drifts on dirty tiles or scattered on the surface of the grey water. One of the rubber horses is burst, lying by the side of the pool, as though its throat has been cut. It is cold now and I look for my robe, the chlorine stinging my eyes. Two policemen are standing by the entrance, politely saying, 'Come along now, Miss, please hurry up and leave' to those stragglers still gathering their things or, in Elizabeth's case, finishing her drink. Brenda emerges, yawning, hair tousled, still with the towel Stephen and I put over her, now worn as a cape around her shoulders. 'Where are we going?' she says. Then, 'Terrific party.'

Outside, Philip searches for a taxi for us, for which I am profoundly grateful. People walk past and stare as revellers in bathing suits, eyes huge and black-circled in the morning light, congratulate each other on a wonderful night and confide that they will 'sleep for a week' even though I know they will not – they will be up and donning more costumes, making more giddy plans, within a few hours. Buses go by, full of people, some surely off to work even though it is a Saturday. It must be after eight, I think, casting an experienced eye over the crowded scene and wondering what on earth they think of what they see. Perhaps, like Jen, they think only that they are witnessing a breed apart, strange and exotic creatures – lemurs, say, that leap from tree to tree and swing by their tails – that are nothing at all to do with the rest of the world.

'Here is your taxi,' Philip says. 'You must keep my jacket. But may I call on you later?'

'Yes, please,' Oonagh says, looking up at him, her face chalky pale in the morning light. Behind them, Violet looks as if someone has snatched the watch from her wrist, the pearls from her throat. *Plundered*, is the word that comes to my mind.

Chapter Forty-one

Soon, Philip is accepted as Oonagh's young man, and everyone is delighted. He is handsome and charming, always beautifully dressed, a keen horse-rider, a good shot, an elegant dancer. His father is a director of the Bank of England and a partner in Lazard's and, although Philip is another younger son, he is so exactly the kind of man Cloé approves of that it doesn't matter. 'He is charming,' she says. And for his part, Philip makes an effort to pay her the kind of attention she enjoys. He brings news of common acquaintance, tales heard at his club that are just the right side of daring, the latest jokes so that she feels included in a society that mostly now she sees only from afar.

Violet talks more, and more gayly, than before of her 'fiancé', Henry Bradley Martin, of letters she has received and plans he is putting in place for a visit. There is a shade of defiance to this talk so that I cannot forget the look on her face in the stark early morning light outside St George's Baths. But I do not see the look again and indeed she appears to enter into the excitement of the romance completely, conspiring with Gunnie on clothes for Oonagh and listening eagerly to her talk of things they have done and places they have been.

Least delighted of all is Maureen. She cannot fault Philip – he flatters her in a way Brinny never would, and so Maureen says he is 'amusing, I suppose' – but she is furious at the amount of Oonagh's time he takes up.

'Always going off to race meetings and outdoor country, horsey things,' Maureen complains. 'She is becoming such a hearty. Everyone is so boring these days.'

'Surely not,' I say. We are walking in the park, briskly, because it is cold and Oonagh did not want to come.

'Everyone,' she says firmly. 'Brenda is impossible now. Always in a jumble and making no sense. Stephen caught up with his jealous old poet. Bryan forever with Diana or studying for his Bar exams, even though he swears he will never practise and only agreed so Uncle Walter would stop going on that he should enter politics. Even Elizabeth – engaged to some dreadful fellow who works in a music shop. She's never been the same since the scandal last year with her Mr Craigie. And of course,' she says slyly, 'Mr Craigie's wife . . . Too funny.'

'Not for Elizabeth,' I say, remembering the hard, scared set of her shoulders that summer evening in the dining room. 'I'm glad she has met someone nice.' It is Jen who has told me that this fellow is 'nice': 'His father was a major, dead now. Denis Pelly is an assistant in a gramophone shop. He seems a steady fellow and just what Elizabeth needs.' This is what she has pieced together from the columns, and she heartily approves.

'Not nice. Impossibly dull. I mean, a music shop . . . ?' Maureen says now. 'And she is becoming dull too. No, there is no denying it, something needs to happen or I will die of boredom.' 'Boredom' is the word she chooses, but I think she means something closer to unhappy.

Oonagh herself is lit up with joy, although I wonder a little at the origins of it. Is it the joy of freedom and approval, or of love? 'So nice to be in Mamma's good books, especially after barely being on speakers for so long,' she says. 'When we are together, she asks after Philip and what he has been doing, instead of picking at my manners or the way I sit. And Papa says Philip's father is "one of the most able men in England" so I feel I have done something terribly clever, instead of just meeting a pleasant chap and letting him take me about.' She is practising dance steps barefoot in the ballroom, occasionally catching my hand and pulling me up from the spindly chair on which I sit to join her: 'you see, like this, and one-two-three, then round . . . ' Philip, she says, likes to dance 'in the old-fashioned way, together and more slowly instead of the mad energy of the Charleston. It's actually quite nice.'

But even though Oonagh is happy to have Cloé's approval, she shuts down her mother's efforts to be involved. 'No, thank you,' she says when Cloé suggests looking at fashions together or tries to offer advice on a new hat. And 'no, thank you' again when Cloé suggests lunch at The Ritz. She is polite but distant, keeping herself apart, keeping Cloé out, so I know it is a small revenge for the many unkindnesses she suffered, for the wretched nannies and constant criticisms, the disapproval, the childish attempts at affection turned aside or submitted to impatiently. I see that Oonagh, now that she feels herself stronger and Cloé weak, is unable to resist being cruel.

'All those years of creeping about the house,' she says when I ask her about this. We are in the motor coming home from the theatre and outside, fuzzy white-gold streetlights flick past as we move, reflections sliding off the smooth undulations of the side and bonnet, the harsh metallic gleam of its paint. Wrapped to her chin in silver furs, hair a white halo, lips painted in a perfect red bow, Oonagh looks like the Snow Queen from Mr Andersen's story. 'Hiding behind curtains and in my bedroom in case she came upon me and started on at me. Those ghastly dinners, with Mamma at the other end of the table, staring at me. The way being stared at like that made me so frightened that I couldn't have spoken even if I had been able to think of a thing to say, and knowing that whatever man was beside me was bored and longing to be elsewhere, beside Aileen or Maureen. I can't just forget all that, you know, and pretend we are cosy and easy together.'

'I think she worried and wanted to help,' I say. I don't really think this, or not exactly, but I don't not think it either. It is, surely, part of what Cloé wanted. And better to bend Oonagh's mind in that direction if I can.

'I don't think she did,' she says. 'And I think only you would be kind enough to suggest it.'

'You do like him?' I ask. 'Philip. Don't you?'

In case the desire to have something, someone, so approved of, is more to her than the actual liking.

'Oh, I do. Ever since that first night.' The party, known to all as The Bath and Bottle Party, has become famous. Indeed, the newspapers made so much of it that now all of London says they were there, even those who mocked 'a party in a public swimming baths, how revolting' beforehand. Aileen has written from Ireland, 'When people talk of the party and I say my sisters were there, you cannot imagine the admiring looks I get!'

'When he appeared, like that, in the doorway, after those dreadful men . . . I was so frightened, Fliss, and so repulsed. I felt I was drowning underwater and couldn't act to save myself. As if I were weighed down and couldn't understand how to struggle free. I felt myself sinking and sinking, with hands all about me; so many hands, clammy like fish, grabbing and pressing. And then, there he was. Like a hero so that I know he will take care of me always.'

'Well, but you are both very young still,' I say.

'Not so very young,' Oonagh says. 'Valsie is my age and she has been engaged forever.'

'Yes, but not married,' I say. 'And engaged to a man in another country.'

'Can I tell you something?' Oonagh looks anxious suddenly.

'Of course.'

'Even though it might make you unhappy?'

'Yes.'

'He reminds me of Hughie,' she says in a rush with an apologetic look. 'Philip. I mean, not that he is like Hughie, not at all really, but the way he looks at me. As if I amuse him and as if he would do a great deal to make sure I can always amuse him. You know, protect me and such.' For Oonagh, who does not talk ever about how she feels, it is a long and quite extraordinary speech. And she is not done. 'I know that Hughie always looked more at Maureen—' She breaks off, awkward, clasping her fingers the way Catholics clasp their rosary beads, an act of faith, then carries on. 'And I didn't mind that. But he looked at me as if he liked to see that I was happy. No one ever looked at me like that before. Except you.'

'Gunnie, surely,' I say gently.

'Perhaps. But I could never be sure – was it for me or for Mamma that she did it? With you, with Hughie, I knew. It was for me. I so badly wanted Maureen to marry him,' she carries on. 'For the longest time, I couldn't forgive her. I know it wasn't her fault that he went away, but I felt it was. That she had quarrelled with him and maybe made him do things he would not otherwise have done.'

'She tried to make it right,' I say, but I don't

tell her how. Or my part in the plan's failure. 'But anyway, it's no use,' I continue. 'There are too many ifs and adding them together only makes more.' What I don't say is that Philip does not remind me of Hughie. Not at all. That he does not have Hughie's seriousness; that the levity that was superficial with Hughie, a shiny surface only, is, with Philip, through and through.

'I know. I understand that now. But why does Maureen never, ever speak of him?'

'She can't,' I say slowly. 'She doesn't look back, you know that of her. Always forward. She is like an adventurer or explorer, scanning the landscape up ahead. Although Maureen scans for fun, not danger. And even less can she look back when something painful has happened. She walks on, fast and certain.'

'Perhaps. In any case, I know one thing. She will never settle for a man who can't quarrel with her.'

'What do you mean?'

'Everyone sucks up to Maureen.' I smile a little at the childish vulgarity of her phrase. 'You know they do,' Oonagh continues, misinterpreting my smile.

'Aren't you wise all of a sudden,' I say with a smile. She stares out the window then for a long time, lost inside those furs, so that I think she is done talking.

Then, 'I'll tell you something else about the way Philip looks at me,' she says suddenly with a wicked grin. 'As if, were no one watching, he would reach out and catch hold of me and snatch me up and, I don't know, *eat* me. Other men have looked at me like that, and I hated it. I don't hate it with Philip, though.'

'You don't?'

'No. I mean, him looking like that gives me a funny feeling, here.' She places a hand on her middle. 'But not hateful.'

'In your stomach?' But like Cloé, she shudders at the naming of bodily parts that aren't arms or legs and turns away. And it is while turned so that I cannot see her face that she says, 'I'll tell you one last thing. I am not the only girl he looks at like that.'

'Oh?'

'No. Valsie, too. But I think men are like that.'

Days later, Maureen and I sit over the papers late on Sunday morning. She has scanned the gossip columns, found the names and stories that interest her, and read them, but without her usual enthusiasm. 'Driberg should really give up if he can't find anything better to write about than Tallulah's new Bentley,' she says disagreeably.

'Well, there's a piece about the Kellogg-Briand

Pact in *The Times*. Mr Baldwin is in Paris for the signing. You could read that.'

'Don't be ridiculous, Fliss.' She sighs exaggeratedly then and leans far back in her chair, head tilted back to look up at the ceiling.

'I don't see so much of Richard these past months?' she says slyly.

'I don't either.' It's true. He calls little these days, even though he has now moved to London.

'Why is that, I wonder?'

'I don't know.' I never told anyone about Richard's proposal. They would have been disappointed. Or approving. They would have insisted on knowing why I had refused. Or they would have been indifferent to my reasons. Any of those things would have been impossible to bear. Once, I would have told Oonagh. But not this new Oonagh. Certainly not Maureen.

'You don't know?' she scoffs. But she isn't interested enough to dig further. 'I wonder is it truly possible to die of boredom,' she says with a yawn.

'Certainly, Elizabeth thinks it is.'

'Elizabeth is more likely to die of the opposite,' she says. I consider reminding her that she blamed poor Elizabeth for being dull just days ago, but don't. Maureen sees no problem with changing her mind. 'But almost, I can see why she tries, so. I am terribly sick of the feeling of waiting and waiting.'

'Waiting for what?'

'For life to begin. First, I thought it would be when we came to London, but it wasn't. All those dreadful debs balls.' She shudders. 'Then, I found Baby and Zita and Stephen and Elizabeth, and I really did think life had begun, at long last. I suppose it did . . .' She looks wistful for a moment. 'But now. Well, I don't anymore.' She yawns widely, not bothering to lift her hands from her lap.

Chapter Forty-two

Over morning tea at the office in Islington, Jen asks me if I have 'thought any more' about taking a flat together. It's been over a year since she first suggested it, and she has been saving all the while, and is now impatient to be gone from her mother's. I tell her I have, that I think often about it, and that in the meantime I too have been saving and saving so that I shall have enough. This is true. I once proposed to Ernest that I might make a contribution with my wages. I think I knew he would say no – what I feared was that he would ridicule me and the tiny amount I was able to suggest, a sum that wouldn't have kept Oonagh in tips for the hairdresser. But he didn't.

'I consider that is very proper of you,' he said, having thought for some moments, tugging at his moustache. 'But I have another proposition to make. I would rather you saved what you earn. You will need it someday. And to that end, I would like to invest your wages, if I may.'

'I don't think I know what that means,' I said.

'No, I don't expect you do, but if you will trust me, I will put your money where it will make more money for you.'

'Very well,' I said. 'Please do. As you say, I will need it someday.' I did not tell him I hoped to need it for rent. That was something for Chloe and the girls first.

'I'm glad,' Jen says now. 'Truth is, Fliss, it is not so very comfortable at home with Susan and George. Mother makes such a fuss of George, of what he has for dinner and whether his slippers are warm, and Peter still has no job. It makes him angry and unhappy, and he has taken to rowing with me because he says women like me and you have taken jobs that should be for men.'

'But does he want to make tea and file papers for Mr White and Mr Pearson?' I ask.

'Certainly he does not.' She laughs. 'Can you picture it? I think he knows he does not, but he is angry at everyone around him. He is ashamed to be unemployed when he is able-bodied and feels that Mr Baldwin's government has betrayed him. He talks about the men who fought in the war with such bitterness. He says that they cannot bear to look at him because he did not fight, even though he was too young. I tell him he is imagining it, but that only makes him angrier. He says there is nothing for him in this country and talks of going to America. He is drinking too much and altogether miserable.'

I remember Bryan: *It's a queer world the old men have left us.*

'I think he's not alone in believing that,' I say. 'It's as if there are two sides – the ones who fought and the ones who were too young and did not, and each thinks ill of the other. Sometimes more than ill.' I am remembering Stephen in his dead brother's army jacket with the chinchilla fur collar and Maureen's major: *You are a disgrace to this country and to those who died in Flanders.*

'Well, I cannot wait to be gone,' Jen says. 'Just as soon as your friends can do without you.'

How does she know? I wonder. I have never said that I am necessary. I have never told her about Cloé's health, her nerves and tempers, or Maureen's demands, Oonagh's fears. Never described the bonds of love and obligation, the warmth of being needed set against the resentment of being used. I have barely told myself how hard it will be to dig up this tangle of roots and extract those that are mine. I fear that, replanted elsewhere, they will not thrive, that the pull of their native soil – not the soil of Wexford and Ballytibbert but the soil of this family – is too strong. But I know I must try.

And then, just as I am wondering what small changes I might make to begin the transplanting, everything speeds up.

It is autumn and once again after the languid summer, a city barely able to raise a shrug, London has energised itself. Those who have been abroad return, rested and cured and newly inquisitive, and fill up the streets and houses and cafés again. The truncated days are made bright in patches with the warm lights of entertainment because everywhere now there is something on offer: a dinner, a dance, a revue, theatre, opera, busy hotels. The city feels as though it makes itself anew every night, sitting down at its mirror to carefully make-up and prepare, donning beautiful gowns then standing to throw open the curtains and announce *Let us begin*.

Soon it's Christmas and the New Year. 'To 1929,' Maureen says, raising her glass. 'A brand-new year.' And if there is a hint of mockery in the inflection she puts on 'brand-new', perhaps that is only to be expected after a Season filled with so many parties.

In the gloomy days of January an invitation

arrives for Zita's wedding, to a grandson of the Duke of Wellington. Maureen sniggers and says, 'Poor thing, she would far rather not,' but refuses to answer when I ask why.

That wedding is quickly followed by Bryan and Diana's so that we are in St Margaret's Westminster two days in a row. Oonagh is a bridesmaid, one of eleven. Bryan's sister Grania, Lady Patricia and Lady Brigid are bridesmaids too. Maureen is not. She has refused or not been asked, I am not sure which.

It is the most talked-about wedding, with throngs of people and photographers outside to see the bride, who is just eighteen but so astonishingly poised and coldly lovely that she could be twice that. Bryan is nervous, tugging at his collar as though it would choke him. He looks tense and haughty and not his usual self. And yet, 'It is the happiest day of my life,' he whispers as he passes by, at which Maureen, beside me, makes another face. 'Sick-making,' she mutters.

Outside, they stand and pose for photographers as husband and wife. I think suddenly how delicate he seems in comparison with her demanding beauty. The crowds have swelled and there are mighty cheers. Diana is smiling now, veil thrown back, but Bryan is stiffer than ever. 'Longing for a drink,' Maureen whispers, adding, 'aren't we all?'

The reception is in the ballroom at Number 11, where the gold and white plasterwork is the perfect foil for Diana's silver-and-white beauty. Walter is now a government minister, for agriculture, and a Lord, and many of those present are men of politics. It is altogether a less gay affair than expected, with the chattering hordes of Bryan's friends replaced by men of gravitas who are Walter's peers. Diana, it seems, is too young to have friends, only family.

'The two youngest sisters have whooping cough, thank goodness, or it would be simply all Mitfords,' Maureen hisses in my ear, then makes straight for Nancy and Baby, who have taken up a spot in the centre of the room and are looking about them with frank amusement.

'Only champagne?' Maureen asks.

'Yes.'

'Lucky I came prepared, then,' Maureen says, taking her silver flask out of her handbag. She so often comes prepared these days. 'Who's in?'

'Oh, very well,' Baby says, 'although I don't see why you bother. Champagne isn't so bad.'

Maureen ignores her and takes a discreet swig before offering the flask to Nancy.

'Goodness no, with Farve here!' Nancy gestures to a craggy-faced man standing at the edge of the ballroom, looking longingly towards the door. 'He's already furious at being here and not at home in Rutland Gate, which is let for the moment. He thinks the enemy' – she nods at Walter and Lady Evelyn – 'have won. He says it's a complete rout: first the engagement, of which he did not approve, then the wedding at St Margaret's, now this. Poor Farve. Too horrible for him—'

'Who's that?' Maureen interrupts, pointing at a man by one of the large windows, face illuminated by a thin ray of winter sun. With him are various older men, some of whom I recognise as friends of Ernest and Walter. They seem to nod a lot when he speaks. He isn't handsome exactly – as I look, Bryan comes to stand with him, and alongside those delicate looks, the wistful, rather forlorn mouth, this man's features are too heavy, too pronounced. He is dark – hair, eyes, complexion – with thick brows meeting almost in the middle. And yet it is an arresting face, a powerful face. Bryan leans in and says something to him and the man smiles and is transformed. The smile goes right to his eyes, pulling his entire face up into an expression of energetic mischief.

'No idea,' Baby says. 'He must be new.' A minute later, when Bryan walks past, Nancy catches hold of his arm.

'Who is that?' she asks, nodding towards the man. 'Maureen is simply dying to find out.'

'Nancy!' Maureen gives her a poisonous look.

'Oh my dear,' Bryan says, turning to Maureen. 'Oh well, my dear. That's Blackwood. Basil Blackwood, Earl of Ava, you know.'

We do know. It's a name we have heard before, from Bryan, from Brinny, even from Ernest and Walter.

'He's a chum of Waugh's,' Nancy says. 'Oxford.'

'Took the Rosebery Prize at Eton, then Balliol,' says Bryan. 'My father calls him "the most impressive young man to enter politics in a decade". And he looks at me in disappointment as he says it.' He laughs but his mouth is twisted.

'Well, he looks a pompous ass,' Maureen says and turns away.

Diana disappears to change – they are to go to Paris and on to Sicily, then back home to their new house in Buckingham Street – and the reception begins to break up. We stand on the steps of Number 11 to wave them off in Bryan's little car, not the same as the one from the days when we watched him out of our bedroom windows but a sassier new red one – and once we have thrown enough rice and called, 'Good luck!' Maureen says, 'Right, then,' and turns to Basil, who stands behind us.

'We're going on, to the Gargoyle. Why don't you come?' She looks directly at him, her blue eyes to his dark brown, and he looks back for a long moment.

'No, I don't think I will,' he says. Maureen shrugs and turns back to Baby and me. She takes an arm of each of us and we set off towards a taxi.

'Did you see how dowdy Diana's going-away suit was?' she says. 'Lucky Lady Evelyn gave her that mink collar or she would have looked like a sales girl setting off for Margate.'

Chapter Forty-three

But that is not the end of it.

'There you are!' Maureen pounces on me some weeks later when I am barely in the door of Grosvenor Place, dragging me with her into the gloomy music room. 'You are so late back.'

'I met Elizabeth and we had tea,' I say.

'Well, never mind that. I say, Fliss, how does one persuade someone that one is a serious person, after all?' she asks, but without looking directly at me.

'And what *someone* might *one* wish to persuade?'

'Someone who is frightfully intelligent himself, and not a bore, not that, but you know, not *so* much of a partygoer either . . .'

'Not one of Stephen's friends, then?' I laugh.

'No, not. Interested in politics.'

'I am sure, whoever he is, he will find you charming just as you are.'

'And I am sure he will not,' she says wryly. 'I need to make an impression on him.'

'You could always trick him, with one of your disguises. The slatternly maid?'

'Nothing bogus. Too shaming. No, I need to find something that we have in common.'

'Does it matter so much?'

'It does, rather.' And the way she is so careful not to say yes tells me that nothing in a very long time has mattered to her as much as this.

Because of that I don't say no a few weeks later when she begs, 'Will you come to the Cavendish this evening with me? Bryan and Diana are back and everyone is to be there.' Nor do I ask who 'everyone' is, but I can guess.

Sure enough, by the time we arrive, Maureen in a dress of palest blue silk that makes her eyes the colour of a holly blue butterfly, Blackwood is already at the bar.

Simply by being there, he makes the room different. The scuffed wooden panelling and smoke-yellow ceiling are the same, the fringed shades on the dim lamps and rickety tables, but instead of the sensation of drifting that room usually gives me, the dipping and soaring feeling of identical conversations being conducted in every group, there is now a corner of the room with purpose. The corner where he stands. Around him, Bryan, Diana looking more lovely than ever in a Paris dress that makes Maureen grit her teeth, Brian Howard and Nancy's writer friend Evelyn Waugh with his wife – who, amusingly, is also Evelyn – look to be drawn firmly, as if the weight that is his has anchored all of them.

Blackwood is evidently a favourite of Rosa's, who shunts him out of her way, calling, 'Move there now, Ava, and don't be taking up space that would be better used by others.' The kind of rudeness she only shows to those of whom she is truly fond.

'Here goes,' Maureen mutters to me as we walk over. And she is brilliant. Her most dazzling self, witty without the malice that can spoil it. More so, she is warm, and the contrast with Diana's silent aloofness is marked; beside her, Maureen is so very human.

And when Stephen, in response to something I do not hear, says, 'Oh, that wretched war! Well, the one good thing is that they talk so much about it that we all know what to expect, and so we can be ready to steer jolly clear if it ever happens again. I'll disguise myself as an old woman and hide rather than join up,' she does not immediately respond, but looks first at Blackwood, who she now calls 'Duff'.

It's the kind of thing Maureen's friends say, as a joke, or a sneer; a way to put distance between themselves and the boring respectable values of their parents. They don't mean it, I'm certain, but no one ever questions them on it, except for the retired majors they despise. Until now.

'You wouldn't do any such thing,' Blackwood says immediately. He looks disgusted. 'You would stand and fight, same as any of us.' And Stephen, instead of making some brilliant, cutting remark so that the rest, Maureen especially, laugh and jeer whoever was foolish enough to expose something earnest and heartfelt in themselves, stays silent. And Maureen does too.

In the weeks that follow, she resumes her habit of climbing into bed with me in the early mornings – lurching across the room in the half-light, dropping clothes and shoes behind her, then falling heavily onto my bed and telling me about her evenings. These tales are now often muddled and meandering, pieced together through a thick fog that threatens her recall of their finer points so that often, I don't understand what she tells. Or she trails off in the middle and falls asleep, snoring heavily, a sweetish smell of alcohol rising from her warm body like the steam that comes from piles of fetid autumn leaves. But what I do understand is that more and more, Blackwood is part of them. There is one story in particular that stays in my mind, even though it is strange and confused and at the time I only half-listen, still heavy with sleep, as Maureen's voice runs on.

'. . . after the Gargoyle Club. Some chaps, friends of Brenda's, said they knew of a party and Baby and I determined to go with them. After all, what was there to do? The club was closing and no one else had any good ideas. But Duff said they were rum fellows, something not right about them, and not to go. Well, I said, I'll go anyway, thank you, and Baby said immediately she'd come with me. We found a taxi and the other chaps got in, then Baby got in and I followed her and Duff said, "Get out, now." When I wouldn't, he took hold of my arm. Well, you know how strong he is. But I tried to resist. I told Baby, "Catch hold of my other arm and keep me steady." But Duff just took hold of both my shoulders and pulled me out as if I were a cloth doll. He tore my dress,' she says with satisfaction. 'And called me "a foul contending rebel".'

'What about Baby?' It sounds like an odd incident to me, although Maureen is clearly delighted, and I wonder what Baby made of it.

'Oh, once she saw the game was up, she came too. And Duff and I rowed all the way back in the taxi. He is splendid to row with. Doesn't give one an inch.'

It is obvious they have found their something in common, but I can't see what exactly it is. Not immediately.

'Duff says . . .' Maureen begins one afternoon.

'"Duff says . . ."' Oonagh mimics. 'We hear so much from you now of what Duff says. You know he is a cousin too. At least Philip isn't that.'

'He may be a cousin, but he's an Earl. One day a Marquess. And such fun.'

'You say that because he's the only person who drinks as much and as recklessly as you do,' Oonagh says pettishly. 'Except Elizabeth, and you can't marry her.'

Chapter Forty-four

In May, Violet is called away, to America, where her fiancé has been injured in a motor accident. 'I must go to him,' she says, pale and important. Oonagh, thrilled by the gravity, rushes around helping her to pack and prepare.

'Just say and I will come with you,' she soothes, squeezing Violet's hand, even though she must know, as I know, that Cloé would never allow it.

'How kind you are, my dearest friend,' Violet says, then dabs at her eyes although I do not see any tears. 'But no, Essex will be with me, and perhaps when I come back, Henry will come too.'

And it seems now that all eyes are on America. There are tense days when something has happened on the stock exchange there that I do not understand, although I hear the word 'correction' spoken often and hopefully. The office in Islington is full of sombre men meeting with Mr Pearson and Mr White. Jen and I hear little, but the faces of these men as they go in and out say much and Jen is twitchy lest the news be bad. 'It will be OK,' I say, 'That's America, not England.'

At home in Grosvenor Place, there are more of these meetings, men who call to see Ernest late into the night. One of these is Philip's father, Robert, who is director of Lazard's bank. They spend many hours in Ernest's study, and I see Lapham go in several times with trays and decanters.

The next day, Oonagh rushes in and up the stairs with Philip more slowly behind her. 'Hot news, Fliss,' she calls to me in my little writing room. 'Come quick, as I have an announcement.' Looking at Philip's more bashful smile, I think I know what it is, and indeed when she has gathered all the family – Cloé, Gunnie, Maureen and I – in the drawing room together, she takes hold of Philip's hand and says, 'We are engaged. Papa knows already. He fixed it up last night with Philip's father. And we would like to be married immediately. I do not see any point in waiting.'

'Oh dear, not St Margaret's *again*,' Maureen says with a careful show of weariness and I know how much it pains her that Oonagh, younger, will be married first.

Later, as I dress for dinner, Oonagh comes to my room with Fidget and sits on the end of my bed, powdering her nose energetically in a gold compact mirror, the dog beside her. 'The date is set for next month,' she says.

'So soon?'

'Yes. It's obvious that Maureen will marry Duff, certainly if she has any say in the matter, isn't that right, Fidget?' She picks the dog up and rubs his nose with hers. 'And I will not be left here alone with Mamma and Gunnie. I will make sure of that. But what about you, Fliss? What will you do? Will you come with me? Fidget would like that, wouldn't you, doggie?'

'You're kind,' I say, 'but no.' It's time for me to leave Grosvenor Place, I know it. 'I shall go and live with Jen. She suggested it, oh, a long time ago, and the time wasn't right. But soon it will be.'

'So you will stay in London? I always imagined you at home in Ireland.'

'So did I. But for now, I will stay. Mummie has no need of me at Ballytibbert.' I said 'no need' because to say 'no wish' would have been too painful.

'And what of Richard?'

'Nothing of him,' I say.

'Is it a pity?'

'No.' I won't tell her how hurt I am that he no longer calls. Or that I hadn't understood that our friendship would end with my saying no to him, and I can't stop myself wondering would I have answered differently if I had known. 'I have been reading manuscripts for Mr Pearson and he says he likes my reader's reports and that I have a future in publishing. The office is to expand, if all goes well, and he says I shall be part of that. In fact, Jen and I had talked of renting in Earl's Court, but it seems we may do better than that. Mildred knows of a place that might do. One of the flats she has been doing up with Lady Colefax; too small for any of their acquaintance. But where will you live?'

'Rutland Gate, close to Diana's parents' house.' She makes a face. 'I cannot love that girl. Nothing like Nancy, is she? Sometimes I think she will eat Bryan alive . . . Anyway, they will be our neighbours, with Fridays to Mondays in Sussex: Plaw Hatch Hall. Can you imagine, like one of those tongue-twisters . . . I hope I never have to say it after too many cocktails!' She laughs. 'And I suppose Papa will buy somewhere in Ireland,' she says vaguely. 'There is a very pretty house in Wicklow called Luggala, like a dear little doll's house. Although Philip will not countenance moving.'

'And you? Will you be happy to stay in London?'

'I daresay. I hope there will be children very soon.' She blushes a little, a reminder that for all her show of sophistication, she is still just nineteen. 'Lots of children. Do you remember when we planned our futures, back in Glenmaroon?'

'I do.'

'And I said I wanted children, and Maureen said she wanted a grand title? Well, perhaps we will both get what we wanted. And you' – she laughs – 'who didn't want to marry, well perhaps you won't, but you have done the most! Anyway, Valsie says it is more fun to be young and married than young and single. That one can do exactly as one pleases.'

'How does she know?' I ask.

'True,' Oonagh says. 'I don't know how she knows. Especially as she isn't, any longer, engaged. It seems that she and Henry won't do, after all.'

'Oh dear. Poor Violet. So, she will be back shortly, un-engaged?'

'Yes. And I rather think it is a good thing that Philip and I are engaged before her return,' she says thoughtfully. I am about to ask more when she says firmly, 'Although she will still be bridesmaid, of course.'

Oonagh's wedding is set for June 24, at St Margaret's again, and Elizabeth, when she finds out, is furious. Because Elizabeth too is to be married in St Margaret's, in July.

'Eleven days before mine,' she says, stabbing at the olive in her Martini. 'Well, how shame-making that will be. Might as well put out a cap and beg.' She looks angrily around the Ritz bar. Her face is chalky and the violet shadows under her eyes are more pronounced than ever.

'But how?'

'A *Guinness* wedding, with one of the Glorious Guinness Girls as bride, in the same church as my feeble affair and only days before . . . There isn't a soul who won't compare: "Poor Elizabeth. So imaginative with her little effort. So *brave*."'

'I don't believe a single person would think any such thing,' I say.

'Well, I do, and that is more than enough!'

As if in revenge, she throws herself into planning a Circus Party to be held two days before her wedding. It sounds the most extravagant and terrifying party yet.

'There is to be a circus orchestra and a jazz band, and a fairground. And real live animals,' she tells me with almost savage delight. 'A Siberian wolf and a dancing bear.'

'Poor things,' I say. 'Not really a party for them, is it? More an ordeal.'

'You are starting to sound just like Oonagh,' she says sharply. 'I had hoped better of you, Fliss: The Modern Girl. The Working Girl. Quite the example to all of us.'

'Well, you work too,' I say mildly. I will not quarrel with her. 'You seem to forget that part.'

'Only because I must. And Denis must too. We must work to survive. You could easily not. Don't tell me Ernest wouldn't provide for you. It's clear he would. Although,' she drawls, putting her head on one side, 'what I don't understand is why? Ah, I see now I have made you blush.'

'Don't be ridiculous,' I say coldly. But she has. Because I, too, have often wondered that very thing – why? Yes, I was useful, particularly when we were all younger. But all I had ever been intended as was a companion for the schoolroom. Why then was I still part of the household? Why did he support me, encourage me, plan for me? I didn't know, and had no one to ask, and greatly disliked Elizabeth's long, speculative look.

'Won't you be tired at your wedding?' I say, to turn her attention. 'With such a big party just two days before?'

'You're so feeble, Fliss.' Then, 'What do you imagine Maureen will give for a wedding present? A fat cheque, I hope.'

Oonagh's wedding, four months after her nineteenth birthday, is just as lavish as Elizabeth had predicted. Ernest nods his approval briskly left and right as he walks down the aisle with Oonagh hidden beneath a thick veil, in a gown of satin that matches the slender arched columns of the church. Behind her, Violet and I in our bridesmaids dresses, elegant variations on Oonagh's, follow with some of the younger attendants in clouds of tulle. One of them, a cousin of Philip's, just six, stumbles and starts to cry and is tugged savagely forward by Bryan's sister, nine-year-old Grania, a veteran now of two family weddings.

Cloé is austere and dry-eyed, exactly as she was for Aileen's wedding, except then she embraced Aileen when she came down the stairs of Grosvenor Place before the church and straightened her veil carefully, arranging it about Aileen's face. To Oonagh, she said, 'Well, I hope you will manage to speak your vows and not just stare silently at Philip with those eyes of yours,' and Oonagh looked ahead, through the front door, already open for her, and said, 'Yes, Mamma,' in a voice without expression.

After the ceremony, when Oonagh cannot be found for the photographs, I find her back inside the church with the crying child, sniffing now, seated on her knee as Oonagh strokes her hair and pets her and says gently, 'You did a splendid job. I couldn't possibly have managed without you.'

'Come on, Oonagh,' I say. 'Everyone is waiting.' She makes a face.

'I'd rather sit in here with this poppet.' She sighs, and she lifts the child down, then stands up, and holds out her hand. 'Come with me, little one. If you start crying again, don't worry, I'm here.'

'And if she doesn't and you need an excuse, you can always pinch her,' Maureen says cheerfully coming in behind us.

Little more than a week later we are back at St Margaret's again, for Elizabeth's wedding. I wonder is it the sensation of sameness or the fact that at least half the guests are still recovering from the Circus Party – which lasted almost two days, ending only that morning for some – that I feel there is a flatness in the church, for all that Elizabeth's parents are radiant. 'With relief,' Maureen says, and I have no trouble believing her. Duff is with us and as always in his presence there is an extra vitality, the spare charge of his energy that fizzes up the air around him. But otherwise, the wedding, outwardly exuberant, is curiously subdued.

Elizabeth wears a dress covered in satin leaves

and pearls that fits her beautifully, and Denis is thin but hopeful in his morning suit. When they say, 'In the presence of God I make this vow,' she looks around at her assembled friends and grins, but he looks straight at her.

Outside the church, the crowds are bigger even than at Oonagh's wedding, something that Elizabeth will certainly delight in. She waves and smiles and turns to show her dress, and now she is truly beaming. 'How blush-making,' she drawls, an arm through Denis's. 'So very many people . . .'

'Fliss?' A voice in the crowd catches at me. I turn, and there is Jen. 'Fliss?' she says again. 'It is you! I thought so!'

'Why are you here?' I ask quickly.

'I came to see Elizabeth married,' she says. 'I thought I would like to see her in person, throw rice and wish her well for married life. But you, what are you . . . ?' She looks more closely at me, takes in my navy silk suit and the string of pearls Ernest gave me for my eighteenth birthday, with Brian Howard the poet, dashing in a white velvet tie beside me, then starts to laugh. 'Oh Fliss. Truly? These are the friends?'

'Well, some of them . . .' I admit. 'I mean, they are all friends, but I only live with some of them. You aren't angry I didn't tell you?'

'Simply furious,' she says cheerfully. 'You dark

horse. All this time. And you could have told me so much more than the *Daily Mail*.'

'I will,' I promise her. 'On Monday. I'll tell you everything. Well, as you're here, come and say hullo to Elizabeth.' I bring her over and introduce her and Jen says, 'I do hope you'll be happy.'

'Aren't you sweet,' Elizabeth says vaguely, eyes swivelling about frantically among her guests, as if dragged this way and that by music only she can hear. Then coming to rest on me. 'Do you know what Maureen gave as a wedding gift? A snuff box. Enamel. Eighteenth century.'

'Very pretty.'

'A snuff box,' she repeats bitterly.

On Monday when I have told Jen all the bits of the story I had previously left out – which takes both our tea breaks, morning and afternoon, as well as lunch – and she has asked me all manner of questions, she says at last, 'You know, Elizabeth was not what I expected.'

'Oh no?'

'No. I had imagined her more gay. Less . . . hunted.'

Chapter Forty-five

The tense talk of financial markets and 'necessary correction' that has rumbled on since March, dying down over the summer, bubbles forth again in the autumn worse than ever until on a gloriously warm morning in late September we wake to the news that the stock exchange has crashed, and, like a great ship going down, will drag all with it. And although the scale of losses is far beyond what I can grasp, I understand the fear in the faces I see around me. A fear so strong that it crawls up and stares out of the eyes of people schooled from birth to show no emotion beyond a mild amusement.

'Will you be all right?' is the question on everyone's lips. Most will not be 'all right'. The stories fall like stones, hard and heavy, and the newspapers are full of those who leap or step or throw themselves from windows. Families are ruined. Fortunes are lost. Futures are broken.

'My mother has lost what little she had,' Jen says quietly, as we sit in the tiny kitchen of the office that is entirely silent so that it feels as though it will never be busy again. 'She now depends on what Susan and George give her, and what Peter can send from America. What about you?'

'I will be all right.' Ernest is not one of those whose fortune is lost.

'Papa will be fine,' Maureen told me that terrible morning, in tones that are, for her, subdued. 'Rupert and Walter too. They say it's the benefit of having a business making what will always be needed.'

'You are to see Mr Ernest in his study,' Lapham says that evening.

Behind his desk, Ernest does not fidget. Nor does he delay. 'Your money is safe,' he tells me. 'I moved it, some time ago. I didn't like the way the markets were looking. People always imagine this can't happen,' he says. 'Why are they such fools, when it has happened before? Though not like this, I admit.' He is rattled, that is evident. He may be 'fine', as Maureen said, but he isn't his usual pleased and private self.

'I'm relieved,' I say. I am, far more than I can express. I think he would be happy for me to leave, but I don't. I think of Elizabeth: *Don't tell me Ernest wouldn't provide for you. It's clear he would. Although, what I don't understand is why?* 'You've been very good to me,' I say. 'And I am very grateful, but more and more, I feel I must ask, why?'

It seems that he won't answer me, because he doesn't for the longest time so that I am about to stand and leave, and then he says, 'I promised your brother. I met him, riding too fast' – even now he has a moment to be disapproving – 'away from the house the day before that party, the last party at Glenmaroon. I had been meaning to speak to him for some time. I already knew he was mixed up in unsuitable matters, and I asked him to desist. He said he wouldn't. I told him I could no longer welcome him to the house, or into company with my daughters, if he didn't, and he said he understood. It may be no bad thing, he said. Then he asked that I look after you. I said I would. I never saw him after that.' I think he only tells me any of this because he's so shaken up by the news from the markets and whatever that has done to his business. 'I hope I have done that?'

'You have.'

'I'm glad, Felicity. It has not been difficult, I don't want you to think that.'

'Why did Hughie say, "it may be no bad thing"?' If Ernest is in the mood to talk, this may be my only chance.

'I assume he knew the risk he took, and he wanted to make sure you would be cared for. He knew what might happen. What did happen.'

'What did happen?' But he just looks at me, so I say it again. 'What did happen?' When he has looked at me for long enough, I understand.

Hughie is dead, and Ernest knew.

When Hughie went, I couldn't face a world without him. A world like that would have been less than half a world. So I kept him in it. I invented a whole life for him – reasons why he couldn't come home, or write, or send word of any kind. I gave him a farm in a place called Venezuela that was only a little bit harder to imagine than his life there; a wife with dark hair and pretty dark children. I gave him happiness and told him I was happy when I told him all the other details of my days. It was the only way I could continue. And through all of that, with every drumbeat of my heart, I wondered, *Where are you where are you where are you*?

Which is why, when Ernest tells me, my heart stops. It must do. Because without the rhythm it has been used to, how could it keep beating? I cannot speak. I cannot move. He does nothing to help. Perhaps he knows I wouldn't let him. Couldn't let him.

'When?' I ask at last.

'I don't know. It wasn't confirmed until some years after his disappearance. And when it was, there were very few details. I was never able to find out what exactly happened. It didn't seem to me that I should tell you.' There is appeal in his voice now. He wants me to say what he did was OK. I don't. 'You were happy. You had put the past behind you. I didn't want to rake up old hurts and remind you of something so unhappy.'

Remind me. Of the thing that never left me. How can he think like that? Is that what it is to be a man of business?

But the truth is, he may have sent Hughie off, but I kept him away, by my failure and my refusal to do what I should have with Maureen's letter.

'I didn't know anything real to tell you,' he continues. 'There was never any credible information. Nothing worth passing on. Just rumour, stories. You know the Irish.'

I suppose he would tell me more if I asked, but I don't. I know enough.

Chapter Forty-six

Grosvenor Place, London, 1930

'Help me, Fliss, quick.' Maureen calls from her room along the hallway. I go to her and she says again, 'Help me, for goodness sakes! I cannot, my hands shake so much. And I have sent Burton away before I boxed her ears, she was so much on my nerves.' She is holding the Dufferin and Ava tiara, constellations of hefty diamonds collected into tall shamrocks dotted through with pearls, and indeed her hands are trembling.

'Let me,' I say. I take the tiara, which is heavy, and set it lightly on her head.

'That will never work,' she says, shoving it down hard. 'You need to be firm with tiaras.'

'You'll hurt yourself, it's too heavy to wear like that.'

'Stuff! If it makes my head bleed, I'll wear it,' she says. 'Now, pass me that glass. In fact, pour me another, from the shaker.' She downs what I pour her, then gestures for another. 'Is Aileen here yet? I do want her to see this. As I recall, she wore a sort of snood to marry the Great Oojah, didn't she?'

'Maureen, dearest, it's your wedding day. You don't need to tease Aileen.'

'Oh, I know I don't. And I won't, not really, but I am just so blissfully happy.'

'Are you really?'

'Yes, really, really.' And she is. She looks as I have never seen her. Her smile, always fascinating, has never been more so than right now. 'If he hadn't asked me, Fliss, I could not have borne it.'

'If he hadn't asked, you would have found some way to ask him,' I say, laughing.

'I'm not sure,' she says, and she is more serious than usual. 'Not with him.'

It is July and there has been some resolution since the Crash of September, but not enough. London is subdued. Thinned out, like seedlings in a tray. The parties have been fewer, the disappearances great. Those who are gone – moved to the country, shut up houses or sold them, seen their grand homes torn down for flats and hotels – leave absences behind them, black holes that cannot be covered over because there are not enough gay young people left for the covering. Those who have chosen to face death rather than disgrace leave deeper wounds.

Bert is one such, Baby's prizefighter. Dead in a way that was violent and shocking and splashed across newspapers even more than when he was alive and chasing clues across London with Baby after the nightclubs closed. He lost money in the Crash – only a little, in comparison with others, but all he had, and the shock must have sent him mad because he left a note for the girl he went about with after Baby, to say he was gone for cigarettes, then climbed onto the roof of the house and jumped. I cannot imagine the speed at which his great bulk must have hit the ground, and I know I will never walk down that street where they lived again.

Bryan and Diana still entertain in magnificent style, inventing elaborate follies and hoaxes to amuse their friends and perplex the public; Oonagh and Philip, too, do their best, throwing frequent, stylish parties, but somehow the heart is not in any of it. Not the way it was. There is a Tropical Party and a Second Childhood Party, and more, but these days they are like shades of the parties from before. I go sometimes, if asked, but mostly I don't.

Even Jen doesn't read the columns much anymore. 'It doesn't feel right, somehow,' she says. 'Not when so many are in such trouble.'

But Maureen is unchanged. The shocks and aftershocks that ran through all of London have left her unscathed, and her wedding will be a brief return to the insouciant glory of the years before the Crash. More magnificent even than Oonagh's or Aileen's. The last of the Glorious Guinness Girls.

Cloé has been in preparation for many weeks, aided by Gunnie. She has been walking more instead of lying in her room, and has taken renewed interest in the trays that go up and down the stairs, devising new diets – 'blackened toast with marmalade, steamed chicken' – so that she is almost like herself again, the elegant figure I first encountered in the drawing room at Ballytibbert.

I try to think what it has all meant. What my life has become because of that day; what it might have been otherwise, but I can't. There's too much in it. Too many twisty ways and paths that branch out and off so that I can't follow them. Who might I have been if I had stayed behind? Where might Hughie be now if neither of us had ever come within the orbit of Cloé's 'girls'? It is a game as futile as unpicking a row of stitches.

'I wish he were here,' Maureen says suddenly, grabbing my hand.

'Who?' But of course I know.

'Hughie. I wish he were here. I always wish that. I didn't even realise how much I still missed him, not for years. Not until I met Duff and began to stop missing him, and that showed me how much I had been, if you see what I mean?'

'I do. I see exactly.' I can only imagine what it must feel like to one day find the endless nagging pain of missing has been relieved. An ache grown used to, that one day isn't there anymore and you can put out a hand and touch the sore place without wincing. It must be like being turned inside out, brushed down and sent back out, new.

'I'm so sorry,' I blurt out. For her, for me. For him.

'Sorry?'

'I'm not sure Hughie ever got your letter.'

'My letter?' She turns back to the mirror, away from me. 'What letter?'

'The one you wrote him. After the quarrel.'

'Fliss, after all this time, how can you still be thinking about that?'

'Because maybe, if he had got the letter, he wouldn't have been in such a fury. And everything might have been different.' I don't say 'he might not have died', because even though I've known for less than a year, I have still never said those words. Not even to Richard, those few times I have seen him, although I wondered often had Ernest already told him and had they conspired, two men, to keep the news from me? And certainly not to Maureen. Perhaps she knows, has known for as long as Ernest. Even so, I can't tell her. I can't say the words to her. What would be the point?

'Fliss, it wouldn't have made the slightest difference,' she says. 'Surely you see that? Hughie was bent upon his path. No letter from me was going to change it. It had nothing to do with me. Or you. Only a child would have written as I did. And that's what I was. A child. It's a long time ago, Fliss.'

It is as much as I will ever get from Maureen, and more than I expected. *It had nothing to do with me. Or you.* I reach out and squeeze her hand. I don't believe her, but it is something to hear her say it.

I go in search of Cloé then, through that house that is empty now of Oonagh, who will come with Philip from Rutland Gate, and Aileen, who is staying at Claridge's with Brinny. They have a daughter now, just over a year old; Neelia, which is Aileen's name spelled backwards, so that Maureen said, 'Goodness, what can she mean by it? Even for Aileen that is too much,' when first we heard. Oonagh has a child too, a boy, Gay, born one month ago.

I won't be returning to the house after today. My few things have already been moved, and after we wave Maureen and Duff off, Jen – who is invited today because Maureen said with arch triumph, 'Now you cannot pretend any longer that we don't exist' – and I will go to our flat in Chelsea, found for us by Mildred.

Cloé is in her bedchamber, putting diamonds in her ears. Her hair is coiffed in a style that is not modern but very much hers, and her face carefully made-up so that the imprint of too many dark and sleepless nights has been disguised with powder and a delicate touch of rouge.

'Is there anything I can do for you before I set off for the church?' I say.

'No, but I will need you to help me later. Afterwards.'

'But I won't be here later,' I say. 'Afterwards. I won't be here.' We have spoken like this many times already; Cloé refusing to accept that I will be gone, me patiently reminding her, knowing that she isn't listening to what she doesn't wish to know, so that it is hard to remain patient. But I must.

'Of course you will,' she says. 'I will need your help.'

'I'm sorry,' I say, 'but I will be gone. You must remember. I am going to live with Jen.'

'But who will be here?' she asks, a tremor rising in her voice as she looks fearfully around her room. 'Who will be left?'

'Gunnie will be here. Gunnie will help you.'

'It's not enough,' she says. And I know it isn't. Not enough for Cloé, not enough to keep her distracted from the reduction in her life, the dwindling circle from couch to bed, punctuated by visits from Dr Gordon. I cannot tell her Ernest will be here, because mostly he won't. The gulf between them that has been growing slowly for years is now too great.

'I will send Robert to assist you down,' I reply. I don't know what else I can say. If I listen to the plea she won't articulate, if I take pity on the desperation in her refusal to hear my plans, then I will never leave. I know now that is what she chose me for – to be a companion first for her girls, and then for herself. But I can't be that.

I can't find Robert. Instead, I come upon Gunnie.

'Cloé is ready to come down,' I say.

'I'll go to her now,' she says.

'I hope you will come and visit me, when I am in the flat with Jen.'

'Perhaps,' she says. She won't. I know she won't, no more than Cloé will. When I leave here today, any kindness that Gunnie has shown to me will be at an end. Once outside the household, I will cease to exist for her. It's the only way she can manage.

St Margaret's is busy as a hive. Duff's Oxford friends, all looking a little green after what I guess was an excessive night. His parents, Lord Frederick and Lady Brenda, who will travel to Le Touquet after this for the casino; Oonagh and Aileen with their husbands and other young marrieds – Bryan with Diana, who looks beautiful and bored; Zita and her husband Arthur, although there are already rumours that all is not well; Evelyn with his wife Evelyn, the novelty of which still makes me laugh. Brian Howard, who scribbles something on a writing pad taken from his pocket, and Stephen, in a pale suit, elegant but somehow wan alongside the ghostly recollections of all his more flamboyant attire. Looking at him, at them all, I am reminded of the peacocks at Glenmaroon: the quivering rage of the crest, mocked by the melancholy droop of tail feathers.

And Richard is here, looking unusually smart. Ernest relies on him more than ever, I hear, and Cloé has begun to talk gratefully of his kindness – he has called to see her many times in the last months. Although always when I am out. He gives me his smile now and holds out a hand. 'You look lovely.'

'Maureen will be glad you came,' I say.

'It was more a summons than an invitation. I didn't feel I had a choice,' he says with a laugh.

'I'm glad you came,' I say. It comes out before I know it's coming. If I had thought about it, I might have hesitated, even stopped myself. Stopped to consider what it would mean, is it fair, how I should phrase it. But there is none of that. I just say it, and then it's said.

'Are you really?' he asks. And I say yes. And I pause there beside him, close to him, for a moment. A short moment that is nonetheless long for us. Long enough, that is.

There are absences too. Elizabeth, chiefly. 'I couldn't,' she said when I asked why not. 'I just couldn't. You see, it was all a sort of game, but not now that Denis and I have so little to live on, and row so very much. Or at least, if it is still a game, it isn't a terribly funny one.' She ordered another drink, and her hands shook so that Jen, who was lunching with us, as she often does, took the cigarette from her, lit it and handed it back, then held Elizabeth's hand tightly to quiet it for a moment.

Sir Francis Laking – the young man who's naked capering brought about Aileen's engagement – is in

St George's hospital, gravely ill after drinking 'too much yellow Chartreuse', according to Maureen.

Brenda, too, is absent. She has been arrested, for bouncing a cheque, and will possibly go to prison. 'She has not been herself,' Stephen says when I ask. 'Even less herself than she normally is. She was to have had a baby,' he explains, picking his way delicately through that convoluted phrase.

'And?'

'And now she is not.'

'I see.'

'So there has been more morphine. Rather a lot more.'

Even Miss Gibbs, Uncle Walter's gibbon, is dead, Bryan tells me. She died in her cage in Dublin Zoo, where she was sent by Walter when age and confusion turned her aggressive, after snatching a hair grip from the head of a child who stood too close to the bars, and swallowing it.

Maureen, however, is defiantly happy. Instead of looking demurely down like most brides, who seem to me to approach the altar as though it were a scaffold, she keeps her head up high, turning it this way and that to catch the eyes of the congregation and smiling broadly.

Afterwards, we go to Grosvenor Place for a reception, where the spectre of Aileen's wedding, then Oonagh's wedding, the financial crash and closed decade seem to add a leaden familiarity to the festivities, dragging them down so that for all the drinking and chattering and flitting of Maureen's friends, it's a subdued kind of celebration. So very much has changed since we stood here last year to toast Oonagh and Philip.

Cloé doesn't even try to pretend, but disappears upstairs almost immediately, Gunnie with her. Ernest makes a brief toast and is then immediately deep in conversation with men with serious faces.

'Do they leave today?' Richard asks me, nodding to where Maureen and Duff are still receiving congratulations.

'They do. And so do I.'

'Where to?'

'I have a flat, with Jen. In Chelsea.'

'I'm very glad,' he says. 'Will you be sorry to leave?'

'It will be strange,' I say slowly, 'but not sorry, no. There is no reason to stay.'

'No reason,' he echoes. He is, I see, shocked at Maureen now. At how brilliant and hard she is, at how loud her voice, how fast she fills and empties glass after glass.

Out on the steps, as we prepare to wave farewell, Maureen calls out suddenly, 'Come and see us off.'

'I say, how jolly, yes please,' her friends call back, and so we pile into cars and drive as far as Croydon.

The day is warm and slow and golden as we gather in a field, cars parked in a circle so that we seem to stand in an arena marked out by silver bumpers and headlights that pick up the swollen rays of afternoon sun and throw them inwards to light our last farewell. Someone unloads a hamper full of champagne bottles with much good-natured rattling.

'I've never seen so much champagne,' Richard says. Corks are popped, a series of cheerful little explosions, with shouts of 'Good show!' But there are no glasses.

'Bryan is bringing them,' says Baby. 'He will be here any moment.' But Maureen cannot wait. 'Hurry, help me,' she calls to me, rushing in her satin heels to Duff's car where she wrestles with the radiator cap, twisting it this way and that until he comes to her aid and takes it off.

She wipes the cap on the hem of her dress, an oily streak through the pure cream silk, and pours champagne into it so fast that it fizzes over her hand and onto the ground, splashing the front of her dress. But Maureen pays no heed. She throws her head back and gulps the champagne greedily from the shallow cap, cheered on by Oonagh, Baby and Stephen, then refills and gulps again, just as savagely.

Maureen passes the radiator cap to Duff, who

laughs down at her, face glowing, and does the same, spilling champagne in great rivers down the sides. Around them, their friends are doing the same, grabbling with car bonnets, twisting, wiping, pouring, throwing back mouthfuls of champagne in between shrieks of laughter.

I watch them, Duff and Maureen, united in the frenzy of their impatience and certainty of purpose, and I think how gay and bright and vital they both are.

I know these Guinness girls can seem absurd – a little, anyway – with the seriousness of their frivolity; childish in the way they stick to the old slang and jokes and giddy life of parties, now that the world has turned sombre around them. But to me they are glorious. I see a funny kind of gallantry and strength in their refusal to hunker down and adapt. They will be the women they were brought up to be, even though the world is changing around them. They are like the great ships, the ocean-going liners, still ploughing through the waters, cutting deep waves and sending them up high on either side. Even though all around them now bob small, sleek craft, the kind that pivot neatly and economically, with little movements and nearby horizons.

I look up and catch sight of Richard. He watches Maureen, but his face is stern, appalled, even, as he sees the pale golden liquid, slicked now with a greasy rainbow shimmer, brim and spill and run down over her hands, falling unchecked into the dirt below. It fizzes up where it mixes with the earth, foaming into a filthy spurt of energy before seeping into the ground and settling, leaving behind a small patch of wet mud. I watch as Maureen absently scuffs the toe of her white satin shoe in the puddle so that the shoe becomes stained and grubby, then steps over it, moving on and forward, always forward.

Epilogue

Glenmaroon, Dublin, 1978

Outside the sky is darker now and the wind rattles the rotten frames more violently.

I dig on among the stable ledgers until I find it. I keep going because I'm certain it will be there. And it is. I recognise it immediately, even though there is no name or writing on the outside and the paper is yellowed. The envelope has never been opened; the lumps of dried glue are hard and knobbly like bone. I hold it in my hand and think I would know the feel of it anywhere, even blindfold, but of course that's nonsense. It's just that I have thought about it so much – what it said, what it meant, the trouble it caused.

What did Thomas think it was when I gave it to him that morning? An idle letter from a girl to her brother? The details of some silly party or game of tennis? I'm sure he didn't think much about it at all. Why would he? Those were serious times, and I had no idea of it.

I open it. It says what I knew it would say, but less.

I'm sorry. Forgive? M

The strokes of her pen are elegant and careful. No one writes like this now. Not even Maureen herself. These days, her letters to me – few as they are – are scratched out in haste, filled with crossings-out and blobs of ink. Often they are incoherent. Spiteful rants against her sisters or jumbled fears that her butler is stealing from her. Stealing what? I once asked. 'Windfall apples' was the answer.

She is most often in London now – her trips to Duff's home, Clandeboye in the North, dwindled after the first few years, and ceased almost entirely after his death. Oonagh is in France with occasional visits to Luggala in Wicklow. Only Aileen stays put in the castle at Luttrellstown that was her wedding gift from Ernest. As for me, I never did settle. Not really. Not in London or back here in Dublin. In London, I was poor, Irish, as much a Guinness appendage as any of the pekinese dogs with their pop-eyes and lolling tongues. Back in Dublin, I thought I would be in my own country, among my own people, but they didn't want me. 'Home' turned out to be a thing to be decided by others, not by me, and my voice was wrong – my accent, I mean, the way I spoke, the words I chose. I had been too long away, in company that was too strange, for it to be anything else. In answer to 'Where are you from?', if I said 'Wexford', that only made the questioner more suspicious. And hostile. So I began to say 'London'. It was easier. Then, at least, I was odd in ways the questioner expected.

But even with that settled, there was the question of what I was. And for that, there was no answer. The Guinnesses had coloured me. 'Stained' was the word I used to myself. Like ink dripped into water, so that even when it has become clear again, the ink is still there, the memory of it anyway, and the water is changed for ever.

That sounds like regret, but it isn't. I'm grateful. Without them, I honestly do not know what I would have become. It's likely I would have stayed at Ballytibbert and slowly rotted with the house, falling at last into a mad heap the way it did – walls and rooms and all the obscenity of domestic life exposed by the collapsed roof and broken windows.

Instead, I had a thing not many women got then: a career. A publishing house where I started low and worked up until I became someone of substance, my opinion listened to, even deferred to. I had their friendship – Aileen's, Maureen's, Oonagh's. And even though it cost me, a hundredfold, in the demands they have made of me, I wouldn't ever have been without it, because it brought good things too. It was a good thing, in itself.

Without them I would never have met poor Elizabeth, dead at forty, from drink. Or Brenda, who lived longer, although we thought she would die sooner. Baby and Zita – how strange to think that they are less than half an hour from where I sit now, tucked away in a cottage in the grounds of Leixlip Castle, where Desmond lets them live as a kindness to his father, Bryan. How even stranger that they are entirely forgotten, their lives worn dry and paper-thin, like the cuttings that drift from this scrapbook, and that I could not go and visit them even if I wished to, because what would any of us say? Stephen, bless him, who burned so bright he should have burned brief, but instead he must have shaken off sorrow as he shook off scandal, and lives still. Sometimes I think he will outlive us all. Nancy and Evelyn, both so gleeful to have missed the first war, both so changed by the second, who have each written books about those days that are as brilliant and funny and sad as the days themselves.

They weren't very many, those years that the newspapers like to remember. That decade of parties held fast in black-and-white photos like the one I dug out from the battered trunk. One-seventh of my life. And yet that decade has put its imprint on all the years since. It was a long, long time before I shrugged off its influence. Their influence.

I remember Mummie, the day I left Ballytibbert, telling me *don't forget what you have*, and when I asked what that was: *You'll have to work that out for yourself, won't you?* I did, I suppose, eventually, but never to my own satisfaction. For a time I tried to be them, and then, after Hughie went, when I tried to be myself, even that was forged in knowledge of them.

I was a collection of 'nots'. Not a Guinness. Not fascinating. Not rich. Not sought-after. Not much considered, except by a very few. But I know Mummie didn't mean any of that. Inasmuch as I understand her, I think she meant the ability I have to accept, to keep quiet but keep engaged. 'You are like a nun,' Oonagh once said, then tried to correct herself in a rush – even then, 'nun' was not a compliment – 'I don't mean that. I mean that you are like a priest – you listen and are wise even though you don't exactly give answers, but women aren't priests of course, so that's why I said nun.'

It's funny. I understand more about Mummie now. I know that today, she would be called depressed. There is a word for it because there are pills and things to give for it. Back then, when there was nothing to give, there was no word either. Or none that anyone would speak. And anyway, if depression was caused by war and loss and grief and lack of money and hopelessness, well, must not everyone have been depressed?

When Richard asked me again, I gave him a different answer. It took him so many years that I didn't expect it, not the second time. By then, there was no one to look at us and wonder and ask what we meant to one another, and so I could let myself simply be in his company, which was the most comfortable thing I knew. Mummie was dead by then, and he was the one person left for whom I would always be Hughie's sister. That wasn't why I said yes, but it was part of it.

We moved back here together, and it was strange to live in a country born of the violence that killed my brother. To accept laws and a constitution created by men who had been his companions and became his enemies. But I can't be the only one – I know very well I'm not – and others seem able to go about their lives without obvious rancour, and so I do too.

'What are you looking for?' It's Trisha. I had forgotten her. I suppose, after all her help, she deserves an answer.

'Some friends of mine used to live here. Quite a long time ago.' It's not really an answer, but I hope it will do.

'Why did they leave so much behind?'

'I don't know. They had a lot of houses . . .' That certainly isn't an answer. 'I suppose they were careless.'

'The Guinnesses, was it?' Still that name has magic. Especially in this country.

'Yes.'

'My grandfather told me about them. He works here too, in the gardens. He used to work here when it was them that had it. Before the nuns.' She grins then. 'He doesn't like the nuns much, but they let him alone.'

'Is it he who does the gardens behind the house?'

'It is. He worked in the stables when there were horses, and in the gardens since he came back.'

'Back from where?'

'Venezuela.'

'Trisha, what's your grandfather's name?'

'Thomas Mahon.'

'Thomas is your grandfather?'

She seems unsurprised that I know of him. 'He is.'

'Do you think I might be able to talk to him?'

'He doesn't talk much.' She grins again. 'But you're welcome to try.'

'Where might I find him?'

She goes to the window and stands on her tiptoes to see out. 'Over there,' she says, pointing. It's the man with the wheelbarrow, closer to the house now, bent over a derelict-looking flowerbed.

'Will you bring me down to him?' I'm shy all of a sudden, an old lady like me. I don't know what I will say to him. Thomas always had that effect on me. He made me feel silly – as if he saw through my efforts to be like the family, saw them for the pitiful game they were. I'm sure everyone saw through them.

We go down again but by the front staircase this time, treading that worn and tired wood, and out the front door. I think for a moment how Lapham would feel to see the casual way the girl tugs it open. The old man – Thomas – is digging a bed close to the house and doesn't stand up at our approach. Trisha has to go to him and whisper something close to his neck before he stops what he's doing. He stands then, with difficulty. I begin to put out a hand to help him, and then I realise that

I am nearly as old as he and it would be ridiculous. I am behind him so he has to turn to look at me. He's as dark as ever, darker even, wrinkles cut deep like whip scours through his leathery skin, and I wonder would they be paler at the bottom were I to stretch his skin tight. He doesn't say hello. Of course he doesn't. People don't change.

'I don't suppose you remember me,' I say. 'I'm Felicity. I used to live here, a long time ago.'

'I remember you,' he says. 'The girl that lived with the Guinnesses.'

'Hughie's sister,' I say. I am still that. I have always been that.

'I know.'

'I see that you kept this,' I say at last, when I have contemplated saying nothing more than 'how are you', then moving off again. I hold the letter out to him. He takes it, his hand shakes, the palsy of age, and it takes him several goes to smooth the envelope out and look at it. *Maybe he won't recognise it*, I think. *Maybe it will mean nothing to him*. But as soon as he has it uncrumpled he makes to hand it back to me. He knows what it is.

'I would have given it,' he says. 'But it was too late.'

'Too late?'

'Yes. Too late. Your brother was gone by the

time that letter ever came to me, although I didn't know it at the time.'

'Gone?'

'Gone.' He won't say dead. I know he won't, because I recognise the not saying of it. 'Within a few days, I had to leave myself. For very many years.'

'Venezuela?'

'Yes. And then I came back, and the country was entirely different.' He looks sad for a moment. 'I went looking, though. For news of your brother. Enough time had gone by that people would talk. But so much time that some were gone themselves.'

'Will you sit down?' I ask. There is a bench on the other side of the flowerbed. I think that we could sit and talk.

'I won't.' And he stays standing even though standing is hard for both of us and the wet, cold ground seems to creep up through the soles of my hopeless shoes, damp crawling up my legs and turning them inch by inch to painful stone. But I stay where I am and listen as he tells me what he was able to discover. His granddaughter stands by, head hanging down, and I don't know if she's listening or waiting.

From what he says, I complete at last the terrible jigsaw of Hughie's final days. It seems he was killed that very first morning, the very day of the party, before anyone understood that he was even missing. Before I passed the letter to Thomas, or Richard reached Glenmaroon. Before any of us even thought to look for him or wonder where he was.

He must have gone out so early that it was still dark, because at first light, the men he was with, making their way on foot into the city with explosives, were set on. There was a fight, one of the many brutal skirmishes in what I now know was a civil war, though at the time that name would have struck me as exaggerated and fanciful. His companions saw Hughie shot and fall into the river, and then they scattered, so far and thoroughly that it was years before Thomas managed to find them and piece together this skimpy account. I suppose I should be grateful that he tried, and kept trying.

I stand there and let the fullness of what Thomas says reach me: Hughie was dead before I woke that morning with Maureen's letter under my pillow. My guilt was not, after all, required. My useless, cosseted guilt that I held tight and that sustained me all these years. My guilt that was a way to keep the heartache alive, and to give myself a starring role that I had never earned. A way to be important in a tragedy that after all I had no part in. Guilt is many things, I know now.

It had nothing to do with me. Or you. Maureen

was right, although she can't have known it, only assumed it, as Maureen always assumed she was right.

He falls silent and Trisha says, 'It's raining.' I hadn't noticed.

'I'm sorry,' he says at last.

'It was a long time ago.' I turn to leave, then turn back again. 'Why do you not tend the gardens at the front in the same way as at the back?'

'Because at the back no one can see what I do. I prefer that.'

Back in the attic, alone now because Trisha has stayed downstairs, helping Thomas in to his tea, I dig for one last time through the papers in case there is something missed, faster now, more careless, sending sheets scattering to either side of the trunk. Nothing. Outside it has started to rain more heavily, and angry drops are clawing at the dirty little window.

I crumple up the letter and put it in my bag along with the photo of the girls standing beside *Fantome*. Neither will mean anything to anyone except me. Even Maureen wouldn't care about the letter because it says so little, and nothing that can touch her. But I want them. They are reminders of years that often seem like dreams but that I don't want to let entirely go.

Richard's footsteps on the stairs now, and along

the bare wooden boards of the attic corridor. He has come to get me.

'Did you find anything?'

'Nothing. There's nothing here. Let's go.' I am weary getting up from the chair and lurch a little in my climb to my feet. He holds a hand out to me and I take it, gratefully, and steady myself against the power of his arm.

'I've got you,' he says.

Author's note

I have been writing about the three Guinness girls – Aileen, Maureen and Oonagh – on and off for over ten years, in newspaper and magazine features. I've been reading about them for even longer. From the start, I was fascinated by all three of them, and the world they inhabited. Fascinated by their privilege, and also the tragedies that they endured, by the stories told about them, the historical background to their lives, and the way they seemed at once real people but also characters in my favourite novels by Evelyn Waugh and Nancy Mitford. Creating a story based around them and their lives has been the best fun I could have imagined.

Authors of historical fiction are always saying how much they loved the research. I'm not sure I ever believed them – it sounded a bit like my history degree, frankly – until I began work on this book. Now, I've joined their ranks. I loved researching this. Every bit of it. The hard part was stopping researching and starting writing.

A word, first, about the Anglo-Irish: the term is used loosely in Ireland to refer to the Protestant landowning class that flourished from the 17th to the early 20th century. Called 'the Ascendancy' in the 18th century, the Anglo-Irish were descended from English Protestants who acquired land in Ireland during the Tudor and Cromwellian plantations, or from 'Old English' landowners, who arrived in the Norman conquest and changed their religion in the 17th century. The Anglo-Irish tended to be Anglican (Church of Ireland). Ulster Presbyterians, the largest Protestant group in Ireland, were called Dissenters – the name refers to social class more than religious denomination. The most prominent Anglo-Irish had aristocratic titles, Big Houses and positions of power, but there were plenty of poorer cousins.

Greatly attached to their lands, estates and regions, they were happy to refer to themselves as Irish but their culture and references were English and they mostly sent their children to school and university in England. Most were unionist in politics – i.e. in favour of maintaining the union with Britain – but a significant minority were nationalists who led the struggle for independence, including notably Henry Grattan, Charles Stewart Parnell and Lady Gregory. The writer Elizabeth Bowen caught their hybrid identity when she described her experience as feeling 'English in Ireland, Irish in England' – it is this duality and tension that has produced so many great writers.

Resentment against the Anglo-Irish flared during the War of Independence and the Civil War with arson attacks on the Big Houses, and many Anglo-Irish felt unwelcome in the heavily Catholic ethos of the new state, and left. By the late 20th century, a more generous, multiple and un-hyphenated definition of 'Irish' had become possible. You still hear the term used occasionally today, but it now suggests fading grandeur – the magnificent, crumbling houses caught in Patrick Cooney's documentary, *The Raj in the Rain*.

As for the political climate of the early section of the book that is set in Ireland – for readers not raised on Irish history, here is a brief rundown: The Irish War of Independence (1919–1921) was a guerrilla war fought by volunteers who called themselves the Irish Republican Army (IRA) against the occupying British forces. It started in 1919 but had been simmering since the failed uprising of Easter 1916. It was characterised by ambushes, isolated skirmishes, and attacks on specific individuals (usually police intelligence), and police (RIC: Royal Irish Constabulary) barracks that were located in towns across Ireland.

The most intense period was from 1920–21, when the British declared martial law in some parts of the country and recruited hundreds of First World War veterans into the RIC and sent them to Ireland. Because of a shortage of proper RIC uniforms, these veterans initially wore a combination of dark green RIC uniforms and khaki British Army uniforms, which got them the nickname of 'Black and Tans'. Their brutality made them notorious.

The War of Independence ended with a truce in July 1921. A delegation headed by Michael Collins (de facto leader of the IRA) was sent to London by Éamon de Valera, president of the self-proclaimed Irish Republic, to negotiate a peace treaty.

Collins came back with a treaty that provided for a self-governing Irish state, but only for twenty-six of the thirty-two counties. The North would remain part of the United Kingdom. And instead of an independent republic, it was to be an autonomous dominion of the British Empire with the British monarch as head of state, and members of the new Irish parliament swearing an oath of allegiance to the British Crown. Collins claimed the treaty gave Ireland the 'freedom to win freedom', but he also knew that the agreement would be divisive in Ireland, writing just hours after the deal was reached, 'Early this morning I signed my own death warrant.'

The treaty was put to the parliament (Dáil Éireann) in January 1922, and was narrowly accepted (64 votes to 57). But to Éamon de Valera and others, swearing allegiance to the Crown was unacceptable. He challenged the right of the Dáil to approve the treaty, saying its members were breaking their oath to the Irish Republic.

A vote was put to the country in the June 1922 general election. The pro-treaty Sinn Féin party won the most seats, but de Valera and his political followers in the republican Cumann na Poblachta party refused to accept the decision, with de Valera saying 'the majority have no right to do wrong'. A bloody and deeply divisive war was fought, with atrocities and executions on both sides, including the ambushing and killing of Michael Collins. It ended in May 1923 with victory for the pro-treaty side, and a legacy of bitterness that was handed down through generations.

That is a very quick sketch of a painful period in Irish history. This is the backdrop against which Fliss goes to live at Glenmaroon with the Guinnesses, and this is the fighting that is intensifying in the years when Hughie is coming to visit her. In this book, Hughie and Thomas's sympathies and allegiance lie with de Valera and the anti-treaty side. Fliss, as would have been common for girls her age at that time, has very little clear idea of what's going on.

This is a work of fiction. There are characters based on real people, and there are invented characters, but all are part of a fictional landscape. Fliss is a completely invented character, as are Hughie and Richard. The Guinness girls – Aileen, Maureen and Oonagh – were real people, of course, as were their parents, their husbands, their many cousins and so on. But the characters in this book are my versions of these people. They aren't the Guinnesses; they are characters based on what I know of them, fleshed out with things I have invented, then put into a story that is also invented, although it contains many real things.

I have stuck closely to the details of the girls' lives, their youth in Glenmaroon, then their years in London society. The Bright Young People of London in the 1920s who become their friends in this book are mostly real – Elizabeth Ponsonby,

Brenda Dean Paul, Stephen Tennant, Baby and Zita Jungman. Evelyn Waugh makes an appearance, as does Nancy Mitford. Bert, the prizefighter who hangs around after Baby in this story, is made up, although he is pretty typical of the melding of social classes that took place during those years, when energy and an appetite for fun and cocktails was all you needed.

The Gunnie and Mildred I have created are both taken from the same source. In fact, Mildred Gunne was a relative of the Guinness girls – she was the daughter of Cecil Guinness, from his second family, born in New York – who came to live with the Guinnesses, first at Elveden Hall in Sussex with Ernest's father Edward, 1st Earl of Iveagh, and later with Ernest and Cloé. Hers is the background on which I based Mildred's character, but I split the real Mildred Gunne into two – 'Mildred' and 'Gunnie' – and gave them each a part of her life. My Mildred is the later Mildred Gunne, who went off and did exciting things – she ran a field hospital during the Second World War, and afterwards worked as an interior designer with Gaby Schreiber. My Gunnie, on the other hand, is based on the early life of Mildred Gunne, where she was a kind of companion/home help to Cloé and chaperone to the girls. In this book,

Gunnie never breaks away in the way that the real Mildred Gunne did.

Thomas Mahon, who plays a small but key part in the plot, is fictional, but based on a real person, Seamus Mallin. He inspired the character of Thomas, because what I found out about him made him impossible to resist. His father, Michael Mallin, was second-in-command of the Irish Citizen Army during Easter Week 1916, and he was executed along with the other leaders. Seamus (also called James) was the eldest son, born in 1904, just months before Aileen Guinness. His cousins, Lily and Cissy Thewlis, lived at the bottom of Knockmaroon Hill, the road that ran underneath the bridge that linked North and South houses at Glenmaroon.

Seamus himself fought on the anti-treaty side in the Civil War. In September 1922 he was arrested with three others after an attack on a Free State troop lorry. His three companions were executed under the new Emergency Powers Act, and Seamus, possibly because of his age – he was eighteen – and his father's sacrifice, was spared death but sentenced to penal servitude. He served two years and took part in at least one hunger strike. He was released in 1924 and emigrated to Venezuela, coming back to Ireland in 1932.

I have woven my story around specific historic

moments, and the challenge of that was to plot a story that took in these moments and made sense of them – a kind of join-the-dots, with fiction weaving in and out of fixed historical points. By and large, I was faithful to the time and dates of these events – I don't see the fun of it if one allows oneself to take too many liberties. The real satisfaction is when a fictional plot works in tandem with life as it happened. The Irish War of Independence, the Civil War, the General Strike, the Wall Street Crash, all these things are the background against which I moved my characters. So, for example, the sacking of the town of Tuam in July 1920 by the RIC, the destruction of the Custom House in May 1921, the shelling of the Four Courts in Dublin in late June 1922, these events all happened as and when I describe in the book. Very occasionally, I have taken small liberties with actual events. Often, this is where there is a lack of consensus around dates. For example, Burton Hall, home of Henry Guinness, was indeed burnt out, just as I have it here, but the date for that is given as 1920, 1921 and 1922, depending on which report I read. So, I exploited the confusion for the purpose of the plot, and I've made it 1920.

As I began to look deeper into the book's time period, 1918–30, which I thought I knew well, I found so much more. The contrast between

Ireland and England was one of the things that really struck me. England – certainly London – of the 1920s was gay and bright and full of fun, while Ireland was poor, and, in the early part, locked in a savage civil war. The way the Guinnesses moved between these worlds, but were insulated from both of them, so that they are observers more than participants, fascinated me.

There are still plenty of people alive who knew the Guinness girls. Thomas Pakenham, for example, whose father Frank was best man at Maureen 's wedding, remembers her well, and her sisters, whom he knew less, somewhat. I thank him for his unbelievable recall. Listening to him bring back the events of more than fifty years ago made me think – enviously! – that the inside of his mind must be like a perfectly organised filing cabinet, complete with all the important details – Maureen's voice, her mannerisms, her personality – laid out and ready to be accessed in an instant. I am very grateful to him for the time he spent talking to me and telling me stories of those days.

I am indebted to the following writers and authors for their excellent research, clever writing and impeccable recollections:

Joe Joyce – *The Guinnesses*

Frederic Mullally – *The Silver Salver: The Story of the Guinness Family*

Michele Guinness – *The Guinness Spirit*

Paul Howard – *I Read the News Today, Oh Boy*

Bryan Guinness – *Diary Not Kept: Essays in Recollection*

Andrew Barrow – *Gossip 1920–1970*

Mary Pakenham – *Brought Up and Brought Out*

Cecil Beaton – *The Book of Beauty*

Robert O'Byrne and his meticulous, invaluable work on *The Irish Aesthete* website, theirishaesthete.com, as well as his brilliant book *Luggala Days: The Story of a Guinness House*

D.J. Taylor – *Bright Young People*

Nancy Schoenberger – *Dangerous Muse: A Life of Caroline Blackwood*

Sally Phipps – *Molly Keane: A Life*

Patricia Laurence – *Elizabeth Bowen: A Literary Life*

Roy Foster – *Modern Ireland, 1600–1972*

Diarmaid Ferriter – *A Nation and Not a Rabble*

Ernie O'Malley – *The Singing Flame*

And I am just as indebted to the following novelists for their exquisite renderings of the period (in no particular order): Nancy Mitford, Evelyn Waugh, Molly Keane (*The Knight of Cheerful Countenance* is a brilliant handbook for an Anglo-Irish upbringing of the 1910s), Elizabeth Bowen, J.G. Farrell, Sylvia Townsend Warner,

Henry Green, Patrick Hamilton, Edith Somerville and Violet Florence Martin.

And you, for reading.

Acknowledgements

Books come about in all sorts of ways – sometimes it's a whole story you're desperate to try and tell, but it can be a character who sets you off, or a mood, or an idea you want to explore. For this book, it was a conversation with Ciara Doorley, my editor at Hachette Ireland. Ciara has been a friend and champion from the very beginning, and it was she who asked, over coffee one day, 'Would you think of writing historical fiction?'

And as it happened, it was exactly what I had been thinking about. I have always loved reading historical fiction; my favourite book as a child, for years, was *Cue For Treason* by Geoffrey Trease, which is set in Elizabethan times, with Shakespeare and Queen Elizabeth as characters (it's still one of the best children's books I've read . . .).

I had written four contemporary novels by that point and was ready for a slight change. I wanted to write a different kind of story, and I wanted to go about it a different way. Historical fiction creates boundaries. There are fixed points you can't mess with, outcomes you can't change; the excitement is finding what you can do within that.

And then Ciara said, 'I've been thinking about the Guinness girls . . .' and the thing was, so had I. A lot. And that was that! I particularly love the 1920s, I love strong, fascinating women, and, I admit, I love a bit of glamour. The Guinness girls brought all of that, and more, and a whole world opened up in my mind almost immediately. Getting it down on paper was obviously far more protracted – and, as always, couldn't and wouldn't have happened without a whole lot of help.

So, thank you, to Ciara Doorley for all the brilliance and energy she has put into this book. To my sister Bridget who read a very early draft of the first half and, as always, immediately put her finger on exactly where it was going wrong. To Sherise Hobbs in Hachette UK for her excellent suggestions; Tess Tattersall for an impeccable edit, Joanna Smyth for her eagle-eyed input. My agent, Ivan Mulcahy, for the immense good fun, and very sound advice. Viv McKechnie who didn't just let me use her printer at a crucial point when all print shops were closed and my own poor yoke was too beat-up and exhausted to handle the 250 pages, she actually took a memory stick and went and did the printing herself. All my wonderful friends, who bring joy and hilarity to my life; if ever the Covid crisis showed me anything, it is how much I miss you when we are unable to meet.

Thanks also to the Irish embassy in London, which now occupies the house at No. 17 Grosvenor Place, where Ernest, Cloé and the girls lived, and especially to Alanna Maxwell for such a fascinating tour.

To Eliza Pakenham for a few glorious days at Tullynally, where I wrote the first chapters looking out at so many beautiful trees. Days of hard work followed by evenings of brilliant chat and fun. The Tyrone Guthrie Centre at Annaghmakerrig, buoyed up by the fantastic food and dinner conversation. My media friends, especially Brendan O'Connor and Mary O'Sullivan who never flag (or not so they let me see . . .) in their support.

All of my demanding, brilliant, infuriating family, and especially my mother. My children, Malachy, Davy and B, who are the point of everything. And finally, David, who, in 25 years, has never stopped making me laugh.

Reading Group Questions

1. Why do you think the author invented the character of Fliss to narrate the novel instead of having one of the Guinness sisters narrate it?
2. *'I suppose she must have quickly understood that my state was usefully close to hers.'* What would you say Fliss's role is in the Guinness household? Is she staff or a guest or does she walk the boundary between the two? Does this vary throughout the novel?
3. *'You're not them, Fliss. And you're the better for it.'*

'Fliss: The Modern Girl. The Working Girl. Quite the example to all of us.'
Do you think that Aileen, Maureen and Oonagh's lives would have been different if Fliss had never joined them at the house? And what impact did living with them have on her life?

4. *'I must go home after all, to Ballytibbert, where I had not been for so long, where my mother didn't want me.'*
   Would you say that any of the figures in the novel were family to Fliss? Why do you think that Fliss had more sympathy for her mother at the end of the book?
5. *'Perhaps it was just that we were older, and the country more violent, but somehow politics intruded into that summer.'*
   What role does Hughie play in the novel?
6. *'Fliss, after all this time, how can you still be thinking about that?'*
   Why do you think that the letter haunted Fliss the way that it did?
7. *'I suppose I had forgotten, too, that there was still so much trouble in Ireland.'*
   'London, I discover, is gay and outrageous and eager to be seen.'

What perspectives of Ireland and London during the period did you get from the novel?

8. *'We wake to the news that the stock exchange has crashed, and, like a great ship going down, will drag all with it . . . Families are ruined. Fortunes are lost. Futures are broken.'*
   How does the financial crash affect the story? Do you think that the sisters took spending their money seriously, both before and after the crash?
9. *'. . . but I understand too well that this is unlikely to come about; what kind of match might a girl in my position expect to make?'*
   Do you think that the Guinness girls all made the 'right' kind of match? Do you think that their marriages were necessary to secure social status?
10. *'I suppose we'll be in the newspapers tomorrow. Papa will be furious.'*
    How much did you know much about the Guinness family before reading the novel? What perspective of them did you gain by reading it?
11. *'. . . deeper in the tattered nests are pages of*

handwriting – letters, lists – and scrapbooks . . . into which we pasted pictures and sentimental rhymes, postcards.'
How important do you think it is to keep physical mementos of the past?